The World-Famous Franky Fritz Band

a novel

C.J. Levesque

Copyright © 2014 by C.J. Levesque
All rights reserved. This book, or parts thereof, may not
be reproduced in any form without permission.

Published by Channel Wind Press

This is a work of fiction. Names, characters, places, and
incidents either are the product of the author's imagination or are
used fictitiously, and any resemblance to actual persons, living or
dead, business establishments, events or locales is entirely coincidental.

Grateful acknowledgment is made to the following for permission to reprint
excerpts from the previously published lyrics to "Who's Sorry Now":

Music by TED SNYDER Words by BERT KALMAR and HARRY RUBY
©1923 (Renewed) BUGHOUSE MUSIC, EMI MILLS MUSIC, INC., HARRY
RUBY MUSIC CO. and TED SNYDER MUSIC PUBLISHING CO. All rights
for BUGHOUSE MUSIC Controlled and Administered by BUG MUSIC, INC.,
A BMG CHRYSALIS COMPANY All Rights for EMI MILLS MUSIC, INC.
Administered by EMI MILL MUSIC INC. (Publishing) and ALFRED MUSIC
(Print) All Rights for HARRY RUBY MUSIC CO. and TED SNYDER MUSIC
PUBLISHING CO. Administered by The Songwriters Guild of America
All Rights Reserved   Used by Permission
Reprinted by Permission of Hal Leonard Corporation

Miles Davis quotation excerpted from *Miles: The Autobiography*, by Miles
Davis with Quincy Troupe, Copyright © 1989, Simon & Schuster.

Cover art: Joshua Budich. www.joshuabudich.com

Book design and pre-press:
John H. Matthews, www.bluebullseyepress.com

ISBN 978-0-9914187-2-5

For Nancy, accepting of me,
and the writing shadow that follows me

PROLOGUE

MOMENTS BEFORE HIS wedding, nothing could separate Franky from his horn. His sweaty fingers clasped his favorite instrument, a Conn Wonder cornet. The piece sported copper tubing on its valve casing, and together with the brass, the two metals gave the instrument a look of polished machinery that belied its ability to blow music. The big horn looked almost comical hoisted near his wiry body. Everyone knew the youthful musician's trumpet always befitted his frame better, anyway.

"Something ain't right the way you're acting," said his best man, Joe. "It just ain't right."

Waiting for the ceremony to start, he and Joe stood alone in a little room off the St. Anthony's altar. Franky's "giant trumpet," as his mother called the cornet, stayed glued to his lips, and his fingers pushed the valves to make a song that sounded nowhere but his head, magnifying the silence that is known in all holy places. He edged over to peek out at family and friends filing in.

"Put that thing down, willya?" said Joe. "You're making me nervous!"

He separated the cornet from his lips and gave it a look. "I don't think I *can* put it down—not until Muriel has my name."

Joe shook his head and went back to his pacing. "I never shoulda signed up for this," he muttered. "This is more stressful than playing onstage."

At three minutes till the hour, the priest shuffled into the room and slipped on his vestments. Joe greeted him with an endless plea to run through his duties one more time, even though the priest had provided him a written copy of the ceremony and explained it to him eleven times the evening before, by Franky's count. As the big moment inched closer, Joe took to his own chosen musical instrument to calm—or express—his nerves: He started drumming with a tooth-pocked pencil he had picked up from a long table that had no apparent purpose except for being the resting place of the pencil and a priest's green stole.

Now it was time. The priest nudged the groom to follow him out into the public area before the altar, but no—Franky grabbed his shoulder. "Do I look okay?" he asked.

The priest, who was about to slip through the curtain, turned around to give him a once-over. He had rolled his eyes at being halted, but then he took notice of the groom as if for the first time. "You look good in a tux," he said.

The bells of the New Orleans neighborhood church *donged* to announce ten o'clock, and Franky jumped: The starting gun had been fired. The snow-haired priest reached through the curtain and yanked the arm of the best man, who in turn yanked on Franky's wrist, pulling him out into the naked vastness of the church. The organ kicked in with a tune that sounded like bad background music, and the entire congregation turned in their pews to at last glimpse the bride.

But then a murmur bubbled up, and a hush followed. Franky and Joe later said they presumed the stirring, which in hindsight was a harbinger of the morning's outcome, to be a collective gasp over the bride's beauty. Sure enough, a figure stood at the opposite end of the endless nave, the morning sun shining on her in a beam of dust.

But the light streamed in too strong. The very instant of her arrival, the lifting sun had struck the church windows to cast a blinding glare, forcing groom, best man, and priest to turn away. In a simultaneous response, they each made visors out of their right hands in order to glimpse even a vague outline of the bride's figure—a shape that at that moment was the only way Franky was able to confirm Muriel's identity. The glare was so strong, in fact, that the three men standing up front before the altar couldn't so much as make out the wedding dress Franky had longed to see. To Franky, the moment of beauty was blind.

Still, there she stood, with only a stretch of Saturday morning sunlight separating them. It was all so strange, he later told Joe:

"Like a dream in real life."

Yet now the guests in the front pews were no longer looking to the back of the church. They were staring Franky's way with a collective quizzical look, and so Joe glanced at his friend too. Standing before the altar, Franky was still clasping his cornet, holding it to his heart in pledge fashion; the groom had never set the instrument down before walking out to face the congregation. Joe, who stood at Franky's shoulder, eased his arm over and reached for the cornet—almost in slow motion to avoid notice. "I can hold it for you during the ceremony," he whispered in his friend's ear, underneath the triumphant quakes of the organ.

That was when the battle started. Joe's gentle pull on the horn met resistance. He looked up to find Franky shaking his head in short, quick movements. Joe pulled a little harder; in answer, Franky held firmer. Next Joe's sly tug turned to a subtle jerk. Franky squeezed his knuckles tight around the brass. The drummer, who weighed two times more than his friend the horn man, began to use that weight in his favor. In no time they were fighting a full tug-of-war, each of their bodies shifting in reaction to the other's pull. First the instrument lunged toward Joe, then it snapped back to Franky. The onlookers in the first pews watched the contest with confused interest. Who would win?

Thwack!

"Ouch!"

It was Joe's voice, echoing through the entire church. At least the organ music covered the shout, for the most part. Forgetting the instrument, he let go of it, shaking his left hand wildly in pain. A pencil had struck him right on the knuckles as he'd clutched the instrument. "I know that feeling from back at St. Francis," he said later. A painful pencil attack had once again come from a religious, although this time the assailant wasn't a nun but a priest.

"Put that thing away," the priest growled, turning to the groom and gesturing at the cornet. "There's no solo in the schedule."

Franky nodded. "I know," he said, panting a bit from the battle. "I tried, but I just can't let go."

With a look toward heaven, the priest turned to face the congregation, and so did the two young men beside him. Horn or no horn, the ceremony couldn't wait. The priest gave a nod toward the back gallery above, where the organist sat hidden from the flock. In a few moments the forgettable melody stopped, and the first notes of the "Wedding March" sounded aloft. More morning minutes having passed, the beam of sunlight was stronger than ever. All up and down the center aisle that would be the bride's pathway, everyone could see floating dust, which on this enchanted day of romance they might have assumed to be fairy dust. Even Joe, never a big Muriel supporter, gazed in wonder at the scene.

But the ethereal dream was interrupted by a distant human voice buried in cotton. The shrill words warbled somewhere amidst the organist's swelling "Wedding March" notes. At first they weren't audible; then, as when someone awakens gradually from a dream, the sharp voice grew louder, until it became a shout:

"Shut up!"

The organ went silent. Just then a cloud must have passed before the sun, for the space darkened. Franky rubbed his eyes to adjust his sight and glimpse both his bride for the first time that day as well as what the commotion was about. Of course, he knew Muriel's voice, so he had to have known it was she who had hollered. But now he not only could hear her, he could see.

That is, he could see the reason for the congregation's initial murmur minutes before, and it had nothing to do with the bride's beauty. Muriel wasn't wearing a wedding dress at all. She stood there, hands dropped to her side, in a faded sweater and blouse. Her shirttail escaped out the bottom of the sweater, untucked, like a messy schoolgirl's, or as if she had just thrown on some clothes from a pile of laundry before finally deciding to make an appearance at the church.

"I can't marrya, Franky!"

The words bounced in an echo, like basketballs down the nave of the church. A hush fell, followed by a collective gasp. Everything had stopped.

"I can't marry you, Franky."

The first time she had shouted it. This time, in the hush, she spoke the words as in a conversation. The groom didn't say a thing. He just stood there, gazing down the dust-dappled aisle of morning sunlight toward his bride. Joe gave him a nudge, which finally unlocked his lips.

"But we're here," he said. "We're in your St. Anthony's."

Even in the dead silence, Franky's voice came out barely audible. Muriel heard, though. In response she threw up her hands.

"Forget St. Antny's," she called down the nave. "I ain't gonna marry you, Franky."

The initial shock waves around the church had begun to dissipate, and a murmur swelled. The groomsmen instinctively circled around Franky, like a football team huddling around its quarterback, and at the back of the church, the bridesmaids did the same. In all the decades of religious life, the priest had never seen such a thing. He stood frozen at the altar.

"All right," he said, gathering himself. "Go home so you can sort this business out."

Franky didn't appear to hear the priest, for he still stood there like a waxen figure. Clustered around him, the murmuring groomsmen bickered over what to do and how to get him out of there. They debated whether to sling him over their shoulders like a fallen soldier from the war they all had just fought, or haul him out on his back, like a man in a coffin.

So over the right shoulder of big Joe went Franky, who still clutched the cornet to his heart probably without knowing it, and the pack of groomsmen trudged off alongside the critically wounded boy-man. To be sure, the scene in the church had become more a funeral than a wedding.

CHAPTER 1

ARIEL'S GREAT ANNOUNCEMENT came on the walk to Franky's rehearsal. And wouldn't it figure, it was the most important rehearsal of the last two decades. Father and daughter had been bickering, just as they had been doing for weeks, maybe months, maybe even years; in fact, all the spats and fights running through Ariel's adolescence might have been viewed as one, single argument that wore on like summer in the deep South.

"I'm not a child anymore," she said. "For crying out loud, I'm almost nineteen years old, so I can take care of myself. I'm done traveling with the band after doing it my whole stupid life!"

Walking through their French Quarter neighborhood, they kept a brisk pace since they were running late, Franky always a half step ahead. Without breaking stride, he scoffed, saying how age had nothing to do with the issue. It was a matter of maturity. "I don't want you lying around the house," he said, before adding with a hammer of finality, "*so you need to come on tour with us.*"

But the issue was anything but finished. Ariel was only tagging along to her father's band's rehearsal in the first place because she wanted to see Bobbi and convince her to go to some bar afterward. The current war, which was happening on the other side of the world, had yet to cause the drinking age to sink to eighteen, but old Louisiana, which itself was sinking, never had to wait for that particular reform because an eighteen year-old could already buy alcohol. Bobbi, who always bristled at the idea of having a drink with the girl she practically helped raise, hadn't yet committed to going.

"Tomorrow morning we can leave for the admissions office about eleven," said Franky, changing the subject. "That way you can sleep in—and maybe we can even grab some lunch at Mid-City Diner afterward." Days before, Ariel had finally acquiesced to registering for fall classes at a local junior college. "Don't you remember how we used to love our trips to City Park to ride the flying horses when we were home from tours? And finish off the morning with lunch at the diner? Ah, those were the days!"

But nostalgia and the change of subject didn't help. Under her breath Ariel started muttering evasive things about college being "boring and worthless."

Franky's voice tightened. "Now Ariel, you made a promise—you said you would at least give it a try."

To save time they were now climbing the clangy fire-escape stairs, Franky first, leading into the building that housed the rehearsal space. That's when she made the great announcement. After merely grumbling and muttering hints of protest, her voice turned firm—so much so that her words echoed about the narrow French Quarter street:

"Forget college—I'm not going. An artist doesn't need college."

Franky stopped on the narrow stair, causing her to practically run into him. "Come on, let's go," she said. "You're gonna be late for rehearsal."

He glared down at her. Unable to find words at first, he repeated hers.

"*Not going to college*," he sneered. "The next thing you're going to tell me is you've denounced my lifelong teachings about love!" He took another step, but then stopped again and looked over his shoulder. "Next thing you know, you'll tell me you want to get married!"

She pulled back in shock, for he had spoken the word he had forsworn for as long as she'd been alive. She leaned on one foot, her hip sticking out a little.

"Nah," she said, shaking her bowed head as if opting out of a fight. "An artist doesn't need men either. An artist's love is her work."

Franky gave a firm nod. "Well all right, then."

Never did he tire of hearing confirmation that his teachings had stuck: Once spurned by Ariel's mother Muriel, he had successfully passed on to his daughter the invaluable trait of bitterness.

"This will be my greatest gift to Ariel," he told Joe before the child had reached the age of five. "The wisdom of love's false promise."

He pulled open the heavy wood door that sported splintering blue paint, and they slipped into the building, one of the larger ones in the Quarter because it lay on the multi-story end of Decatur Street, near Canal. The evening only prolonged the sluggish ninety-six-degree day that had just passed. Darkness had knocked off a mere six degrees of the blood inside the old thermometer that hung near the building's stoop even though the clock now said nine o'clock, and the big black standing fans in the room blew nothing but watery, boiling air. Franky wanted to save money during these lean times by renting rehearsal space with no air conditioning, and so they found themselves in a mostly vacant brick building from an unnamed architectural era that knew a maximum of six stories. A couple of the rooms had window air-conditioning units, but not this one, which did, on the other hand, come with the necessary folding metal chairs.

Clad in his usual tuxedo even though it was only a rehearsal he attended, Franky stooped before a music stand as the band members took their seats and chatted; after the flare-up with his daughter, all was settling into comfortable routine. But he couldn't get college off his mind.

"Everybody," he announced over the din to get their attention, "I just thought you'd all like to know: Ariel isn't going to college."

The band members fell silent, looking toward him. Then they turned toward Ariel, the band's perennial "little girl," who sat in the back of the room in one of the metal folding chairs—glaring at her father, eyes wide and mouth open, incredulous. After freezing her face like that for the audience, she slouched back in her chair, waved her hand, and whispered something to Bobbi.

"*Artists* don't need college," Franky continued with a sardonic chuckle. "Just like musicians don't need to learn their instruments, right, boys? Come to think of it, those kids playing rock 'n' roll never learned to play, so I guess it's the way young people do things these days!"

The group stirred, and Joe's voice rose above the others in a gentle tone: "Ah, Ariel, that ain't true. College'll be good for ya, I just know it. You go to college and—and, and speaking of 'these days' like your daddy was sayin'—these days a girl can be anything she wants. That's what they're sayin', anyway."

"Let's you and me get that drink after rehearsal, darlin,'" said Bobbi. "We can talk then."

"You be quiet, Daddy," said Ariel, passing over their remarks. "This is between you and me. We'll discuss this when we get home."

"Oh yes we will," said Franky. "Oh yes we will."

CHAPTER 2

ON THE MORNING after his foiled wedding, the young groom awoke alone in the twin bed of his childhood. Later that day he told Joe how the single thought that kept coursing through him like blood—aside from the nausea that made him beg for death, aside from the jazz beat of "So long Betty-Betty" bumping with a nervous pulse that was about to drive him insane or make him sick, aside from the pounding ache in his head that kept tempo with the "Betty-Betty" beat—aside from all these things that he could not rid from his head, was, strangely, a novel. *Great Expectations.*

"I hate that book," he told Joe. "I'll always hate that book."

His ninth-grade English class had been reading the novel at the time he'd first met Muriel. But why did that damn piece of harmless make-believe put him on edge—which pretend character haunted him? It wasn't the beautiful Estella, who certainly did captivate him, for she was the obvious Muriel of the story. Nor was it Pip, the lovesick boy in whom he saw himself, thanks to the Brother Thomas High School English Curriculum Committee, which by cruel design had assigned a book whose main character was about the same age as the students reading about him. Pip was the one reason he hated the book: He was a peer of Franky's, also spurned by a girl. But something else about the book haunted him. Something lured him to the story while he simultaneously loathed it.

"No, it's not Estella and Pip I keep thinking about," he told Joe, who had sat through ninth-grade English with him. "They're harmless. They're just kids."

But nor was it the obvious adult candidate in the novel, the evil Orlick. "By the end, Orlick's harmless too," Franky said, "because he gets his due."

Great Expectations or no, it was odd that he even attended a Catholic school. Franky came from a reasonably wealthy Jewish family who lived in one of the smaller homes uptown on Pine Street. Muriel came from an *un*-wealthy Italian family who lived in a duplex shotgun in the Ninth Ward off St. Claude Avenue, near the Industrial Canal. At the time, the best boys' high school in the city was Brother Thomas, so that was where little Franky had to go. Jim Liusa, meanwhile, scraped together the tuition money to send his daughter to St. Bernardine High, then the premier preparatory academy for girls and the sister school of Brother Thomas. Women neighbors murmured that Mrs. Liusa was sending her daughter there "to meet some rich Catholic boy" from Brother Thomas. She met a boy, all right, but not a Catholic one.

Aside from those thoughts of *Great Expectations*, there was one other tiny detail he always recalled concerning that Sunday morning after the wedding: Rising out of bed, he never noticed what he was wearing, what clothing still hung draped on his frail, booze-saturated body, until he had staggered from his bedroom and downstairs to face his parents alone for the first time since the ceremony. The night before, his buddies had dragged him to the French Quarter for eleven hours of boozing after the aborted wedding, and so it was almost noon before he started making his way down the hardwood stairway that was dressed with a floral runner. He held the railing every step.

When he'd accomplished three steps, his mother passed below with a feather duster in her hand. The *swoop* of the duster stopped when she put her hands on her hips and gazed up at her son, the deserted groom.

"Franky, you're still wearing your tuxedo!"

As any drunk might do, after being dropped off from the long day and night of drinking, he had stumbled up to his room and collapsed immediately into bed, never minding the formal costume on his back. Now, stopped on the third step from the top of the stairs, he held up both arms and looked down his concave chest to notice the formal wear for the first time. Then step by step, he restarted his trek downward. "You need to return that thing so you don't get overcharged," his mother added.

"I don't have to return it," said Franky, concentrating on the stairs. "I bought it."

That was a story in itself. On the Friday afternoon before the wedding—just two days ago—Muriel had asked him what sort of tuxedo he had rented.

"Tuxedo?" Franky answered.

Not having attended a wedding before, he hadn't thought to get one. And besides that, the event had been planned so fast that whispers had even started about an accidental baby on the way—in other words, the young groom had almost no time to learn about weddings.

"Yeah, what's it like?" said Muriel. "Is it nice?"

He hesitated. "I believe it's black."

Within minutes Franky found himself scurrying downtown to Mintz Formal Wear on Canal Street, trying to arrive before the store closed. He passed through the door at four minutes till the closing hour, shirt clinging to his back from June-day sweat and chest heaving. But to no avail. With his lungs lurching, he listened gape-mouthed as Mr. Mintz explained he had nothing left in Franky's size. It was the peak of wedding season; moreover, Franky had "a unique build," Mr. Mintz told him, and so he didn't carry many tuxes that would fit him in the first place. Dejected, Franky bowed his head and started to turn for the door. "But wait," the shop owner said with a wag of his index finger. Fortunately, he did have in stock a single tuxedo from his sparse and picked-through *For Sale* shelf that might work, one made for "young men who hadn't filled out," as Mintz put it: "Usually boys about fifteen." Franky took a couple of beats to figure out, as with a math problem, the man's comment.

"I didn't know that guys *filled out*," he answered.

The shopkeeper didn't hear him. "A guy like you is better off buying anyway," he said, examining Franky's quirky, rail-thin frame and putting a tailor's tape across the young man's shoulders. *Jeez*, he muttered to himself, shaking his head. "I've never seen anything like it."

When Franky reappeared from the dressing room wearing the pants, Mr. Mintz helped him into the jacket and then took a step back to size him up. As everyone saw later, the jacket had miraculously strengthened his shoulders, and the black tone of the ensemble worked wonders on his pink skin.

"You look good in a tux," said the shopkeeper. He took a step back again and studied the groom some more before giving an approving nod. "Better than you look in regular clothes."

Mintz stepped over to a cash register and began punching the round keys atop their long metal fingers. Following him over, Franky questioned whether he should be buying an outfit he'd never get a chance to wear again, but Mr. Mintz insisted it was the best route. "You're young. You'll be able to get some use out of it and save money in the long run."

But when will I need a tuxedo ever again? Franky asked. Mr. Mintz was adamant. He'd known Franky's father for years and he wouldn't steer him wrong, which was true. "Trust me," he said. "A guy like you is better off buying. Just wear the tux every chance you get, and it'll pay off."

But right now Mrs. Fritz, at the bottom of the stairs making her feather duster dance, droned on about who in their right mind would buy a tuxedo that you'd never wear again. Franky stopped listening within seconds. For the rest of the morning, he looked so downtrodden and despondent that even Mr. Fritz made an attempt to buck up his son. Franky had refused breakfast from his mother and returned to his room, where he lay in bed staring vacantly up at the ceiling. Mr. Fritz, who was enjoying his only day off from his shop on Canal Street that sold ladies' shoes, eased open the bedroom door. The emptiness within was filled by the whir of Franky's TornadoFan. After slipping inside, Mr. Fritz pulled out his son's desk chair, planted his shoe on the seat, and folded his arms over the back. From that stance he tried to console Franky the only way he knew how: by teaching a lesson through a story.

Mr. Fritz spoke of a great hurricane that hit the city a long time ago. The floodwaters rose, invading the streets and even people's homes. The water climbed so high that coffins from the below-sea-level cemeteries for which the city was famous escaped their resting places and floated down the streets like pirogues. Anyone with any kind of forgotten boat lying unused in the backyard hopped in it to escape the rising waters. One man who had a small rowboat even took a dresser full of clothes with him. He had room in the boat for his dog too, but the man liked the dog only somewhat, and he wasn't sure how he would be able to feed it anyway, so he coldly left it behind on the second-floor porch with just a few scraps from the previous night's supper. The mutt watched the boat drift away down the street, the same stretch it had walked a thousand times on a leash with its indifferent master.

Days later, rescue workers found the thinning and famished dog still sitting at the high spot on the porch, gazing down the street in the direction that his master had floated. The dog was still hoping for his return.

Once the waters had receded, new owners were found for the dog. The good mutt grew healthy and strong again—and grew accustomed to his new life and new owners, a childless and old married couple, who loved him very much. One day, though, while on a walk with his new master, the dog spotted his old one, the man who had abandoned him. In a flash, the mutt bolted over to the former owner, tail fluttering like a hummingbird's wings, and threw its front paws onto the man's legs, licking him like a sundae.

And that, to Franky's surprise, was the point at which Mr. Fritz abruptly ended the story.

"You see?" concluded his father. "Love is stupid."

The tale had succeeded at least in the sense that it had drawn the interest of the near-comatose Franky, who asked his dad to tell him what happened next. Did the old owner take him back? Did the new owner protest? Did they have an argument, or perhaps did the old owner turn his back on the dog? But Mr. Fritz said he was missing the point. "Never mind all that," he said, waving his hand. "The point is, love is stupid. Always remember that."

A little while later, Joe rode over on his bicycle to see how his rejected friend was faring. As he always did, he used music to snap his friend out of his funk.

"Now we can finally get the band going," he told him. Joe sat straddling Franky's desk chair, his forearms resting on top of its back. Joe had spent hours at that desk up in his friend's room, the jittery kid tapping his Keuffel & Esser Co. slide rule and pencil as he fought off panic attacks and struggled through hated math problems, while Franky breezed through homework on his bed and then waited for his friend to finish. Now Franky lay facedown, one leg straightened and one knee bent up to his hip. "No girls, no distractions," Joe continued, speaking to the corpse on the bed. "So maybe what Muriel did was meant to be."

"Nothing," intoned Franky, "was ever meant to be."

Joe, whose eyes had been wandering around the room out of the boredom that comes with spending time with a depressed person, turned and took in his friend.

"Jeez, you do look pale."

"That's because she stole my soul. I'm only a ghost anymore."

Joe noticed something else about his friend. "Get rid of that tux and put on some regular clothes so we can go out and get you some fresh air."

All his clothes were at the apartment, Franky said. The week before, he may have forgotten about his tux, but he remembered to attend to one important detail that no young groom would forget: He rented a modest apartment outside the French Quarter on Frenchman Street, where his bride and he would consummate the marriage and begin life.

"You'll want to move your things in before the wedding," he told her. "That way when we get back from Bay St. Louis—"

"Daddy says it's not proper to move in until after the wedding." Still, she snatched the key from his hand. "But I'll have a look at the place anyways."

Now, as they idled in the bedroom figuring out what Franky would wear, Joe returned to studying the ex-groom. "You look good in a tux," he said.

At first Franky didn't answer him. In his supine grief he had been leaving many of his friend's comments lingering without responses. "Too bad I'll never get to wear one again."

"I don't know, I think the bandleader should wear one onstage. It's classy."

"Bandleader…" His voice trailed off as he briefly considered the concept. "No," he said after a few beats, and then added that he didn't have the wind in him to play a horn anymore: "I can barely even breathe."

Joe grew almost desperate—for both of them. "Come on, Franky," he said, "I need you. You're the leader, you're a natural. You gonna let your buddy down? You know I can't do it without you. What am I gonna do if I don't play music? Christ, I barely made it through high school."

Joe tried everything—from the allure of stardom to the guilt of deserting a friend—to pump a little air into Franky's deflated soul, but nothing was working. Booze nausea had sapped any physical strength that grief hadn't already stolen. But at last the drummer thought of something that might help. He conjured a word—or really a *name*—that possessed truly magical powers over his best friend.

"Bix had pain too, you know."

"Huh?" Franky pushed himself up to lean on one elbow.

"Bix took his pain and poured it all right through that cornet of his."

Joe was speaking of Franky's boyhood hero and obsession, the great Bix Beiderbecke, who'd died young, killed by drink. The failed groom's flaccid voice suddenly turned firm. "Don't bring Bix into this. Bix was a genius."

"And Gene Krupa. Look at Krupa with the drugs and the cops and everything. Now, he's gotta know pain."

"Krupa is a drummer," Franky answered, finding more strength. "Like you, he can beat out his pain."

"You got that right," said Joe. "I follow Krupa's beat. And your guy is Bix. Every player puts his pain into their music, and Beiderbecke did it as good as any of 'em."

Franky almost started to nod, but then his body collapsed back down on the bed and he shook his head, saying, "Bix Beiderbecke never met Muriel."

The two began to argue about which musicians had endured the most pain. Franky grew cantankerous, but at least he was no longer comatose. Cantankerousness, Franky was learning, was the force easiest to grasp for survival.

"Bottom line," Joe said, concluding the debate, "ain't no pain, ain't no girl, ain't no nothing—woulda kept Bix from his music."

"You're damn right nothing would."

The ghost of Bix Beiderbecke had come to resurrect Franky. With his best friend roused, Joe coaxed him out of the house for some fresh air, of which there was none in summertime New Orleans unless one could accomplish movement. So they hopped the streetcar, and Joe tossed around ideas of what clubs their band would play first. Franky, still skeptical that he had the breath in him to blow a single note, looked out at the passing homes on St. Charles Avenue and only half listened. The breeze coming through the open streetcar window did him good, and then Joe dragged him over to the river, where they picked up a free boat ride on the Algiers ferry, which took them across the river and then back where they started. This additional breeze from the ride offered him a further breath of life, as did the diesel fumes he inhaled and the white water they watched spitting and churning below as they leaned over the rail at the vessel's stern.

A few minutes later, fourteen hours after he had attempted to drink the disastrous wedding away in the bars of the French Quarter, he found himself once again walking the pavement of the oldest neighborhood in the city. Today, though, the Quarter, where he and his girl had reached so many milestones (first kiss, first and only lovemaking, etc.), did not smell so much of his former fiancée. He had walked those streets so many times since childhood that they harbored countless shards of the past whose colors blended together like mosaic glass, tempering Muriel's memory. Franky had loved the Quarter and Canal Street for as long as he could remember. He had shopped with his mother at the department stores that lined Canal, especially the one with the big clock, and enjoyed simple lunches with his father at the oyster house on Iberville that everyone knew. As adolescents, he and Joe would head to the Quarter with but one destination in mind: Roussel's Music Shop, where the two boys' hearts would palpitate and their palms perspire upon passing through the Decatur Street doors that led into the musicians' den. Because of those memories, Franky's visit to the Quarter with Joe that day had a medicinal effect on him. The familiar environs served as a subconscious reminder that his young life history already encompassed much more than just Muriel.

"Let's check this place out," Joe said, stopping him in front of a decrepit door a half block off Bourbon. "We might have a shot here."

"I've never heard of it," said Franky.

"That's why we might have a shot."

Joe led his tuxedo-clad friend, who proved too depressed to object to anything, through the entrance. With the bright sun branded on the two boys' pupils, the room came through almost pitch dark. They could barely make out the outline of the bartender and one man sitting at the bar. With Franky in tow, Joe asked to see the owner, who appeared a minute later from a mystery door.

"We've got a band," said Joe.

"You're a kid," the owner answered. "Come back in five years."

"This here's Franky. He's the bandleader."

The unshaven man looked Franky up and down. "You look good in a tux."

"Thank you," said the otherwise silent Franky.

The man considered him some more. "You must not be too bad, if you're out playing. Maybe come back in two years."

The two boys looked at each other. The owner thought that Franky had just finished a gig because he was wearing a tuxedo. Franky was a pro, he assumed.

THAT NIGHT BEFORE going to bed, after wearing his wedding costume for two straight days, Franky finally shed his tuxedo. In the ensuing weeks, whenever he walked into a live-music venue sporting the formal wear, his burgeoning source of identity and luck, people assumed he was either with the band or perhaps was some established musician who had come to check out the act after playing somewhere else. Of course, for Franky the tux also had become a badge of honor, a melodramatic symbol of his wedding that never was, of a love never realized.

So as his rich music life unfolded following his foiled wedding day, it became clear which character in *Great Expectations* affected him most. The character Charles Dickens had burned deepest into Franky's tormented mind was not Pip, Estella, or Orlick, but a cold, old woman: Miss Havisham. He could not forget that brittle, graying wedding gown which she wore within the confines of her dusty house.

"I like her," he told Joe during one of their countless conversations about that defining ninth-grade year. "I like that mean old woman." And for months after, whenever questioned about why he wore his tuxedo, he answered that even though the tux was stiff and formal, it was comfortable. It fit to wear what he felt.

CHAPTER 3

NEVER MIND ARIEL and college. The members of the band loved her, but they had their own matters to fret over.

The wet heat, combined with the reality that the players had passed through a career's worth of practices and rehearsals that numbered in the thousands, caused them to hang out and gab with listless energy. But maybe their indifference was just a musician's mask of nervousness. Like a gig of a lifetime, everything rode on this night of rehearsal number one-thousand-something, which doubled as an audition, a chance for an anonymous player to try and impress them. The band, struggling after all those years of success, had but one more player to evaluate after a stream of them had come through the doors only to fail Franky's esoteric music test or keep any of the other players from yawning. So if the concept of infusing new blood was the group's last hope, this player scheduled today was the last hope for them to find the right match. They had already listened to no less than thirteen prospects, all of whom failed at the impossible riddle Franky had given them of playing two songs at once. In fact, the ad that he had placed in a local music tabloid demanded that Orpheus himself walk through the door:

> *Brass needed for professional band. Must be able to play jazz, blues, rock, classical, Cajun, and everything else impeccably, but especially rock and jazz.*

Folks weren't talking so much after the little public spat between father and daughter. Those uncomfortable family moments had grown all too familiar starting with Ariel's ninth-grade year, but the players never had grown used to them. Thus, they could have used a nice, smooth rehearsal that evening.

But then on cue the next source of conflict came sauntering through the door. With a saxophone case held aside his blue jeans torn at the knee, the last man auditioning strutted in, moving in a slouchy way that resembled Ariel's gait. Franky wasn't sure whether this modern way of moving—never before seen until Ariel's generation, most believed—spoke of nonchalance or poor self-esteem. But the newcomer quickly answered that question.

"I liked your ad," he said, setting down his sax. "I'm up to the challenge, man, so give it to me." He didn't seem to notice or mind how the other musicians slouched around him with their arms folded, not bothering to introduce themselves because they assumed he would be as unimpressive as the other thirteen auditions. "I'm Evan," he said. "Evan Macon from California."

One of the men, either Tim or Al, snickered a little, and Franky started to open his mouth, ready with a witty comeback to put the young fellow in his place. But someone interrupted:

"Let's hear it. Show these old-timers what you can do."

It wasn't Tim or Al speaking. No, the voice, a feminine one, came from the back, and it didn't come from Bobbi, their vocalist. Still slouching back in her chair with her arms folded, Ariel was smiling shyly while looking directly at the invited imposter. Everyone had turned her way.

"Come on, let's hear it," she repeated, a lock of brown hair twirling in her finger.

Stunned, Franky had no choice but to echo her. "Show us what you can do."

What stung him, he later told Joe, was the look that came over her face at that very moment. "Here I am, her father," he explained, throwing up his arms, "and I'd never seen that exact smile. She'd never revealed that one to me!"

But he didn't express that sentiment at the time. Rather, his fears—or perhaps a sense of doom—welled up from his gut and out of his mouth:

"The Devil was a musician."

It came out in a mumble, though, so only the band members closest to him heard. Meanwhile, there was business to attend to.

"Yeah, show us what you can do," echoed Tim, and a couple others murmured in agreement, slouching back in their chairs and readying to only half pay attention.

"He's just a kid," Tim said skeptically to Franky. "He can't be much older than Ariel."

"That's the idea," said the bandleader, watching the musician lift his sax out of its coffin. "That's the idea."

Franky's vision for the godlike recruit they needed to find came to him at the beginning of another recent pre-tour band rehearsal. Standing before his fellow players at his music stand, he literally saw the answer, and this idea was believed to be one of his great epiphanies. Strangely, though, what lay before him, the very source of the moment's inspiration, he had seen a thousand times before: the mere faces of his old friends.

He was thumbing through the sheet music with his head bent downward when a nickel escaped from the pocket of Joe's loose pants as the drummer squatted down to take his place behind his kit. The bouncing nickel jangled on the tile floor, causing Franky to glance up before returning back to the musical score.

That's when he had the epiphany. After going back to his sheet music, he took a double take at what lay before him—not at the nickel but the group of assembled musicians. One by one, they saw him studying them and so they turned silent, waiting for him to say something, like a classroom of kids noticing their teacher's silent glare. And say something he did.

"We got old," said the bandleader. He regarded them, astonished, as if the aging process had just happened right then and there. Then, the astonishment having passed as quickly as it had come, he nodded firmly. "We need some youth."

When they asked what the hell he was talking about, he elaborated. "We're not kids anymore." That is, they no longer possessed an overflowing supply of sexual electricity to burst forth through their horns and send an audience into a tizzy of fun and excitement. Moreover, they had no young fellow to draw youthful audience members.

"To a young person," he said, "we're old farts."

So he ran the ad in the tabloid, demanding an Orpheus-like player who could master old and new. When the publication came out, Joe was stupefied. "But Franky," he said, studying the ad and its reference to a certain form of modern music, "you hate rock. Your life's mission is to beat it."

"I know," Franky said, nodding. "That's the trick: to get someone who's great at that garbage but keep him from playing it."

The principle was the same as with Bix, he explained. The band never really played all that much of his hero Bix Beiderbecke's music, yet the Bix-style energy still flowed from their bandstand. Similarly, the new player, if he was talented enough, would infuse the young people's sound into the band without actually playing their music. Dismayed by Franky's embrace of rock, Joe looked at his friend as if he'd lost his mind, and hardly for the first time. But then the drummer nodded his head in understanding when Franky put it this way:

"I'm opposed to rock, but I'm not opposed to its beat. I'm not opposed to its energy."

Franky always started off auditions trying to trip players up, and this time was no different. "He definitely looks like a rock 'n' roller," he whispered to Joe. "We'll start him off with something else."

Everyone sat up in their seats, and the cacophonous sounds of a band coming to life rose up into the space.

"All right, kid," said Franky to the sax player. "We're gonna do a tune that by the looks of you I'm sure you don't know, but it was actually a minor hit for us—it even charted. Now, it's called 'My Baby's Gonna Cry.' It's not exactly Duke-quality, but it surely beats anything *you've* ever played."

The player acted as if he didn't notice the insult. Instead, he insulted the band members.

"Yeah, I've heard that one," he said with a shrug. "My parents used to play the record all the time when I was a kid."

But while some of the others grunted, Franky didn't appear to mind the reminder of their age. He raised his eyebrows in interest.

The players put their instruments to their mouths as they had done ten thousand times before. Franky gave the count: *uh-one, uh-two, uh-one, two, three, four!*

Not only did the invitee know the song, he *knew* the song—musically. From the moment his teeth bit down on the reed of his mouthpiece, he more than kept up with the band; he added his own electrons. He zipped through "My Baby's Gonna Cry," playing in perfect sync with the rest of the players and—since, after all, he was auditioning and needed to showboat a bit—flavoring up the tune with little runs and accents that he weaved in and out of Bobbi's vocals.

"Hey, not bad, kid," the singer said after the last note sounded. The others followed with modest nods and shrugs of assent.

"That's the best I've ever heard that dumb song," Ariel chimed in from the peanut gallery. She received two faces: The young player nodded and smiled at her, while her father glared.

Now it was time for part two of the audition: He would need to play solo.

"Sure you can play the old way," said Franky, turning back to him. "Now let's hear you do some rock 'n' roll."

The musical guest sat up eagerly. "Old stuff or new?"

"Both."

"No prob, man. Whatchya wanna hear first?"

"Both at the same time."

The young musician took a drag on the cigarette he was smoking and studied Franky with a squinted eye. Mashing it in a glass ashtray on the floor by the leg of his chair, he glanced over in Ariel's direction, then nodded with a smile of aplomb and said, "I like this guy."

With that he stood up and dove into Jimi Hendrix's moody "Little Wing," only the guitar was a saxophone, a saxophone no one had ever heard before, at least anyone in the room. Franky couldn't help his mouth from dropping open a little at first, but then he caught himself, sobering up with a frown. The song was slow, lacking the kind of energy he wanted injected into the band, the rock 'n' roll energy he sought. But then the young musician segued to a different tune that Franky was sure had to be a Buddy Holly number. Folks started nodding their heads and tapping their feet, then before they knew it, he eased up on the gas pedal and slipped back into "Little Wing."

"You're alternating between the old and new tune," Franky called over the rolling sax. "You're not playing both at the same time."

The player looked too consumed with his music to hear. He swung back to Buddy Holly, then back again to "Little Wing"—and so on and so on, with each change coming closer together until he *was* almost playing the tunes simultaneously. The little audience began stomping their feet and clapping to the beat. Ariel, meanwhile, emerging from her perennial state of blasé, jumped up out of her chair and grabbed Bobbi's hand. The two started grooving and dancing together to the solo sax, which sounded almost like a full band once the onlookers' clapping and stomping kicked in.

At last the one-man band pulled the unified tune into the station with one, long flickering note.

"Hooray for Evan Macon from California!" said Bobbi.

"Yeah!" Ariel exclaimed, clapping. "It's about time you guys got someone who could play."

The band members followed with nods and a scattered round of applause—all except for Franky, who had picked up off the floor the blasé look that Ariel had discarded. Everyone watched. They all said later that they thought the young player didn't stand a chance of getting in the band because Ariel was acting flirty with him. Sure enough, Franky marched over to the young musician and grabbed his shoulder while staring him in the eye, looking like he was about to tell him to beat it, hit the road, kid. The two couldn't have looked more different, standing there facing each other—one in a tux of solid black and white, the other in old, torn jeans and an untucked shirt with a tiny floral print.

Franky grabbed Evan's hand to give it one single shake. "You're in," he told him. He made a sweeping gesture with an open palm as if presenting him to the band for the first time, and then he turned back to face him square on. With a lowered brow he added, "But get rid of those ripped-up jeans. Get rid of the jeans, no girls allowed, and don't play that garbage ever again."

CHAPTER 4

FOR FRANKY, WHEN he was Evan's age, a Goodman on clarinet was, of course, just as exciting as any electric-guitar virtuoso that came later. Within weeks of the wedding he had dived far into music's endless depths, coming up for air for but one meal at twilight and for sleep, which he took only once the night's darkness started to glow with the first hints of daylight and all any ear heard was the morning streetcar clattering in perfect rhythm. He and Joey and formed their band during these months, putting together the nucleus of what was to become the great, touring Franky Fritz Band. He designed no master plan to craft a career in music. Possessing the nearsightedness of most nineteen-year-olds, he just wanted to play jazz, and so he did everything he could to play as much of it as possible. With a little luck to neutralize any minor immaturities, a dash of success followed.

The professionalism of his musicianship came thanks in part to Uncle Sam. Upon high school graduation, Franky was just like the rest of the New Orleans boys who participated in the lottery of their lives, the one where the winning tickets came from the national government and the odds were stacked toward most of the boys winning. He received a letter directly from the president: *Your friends and neighbors have selected you, of strong body and mind, to serve your country.* He shuffled down to the draft board that had been set up at Alcee Fortier High School, holding in his hand that piece of government paper that had on it a serial number that was special even though it was in the thousands. Within three days, he was headed for Camp Beauregard in Alexandria. But when he arrived, they took one look at him and acted disappointed in the specimen before them.

"Can you do *anything*?" said the drill sergeant who greeted him. Franky had passed the minimum weight requirement, but only barely. Standing in front of the sergeant, his height, which had surged in recent months, made him look even thinner than his weight indicated on paper.

"Sure, I can do something," Franky said. "I can play any horn you can name."

And that was that. The day he finished his basic training, he was being shipped off somewhere different from everyone else.

"Get 'im outta here," said the drill sergeant, dismissing the sack of skin and bones before him.

Where he was going: Off to play music in a military band to boost the spirits of his fellow soldiers. These were the first touring gigs of his career, the ones that made him fall in love with the road.

Thanks to one seminal experience, he became known as an asset to any act. He could play any piece of metal put before him—whether trumpet, trombone or cornet—and so he acquired the tagline "Man of Many Horns." That's what a certain famous wartime entertainer called him once when Franky's military band shared the bill with his act, and the moniker stuck with him among the players.

It happened just after Franky's band came offstage and minutes before the entertainer's set was supposed to start. His trumpet player—who was crucial to the comedy routine because he played a key burlesque solo when a voluptuous woman was to walk onstage—had caught a fever that was so high he couldn't even stand up. Sauntering offstage with his trombone in hand, Franky witnessed the emergency situation unfolding before him like a stage play. It was a true showbiz drama, with the famous entertainer barking orders about going to find him a horn player, I don't care where.

"I can take his place!" Franky announced, raising his finger.

The entertainer stopped barking and turned. He gave him a once-over—everyone, it seemed, always gave the poor, emaciated boy a double take.

"All right, kid," said the entertainer with a roll of his eyes. "We'll never find a real man in time."

The show went off without a hitch. The voluptuous woman slithered out onstage, Franky played the sultry solo, the crowd of soldiers cheered in sexual ecstacy, and the performance went so well that the whole crew cheered out of relief and joy when it was over. Meanwhile, the voluptuous woman smacked a big, wet kiss on Franky's lips out of thanks, or maybe even arousal caused by the solo blown by the emaciated boy-man. She must also have been impressed with his dexterity: After his trumpet part, Franky had taken up his cornet to add color to the next number, and then he'd improvised on his trombone to boot. That's what got the attention of the famous entertainer, for like a football coach, any bandleader can use a versatile player.

"Well, I'll be," he said. "It's the man of many horns."

From then on the famous entertainer, whose name was Bob Hope, would call out: "Hey, Man of Many Horns, get over here and let's rehearse this song!" "Hey, Man of Many Horns, nice playing tonight!"—and so Franky caught on with his band. Continuing his tour of duty, he hopped as many as three islands in the Pacific with Hope and his act. The gig probably would have stuck for the rest of the war, but after the third island, one of Franky's sarcastic witticisms got him kicked out of the ensemble because he happened to direct one toward Hope himself. He played out the rest of the war with a much lower-profile band, although he insisted for decades afterward that with his new act "the musicianship was better anyway."

Now back home, he showed eventual signs of becoming an independent bachelor, waking up at the end of every morning and adding a second meal to his day, a square breakfast: two eggs, a slice of ham meat from a can, and a potent cup of coffee with chicory. Even his evening meals became lavish and modern: wieners that also came in a can, but with an individually packed "Sack-o-Sauce" for each dog. All that was left of Muriel was a small framed black-and-white photo that had been colored with touches of paint, as they used to do back then.

Before long, the ensemble, composed of a cluster of old high-school band friends, was playing on a fairly regular basis, with Joe on drums, Franky on horn (trombone, trumpet, and cornet), Al Butkus on trumpet, and Tim Callahan on saxophone. They generated interest by developing a repertoire of familiar songs from artists like

Goodman, Basie, and Berlin. Franky had designed one rule for their play lists, and that rule was getting them repeat customers and more gigs:

"Make it fast!"

The band picked only songs that were danceable, songs that shot energy like flares onto the dance floor. If they wanted to do a tune that pulsed a bit on the slow side—well, they just picked up the tempo and injected some spunk into the number. For a while during their performance learning curve, they were running through all the tunes at the scrambling tempo of Duke's "Hot and Bothered." But they didn't play only fast songs; it was the in-between tempos that they avoided. Always watching the mood of his audience from his band perch, Franky developed a keen sense for precisely when to throw in a slow romantic number to appease the lovebirds and the lovebird hopefuls, something more along the lines of "Mood Indigo."

As his burgeoning confidence fed his creative energy, he even began doing a little composing himself. He was especially proud of one particular song, and so the band had actually learned it. But while he and the rest of the players liked the tune well enough, they couldn't get up the nerve to play it in public. Besides, they hadn't even come up with a decent name for the tune.

Covering up any immaturity that he may have possessed (including his prepubescent frame) was the tuxedo, which continued to drive forward his developing career, for it gave him credibility in landing those early gigs. When he approached bar owners or met with engaged couples planning wedding receptions, they did not see a scrawny half-man, half-kid. What they saw was a musician so serious about his trade that he wore his stage clothes at three o'clock in the afternoon, ten o'clock in the morning, or whatever time they happened to be meeting with him.

To his band friends, though, the tux was a concrete manifestation of an elephant in the living room: Muriel and the wedding. Franky never brought up those topics, and so in the masculine form that sensitivity takes, his friends and fellow band members followed suit. Franky hadn't seen or heard from his almost-bride for several months.

Soon the band landed their first weekly gig at a place called Nick's, a tiny bar in the Marigny neighborhood not far from Franky's apartment. The joint was usually so dead that the owner, a sweaty growler who had *business failure* written all over him, was willing to try any easy fix—in this case, a few novice performers—to increase business. Without hearing a note of their music, he simply told the boys to be there on Tuesdays.

"If anyone leaves while you're playing," he told them, "you're done."

That frightened the young musicians on the first night—especially Joe, who was so jittery that everyone worried he might not even be able to play.

"My entire career's at stake," Joe fretted. "If we blow it tonight, I'll have to go find a job at the shipyards."

To calm Joe sufficiently enough to play, Franky came up with a quick solution. He quietly suggested to the lone customers, two men who had been sitting at the bar lethargically complaining about being out of work, that the band would pay for one free beer at the end of each set. The cash-poor patrons stayed all night—and applauded, although who knew whether the clapping was for the music or out of enthusiasm for the impending beers.

For Franky, his life's road was settling down into one of those straight and comfortable stretches of stability, or so it seemed. Then came the phone call at Nick's.

The band was playing their weekly gig at the dingy joint, where Franky's tuxedo and hair tonic always stood out. He was feeling especially good that night—so good that he had been trying to convince the boys to lead off one of the sets with the song that he'd composed. But the other players were still too skittish about playing anything original. At the end of the first set, Nick whistled Franky over to the bar.

"Hey there, horn man, you got a lady on the phone for you. She keeps calling while you're playin'. I been telling her you're busy, but she won't quit bothering me."

Franky, who was getting a taste of the social fruits of musicianhood, grew excited and flattered at the news of a phone call from a "lady," as Nick had said. He was not dating anybody, but he might chat with a girl at some wedding reception or other after she sent a shy smile his way from the dance floor as he played. Therefore, he likely hoped the caller to be one of those passing acquaintances whom he might have told, "We play at Nick's Tuesday nights."

But the identity of the caller stretched beyond the furthest reaches of his imagination; he wouldn't have been more surprised if Rita Hayworth herself was calling. Rita Hayworth wasn't calling, of course, though the mystery lady didn't bother identifying herself or, for that matter, even saying hello:

"Your mama said you was gonna be there. So whenya gonna come back?"

The barked words, shooting through the black-coiled cord that stretched across the bar, reverberated from the phone. The nasal voice was instantly known.

"Muriel?" he said after fighting to swallow the lump in his throat.

"Whenya gonna come back, Franky?"

He swallowed again. "Well, I don't think I was the one to leave in the first place, but if—"

"No, whenya gonna get off work and be back at that apartment?"

His eyes bulged, and he put his hand over the phone. "Hey, fellas," he called to his bandmates, "she wants to make it with me again."

The boys all rushed up to the bar to witness the amazing phone call. "Ah jeez," Tim murmured. "He said she wants to make it with him *again*, so that means it's Muriel."

Franky lifted his hand from the phone. "Well," he said, casually slouching back against the bar as his friends watched him. "I guess I can be home around quarter past one."

"None of this *around* business," Muriel said. "Let's be safe and say be there at two o'clock—exactly, and I mean *exactly*."

Franky nodded and threw the boys a smile. "If you want me there at such an exact time, you must have a surprise for me."

A couple beats of silence passed through the line. "Yeah, that's right. I got a surprise."

"But—" Franky stammered before gathering himself to try and play it cool. "Where will you wait if we both have to be there at such an exact time? A girl can't be waiting on my doorstep, outside by herself in the middle of the night. Maybe you should come—"

"I still have a key, remember?"

And she hung up.

Her off-putting manner was only a continuation of the ambiguous engagement that had been. At the time Franky returned from the war, marriage-license sales were shooting up like a New Orleans thermometer. In that spirit, his proposals to Muriel began coming via the U.S. mail, when he was off fighting the enemy with a full arsenal of horns. Like thousands of other boy-men who held their white-knuckled grip to thoughts of reuniting with loves back home, Franky lived on Muriel's memory during those months; that's what his letters to Joe indicated, anyway. After the first proposal, she didn't write back at all for some months, and Franky blamed it on the army mail's lack of dependability.

"Don't they know guys have got girls back home?"

When it was time to go home at last, he spent hours on the train with beating heart and sweating palms, envisioning himself as one of those soldiers he'd seen in newsreels being embraced by a girl in some train station or seaport, ticker tape falling around the reunited couple. The scene at the train station on Annunciation Street where he arrived was not unlike that—at least the air was sparked with a festive spirit, with families and lovers embracing and folks practically bowing to the hero soldiers who had fought for their country and won.

But no seaport embrace among throngs of other lovers greeted Franky: His mother and father picked him up in their Terraplane. His mother hugged him and his father gave him a handshake and took his bag.

"Come on," said his father, "let's get out of this mess and go home."

"Muriel is at work," his mother explained as they started off to the car. "She said she'll see you tonight."

Boy, did he doll himself up for the big date. He shaved not once but twice, using double the lather each time, and then showered first with hot water until he sweated and then with cold until he returned to room temperature, which was hot. Next he splashed drugstore cologne he'd bought that afternoon onto his neck and face even though it stung from his having shaved too much, ironed his pants while standing on his spindly legs in his army-issue boxers, donned a white-pressed shirt, tied his tie, and slipped on a blue blazer. Finally he stopped to inspect the finished product. Looking in the oval mirror hanging above the dresser, he examined himself from the waist up and, meeting his own eyes, spoke to the reflection.

"Your life starts now," he said.

He sure was right about that. When he appeared at her door, she greeted him with a perfunctory hug. Perhaps he wouldn't propose after all; perhaps it was all a mistake, he would later recount to Joe. But his hurt vanished as they were seated at the perfect table at Lucy's in the French Quarter, in a nook more secluded than the other booths. Looking at the menu, Muriel said something so flattering that Franky almost questioned whether someone else sitting behind her had spoken.

"You went off to fight," she said to him without glancing up from her menu. "You're a war hero."

After their meal, as he had planned, he walked her to the garden behind St. Louis Cathedral, where a statue of the risen Christ, arms uplifted and palms open, cast a great shadow on the wall of the giant church. Franky, in neither his sweetest dream nor cruelest nightmare, could not have imagined Muriel's answer there in the garden, for it was neither yes, no, nor even maybe.

"Muriel, will you marry me?" he said, kneeling before her with the ominous God shadow looming behind him. He held his breath.

But instead of answering his question, she spoke to the *other* urgent question veterans often asked their sweethearts, one he hadn't mentioned:

"We're going to a hotel!"

He gaped up at her, then at the resurrected Christ, then at Muriel again, and then they both turned and started walking arm-in-arm. To the *clock* of Muriel's heels, they passed the din of dinner crowds, their unified voice streaming out of restaurants with open square frames where windows should be, and the occasional shouts of drunken men echoing off buildings through the narrow streets. Once they were back in the square in front of the cathedral, she stopped before another statue—not of Christ this time but of another mortal god: Andrew Jackson, who sat fierce atop an angry horse that bucked high on its hind legs. Tourists and locals passed by around them, while youthful couples reunited after the war walked hip to hip with streaming smiles.

"You're back from the war," Muriel said. But she was looking up at the Jackson statue. "You deserve this."

Arms clutched together, the two marched to the nearest hotel he could find, a nondescript but respectable place on St. Ann Street that was only about a half block off the square and boasted a courtyard of giant flowerpot urns and tranquility, like so many other French Quarter inns.

Years later, Joe and Franky would discuss what must have been going through her mind. Perhaps she thought it was her duty to give herself to a veteran. She wouldn't be the only one offering that sort of welcome. Girls from New Orleans to New England, from New York to New Mexico, were welcoming boys home with the gift of their own bodies. A great sea wave of physical love acts had begun to build, resulting in the tsunami of a baby boom. But beyond that explanation, it was possible she did so out of guilt. He had been unapologetically devoted to her since the ninth grade.

Those reasons might have had something to do with it, said Joe, when they were talking years later. But the bottom line, he explained, was that she was just stalling for time—or, in short, "She'd rather sleep with you than answer your question."

Now at the hotel, Franky delighted in doing it three times through the night, and he always swore afterward that she welcomed him in with gusto and pleasure.

"So this means you'll marry me?" he asked in the darkness.

A lone, anemic streetlight that flickered outside offered but a shadow of visibility. Muriel's eyes opened up, and a crease formed in between her brows, as if someone had dared switch on a light and awakened her from a deep sleep.

"All right," she said. "I'll marry you. You're back from the war."

Then she turned away and slept. Excited by the evening's unexpected turn of events, he lay awake, eyes sometimes wide open and sometimes wide shut, with both the dim ceiling above him and the insides of his eyelids alternately serving as a movie screen. He would later recount how across that screen ran footage of the couple's idyllic future lives together, and in just a few seconds of reverie, he had painted a complete picture. Since he believed he loved her more than music itself, the aspiring jazzman would happily give up a career as a professional musician to offer her stability by becoming a school music teacher after attending the teachers college. The pay would be modest to support a family, but it would be a stable vocation, and he could supplement his income by giving piano lessons and perhaps even playing gigs with Joe and others around town, especially during the summer when school was out.

He finally fell asleep just as the birds, anticipating the impending daylight, began to chirp in the darkness. When he awoke with the harsh Louisiana sun annoying his eyes, the bed felt big. He had never slept in a double before. But that wasn't the only reason. The bed felt big because he was the only one in it. Muriel was gone.

Having been up most of the night in reverie, Franky must have dozed for no more than an hour. She had been waiting through the night for him to fall asleep.

WITH THAT SORT of history, he should have known crazy things would happen anytime Muriel was involved. Once the last set at Nick's finally ended, Franky jumped off the little stage, flying through the air like a scampering cat, and stuffed his prized instruments into their cases as if they came from the five-and-dime.

The rest of the story, leaked to one close friend before congealing into legend among all who would ever know him, became a staple about the Man of Many Horns. He reached his home at 1:58, according to his watch. Muriel had been strangely adamant that the timing of his arrival be precise, and so, not wanting to take the least risk of derailing her fleshy surprise, he stood at army-attention on the doorstep for two-and-a-half minutes. The window shade, which had been pulled shut, glowed a sepia color, the sole lamp in the front room having been lit so that the window shade recalled brittle paper on which lost letters are written. Taking a breath so that his chest ballooned as it did when he blew his trumpet, he knocked with three strikes and then waited for the sound of arriving steps on hard wood.

All he heard, though, was the distant bark of a dog complaining at nothing in particular. He stood there, hard with hope.

"Hello?" He waited for an answer. "Muriel, I'm home."

The idealized cliché chimed with a future he had once envisioned, when he saw himself arriving home from teaching in some high-school band room. He listened for an answer, but heard only sounds coming from outside the house rather than inside: the barking dog, a demanding cricket blaring at hi-fi levels, the drone of a car passing two blocks away. She's probably in the bathroom getting herself ready for me, Franky thought, and so he waited one more minute before knocking again: still nothing. Yet the quiet house didn't dampen his confidence. After all, the light was on, and so she was obviously in there waiting for him. Two more minutes he waited, and then followed with three more firm knocks. All stayed still. At that point he thought of something: She had never instructed him to knock—why would she? It was his own home. At this very moment she must be lying in his bed, waiting for him in her weightless gown. So he pulled his key out of his pocket, slid it in the lock, and eased open the door.

"Muriel, here I am."

Silence, save the empty ticking of a grandfather clock, given as a wedding gift by his parents.

"Muriel?"

At that point he sensed the emptiness of the place. But wait—something had stirred.

"Hello?"

Still standing in the doorway, he glanced toward the far corner of the room, to his dining corner near the kitchen. There, atop the rickety metal table sat a wicker basket with a pink blanket spilling over the side. It couldn't be.

The walk across the small room was a short one, but as he would later tell Joe, it seemed as if entire minutes passed. Finally, when he was just a few steps away, the side of the basket ceased to obstruct its interior: yes, a baby lay inside, fast asleep. He stared at it, so tranquil, as if the child was still in its mother's womb, still insulated from the world that Franky had begun to see as harsh.

Only when another dog barked outside did he see in his peripheral vision a note, written on a lined sheet torn in half from a school notebook, lying on the table. Rather than being an exhaustive missive offering a cathartic and in-depth explanation of the special delivery, the message lasted only three lines, favoring logistics over sentiment:

Was just fed.
The people over there at Charity want you to come tomorrow so you can put down a name, I left that part blank.
Muriel.

Frozen in shock, he took no immediate action. For what was left of the night, he just stared into the basket, first standing over it with his hands in his tux-trouser pockets. Quietly, he pulled the chair, with its chrome-metal frame and padded vinyl for a back and seat, out from under the table to sit in silence before the basket as if it were a statue of worship. His voice broke the nighttime quiet only when he uttered something that might have shocked anyone who would have heard it:

"She's the devil come to earth."

Franky repeated those same words to Joe not long after that, sharing his first thoughts upon seeing the baby. Shocked, Joe scolded him: How could he say such a thing about a sweet little baby. He ought to be ashamed of himself!

"No," said Franky darkly, "I was talking about Muriel."

So he was free of his Muriel addiction—but he would end up purchasing that liberation only by surrendering a freedom of another kind. After staring continuously at the baby for some time, he fell asleep at a point at which he couldn't recall. He discovered his own head resting on its side beside the basket only when the new sun had turned the room pink and his ears registered the *tonging* of the grandfather clock. After passing his hand over his cheek, which had grown numb from being pressed into the table, he lifted himself up and peered inside the basket to see if what he recalled from the night before had all been a dream. But no, the baby was still there all right, gazing out into the real world with its vacant blue eyes, wide awake but quiet. The child luckily had yet to cry during the couple of hours that Franky had been serving as de facto guardian.

Stiff from sleeping in the metal chair, he hobbled into the kitchen and put on some coffee. Set on the counter was a brown-paper grocery bag, in which he found assorted baby supplies: a box of evaporated milk and other ingredients to make formula, a baby bottle, some cloth diapers. Parked in the corner of the kitchen, meanwhile, was a baby carriage—secondhand, by the looks of it. For the first time, the baby began to cry, and so Franky, seeking an obvious solution, reached for the evaporated milk and bottle, taped to which was another piece of scrap paper with Muriel's handwriting: directions for preparing the solution. The magically transparent cellulosic tape made an impression on Franky, he later said when recalling the moment: The tape was apparently plentiful again, after previously being gobbled up by the war effort. Once finished with the preparations, he touched the thick-glass bottle's nipple to the tiny lips of the needy child, who accepted it and went quiet again. That was when he spoke to the child for the first time.

"Good thing I don't have a gig today, baby."

Up until now Franky hadn't much time to think. After the baby had cried its first brief tears, he might have been due for a good panic attack right about then. But the note from Muriel, which he noticed still lying on the table, gave him some administrative tasks on which he could focus his mind: He needed to go to Charity Hospital to fill out some paperwork. He probably would be returning the baby right then and there, for he was just a man; he wasn't a mother. Surely hospitals offered that option.

"Okay, baby, let's go see what we're going to do with you," he said, downing the last drops of coffee in his cup.

So began Franky's unceremonious initiation into parenting. He put the baby supplies back in the brown bag and then, picking up the newborn for the first time, gingerly settled it in the carriage. After he'd shut the door behind him, he looked down at his companion and then back at the door, where he had stood waiting for Muriel the night before, anxious and hard. Those moments, when all he could think of was sex, had become a time that was years ago. Meanwhile, the previous night's memory of the infant perched on the kitchen table in the basket conjured up a story learned in childhood.

"This is sort of like Moses," he said, studying the contents of the carriage.

CHAPTER 5

"Dad, I'm going on tour with you, okay?"

Stooped over the kitchen sink with dishrag in hand, Franky's head jerked up. Just yesterday on the way to rehearsal he had demanded she go, and she'd pushed right back. But things were different now.

"Did you hear me?" she singsonged from her bedroom. "I'm going, all right?"

Franky set the dishrag down and stepped into her doorway. She was sitting cross-legged on her bed, thumbing through various sketches and paintings that surrounded her.

"I haven't been to the beach up north in forever, so I wanna come." Her head stayed bowed, focused on organizing her art in some unknown way. They were always on opposite sides, those two. And now, with her having changed her mind about the tour, he made an about-face as well.

"You are *not* going. You need to stay home and get ready for your classes." He hesitated, then added, a bit softer, "Besides, you said you wanted to spend the summer working on your art."

Of course, in the ensuing days everyone knew the real reason why she suddenly wanted to go on tour, and everyone knew why for the first time in her life, he suddenly did *not* want her to go. A quiet buzz among the band members would rise up.

"There's nothing to do to *get ready* for classes," she said. "And *if* I decided to enroll, they have late registration in the fall."

A fight was bubbling, for they had broached the subject they'd avoided since the rehearsal. But now she turned clever, and it was a good thing too. Otherwise, surely they would have started bickering, the other flammable topic (Evan) would have surfaced, and Franky would have refused until his dying breath to let her go.

"Come on, Daddy, this may be one of the last times I get to go on tour with you. I'm grown up now, and I'll be getting a job, and—who knows, probably going to college."

Franky's tone stayed taut, as did his body, like the soldier he once was for a brief time. But in the end, *college* was all she had to say to disarm him.

"*I* decide who goes on tour," he said. "It's always been that way. I bring the best players I can find, plus whoever else I think is going to make it a better trip—or at least isn't going to hurt it."

She turned back toward her artwork on the bed, offering only a conceding nod, while he leaned against the door frame, shaking his head and folding his arms.

"It's a big tour for the band," she said, raising her eyes. "Would you take the band out on tour this time without its good-luck charm?"

Head still down and eyes up, she offered a shy smile. She was right about being the band's good-luck charm, having garnered that role practically at birth. After staring through her, he sighed and came to.

"I'll let you go if you promise me one thing," he said. She looked up at him, awaiting the condition. "You can come with us if you promise to enroll in September for the fall semester."

He watched her. She shrugged and went back to her art.

"Okay," she said.

Franky stayed in place, arms folded and leaning against the door frame. Then he nodded slowly—still studying, questioning—before heading back to the kitchen.

HE HAD BEEN right to be concerned. By the second day of the trip, Ariel and Evan were inseparable. They sat together and talked nonstop on the tour bus, and they hung out before and after gigs. Franky couldn't stand it. "A musician!" he said. "My daughter is with a *musician*!"

Bobbi rolled her eyes at that one. "What the hell you think you are, old man?"

"A musician," he answered. "That's how I know how bad they are."

She waved her hand at him. "You should learn a thing or two from your daughter," she said. "There's something special about those two. I can tell these things."

He grumbled that there was nothing special about them "except for lust."

"Oh, grow up, Franky," Bobbi shot back.

Evan couldn't be blamed for hanging out with Ariel, regardless of any romantic interest. He was twenty years younger than most of the other players, and she was someone his age. On the road in the bus, at a meal in a diner or anywhere else the band gathered, there were bound to be occasional whispers dividing old and young—especially during this new era, when for the first time in history the young decided they were more relevant than the old.

"Thank God I have you," Evan told Ariel. "Being around a bunch of old farts isn't my thing, man."

But like winning in sports, success in music covers up conflict. The night before they'd played to an electric crowd, and it seemed that at every tour stop Evan, who had begrudgingly made peace with Franky about his torn blue jeans by buying a pair of black slacks at a thrift store, knew a handful of friends to call and conjure to the gigs. "Bring as many people as you can," he would tell them, and a gaggle of younger folks would show up. One gig outside San Francisco, which was near his hometown, even turned into a swarm. They now were only about halfway through the trip, with ten or eleven dates still to play, but everyone felt good about how things were going. Sure, some bickering on the bus or during sound check erupted between the two generations, but once they started playing before the eager audiences that were starting to show, everything slipped into the groove of camaraderie, the kind that playing onstage can generate among people who like one another only in music, but not in life.

"Evan, you're our ticket back to success!"

Setting up his drum kit for the evening's gig while the others mulled about and pulled out their instruments, Joe couldn't hold himself back. He hadn't been so excited in years. Others chimed in as well.

"Yeah, if you don't watch it, Franky's gonna have to give you a pay raise," said Tim, and the others laughed.

"Don't give him any ideas," Franky warned. "We already have a hard time fitting his head in the bus."

Acknowledging the attention with a smile, Evan brushed them off by swatting his palm forward. "Hey, Franky," he called. "Check this out."

He was bending over, unsnapping the buckles of his sax case. Before the conversation had turned to him, he had been chattering to anyone who would listen, but mostly toward Franky, who ignored him by scribbling down the set lists on a music stand.

"Check out this new tune I've been working on."

Putting the reed to his mouth, he closed his eyes, and a few bluesy notes snaked into the air like cigarette smoke. Then the notes jumped into a bucking horse of a rhythm, causing Franky to look up.

"Hey, that's hot," said Tim, looking Evan's way.

"Yeah, keep going," said Joe, tapping his foot.

"Not bad, fella," said Bobbi, nodding.

Franky, forced to acknowledge the stir of interest, glanced up from the music stand and affected a bored look. "Clichés," he said. "Nothing but clichés."

"Nah, that sounds good," Al said. "I like it."

Evan stopped and nodded. "Hey man, what do you say we learn it and play it some night this week?"

The other players nodded and murmured in agreement, and they started chatting about parts and arrangements. But Franky stopped them.

"You can forget that idea," he said above the din. "No new tunes. No new tunes while things are just starting to get rolling again."

The others grumbled at their parade being rained on. "But, Franky," said Joe. "That's how we got our biggest success back in the day—by doing some of your originals."

"No new songs!"

Franky spoke louder than he'd intended; they saw this because he started rustling through sheet music. "At least not when when they're clichés," he added, flipping through the pages.

After that, no one seemed to want to chat anywhere in the vicinity of the grump. One person, though, seemed unaffected by the outburst.

"Yeah, those old tunes are hot anyway," said Evan, his voice bouncing. "I should know." Before gigs, the disposition of the otherwise slow-talking sax player, the others had noticed, changed color like a mood ring. Anticipation and adrenaline bubbled up from inside. So now he spoke faster than usual: "You know, Franky Fritz music is a real part of me. I mean, it's at the center of my *being*, man."

Franky, who had resumed his work on the set lists, raised his brow, only half-listening. The others, put back at ease by Evan's way, started setting up again.

"I've got it right here," Evan continued, standing back up and putting his hand to his heart. "It's in my flesh, it's in my bones."

A hint of a flattered smile surfaced on Franky's face, and he uttered a skeptical "Oh really?"

"Yeah, man. I was, like, created out of your music."

A guffaw erupted from behind Evan. Ariel sat slouched at a table, smoking a cigarette. When Franky looked over, she was smirking. He looked back and forth between the two. "That's a disgusting habit you picked up on the road with us," he said, gesturing at her cigarette. "One of my two regrets about raising you on the road—the other being that filthy mouth of yours."

"No, I'm serious," said the sax player, too insistent to pay attention to the father-daughter dynamic. "No poetry. I mean *literally*—I was created from your music."

Franky sighed and dropped his pen, showing that he wasn't being allowed to concentrate, but Evan didn't seem to notice.

"Yeah, my parents told me the story a million times. They used to love your music. Said it was old even back then, but somehow it sounded different from the other old bands."

Ariel squirmed as if she knew a secret. Nevertheless, having been complimented, Franky gave a nod, and he relaxed a little, returning to his writing. "They knew their music."

"Right, so get this." The bandleader still refused to pay him the compliment of looking his way, but Evan shot straight to his punch line: "My parents *made it* one night because of you."

Ariel could hardly contain herself. Franky slapped his pen down and glared; Evan finally had his full attention. "*What* are you talking about?" said the bandleader.

The young sax man shifted gears, returning to his usual matter-of-fact cadence. "Yeah man, they made love for the first time after they came back from a Franky Fritz Band show. And they put on your record when they got home. *You* turned them on, man. That's what they said: It was the music that did it."

With the punch line out, Ariel stopped trying to hold back her laughter and delight.

"So my parents always tell me … " He stopped for dramatic effect. "I was conceived from the loins of your music!"

Franky now clenched his pen, which hung frozen in midair.

"Yeah, man, isn't that a cool story? Matter of fact, that's why I wanted to audition for this gig and play with you guys. Your music is in my blood, man, it's in my soul!"

A swell of murmurs rose into the air, with a few nervous chuckles and *well, what do you know* comments surfacing above the din. And then Franky muttered aloud to himself in revelation:

"I spawned my daughter's demon."

The time to go on stage couldn't come soon enough. But that night they sounded hot for sure, and for the time being the weird vibe going on outside of the music was forgotten. At the end of the night, they closed out with "My Baby's Gonna Cry," as they always did. Not a patron was sitting in a chair, for everyone bounced and skipped on the dance floor—even the young kids that Evan had coaxed out to the gig.

"Take it to the bridge, boys!"

The band members, some of whom had played the song a thousand times, looked over toward the front of the stage because it wasn't Franky or Bobbi's voice coming through the speakers. Evan was standing there, center stage, craning his neck to reach past Franky to his mike.

"Take it to the bridge, boys!" he repeated.

The others shrugged and, instead of closing out the tune, they played on for one more round of the refrain, then another. Evan used the extra bars to dive into a sax solo that rollicked. "I got chills," said Joe afterward. "I tellya, I got chills."

The song ended, and everyone cheered—the audience and even the band members. But when the tune ended, Franky pulled Evan aside.

"Don't ever pull that nonsense again."

"But I was just flowing with—"

"You heard me. Don't ever pull that baloney again. A band's got to have one guy calling the shots—and I don't want you messing with my song, besides."

Evan did not give his trademark shrug this time. Instead, his jaw turned firm. "Whatever you say, man. Whatever you say."

* * *

CHARITY HOSPITAL DIDN'T go as planned. Baby wards sure were busy that year, what with the men coming back from the war. No hospital had any time for nonsense, let alone one with the name Charity.

"Sign here," said the nurse, handing him a clipboard without so much as giving him a glance. Franky obeyed. "And fill that out," she said, pointing to a blank space under which appeared the typed words NAME OF CHILD. Again, Franky obeyed. "Congratulations, Daddy," she said.

"But where do I leave the—"

"Here you go." She pushed a small bundle of cloth diapers, along with a bag that rattled with thick glass, into his hands. "You get some free supplies."

So they sent him off on his way before he realized he was the proud owner of a new baby. It was as if a fast-talking salesman had just sold him a car when he had only walked into the dealership for some information.

As for filling out the name, good thing he had one in his head, thanks to a stop along the way. On that walk the newborn baby met the French Quarter for the first time, with all its smells, both delicious and rank: andouille sausage and bell peppers buried in rice, draft beer turned oily-black in the gutter, crawfish boiled red in Creole seasoning, and the previous day's garbage, cooking at 85 percent humidity, waiting for the prisoners to come by on their rounds to pick it up. Considering that a newborn's smell sense—the most primitive and powerful of memory links—was already functioning fully, the experience seeped straight into the baby's soul. Through the French Quarter world they strolled leisurely, watching it all pass by: the pedestrians, the shops, the narrow storefront windows no bigger than a home's.

But the dream ended when a sight jarred him awake. They came upon a used-book shop, a little establishment that Franky had passed a hundred times before. This time, however, what he saw in the shop window brought him to a halt. On display, standing defiantly upright, was a book cover all too familiar—a face that followed him, as when enemies reappear again and again in life, like magnets with mysterious powers. The shocking title was emblazoned in gold on a maroon cover that recalled dried blood:

Great Expectations
by Charles Dickens

Franky glared at the novel and then looked down into the stroller. Uncannily, the baby, who lacked sharp vision and focus at this stage of development, seemed to be staring smack at the novel, transfixed by its red color.

"Stay away from that book at all cost," warned Franky. "And while you're at it, stick to nonfiction."

Peaceful and quiet up until now, the baby erupted with a cry of protest. Franky started to move along to leave the novel behind, but another book in the window caught his eye. It sat immediately beside the treacherous Dickens novel, this one a testament to the practical value of nonfiction:

Westfield's Book of Baby Names

"Now, there's a book that has a use," Franky said.

He pushed the stroller over the unexpectedly high ridge of the shop entrance and through the doors. The proprietor, a gentleman with thin white hair and reading glasses set on the tip of his nose, sat perched on a stool by the cash register, reading one of the shop's books. Franky asked for the copy of *Westfield's* in the window.

"Beautiful little girl you have there," said the shopkeeper, reaching into the window display.

Franky was seized with confusion. "Beautiful girl?"

"It's a girl, why, isn't it?" said the man, peering over his spectacles into the stroller. "She's all wrapped in pink."

"Right," said Franky. It's a girl."

After taking *Westfield's Book of Baby Names* from the man's hand, Franky gave a curt thank-you and slipped into the privacy of the shop's towering shelves. Sitting on a footstool, he went straight to the section *Girls' Names*, located less than halfway through the volume, and began running his long index finger down over the endless list of entries: ...*Abigail*... (too old, eighteenth-century sounding)...*Adeline*...*Angela*... *Ariel.* Ariel. *Ariel.* Franky stopped on this entry to read further:

ARIEL. The most notable possessor of this name is the airy spirit in Shakespeare's The Tempest. *Parents considering this name should be forewarned that the Shakespearean Ariel is a mischievous (yet blithe) spirit; however, there is probably little danger of social stigma as the non-literary general public may not be much familiar with this Shakespearean character....*

Ariel. *Ariel.* It had a ring to Franky's musical ear. But beyond its lilting sound, there was another obvious reason why the name rang sweet, although he couldn't have consciously realized it. If he had, he would have skipped over it with a shudder: *Ariel* paralleled *Muriel* in rhythm, sound, and syllables.

FRANKY WAS SO naïve, or so in denial, he didn't consider that a baby would probably end the glorious music career he envisioned for himself before it had even started. To his father, no more music career was not only a possibility, it was a certainty. It was an obligation.

Naturally, the newly minted boy-father called his parents right away—on the telephone from Charity Hospital. But he didn't beg for help outright. He had told them earlier in the week he wanted to stop by to pick up a jazz magazine he'd left over there, and so now he said he was calling to let them know he would catch the streetcar and swing by today to get it. Oh, he said, and by the way:

"I'll be bringing a baby with me. I have a baby now, so you might want to heat some water."

Heat some water hopefully gave the appearance he was knowledgeable and in control, but never mind that. The Fritzes wanted to take immediate control of the situation themselves and fix it with one swift phone call of their own, to the Liusas. They said the child must be shipped right back where it belonged: to her mother!

So Franky, weighed down with a baby in one arm and a complimentary bag of Charity Hospital diapers and supplies in the other, shuffled up the walk to his old home. His two parents stood inside the screen door, watching him approach. They must have been waiting there the entire forty-five minutes since their son's phone call.

It was all over. Mrs. Fritz caught sight of angelic Ariel, and by God, she would keep those terrible Liusas away from the child. (That was fine with them, it would turn out.) But now the details of everyday life had to be worked through. Franky needed a steady income, and his father would be able to help with that.

"You can start in the shop on Monday, and I'll pay you on Fridays," said Mr. Fritz. "Come ready to learn ladies' shoes."

Franky about dropped his baby.

What?" he protested. "I already have a job: music!" The shoe store might be okay for part-time work—"maybe two or three hours a week," he said—but in fact he had a gig on Monday, and so "I'll need to start another day, thanks." Using two of his father's favorite expressions, he added, "Work comes first, and the the show must go on, right?"

"Gig, nothing," said Mr. Fritz. "You're a father now. Your gigging is all over, pal."

Franky took a breath to gather his wits. Making a go at appealing to his father's practical nature, he explained the bottom line: He was making better money as a musician than the wage at which Mr. Fritz would start him—and besides, he reasoned, "A musician works less, so he can spend more time with his kid."

Mr. Fritz shot back that there was "no security in music." Franky might be making more money today, but tomorrow he might be making nothing.

"I'll make a deal with you," said Franky.

This was the unwritten contract they entered: The year that Franky earned less income with the band than he would have at the shoe store (including 5-percent annual raises), that would be the year he would have to quit music.

Of course, Franky could do what he wanted; he was living on his own now. But in a confessional moment while speaking to Joe, the boy-father voiced a dormant but realistic fear. Franky, who had naively embraced the responsibility of parenthood without giving it much thought, was hanging out with his friend in his new bachelor pad, just as the two friends had done up in their childhood bedrooms in past years. The conversation had paused, and they both were watching Ariel, still in awe of the helpless infant who gazed steadfastly at her father.

"I'm really going to need my *own* parents," he said. "They've already been parents."

"You sure are," said Joe, gazing at the baby. "You sure are."

During those first days Ariel, already deserted by her mother, must have been working to win herself a home with good behavior.

Because after that, all she did was cry. And when she cried, she cried longer and louder than Franky could have ever imagined. Worse, her crying bouts poured out unique and varied: She was a composer discovering new scales. Sometimes her cries jolted up and down like the teeth of a wood saw, sometimes they wailed like a police siren. Other times they sounded like some grieving sea mammal in the night, calling long and sonorous pleas for its dead lover. And like the jazz that often surrounded her, sometimes her crying was even musical: dirgelike, that is. Like a jazz funeral going down Orleans Avenue.

In spite of Ariel's colicky disposition, Franky didn't get off to such a bad start in his parenting. He certainly had greater success in making her stop crying than did his parents. His education on crying bouts began almost immediately—in the middle of the night after his first day with her. After her wailing called him out of his half-empty double bed, he responded to the problem with naïve aplomb. "Calm down, Ariel," he said. "I'll just give you a bottle and everything will be all right." Only problem was, she wasn't hungry. Nor did her diaper need changing. Nor did picking her up help. He had reached a need for a fourth answer that every new parent inevitably faces for the first time.

The cry this time was of the grieving sea-mammal variety, and it reverberated off the walls and right out the open windows of the apartment. It really *must* have sounded like an animal because before long, a nearby dog began howling in unison right along with her—in the same key, Franky noticed. Then another dog joined the chorus, then still another. Hearing the dogs' howls over hers, Ariel cried louder. The choral piece lasted for several minutes, until it gave Franky the bright idea to interrupt the mourning song with a tune of his own. He jumped right in with the first bars of "Lovable" as performed by Bix. In a few seconds Ariel, who was preoccupied with her own overpowering music, became cognizant of her father's singing. Her tiny mouth, which had stretched almost as wide as her head, closed shut as the vibrations of the Beiderbecke piece, a tune sung by the now familiar voice of her father, landed in the little baskets that were her ears. Without the baby to lead the chorus, one dog stopped howling, followed by the second more distant one, and so on, until quiet came, and all the dogs in all of New Orleans probably stopped barking, easing into a slumber.

Then came a moment almost haunting in its oddity: Ariel was listening to her father with a disturbingly adult look of auditory concentration, as if she were a musical fanatic in some café hearing Bach on a set of headphones. For a fleeting, prescient moment Franky would later retell, he caught a glimpse of his baby daughter as a woman, an artist. But a more earthly and paternal thought struck him a moment later.

"Why, little Ariel," he said, embracing her in his arms, "you love Bix too!"

Excited by the revelation, he jumped into another tune associated with Bix: "I'm Proud of a Baby Like You." Father and daughter filled the coming days and weeks with such moments of bonding, which proved a love medicine having supernatural powers in its ability to render his ears almost immune to her piercing crying bouts. With that medicine neutralizing the noise, he loved her more than ever, and everyone said that was a true miracle considering the sensitivity of Franky's musical ears. But others weren't so immune.

"She definitely inherited her father's lungs," Mr. Fritz would say. "Never give that girl a horn."

The irony was that Mr. Fritz was responsible for his son's music passion, including the Bix Beiderbecke fixation. When the little-boy Fritz developed an interest, he fixated upon it day and night. From the time the first words came out of his mouth, he had to learn every detail there was to know about whatever caught his interest: biplanes of the Great War or dinosaurs in prehistory or crawfish and other life in swamps. One interest was set aside only when the next came along, or the next seemed to cosmically appear at the very moment the previous subject had been exhausted. In more modern times they would call such interests healthy and say things like, "The child is showing exceptional intelligence." Back then, however, Franky's one-track mind syndrome was cause for concern, particularly to Mr. Fritz, who said, "Our boy is strange." The final three obsessions of his youth—the ones that left permanent marks on him—were music, Muriel, and, strangely, St. Francis of Assisi, not in that order.

As for the music obsession, occasionally Mr. Fritz came home with a couple of records, a favorite being a release from Louis Armstrong and the Hot Seven, recorded in 1928. Even as a toddler Franky was swaying to Mr. Fritz's records: Armstrong, Jelly Roll Morton, the Original Dixieland Jazz Band, and others. Franky always loved music, rocking back and forth on his knees and banging pots with wooden spoons to radio programs long before he could walk. But one day something special happened. Around the time he was beginning to grow bored with crawfish and swamp life, his father brought home a record with a name on its cover that looked different from those on the rest of the records. While the sound of that name—*Bix Beiderbecke*—resonated, he didn't actually know the man's music. Perhaps the name's comfort merely came from its sounding like those of his parents' friends.

"What kind of music is that?" Franky asked, pointing at the record. "*He* can't be a jazzman."

"Of course he's a jazzman," his father answered. "He's a Jew."

Beiderbecke had died a tragic death some years prior—almost a lifetime to a kid—succumbing to alcoholism before he had reached the age of thirty. Franky didn't know Beiderbecke's story at that point, but the sight of the record's dust jacket sparked a fire that led to an obsessive study of the man and his music, an infatuation more acute than any prior. Years would pass before he learned the falsity of his father's claim about the ethnicity of the mysterious Beiderbecke, whose career spanned a brief eight years and whose modest level of fame failed to inspire interest and post-mortem study until later. But knowledge, even the dubious kind, can set fateful forces into motion. Thus, the launching of the little boy's new obsession started with a single question:

"Can a Jew play jazz?"

Of course! his father told him—this was America, and people can be anything they want in America!

After a couple of beats of thought, Franky answered with such finality that it visibly shook his father.

"Then I'm going to be a jazzman too," the little boy said.

Mr. Fritz brushed off his son's prophetic announcement with a nervous laugh. "*You* can't be a jazzman," he said.

"I thought you said Jews can be jazzmen because this was America."

Mr. Fritz grabbed his newspaper, gave it a nervous shake, and started reading. "Well, maybe," he said. "But only the ones that haven't got a good shoe-store job already lined up."

One other thing about old Bix Beiderbecke seemed contradictory. Because Franky hadn't heard of him before, he certainly wasn't a New Orleans jazzman. Therefore, he reasoned, "He must be from Chicago."

"Nope," his father corrected, "he's from Davenport, Iowa."

Franky had never heard of Davenport, and all he knew about Iowa was the one and only thing his school taught about the state: They grew corn there, sort of like how in Louisiana they grew sugarcane.

"How could Bix be from the boring corn state and play like *that*?" Franky once asked as Bix's cornet blared on the phonograph in the background. Like all omniscient fathers, Mr. Fritz conjured a ready explanation.

"Davenport and New Orleans are connected," he said. "Davenport is on the Mississippi."

Oh, said Franky with a nod. That explains it. And for emphasis, Mr. Fritz provided proof that the Mississippi connected Bix with the "real jazz" of New Orleans. Even though Bix had recorded "Davenport Blues," he also had done "Way Down Yonder in New Orleans"—Mr. Fritz's favorite.

So, consumed with music and Bix, Franky used his only-child powers to convince his parents to buy him music lessons.

"I thinkest that I should own an instrument," he told his parents.

He had been speaking a stilted, antiquated English thanks to his previous obsession of reading old biographies of Francis of Assisi, the great Catholic saint. As fortune would have it, the formal speech played in Franky's favor.

"If we let him learn an instrument," reasoned the worrying mother of a lone child, "maybe he'll stop talking funny."

Naturally, after listening to his father's Bix and Louis Armstrong records over and over, he wanted to start with a horn, but his mother had other ideas.

"There's already a piano in the parlor," she said.

The piano wasn't what Franky wanted, but it would turn out to be a good musical foundation for him, a step toward band leadership and composition. He took to the piano right away, practicing hours beyond the forty minutes a day required by his teacher. When he wasn't playing, he was listening to his father's records, tuning in to swing-band radio programs, and hunting down any scant magazine mentions he could kind find about Bix Beiderbecke. Eventually, the older Fritzes grew concerned about his overzealousness for the piano. Already having endured countless other fixations of his son's, Mr. Fritz would look at the ceiling, shake his head, and toss up his thin merchant's arms, exclaiming, "Why can't he just play baseball?"

The music fervor continued until the moment Franky's destiny was poured in concrete like the foundation of a New Deal bridge: He stumbled upon Roussel's music shop on Decatur Street for the first time. Surely he had passed the shop before, but now its contents meant something to him, making it a toy store seen for the first time. Adding to the mystique was that the shop sat just inside the French Quarter off Canal Street. The district was wild back then, but little Franky didn't notice. Even at that age he loved the locale because it looked to be from a different era. He was walking with his mother, who had taken him on one of their department-store shopping trips on Canal, when they passed the shop window in which stood a big, brass tuba. With the display case sitting a few feet above street level, the great, shiny instrument towered over little Franky like the St. Francis statue in front of his school.

"I want to go in *there*!" he said.

Okay, Mrs. Fritz replied after resisting at first, but just for a minute. As he would share with Joe years later as a teenager, from the moment Franky entered the shop, he knew he had come home. One or two customers were lounging around with the shopkeeper, clanging cymbals and blowing bluesy notes as they moved from horn to horn and snickered about a drunk broad at last night's gig. Busy chatting with the two music pros while simultaneously eating a roast beef po-boy, the shopkeeper barely glanced up as Franky and his mother stepped about his store. Amid the chipped, dark-stained shelves that housed sheet music and instrument paraphernalia, and under the hovering smell of the po-boy, Franky discovered a gaggle of living, shimmering brass: trumpets, trombones, cornets, saxophones, tubas, not to mention clarinets, flutes, guitars, you name it. Being a New Orleans boy, he had seen plenty of horns before—in marching bands at Carnival time, in jazz funerals, anywhere on the street on any given day. But to see so many of them stacked together—shimmering, brand-new, and flaunting themselves for sale—was a new experience. From that day forward, Franky bugged his parents about buying him a horn for his birthday. He preferred a cornet—Bix's horn—but any piece of brass would do. At first they resisted and argued with their son as usual. "I'll get you a new baseball bat *and* a mitt instead. How do you like that?" said Mr. Fritz. The truth was, a baseball bat and glove already lay dead in the coat closet with their tags still attached.

So Franky said no, he didn't want another bat and mitt; he wanted a *horn*. Eventually the honking calls for a horn from the only child got him what he wanted. Rationalizing that a horn would at least get their son away from the piano, the Fritzes acquiesced and bought him a trumpet from Roussel's. Next came the Conn Wonder cornet that later would find its way into his clutching hands at his own foiled wedding. Franky took to the two instruments immediately, seizing his budding musical knowledge from the piano to gobble down practice books for brass. Before long he was playing along with records on the phonograph, picking up chops from the pros in bits and pieces. And so years later, whenever he played, he thought of the legendary cornet player from Davenport, Iowa, who had permeated the core of his imagination. But as far as Franky knew, Bix Beiderbecke didn't have a baby to look after.

CHAPTER 6

ANY MENTION OF Evan—or, worse, Ariel and Evan—set off the verbal tic.

"I did it," Franky kept muttering the next day, bowed head shifting back and forth in a continuous no. "I did it." Out of the blue, when he was breakfasting with Bobbi, or climbing onto the tour bus, or driving the gang down the interstate highway—a big new road where the rattling old bus didn't feel it belonged—the phrase kept coming out: "I did it."

On the trip Ariel had been staying in Bobbi's room; she had done that on a regular basis ever since she was a baby. So on this tour, all through this agonizing stretch of Ariel and Evan, Ariel and Evan, nothing but Ariel and Evan together all the time, Franky hadn't had a moment alone with his daughter. Tonight, though, it would be different.

"You're staying with me tonight, young lady," he said. "I'm the manager of this trip, and I decide the details."

Despite his tone, she didn't protest except mutter a "fine" under her breath; apparently young love was proving a tonic for an annoying father. They had spent so little time together that they hadn't had the chance to reach the point of being at each other's throats. So there they were the next morning in their motel room, father and daughter getting ready to meet the others for breakfast. But so much for some bonding time; they'd hardly talked at all, instead just shooting mutters and grunts each other's way like a husband and wife in a marriage gone cold. And even in her presence, Franky couldn't quite keep a lid on his *I did it*s.

"I did it," he now muttered.

"You did *what*?" asked Ariel, annoyed. "You keep saying that."

Clad in his tuxedo slacks and a tank-top undershirt, he was folding clothes and putting them into his suitcase. Ariel lay on her bed with arms folded, watching the color television that was advertised outside in neon letters on the motel sign, underneath the word VACANCY.

"I did what?" he repeated, standing up straight after bending over the suitcase. "I did what?"

"You've been saying that for the last two days."

He slapped a folded shirt onto the bed. "I'll tell you what I did. I caused the birth of my own daughter's downfall—that's what I did!"

Ariel froze. She fixed on him, her mouth open and her eyes round. Then she burst into tears.

"You take that back!" she said, arms straight at her side and fists clenched. "Evan's wonderful—and he's the best thing that ever happened to your stupid band, besides!"

"Oh, for crying out loud," he answered to the air, going back to busying himself with folding clothes. "I can't believe this."

Talking to his friends, he had always expressed wonder at how as a toddler, his daughter could cry as if she had just experienced a tragic death at one moment and then the next continue on blithely about her day. But unlike most people when they grow up, the trait never left her.

"Why are you mad that I'm happy?"

She waited for an answer. But he responded by pacing about the room: grabbing a comb and some pocket change from the top of the dresser, picking up a stray sock sticking out from under the bed, collecting his shaving kit at the sink.

"Go on, tell me. Why are you so mad?"

"You know good and well why I'm upset." He now faced her. "You've forgotten what I spent my life teaching you!"

She hopped off the bed and switched off the television. Wiping away leftover tears with the back of her hand, her face turned dry and firm. And then she made Franky, who was still pacing about the room, stop in his tracks.

"No. I didn't forget. I just found out you were wrong."

It wasn't often Franky ever missed a beat with a comeback. His mouth started to open so that one strand of spit connected his two lips. But as if on cue, there was a knock at the door: Joe was getting them for breakfast. Their alone time was over.

* * *

A FEW WORDS threatened to ruin Franky's music career. Mrs. Fritz must not have told her husband that his granddaughter would be spending the night with them, while Franky played a gig. So when Mr. Fritz opened the front door to see Franky and the baby strolling up the entrance walk, his pupils drifted upward like two helium balloons released.

"There goes my good night's sleep," he said.

That did it. Mere steps away from the stoop, Franky stopped. "Never mind, she's staying with me tonight." And he made an about-face and marched right back down the sidewalk.

Where was Mrs. Fritz? Not at the door. Otherwise, she would have diffused the situation, telling Franky to ignore his father and coaxing him inside with little Ariel. But instead only Mr. Fritz stood there, and so he lobbed a smart comment at Franky's departing backside:

"Good luck with the baby tonight. I guess I'll be seeing you at the shop, after all."

Franky stopped again. "Ariel," he said, looking down into the carriage, "I'm sorry that your grandfather doesn't love you."

Franky had won the last word. Since Mr. Fritz came from a time when men didn't speak of love except for the short stint when they courted a girl for marriage, he just grumbled something inaudible and shut the door.

Franky had fired a smart comeback, but he had just done something stupid as well. He had a gig in a few hours and nowhere for Ariel to go. What was he to do with her now? *The show must go on,* he loved to say. Now he had done it. Ariel hadn't sabotaged his career; *he* had. To make matters worse, Ariel, as if she were aware of the stress she was causing, erupted in one of her crying fits as the two made their way back to the streetcar line.

"Darn it all!" he exclaimed.

In desperation he jumped into a humming version of "Loveable." In the middle of the sidewalk, he leaned into the carriage and kept humming away, gazing upon the baby with his face inches away from her. And once again it happened: she quieted.

"Well, I'll be," said Franky.

But even the musical *puh-pat* of the streetcar ride home failed to give him any ideas for a babysitter that night. Besides, Ariel was practically famous across the city for her wails—at least within any circles that the Fritzes might travel. He could never bring her to Nick's, for the owner would hit the roof if he found out that his dark establishment, which was the kind with a pungent adults-only smell, was doubling as a babysitting service for his employees. But the show, after all, must go on, and so he stacked his horns by the door and then set off—carriage preceding him.

When Franky pushed the carriage through the bar's splintering doors, all of his bandmates acted predictably. Tim was the first to glance up and see the pair.

"Ah, jeez," he said, throwing his arms down. "What is this—a night with the ladies' sewing club?"

As expected, the tiny baby entirely knocked the wind out of Joe. "Nick's gonna throw us out," he gasped between hyperventilating breaths. "I just know it—we'll never play in this city again!"

Franky, who had stopped in the doorway to absorb the blows of reaction, started a purposeful stroll, pushing the carriage through the dank joint as if all was perfectly normal.

"It's okay," he said. "She doesn't cry when I sing."

He received nothing but shaking heads and disgusted calls for Jesus. But Franky persisted with his logic: Ariel had inherited his musical gene, he explained to the boys, and so she always magically responded to her father's singing. And wouldn't fortune have it that he was scheduled to sing that very night!

"But, Franky," Al interjected, "you only sing one song."

And the lone tune, "Who's Sorry Now?" wasn't coming until the final set. The band knew no other songs that used Franky's vocals.

The boys started to gang up on him, with Tim even suggesting they needed a new leader and that maybe Franky needed to take some time off.

"So you can be a mama," he said, gesturing at the carriage. "I can see you make a good mama, there."

Insults fueled the exchange, and so the grumbling became bickering, and the bickering became a full-blown argument—all in undertones so that Nick wouldn't hear from the back. The boys, led by Tim, lunged into Franky with verbal smacks, and Franky shot back. But before long the fight waned. The jabs at Franky wound down to mutterings pointed less at the bandleader than at the air, which in New Orleans absorbed discord almost as well as it did water.

"There goes my playboy image," said Tim. "There goes all the girls."

"There goes our gig," said Al.

"There goes my music career," said Joe. Shaking his head and fighting tears, he added, "There goes my *life!*"

Franky had to do something; he just hadn't figured out what. He nervously started humming a favorite tune while he and the boys got back to setting up, this time in silence. Joe sat behind his half-assembled drum kit and stared back and forth between Ariel and

Franky with his face scrunched. His foot tapped feverishly, the nervous energy scrambling all the way down to his lower extremities to find an escape hatch. After a few bars, Franky's humming merged comfortably into the beat set by Joe's foot. The two had played music together for so long that such an occurrence happened naturally, like migrating birds floating into formation, until eventually the tune drifted into the one they had planned to open with, "Yesterday's Boogie." The improvised music must have pleased Ariel, for she stayed quiet. Her eyes grew wide, transfixed by a beat that was a brand-new addition to her father's familiar vocal croon, and so Franky kept at it.

By the time the boys were all set up, the medicine of humming and drumming had started to wear off on Joe, and the Ferris wheel of the same old questions started up again: "What are we gonna do with her, Franky? For crying out loud, even if she stays quiet, Nick's gonna *see* her!"

"Never mind *for crying out loud*," Franky answered, and then with a wink and a forced grin added, "I already told you: She won't be crying out loud—she's going to be quiet." But the boys didn't laugh at his attempt at levity, so he got serious again. "All we need to do is make sure he doesn't see her, that's all."

"Oh yeah?" said Tim. "And how you gonna manage that?"

Franky looked around the room for a couple of moments as the boys stared him down. "We'll commandeer that table over there, that's how we'll manage that," he said. "Come on, grab your cases, soldiers." He picked up his own horn cases and lugged them to the table. Shaking their heads, Tim and Al followed, while Joey sat behind his drums looking like his mother had just died. One by one, Franky took each of the cases from the hands of his bandmates and stacked them around the table in between the nooks and crannies of the wooden chairs, forming a little fort. He then grabbed his baby and slipped her under the table, inside the wooden chair legs and the walls of what had just become Fort Ariel. The boys ducked their heads to peer underneath. The infant looked both content and intrigued, impressed with her new surroundings, like a smug cat finding pleasure in the security of a protective nook. The sight offered a passing respite of hope, for the boys momentarily stood in silence around the table.

"If we can make it through this night without getting thrown out," Al said, breaking the brief quiet, "we'll *definitely* hit the big time."

For the next twenty minutes or so, Franky stuck by the table and hummed tunes for the infant. There he sat in the chair, ducking his head to peer through crevices of the fort, all the while rocking the bassinet with his foot to the beat of his hum. By now a few customers had strolled in, while Nick had taken his slouching stance behind the bar and was glaring at the boys to get started so that no customers would leave before they did. Joe's drums and cymbals had begun their sporadic thumping and swishing, while Al and Tim's brass blew out random song fragments mixed in with musical scales ascending and descending. The simmering sounds of a band coming to life beckoned Franky to the stage, but he still hadn't gathered the nerve to leave his baby, even though it was four minutes past the hour.

"Come on, get your ass over here! Nick's gonna start bitching."

Tim had come up behind Franky, who was still gazing down under the table. It was time to say good-bye. Now he had to leave it to fate as to whether Ariel would cry and make herself known to Nick. Tim grabbed his shoulder to get him to turn around and get going.

"Relax," said Franky, staring down into Fort Ariel. "I'm getting inspired."

He whispered one last good-bye to his baby, told her to "please, *please* be good," and then hummed his way up to the bandstand, augmenting the volume of his voice as he moved farther away from the table so the sound would continue to reach Ariel's ears. Two customers sitting hunched over the bar turned to get a look at the random song maker.

"Stick to the horns," one called out.

"You stick to your seat and stay quiet," answered Franky without breaking stride. The man slipped off the bar stool as if he were going to come over and deck him, but then Franky added, "Because you won't want to miss the show!"

He skipped up onto the little makeshift stage of boards on cinder blocks, which made a hollow knock upon the strike of his dress shoes, and met the eyes of his bandmates. They each returned his look with a sigh—some being of the relieved variety (Joe's), others of the annoyed kind (Al and Tim's). He surveyed his little audience: five occupied tables and the two lone drinkers at the bar. Blue-collar folks, some with dates, occupied most of the tables, but the band, which had been playing there a few months now, was starting to bring in a few varied patrons as well. A couple of guys about the boys' age had strolled in, and Franky was beginning to know the type: college students, probably from Tulane, who undoubtedly prided themselves on going to the seedier bars to hear decent music for nothing but the price of a cheap glass of beer.

"Thank you for coming out this evening, ladies and gentlemen," said Franky to the living room-sized gathering. "We're going to start out by treating you to a number that is particularly near to my heart: 'Who's Sorry Now?'" He glanced back at Joey and started snapping his fingers. The drummer, however, returned the look with saucer eyes and dropped jaw, and the rest of the band shot him looks of surprise.

"What the hell are you doing?" said Tim, leaning into Franky's ear. "We're supposed to lead off with 'Yesterday's Boogie.'"

"Never mind 'Boogie.' Tonight we're going with 'Who's Sorry.'"

Shaking his head, Tim stepped away, muttering, "Since when does a baby decide our set list?"

"When the baby is my daughter, that's when."

Glancing back at his drummer, he snapped his fingers, which pulled the band taut like an arrow in a bow. At last he gave the order to fire: "*One, two, one-two-three—*"

"*What the hell is that over there?*"

Nick's bark silenced the band before it had begun—except for Al's trumpet, which blurted out a lone note that escaped before he could retrieve it. Everyone in the room turned to look toward the bar. His fat, seething arm extended, Nick was pointing straight at Fort Ariel. Franky's deft verbal talents were instantly frozen. The audience members looked up at the band, and the band members looked at one another. With Franky's lips paralyzed, words came to Tim first, but his answer was only a statement of the obvious.

"That's our stuff on the table," he said.

Nick seemed to be peering through the cracks between the instrument cases that blocked the underneath area of the table. Had he glimpsed the bassinet?

"What do you mean, that's your stuff?" he snapped. "What kind of a mess is that? Tables are for customers!"

So Nick still hadn't seen Ariel. All eyes turned to Franky, both the cause of the problem and the one who usually served as their agile spokesman. But again someone else took up the spokesman role—this time, a customer. It was the same man at the bar who had heckled Franky's humming:

"Ah, for crying out loud, Nick. In the seven years I been comin' here I ain't seen one damn customer at that table in the corner."

"Ain't that the truth," muttered his companion, and rumblings of agreement among the other customers followed.

"Give the boys a place to put their stuff, for chrissake," someone said above the murmur. Making a broad, sweeping motion with his palm up as if gesturing toward hundreds of fellow patrons, he added, "Jeez, half these people in here wouldn't be here if it wasn't for the band."

All heads turned back to Nick. Everyone in the room could see the embarrassment in the barman's gnarled and reddened face. Somebody was going to pay, and all witnesses waited to find out who.

No doubt Franky wouldn't have thought the moment could get more miserable, but it did. As he waited through those stilled seconds for Nick to respond, a tiny noise broke the silence. Ariel hadn't heard the comforting humming of her father for some time now. From over at the table came a stirring, the first rumblings that preceded a good cry. Franky scanned the room for others who may have heard the noise. Yes, a few patrons had turned toward Fort Ariel.

Finally, Nick, whose ears were dull to not only music but all sound, brought the standoff to an end. "Just shut up and play," he growled at the boys, grabbing a bar rag. "You're already ten minutes late getting started." He turned to the band's defender at the bar. "And *you*—no more beers for you if you're as drunk as you're making out to be!"

Before Ariel could launch into a crying bout, the band jumped into "Who's Sorry Now?" and the situation at Fort Ariel spurred them to hit the tune with an energy only nerves can conjure. Instead of making the band sound jittery, those nerves added several drops of Tabasco to the music. At first Franky's voice shook a bit, but he was able to steady it as the song progressed, even singing with a little flair. When it came to his voice, he was the first to admit it was lacking. But at least he could carry a tune, and so during these days he sang based on the business knowledge that an audience wanted vocals. He also knew that his own limited voice was but a short-term solution.

"If we're going to make it big, we need a real singer," he'd often tell Joe and the boys, "preferably, a chick singer."

But for now the band would have to settle for Franky's voice, just as Ariel had come to do—and tonight the audience loved it. At the end of the song they answered with a great cheer followed by applause, drowning out any crying that might be coming from Ariel's way. The rest of the band, meanwhile, soaked up the audience's appreciation and then pumped it like gasoline right back into "Yesterday's Boogie," an instrumental they attacked with harnessed abandon. The quartet cooked along, and Franky, still preoccupied with thoughts of Ariel, at first struggled to keep up. By the end of the number, though, he too became caught up in the breathing music and the audience that fed it. If Ariel was crying, the music was drowning her out. In between songs, Franky listened for any protests from his daughter but heard nothing. A few more customers trickled in and joined the exchange between players and audience. The band rolled into the third song of the set, and then the fourth. By now the music had lifted Franky into the air and floated him to another world, a place where the pressures of fatherhood were momentarily forgotten. But the respite couldn't last for long.

CHAPTER 7

WHAT AL SAID came out innocent enough: "Let's debut Evan's tune tonight."

They were getting ready to go onstage. One recent evening on the tour Franky had walked in late for sound check only to find a few of the band members toying around with Evan's piece, and they were obviously enjoying working with the new material. Franky, who might have exploded but didn't, even had to admit it sounded "okay."

"Come on, let's do the song—maybe in the last set," said Al. "I bet we could make our way through it. Hell, Franky, you're the improv master. You could find your way through and make it sound even better."

"Yeah, let's play it," Joe said, and the others murmured in agreement.

"It's time for a new one," Bobbi said. "Evan's been good for the band, so this will be good for us too."

Franky, who had been trying to ignore the conversation by peering out at the audience from backstage, could ignore the groundswell no longer. He spun around.

"No new song tonight! End of story."

The others rolled their eyes, but not Evan, who hadn't spoken the whole time. "That's cool," he said. Yet his mouth closed with a firmed jaw, betraying his words. "I'll just work within the framework of the tunes we play, that's all."

"Thata boy," said Franky.

The others went on milling about as they waited to go on. Standing next to Joe, Franky studied Evan from across the room.

"He's finally accepting his role and settling into the band," he murmured. "For a while there, I didn't think he was going to work out."

But Joe slowly shook his head in a foreboding way as the two of them watched the young player strap on his sax. "Sure, he does what you tell him now," he replied, "but he doesn't smile anymore."

Once they were onstage, Evan didn't really do what Franky told him, anyway. He never seized the mike and directed the band to play entire extra refrains as he had done that one night, but he kept pushing the limits in a constant search of where Franky had randomly chalked lines for him not to cross. In some places he played extra notes beyond where his part was supposed to end. In others, he hesitated for a measure before jumping into a run. Most times Franky turned and shot him a glare, and on occasion the bandleader let it slide. But by the final set Evan was doing pretty much what he wanted, never so much as bothering to glance over at Franky to see how he would react. For that matter, Evan never glanced at him at all the whole night, as if refusing to give his leader that minimal gesture of respect. The final note of the final tune sounded.

"Your solo only lasts two bars!" Franky said backstage. "What the heck are you doing waving off Bobbi so you can go for more?"

Evan just shrugged. "I was hot, man. You of all people should know how that feels."

"Yeah, Franky," said Bobbi, jumping in. "What's gotten into you? We didn't used to be so rigid. That's part of the problem nowadays. We used to have fun with the songs."

"I don't care if you're a blue flame in hell," said Franky, ignoring Bobbi. "I'm the bandleader around here, and you're going to stop playing when I tell you to!"

Shaking his head, Evan muttered, "You bet, man."

"*You bet*? I'll tell you about *you bet*. You bet I'll cut out your solos if you don't shape up—*man*."

The young sax player didn't answer. Instead, his head dropped so that his brown hair, parted down the middle, hung over his face. For weeks he'd been letting Franky's hostility just roll off, but it was now apparent how it had been taking its toll underneath, for he muttered to himself and maybe Ariel, "I don't know how long I can take this."

Yet the next night, Evan did not stray one bit from Franky's direction—so much so that a couple of players asked him what was the matter and why had he played "like you were bored out there."

"Preoccupied is more like it," answered Evan. And that was all he said.

The laxness continued the next few dates. "You're like a loose guitar string out there," Joe said, studying him up and down. "You don't sound taut no more." But Franky, the leader who usually demanded his players' souls, didn't seem to mind the sax man's uninspired playing. As they put away their instruments, he commented, "So you decided to get with the program, I see. See how good we can sound when we all stay with the plan?"

"Yep," Evan said.

The gig finished, the players started to go their usual separate ways. Evan shot toward the restroom and changed into his blue jeans the moment he got offstage, and he and Ariel said they were going to hit a diner, but they wouldn't say where; the night before they had found a favorite hideaway. Up until now, they hadn't shown themselves to be a young, secretive couple who hid themselves away; on the contrary, they went out and socialized, usually with whatever group Bobbi happened to choose, whether it be the bar crowd or the diner clan. This time, however, was different. In their failure to reveal their destination, they made clear they wanted to be alone.

THE NEXT MORNING at breakfast in the motel restaurant, Bobbi announced the news.

"She broke her promise," she told Franky across the table. "She didn't come back to the room last night."

Franky's eyes popped; he grabbed the edge of the table with both hands.

"Don't worry, she's all right," she added, taking a drag on her cigarette. "She finally came in—"

Before finishing, she exhaled the cigarette smoke. Franky too started to exhale, and his body slouched in relief.

"—when I was getting up."

He jerked back up. "What?"

"Yeah, she rolled in just as I was getting up."

"That's it," he said. Evan needed to go! Or his daughter needed to go. "No daughter of mine is going to be out all night with a boy, I tell you! Not on my watch, any—"

But Bobbi snuffed out his rant before it truly kicked in. "No, no, it's not like that," she said, waving her hand. "They were sitting in the diner all night talking."

As Franky simultaneously tried to digest all the pieces of news and decipher whether the sum total was good or bad, she explained how she had given Ariel a lecture about not getting pregnant, the lecture that she'd given her a thousand times since the dawn of the girl's adolescence.

"But she stopped me and shared the kind of night she had," Bobbi said. "And you know she's never lied to me."

Franky went back to his scrambled eggs and started grumbling about how "those two need to go, or one of them does."

"Evan's not a bad kid, you know, Franky. They're two nice kids who care for each other, is what they are."

Franky grunted. "Well, he'd better behave himself because if he doesn't, he's out of the band."

Bobbi poked her fork in and out of the stack of three pancakes that had just come. "You don't have to worry about that none."

Looking up, Franky gave her a quizzical look, waiting for her to elaborate. She let go of her fork so that it clinked on her plate.

"Evan's gone," she said. "He left."

* * *

AS THE BOYS closed out a tune, Franky thought he heard another noise coming from the direction of Fort Ariel. It wasn't all-out crying, but it did sound like the first tremors of what might become one of her notorious wails. The band was now in between songs, and so the moment was ripe for a good cry just when no raucous music was playing to drown her out. Beyond bolting straight to the table to appease her, Franky could think of but one option to keep the baby unknown: make some more noise.

"Thank you, thank you!" Franky barked at the audience, patting his forehead with a handkerchief. "Whew, that number was hot!" he said as an aside. "Ladies and gentlemen, that was Joey on drums. Everybody clap your hands loud for Joey." The crowd answered with a noisy round of applause—noisy enough to drown out Ariel. "Joey, let me hear you!" Looking at his leader with a quizzical shrug, Joe answered with a few taps and rolls; Franky had never done such introductions before. But the small gathering loved it, letting out a loud cheer followed by laughter at the irony of the bigtime showmanship before a living-room audience.

"Hooray for Franky!" a woman called out. "Just like Louis Armstrong!"

"Yeah, or Benny," a man yelled.

"No," answered Franky. "Like Bix. Just like Bix." He spun on his heel toward his band. "Let's hit it, fellas. One, two, one two three—"

Off the band went into the final song of the set. The reason for the sudden urgency to start the next number was lost on the boys—only the parental ears of Franky had heard rumblings starting at Fort Ariel—but they jumped right in, always looking to their leader to do the launching. The pace he set was so frenetic that one couple jumped up and started dancing, the first time that anyone had done so at one of their gigs other than at weddings and bar mitzvahs. The boys loved the scene before them—all except for Franky, who blew his horn with eyes fixed on the table in back. The band was rolling through this last song before the break, and so he needed desperately to find a way to get back there to see if she was crying. With no music to drown out a wailing baby after the set, everyone in the bar—including Nick—would hear her, even before Franky would be able to fly to her side and quiet her. Worse, Franky had a short trombone solo toward the end of the number, and so he wouldn't be able to slip off the stage to pacify the baby as the other boys closed out the piece with a mere missing horn. The evening could end right there.

A slick of sweat surfaced on his forehead. Another couple, feeling the energy, jumped up and started to swing. Now two couples were hitting it on the improvised dance floor. Meanwhile, the remaining people in their seats tapped their feet to the beat and some clapped their hands. The band had heated up so much that even the slouched drinkers at the bar had turned their heads to watch the boys pumping out the voltage on stage.

When Franky's solo came, it was a wonder he was able to start it at all, given everything nonmusical on his mind. At first he stumbled through a few mistakes, but only he and his fellow musicians could hear them. Certainly the audience, intoxicated by the potent mix of booze, music, and fun, hadn't noticed.

"Ladies and gentlemen, Mr. Franky Fritz!" improvised Tim in the middle of the solo, and claps and cheers followed.

"Go Franky!" called out one of the university students. "Keep playing!"

That, Franky later said, was when he got his idea for how he would check on Ariel before the song ended. The solution lay in the very solo he was playing. Only problem was, by this point it was almost time for both solo and song to end. Out of desperation came the solution.

"I just can't stop!" he hollered to the audience above the pulsing music. "Take it to the bridge, boys!"

Still playing their instruments, they watched Franky out of the corner of their eyes. What was he doing? The young pros had never veered from the normal progression of a song ever before. At this stage in their public careers, they were not improvisers. Not to mention that their reserved leader had lost his mind.

"Let's take it to the bridge, boys!" repeated Franky, bulging his eyes back at them.

The other members needed to make a decision fast—and in unison. The end of the tune was coming in a matter of mere measures. In the final moments, they looked at one another, shrugged, and then instead of heading toward the song's closing notes, went back to the bridge. Franky could now double his solo time. Launching into round two, he leaped off the one-foot stage and continued to work his trombone slide among the dancers and other audience members. He danced and pranced around them, and they loved it. Meanwhile, the other players stayed in their stage positions and kept chugging along on their parts, all the while laughing at the skinny soloist's antics. They had agreed that Franky would be the bandleader, but never did they realize that their shy buddy in the tux would possess such showmanship.

Franky kept at it, orbiting the group of dancers as if they were a sun. He began by almost brushing their shoulders as he moved around them, and then with each orbit traveled, he drew a bigger concentric circle. Yes, the music had taken him, but he knew exactly what he was doing. His circular path widened with each orbit, drawing closer to Fort Ariel with each pass. By now he roamed so far from the stage and even the dancers that many shrugged their shoulders as if to say, "Crazy musician!" Now almost in the back of the room, Franky could actually hear the baby over his blasting horn. Yes, as he had feared, she was crying, revving up for her dreaded sea-mammal wail. Still working his horn, he danced around the table as if it were a pagan fire, all the while attempting peeks inside the fort so that he could make eye contact with his baby. If the music wasn't appeasing her, perhaps the sight of his face would. But she kept crying. She likely never saw him anyway, because her crying eyes stayed scrunched like two tissues. Besides, perhaps only his voice, and not his face, had magical powers over his daughter.

Desperate measures, then, for desperate moments: If it was his voice that Ariel demanded, then that's what she'd get. With all of the audience members still turned toward the back of the room to see what the mad soloist would do next, Franky took the horn from his lips and started *voicing* the solo, working off the main melody line of the song and regularly peeking in to look for a response from his daughter: *Be-doop doot-do. Doo-doot-dee-do, do. Bop-bop, bah....* The audience members naturally had no clue what in the world the player was doing by circling a lonely table in the back of the room, but they loved it nevertheless. To them Franky simply came off as an eccentric musician who marched to the different beat of Joey the drummer. His enigmatic antics, however, did solicit a comment from one of the drunks at the bar.

"That marijuana makes you go mad," Franky heard as he passed by the bar on his orbit. "I seen a movie about it."

The man was talking about that old 1936 film, *Tell Your Children*—aka *Reefer Madness*. But no marijuana was transporting the horn man so. Franky was trying on his rendition of scat singing, a style first heard via Louis Armstrong and His Hot Five's 1926 recording, "Heebie Jeebies." Mr. Fritz had played it over and over on Saturday nights after dinner, until Franky started putting it on the phonograph himself every other evening of the week, finally tiring of the tune long after the shellac record grooves had worn down so much that Armstrong and his band's instruments lay burried deep in a soft blanket of cotton.

Seeing their leader bopping around the table and peering into the fort, the rest of the boys nodded to each other in understanding. Tim winked at Franky, and the other boys nodded at him when he caught their eye. Joe, meanwhile, just pounded harder on his drums in an effort to do all he could to cover any crying from Fort Ariel. With their leader still wandering in the hinterland far from the stage and the solo about to end, they took the tune back to the bridge to extend the solo break for yet another round. The audience, loving every second of the scene, at this point simply assumed the band was just going all-out for its last song of the set. The boys were hot, and nothing was going to make them stop.

All this time Franky kept singing the lyricless melody for his daughter. As usual, it took Ariel some time to hear her father's voice above her own crying, but eventually she did. At last her scrunched eyes unsealed into two inquisitive slits, lured open by the familiar voice. The wailing turned into a sputter, then a mere series of coughs. Within a few moments it had abated completely. Franky kept at it for a while, until he was sure that Ariel had calmed down. But he needed to return to the horn soon because the song needed to come to a close.

Yet he knew from experience the crying would resume the moment the sound of his voice stopped. Gathering his nerves, he brought the horn back to his lips and picked up with the melody that he had been voicing. But before Ariel could take notice of the change, he dropped the horn from his lips and went right back to the vocal improvisations—and then back to the horn again. He continued to alternate back and forth between horn and voice, horn and voice, each time making the singing intervals shorter and the brass stretches longer. The baby's interest didn't wane during the horn stints, for she followed the transfer from voice to horn and back as if she were a choir member learning a new melody by hearing the notes explained on piano. Eventually, he eliminated the singing completely and just blew the melody through his horn. Even though his voice was no longer creating the tune in her ears, the sounds nevertheless came from that big shiny thing stuck to her father's mouth. The link between horn and daddy had been cemented, or at least so Franky hoped.

It was once again coming time for the solo to end, and Franky needed to get back to the stage. If the players took it to the bridge yet again, they would no longer sound hot to the audience. They would sound either boring or deranged. Blowing into his trombone at full strength to assure her that he was still near, he departed Fort Ariel like the lunar module leaving the moon years later, and restarted his orbit. He circled the table, at first sticking close by and then widening his path around the center point with each pass to bring him closer and closer to the stage. Finally, the ever-widening concentric circles returned him safely to where the rest of the band awaited him—just in time for the closing notes of the song. Like an old pro, he had ventured out among the audience and then returned to the microphone in time to sing the final notes. The band, steaming hot just moments earlier, brought the song to its conclusion like an engineer easing a train into the station. On the final note, Franky leaped right off the stage and beelined for the back table. Realizing the situation, Tim jumped in to fill the bandleader void:

"Thank you very much, ladies and gentlemen. We're the Franky Fritz Band—featuring the Mad Soloist, our very own Franky Fritz."

It was the first time that anyone had referred to the ensemble as the Franky Fritz Band, and from then on, the name stuck. The boys had always accepted Franky, the best musician of the group and the originator of the idea to start a band, as their leader. As of this night, however, he was not only the musical director, he had become the natural showman—the front man—of the group. Moreover, the Franky Fritz Band had a ring to it, and so that was that. As for the nickname Mad Soloist, that stuck too, right along with Man of Many Horns.

Before Tim had finished thanking the audience, Franky was already sitting down at the back table, sneaking a look at Ariel. The sudden bolt offstage had caught the attention of a few of the audience members, who gazed back at him with questioning looks.

"Boy, that wore me out," said a panting Franky, slouching full back in his chair and head dropped back. "I sure needed this seat, all right."

The college students, who were sitting nearest to the table, looked at each other. "Wow," said one, "the music made him so hot, he almost collapsed."

"Good thing Nick let the band have that table," said the other, nodding. "Otherwise he'd be laid out on the floor."

Franky could do no wrong. He had a solution for every problem that arose, it seemed, and so he brimmed with confidence, ready to take on the world. When the boys congregated at the back table to briefly critique the set, he shared a bold idea.

"Next set, let's play the original tune," he said.

"No!" cried the boys in unison.

"Jeez, Franky, we've had enough stress tonight already," Joe said.

During the break, while Franky surreptitiously kept Ariel company, the boys wandered about the bar to enjoy the fruits of fifteen-minute fame, which didn't have that name yet. They mingled with the customers, who invited them to their tables, bought drinks for them, and showered praise on their performance. Up on stage Tim asked Al if he'd seen that swell-looking blonde and then tried to talk to her at the next break. With the Ariel problem suppressed and the audience feeding their performance, the band finished out the evening strong, playing with a musical power that each player had known only when practicing in his respective bedroom. It had been a great night—and they had even won an important concession from Nick: a table for the band. From that night on, the boys would have a table of their own to store their instrument cases and congregate during breaks. After the gig was over and they were putting their instruments away, Joe, glowing over the victorious night, summarized Nick's ultimate acquiescence, which had allowed the boys to successfully hide Ariel from the bar owner.

"Kindness saved the gig," he said, attempting to mimick his best friend's eloquence.

"No," corrected the bandleader, returning his trumpet to its case, "greed saved the gig." Joe started to protest the cynicism, but Franky was adamant: "Trust me. The only thing that can save you from a jackass is his own greed."

Regardless, it was the most successful gig the band had enjoyed. Franky, Tim, Al, and Joe were all taking steps toward becoming vocational musicians. Strangely, while the boys would never have uttered the notion to one another, Ariel, the little time bomb swaddled in pink, had turned out to be their good luck charm.

CHAPTER 8

ARIEL, AS YOUNG lovers do when they're apart, knew only the present. At one given hour she lived in an adolescent-like rage and blamed Franky in fiery diatribes for her lost love. The next hour she was a forlorn woman, silent and perched in her widow's walk, waiting and watching the gray horizon for her man to return from sea.

Bobbi had heard the details of Evan's departure the next morning, when Ariel finally showed up at the motel room after being out all night talking with the young musician. Just when he was losing patience with Franky and his band, he'd gotten a call from a friend in a blues-rock outfit whose sax player had abruptly quit. But he would come back, he promised her. He would soon meet up with her again in New Orleans.

"I'm leaving because I can't take him anymore," he told Ariel that night in the diner. "But so help me, if I ever leave again, I'm taking you with me."

Franky and Ariel now found themselves in the confines of another motel room that looked and felt the same as the other ones. After the night's gig, Bobbi, gently refusing to have Ariel stay with her that evening, had nudged her in the direction of Franky's room "so you can mend things between the two of you." But father and daughter hadn't spoken a word from the time they said good-bye to everyone after the gig and walked together in silence back to the motel, straight through the six minutes Franky took to brush his teeth and wash his face at the sink.

The running water ran, a motel glass clinked on the sink, the television droned. Mundane sounds augment silence, building tension. Ariel slapped her hand down on the bedspread.

"You just don't want to see me happy, that's what it is!"

The thump broke the silence of everyday sounds. But Franky, acting as if they had been chatting the whole time, didn't waste a beat to say he didn't know what she was talking about.

"*You* know what I'm talking about," she said.

He dismissed her by swatting his palm down. "What, Evan leaving? That's the best thing that ever happened to you. Now you can concentrate on college."

"You've ruined my life!"

Her neck jutted out, ridges forming on it that reached to her collarbone. But he didn't look her way. Refusing to acknowledge her outburst, he traipsed about the room, tidying up.

"Ruin your life? You'll ruin your life if you don't go to college."

Ariel folded her arms. Now she was almost hugging herself, either to protect and sooth herself or hold in her own rage. Franky had refused to acknowledge her emotion. He hadn't once looked her way, and both his tone and volume had stayed consistent, like a flat song.

Audible enough for her father to hear, she spoke mostly to herself through clenched teeth. "I've got to get out of here," she said. "Just watch me."

Franky stopped. He looked at his daughter for the first time instead of busying himself about the room. She had spoken a threat—though sometimes threats are desperate pleas. He raised a finger as if to say something. But no. He turned away with his nose in the air and sauntered off back to the bathroom to finish getting ready for bed.

Sticking nose in the air, followed by an about-face—she herself had taken to doing that at the dawn of her adolescence, and so Franky at that moment had borrowed the gesture from his daughter. In fact, it had become one of her trademark moves—which, whether by gene or daily observation, by nature or nurture, she had actually taken from him. The family dynamics were dizzying.

* * *

BACK IN THOSE older days, Mr. Fritz never answered the phone because, he said, telephones were for women. Only by a whim of fate did he pick it up this time. Mrs. Fritz's hands were deep in dirty dishwater, so she had asked her husband to "Get it, will you?" She had already briefed him on their babysitting duties for the evening, and so he answered the phone with a sarcastic question, without even saying hello and confirming who was calling: "What time are you coming over to drop off the Town Crier?"

With Mrs. Fritz working the dishes in the sink, Mr. Fritz listened for a moment to the silence on the line, filled only by the hiss provided by the New Orleans telephone company.

"I'm calling because Ariel isn't coming," Franky answered. "She told me to tell you she's busy tonight, and she doesn't want to see you."

Of course, Ariel still was not talking by then. Regardless, it would be another babysitting evening at Nick's for the Franky Fritz Band. When Franky showed up at the bar once again toting Ariel, the boys bristled, but they nevertheless accepted the intrusion. They had been through the routine before. And besides, maybe having the baby around would once again bring them good fortune. Sure enough, by constructing another Fort Ariel at their back table, they made it through the evening with relative ease, except for a minor incident or two. On one occasion, when Nick went out to the back alley to throw out a batch of cardboard liquor boxes, he noticed a baby carriage parked neatly amidst the metal garbage cans and empty beer kegs. He stomped back to his station behind the bar as the band was just wrapping up a set.

"What the hell is a baby carriage doing in my alley?" he hollered.

He had no way of tracing the mysterious vehicle back to the boys up on the stage, but nevertheless they all froze in their guilt—and then looked toward Franky for an inventive response. The direction of their gaze caused Nick also to focus on the bandleader, as if he were the culprit. Then a surly grin came over his face.

"Hey, Franky," he called, "I didn't know you was a mama. I bet you make a good one!" A burst of his own laughter punctuated the remark.

"I brought the carriage for you, actually," said the Mad Soloist. "It looked quite comfortable, and so I thought you'd like it."

Still laughing at his own anemic joke, Nick didn't pay attention to the answer, but some of the customers did hear it and laughed. Nick, who thought they were laughing at his wit, strutted behind the bar and laughed some more. The moment foreshadowed a dimension of the band's eventual success. As the ensemble evolved into a true professional act, the fun of going to see the Franky Fritz Band would involve not only listening to what would erupt from the players' horns but anticipating what repartee would come out of Franky's mouth.

He owed his skill of verbal acrobatics to St. Francis. Or at least his St. Francis fixation. "Franky's problem," as his parents called their son's pretentious speech, started way back in the third grade at St. Francis of Assisi grammar school, where the Fritzes had enrolled him because of its stellar academic reputation. Sister Marie Joseph introduced her students to their school's namesake by reading to them G. K. Chesterton's biography of St. Francis, written, as all biographies were at its time, in lofty English. From the very introduction of the book, Franky was marked for special attention. The young Sister Marie Joseph—who was rumored among the teachers to have an interest in St. Francis that bordered on the sexual thanks to the saint's shedding all earthly possessions including the clothes on his back—looked straight at Franky and announced for the entire class, "Master Fritz, pay special attention to this story. This is the saint after which you were named."

The Jewish boy replied, "My parents said they just liked the name."

The innocent remark didn't cause the nun to so much as blink. "Yes," she said, nodding knowingly. "But their fondness for the name came from God."

From then on the enthused Sister Marie Joseph continually glanced at Franky whenever she read the biography to the class.

"My life is ruined," the frail eight-year-old told his parents at supper that evening. "I have a saint's name."

Yet Sister Marie Joseph captivated the class with her histrionic reading and even embellishment of the text, which might have been excusable to captivate third-graders. Even so, the colorful life story of Francis, particularly when the saint talked to wild animals of the forest, appealed to children of that age.

"Never mind that make-believe Doctor Doolittle," the nun told the students encircling her for reading time. "Saint Francis was *real*."

St. Francis's superpowers inspired both Franky and Joe, who had met each other that year. With St. Franicis's abilities, "Then me and Jack could conversate," said Joe, referring to his dog. The two friends were walking home from school. "I could find out what he's thinking."

St. Francis inspired Franky as well—so much so that he read and reread the book after Sister Marie Joseph awarded him the class copy "for being the best listener." So when his parents would yell up the stairs about his failing to pick up his clothes, he would respond: "I seest that my room is in ruins. I shall go and restore it for you."

That would send Joe, who was often there lazing about in Franky's bedroom, into hysterics—instant stage feedback for Franky, whose learned language patterns later translated into a unique stage presence that left audiences captivated, but in a perplexed sort of way. Of course, once Franky's music-and-Bix obsession took over, he left St. Francis behind, save for the remnant language patterns and a lifelong respect for the holy man. Sister Marie Joseph, however, became upset when she got word from Franky's teacher the next year that her favorite student was now more interested in a Jewish drunk than a Catholic saint.

BEYOND THE BABY carriage in the alley, Franky and the boys had to overcome other complications that night—namely, a couple of Ariel's crying bouts. To Franky's horror, on one occasion she began to erupt right in the middle of the band's second break, when no music could overpower her lungs. Fortunately, Franky saw it coming, when her inevitable wail was still only an engine sputter. He looked around for help, but the rest of the band was scattered about the bar. He needed to get their attention and he needed to do it right then. He was left with no other option but to holler across the room, even though it would draw not only the boys' attention but the entire bar's. So that's what he did—he barked out the naked truth, intending for the statement's candor to bypass the customers:

"My baby's gonna cry, boys!"

All eyes turned toward the back of the room, including those of the band members, who froze in shock. Each one of them stared pop-eyed at their leader. But it turned out to be an ingenious statement for its misleading frankness. One of the college students interpreted the announcement in his own way.

"'My Baby's Gonna Cry,'" he said, repeating Franky's words. "I think that's an old blues tune."

Hearing the comment, one of the men sitting at the bar glanced over his shoulder, and chimed in. "Yeah, get up there and start playing again. But none of that old colored music."

Franky turned his head sideways to roll his eyes in private. Then he responded, "We're a jazz band, fella. You're already listening to it."

The boys, meanwhile, had already jumped up from their seats and grabbed their instruments. Nick was glad to see the band back onstage early, for he never understood the concept of musician breaks.

"All they do is stand around and play," he was often heard muttering to anyone nearby. "Men working in the hot sun don't get that kind of pussy treatment."

The band was now poised to start up. But what song could they do? Franky had just announced "My Baby's Gonna Cry," a song that didn't exist. That gave him an idea.

"We'll have to do the original," he whispered to his bandmates. "It's the only tune we've got they won't recognize." They glared back at him but nodded. "Ladies and gentlemen," said Franky, facing the audience. "Here's a little number we like to call '"My Baby's Gonna Cry.' Hit it, fellas!"

The band, until that moment too fearful to play Franky's original tune, launched into the newly dubbed piece, "My Baby's Gonna Cry." Everyone was all nerves, though, even Franky.

"I've got to keep moving!" he barked into the microphone in the middle of the instrumental tune.

It was as if his thoughts had escaped through his mouth. That was the verbal escape for his nerves, but a far superior valve is a physical one, so his desperate body jumped into motion without instruction from his head. The bandleader harkened to his soldier days by commencing to march across the front of the stage, only to put his nose in the air because he was blowing his horn, a stance that had the unintended effect of hiding his fears and making him look arrogant about his playing. The onlookers cheered him, so when he got to the far end of the stage he made an about-face and started back the other way, keeping his nose held high even when he didn't have the trombone attached to his mouth. The audience cheered again. It would become a trademark Franky Friz move to be employed whenever he played the song. The rest of the night went off without a hitch—although Franky did have to spend a little time playing the role of the Mad Soloist and orbiting over to the back of the room so that he could appease Ariel with his scat singing.

The baby, incidentally, did something that night Franky would never forget. To her father's astonishment, coming over her face during those moments of listening was the look that Franky had seen before: the disturbingly adult expression as if she were a woman in a café listening to Bach on headphones. The face was neither tranquil nor happy. It was one of intense concentration, perhaps tinged with a touch of melancholy—but that would be impossible because melancholy requires a past. Perhaps, as Franky would recall later, she was reminiscing about her better days in the womb.

OTHER THAN A female vocalist, the band still needed musicians of every ilk to build on their nucleus of players—if, that is, they were going to do justice to the big-band music they tended toward. For one, they needed a bass player, and of course they always could use more brass even though the Man of Many Horns was doing a stellar job filling in with his trumpet and trombone and cornet, sometimes sounding as if he were playing two instruments at once.

First came the bass player, who appeared thanks to Franky placing a *Times-Picayune* classified advertisement, which ended up being nestled somewhere in between a listing for an ancient hunting rifle and a reward offer for a lost Labrador from Mid-City.

"With our luck, the *dog* will show up for the audition," said Joe.

"At least we'd be able to collect the reward," Al pointed out.

Only one person showed up at Nick's for the tryout.

"I'm Big Jim Hebert," said the newcomer, shaking Franky's hand. As if the giant instrument that he'd wheeled in alongside him were somehow invisible to the boys, he added, "I play the bass." The boys noticed that the nickname didn't match his body, for he carried a build that bore a resemblance to Franky's frame. Thus, the bandleader looked him up and down in much the same way that he himself had been examined so many times. But unlike Franky, who walked with a board-like back and raised chin even back then because of the feel the tux gave him, Jim Hebert carried his lanky body in a way that formed a concave *C*, which curved comfortably around his instrument when he played it.

"*Big* must be for the instrument you play," Franky said to the job candidate, "because it sure has nothing to do with you."

"No," answered Jim. "Big is how I play. I play big."

"We'll call you Slim Jim," Franky said. "That sounds better."

As it turned out, Jim didn't play so big during that first audition. But he did seem to be a nice enough fellow, and he would add a solid if simple pulse to the band's sound, rounding out the boys' higher-register instruments with his understated thumps. Slim Jim Hebert, more or less, was better than nothing. And with all the gigging they did, he sure got better, just like the rest of them.

Other musicians passed through the band's ranks, coming and going for one reason or another ("The fit has to be right," said Franky, and the others agreed). But one night at Nick's they found another player who stuck, or the player found them. The story of how he became a core member was as random as any of the other players that caught on with the band. The young guy, about the boys' age, had been sitting alone the whole evening drinking a Barq's root beer and listening to the band with locked eyes, head nodding like a bouncing ball to the beat.

"Who's that weirdo sitting in the back?" Al asked as the boys left the stage following the last set. "He hasn't said a thing to anyone all night."

"He digs the music," said Joe. "He never stopped tapping his foot to my beat."

Franky noticed something else as well. "A teetotaler at Nick's on a Tuesday night? I bet he plays music himself."

As they strolled back to their table to put away their instruments while the customers trickled out into the steamy night, the kid drinking the Barq's still sat there, tapping his foot and bobbing his head as though the music hadn't stopped. Occasionally he glanced back at them, like a shy would-be lover stealing a look at his crush.

"What a freak," Al said.

"He's not a freak," insisted Franky. "He's a musician."

The kid, whose name was Ted LeBlanc, eventually found the courage to step his way over to the boys' table and, after the exchange of a few words about music, ask if he might stop by a band rehearsal some day with his alto sax.

The boys learned Ted's story only months later. A Cajun from Lafayette, he'd come to New Orleans the previous fall to attend Loyola University, the Jesuit institution that his parents had always dreamed their son would attend. They had saved every penny to pay for the Catholic college—yet while he sat in biology or English lit, Ted heard not a word of the professor's lecture; he heard only music. As soon as he arrived in September, he stepped off campus to seek out his love. He dipped into his meager spending money, which his mother had divided into equal weekly lumps to last the entire semester, to satiate his insuppressible hunger for hearing all the best jazz bands in the famed music town. When money evaporated, he took in the sounds of players on the street, stood outside bars listening to syncopated melodies pulsing out doors, walls, and windows, and hunted down the anonymous bars absent from the music map because they weren't music bars at all. In other words, he sought out places like Nick's.

The cancerous disease of music having conquered him, Ted was failing most of his classes by the end of the first semester. His nadir came when he plodded across campus grass to the registrar's office and signed the official papers to withdraw from school. The next stop after the registrar's office, coming in the weakening daylight of an overcast November afternoon, was the school chapel, where he chattered the Rosary in a desperate request for help from Mary the Mother of God. By dusk he had moved his one bag of possessions from his dormitory room to a rundown boarding house on Basin Street, thus putting off the impending Greyhound bus ride back home to Lafayette, where he would have to face his parents. And then, under the camouflage of night, always ideal for denial, he wandered out to find some music for the price of almost nothing, music that would conspire with the dark to help him forget his dire situation. It turned out Mary showed mercy, watching over him like his own mother: He found Nick's and a new home in the Franky Fritz Band. To be sure, not only did Mary approve of Ted's music, so did the boys.

"Shit," Tim exclaimed at that first rehearsal, "this cat can play!"

So by the time the band had reached its first anniversary, it had grown bigger in size, sound, and ability. The band members were all still infatuated with the music that had surrounded them as they were growing up—primarily big band and swing—and they put all their energy into developing those sounds that conjured adolescence. Only problem was, while the group was adding players, they weren't getting more gigs, nor were they earning more dollars for each outing. Their music was already on its way out, and big band was never New Orleans's trademark sound anyway. These forces made them a band with an out-of-step identity. At this point neither Franky nor any of the other band members were businessmen. They were strictly musicians of the passionate kind: If they could make the band sound better with another player, they would add one, for it was all about the music. But time was ticking. Ariel had just turned one, which meant that he now had an income benchmark to beat for the coming year under his contract with his father. That document, which lived only in the unspoken airwaves between father and son, required him to take in more money from his music with each passing year—or face the end of his music career and the dawn of a life selling women's shoes.

As life's roller coaster demanded, harsh reality hit on the heels of a career crescendo. After a scarily slow period, the band got a massive surge of life when they were booked as many as four or five nights a week, even playing some sets at the Blue Room in the Roosevelt Hotel. But they were fooling themselves about their success: The reality was that the boys had been landing so many gigs mainly because it was Carnival time, when the demand for music peaks in New Orleans. On Fat Tuesday itself, the band bounced between no less than three different gigs through the day, heaping up big servings of New Orleans-style jazz, the music everyone expected to hear during Carnival. The boys were growing awfully tired of playing the same kind of music, but nothing could beat the nonstop schedule. Several days prior, one gig even took place while cruising down the far end of Canal Street on the festooned bandstand of a parade float. (The boys had landed that gig only because Tim Callahan's father knew someone who was a member of the Krewe of Mid-City, the social club putting on the parade.) Ted LeBlanc, the out-of-towner and most recent addition to the band, stood most awed by the sights as he gazed from the float bandstand down at the festive crowds that lined the streets. During a quick break between tunes, he took the opportunity to inhale the scene with a full breath, which had the effect of completely intoxicating him.

"We're almost famous," he said with mouth agape and eyes dazed.

Having grown up in New Orleans and experienced Mardi Gras year in and year out, Tim Callahan told Ted to shut up and play.

"They're not here for you," he said of the crowds. "They're here for the party."

At the conclusion of Mardi Gras, the gigs washed away almost as quickly as the city workers hosed out the French Quarter when the clock struck midnight to mark the onset of sobriety and Ash Wednesday. The band members had fooled themselves into believing they were making a name for themselves in the jazz town, when employers had only been filling extra slots opened up by the festive New Orleans season. During its Carnival run, apparently the Franky Fritz Band had left no impression at all.

"It'll be a miracle if we even make it to next year's Mardi Gras," said Joe one day. "They got too many damn bands in this town."

He and Franky were standing outside a church hall after having finished playing a wedding. Rice, strewn all over the church sidewalk, slipped and slid under their black leather-sole shoes. The rest of the band had already left, for during the bleakest moments, just Franky and Joe inevitably were left talking. From that day forward spread the barren white plain of a dateless calendar, other than their regular Tuesday-night gig at Nick's. Worse, just around the corner was summer, when the oppressive heat brought the city to a crawl and even its music quieted some.

"Maybe we should head to Europe for the summer," Joe said, "just like the best bands do."

"No offense," said Franky, "but that's the stupidest thing I've ever heard you say."

While Europe was eating up jazz, which had taken the world by storm like no other American art form in history, the boys not only lacked the money to get themselves and their instruments across the ocean, the idea of a few nameless punks from New Orleans landing gigs in Paris just didn't seem plausible. But the notion of travel seemed to hold some unknown promise, and so it lingered above their heads.

A few days later, the two young men were talking up in Joe's Bywater bedroom, which, along with Franky's room, had over the years become the place where all ideas arrived like the mail. It was Monday, and they were waiting to be called downstairs for Joe's mother's weekly red beans and rice supper, after which no good ideas ever arrived because they felt so slow and content afterward that they couldn't put two thoughts together. Their pessimistic conversation about the band's future had been running continually since their chat on the church steps, for their open calendar had left them with plenty of time to think in a loop. This day seemed particularly dire because Al Butkus had just stopped by to tell them he was thinking about quitting the band to learn the electrician's trade from his uncle, who happened to be looking for help. Or maybe he would attend the school boasting the venerable name Cambridge "Extension University," which offered many programs, marketed to veterans, that all piqued his interest probably because of the important-sounding suffixes that capped their names: Salesmanship, Foremanship, Executive Management, and Traffic Management.

Joe was lying in his bed and tossing a baseball up in the air while Franky sat at the little desk with his back to him. In their school days, Franky might have been lying on the floor, looking upward and conjuring a movie reel of their dreams against the white of the ceiling. But those films had been growing blurrier by the day. Joe's eyebrows scrunched downward, and a crease formed in the baby skin between his eyes.

"I just know it," he said, shaking his head. "I'm gonna end up an old man who don't play nothing but Saturday-afternoon weddings on the side."

The surface of the desk was all but empty, save the worn Keuffel & Esser Co. slide rule that Joe had used both in heroic attempts at performing calculations for math classes and as a drumstick to perform countless nervous beats while attempting those calculations, which he believed lay far beyond his ability. Franky had picked up the slide rule absentmindedly as the two talked. Gashes along the edges of the blond wood catalogued in detail the years of its violent history of music and math anxiety.

"And even worse," Franky said, building on Joe's thoughts, "because of fate, we're doomed to play New Orleans jazz."

Franky studied the slide rule while his mind drifted. The businessmen at Keuffel & Esser had manufactured that piece of wood with the intention of helping some student stand a better chance of landing a decent job after graduation. At this moment, however, it seemed unfortunate that drumming was the only career for which the slide rule had prepared Joe. As if passing the conversation's baton for Joe to make the next bleak comment, Franky tossed the math instrument to his friend, who caught it with the ease of a veteran drummer snatching his sticks out of the air without thought.

"Yep, and Dixieland is back—all over the country, even," he said, accepting the baton. "We can't get away from it. Pops's movie made sure of that."

As idle as it sounded, this comment of Joe's sparked Franky's revelation. Joe was referring to the film *New Orleans*, which had been released some time before. Louis Armstrong—aka Pops—appeared in the film, performing the music he'd grown up playing, and Dixieland was enjoying a bit of a revival among the general public and critics alike. The traveling big bands, meanwhile, with their high overhead were riding into financial troubles; even the biggest of the big bands sadly were coming home from the road for good. In their place smaller ensembles were forming, some of which were forging new musical ground with their improvisational styles and rediscovering the vibrancy of older forms. It didn't look good for the stuck-in-an era Franky Fritz Band.

Then came the breakthrough—albeit not in final, usable form. Franky snatched an idea out of the air that all along had hovered above him like an unlit firefly. Everywhere, it seemed, New Orleans jazz was enjoying a bull market—except in New Orleans, where supply satiated demand.

Franky flipped himself around and straddled the desk chair so that he faced his friend. In his soul, he had long since become a musician. At that moment he became a businessman too. He started flipping through a travel-and-exploration magazine he found on the desk that pictured the wilds of South America alongside ancient peoples living in Africa. Embedded in that colorful tapestry of strange lands, one ad caught his eye: *"Go Abroad" to Louisiana.*

In sharp contrast to the faraway worlds pictured on every other inch of the magazine, the ad included boring images in watercolor of shrimp boats and the French Quarter. Those sights, so mundane to his eyes, apparently looked exotic to the rest of America.

"We were born in New Orleans," he said, straightening up, "so that means we're a New Orleans band."

"You're still sounding like a scratched record."

"A real New Orleans band could get a gig just about anywhere, I bet."

Joe looked at his friend in concern. The slide rule that tapped on his knee grew more rapid, while his shaking head nearly became a tic.

"We can't move somewhere else," he said. "My mama's here."

Franky rolled his eyes. "You're not going to have to leave your mama. What I mean is, we can get better gigs *everywhere*."

"I don't get it."

"We'll be a touring band," explained Franky. "And we can be based here. You can see your mama all you want when we're not on the road."

Like a Ferris wheel slowing to a halt and reversing direction, Joe's head-shaking tic abated until it shifted into a soft nod. "Hmm," he said. "But how we gonna get these faraway gigs? We can't exactly just catch the streetcar and ask for the owner."

Franky thought a moment. "Beats me," he said, shaking his head in defeat. "Beats me."

CHAPTER 9

I've got to get out of here, Ariel had said.

And she did. She caught a bus home first thing the next morning. But never mind the spat with her father: As Bobbi pointed out, she would have split anyway, for now that her true love was gone, she had no reason to tag along with a bunch of men her father's age to places she had been a million times before, places where she needed to find ways to fill endless hours of empty time.

"I bet she misses him even more on the road," said Bobbi, fiddling with the straw in her cola. "The road can make you lonely."

They were sitting at dinner, just she and Franky, eating their pre-gig meal at a family steakhouse where ropes and spurs hung on the walls. What was disturbing, said Franky, was that they had eaten in the exact same room, in the exact same restaurant, two nights before—but in a town five hundred miles away.

"Even restaurants are becoming chains," he grumbled, looking around at his surroundings. "They're like A and Ps now."

Bobbi wasn't talking much this meal, and so she didn't answer now. She just cut her baked potato with her steak knife in six slices like a pie and then mashed and dressed it. So Franky continued, reminiscing about the old days when Ariel, Bobbi, and he had such wonderful times on the road together. And then came his daughter's adolescence.

"I could never stand these battles with her. She's the only one who can beat me at being stubborn."

Bobbi dropped her knife and fork. "You nitwit, it's got nothing to do with being stubborn," she said. "She's in love."

Franky stopped eating and looked up. "You know good and well never to speak to me about such nonsense." He went back to his steak, napkin tucked in shirt to protect his tux. "Besides, I thought you were on the same page as me about this."

"I'm not on any page with you, Franky Fritz, that's for sure. I'm sick of your silly notions. Sick of 'em!"

With Bobbi he knew when to shut up. They finished their meal and paid the check without talking further.

The gig that night wasn't much to speak of. In fact, whether due to Evan's absence or good-luck charm Ariel's departure, or just the unspeakable possibility that the band was dying, nearly every one of the remaining dates brought weak audiences. Franky plunged to his spiritual nadir one day at suppertime when they were traveling west, after they had finished with the Indiana-Illinois leg of the trip. It happened as they filed into a roadside café somewhere in Iowa. Joe was the first to spot the messenger, which was nothing more than a mundane flyer tacked onto a cork bulletin board. At the moment the ominous harbinger revealed itself, Franky was in the middle of one of his great music lectures, telling Tim about where jazz was going and how rock 'n' roll, even though it had been afire for well over a decade now, soon would be nudged aside—by none other than jazz, which would reclaim its position as *the* American music, "king of both quality and popularity," as Franky put it.

"Hey look," interrupted Joe. "There's your hero!"

Everyone turned to where he was pointing. The flyer flapped in the diner's narrow entranceway, made anxious by an Iowa draft. "Maybe you're right about jazz—maybe this is a sign!"

It sure seemed so. Joe slowly sounded out the flyer aloud as the others gazed at it:

The Davenport Jazz Festival
Presented by The Bix Beiderbecke Preservation Society
-featuring the music of Bix-
Come Experience the Legend of Davenport!

Bix had always been Franky's talisman of good fortune and inspiration, and so Joe and the other band members waited for their leader's face to light up. But it didn't; on the contrary, it turned ashen. He repeated but one word from the sign.

"*Preservation*," he muttered, still gazing at the flyer. Then he turned to the rest of them. "It's official. My music is a relic."

No one had ever seen their bandleader show any sign, no matter how tiny, of defeat. After a beat or two, though, Bobbi answered with an edge, either because she didn't know what to say after hearing, for the first time, Franky take pity on himself, or because a surge of compassion spurred her to show affection through a barb.

"Well, that don't make no difference," she said with a shrug. "Your music was a relic back when you first started playing it."

* * *

AS THE DATELESS calendar lengthened, Franky did everything he could to avoid having to go to his father for money, even sending away for a promotional offer seen in his mother's magazine for free samples of baby cereals and strained foods. But the grave day came: He went to his father and asked for help to pay his rent and feed Ariel.

"Get yourself ready for the shoe business in two months," Mr. Fritz warned when he handed over the rent cash.

With gigs hard to find, the band fell back on its Tuesday-night staple: Nick's. The players spent those weeks at the bar sharpening their chops, while Franky also continued to hone his stage skills, singing more often and interacting with the small audiences from the stage with increased frequency. One time those interactions reached an intimate level. The encounter would turn out to have a fateful impact on both Joe and Franky, although the marks left on each showed opposite on their respective persons. The imprint appearing on one turned whole and blossomed, while the mark left on the other formed fragmented and sharp, like a thorn.

The encounter came one night when the band was in between sets. Franky, accustomed to going off by himself to tend to Ariel during breaks, had taken to sitting alone at the band's back table even when Ariel was away with her grandparents, as was the case this night. The Mad Soloist refueled during these moments alone, watching the others mingle with audience members while his head kept busy with other matters: wondering whether his daughter was sleeping or crying, critiquing each song of the previous set and playing out the coming batch of songs note by note. At this fateful moment, he recalled later to Joe, he was imagining Ariel crying in his mother's arms.

"You're the only one in a tux. But you look good in one."

Franky about jumped. People rarely approached the table at all—and this voice was feminine. Smooth and low and feminine. When he looked up, he found a curvy stranger standing over him. She must have been at least five years older, so maybe the compliment seemed excusable in its forwardness. But in an instant, heat filled the space between them. The only feeling to which he could liken it was when he'd sat in the blackness of a movie theater and watched Rita Hayworth shake and sing "Put the Blame on Mame." She stood over him as if she were challenging him to a duel. And perhaps she was—a duel, that is, of one kind or another. For the first time, he was experiencing flirtation of the purely sexual kind.

"How about a thank-you? I said you look good in a tux."

"Thank you," he stammered. And then, as if voicing his own thought, he added, "Unless I'm going to bed, I'll never take it off again."

Without thought he had spoken with the conviction of a man taking an oath, and an oath it turned out to be.

"You know, you should sing more. Or at least find someone to sing more."

He was fumbling for words, and his mouth couldn't make sounds. But what she said—her mentioning his singing—brought him back to thoughts of Ariel, who gave him an idea of something clever to say.

"I would sing more, but I haven't even learned to speak yet. That's why I just sing *do-be-do-dah* and things like that."

The woman giggled seductively, and Franky's temperature jumped another 10 degrees. A break in conversation ensued, but before it could get uncomfortable, she slid around in her seat and started waving toward another part of the room. Almost immediately a woman, already looking toward Franky's table, answered the wave by jumping up out of her seat—rising above the chairs and tables like someone announced for an award. As this stranger shuffled over in heels that made her walk awkwardly, purse in hand and toes pointed inward, the woman standing by Franky introduced herself as Sondra and handed him a lighter so shiny that he could see his reflection in it as clear as a mirror. Sondra, who wore a low-cut blouse that showed a tan line across her breasts and pushed the era's modesty limits to the brink, leaned over with a cigarette between her red-painted lips for Franky to give her a light. She did all this without saying a word, and so at first he failed to oblige her, until finally he started to fumble with the shiny metal contraption. The world had slowed to a drugged dream sequence, and still he was struggling to keep up with it. Before he could snap a flame out of the metal box, the friend arrived at the table—doubling the number of lovely ladies standing before him.

"Aren't you going to ask us to sit down?" Sondra said.

He nearly choked from his social blunder. Yes, of course, please sit down, he said, and Sondra introduced her friend as Marcie. Even though he had little money to spare, he heaved aside his embarrassment by buying drinks for the girls when Nick came around. Like sisters who had been out together a million times before, they asked for martinis without breaking conversation; for himself, Franky ordered his usual iced tea. He hadn't touched a drink since his wedding night, thanks to both bad memories and, earlier, taking in the sad story of Bix and his booze at an impressionably young age.

"Thanks for the drinks," said Marcie. Then she turned to her friend and added, "You see? A real gentleman—you should try one sometime."

The indirect compliment was enough to help Franky claw himself back up to emotional ground level. "A girl like you," he said to Sondra with some hesitation, "I can't believe you're not with a date."

"She just got done dating a jerk," said Marcie. "So *I'm* her date tonight."

Her head punctuated the comment with an emphatic nod as she chewed her gum. Sondra, meanwhile, didn't express any disagreement with her friend's assessment of her former boyfriend. She just took a slow sip of her drink.

"Besides," she said after a moment, "I prefer a man who plays music." She scanned him once over by starting at his feet and ending at his eyes. "Especially one in a tux."

The sex in the air was so strong that it got into his mouth with his next breath, and so it anesthetized his tongue. Sondra slipped her still unlit cigarette back between her painted lips and leaned forward toward Franky, giving him a striking view of cleavage. But then a faraway voice broke through to awaken him from the surreal experience:

"Come on, Franky, let's go!"

Al was calling from the stage. Wouldn't it figure: They had to start the next set. Rising from his seat, Franky excused himself and made his way to the stage with arms crossed over his burgeoning self. The opportunity had been blown, for the girls would surely leave his table now that he was gone. But they didn't leave right away, and so he kept one eye on them while he blew his horn. Only the other musicians noticed how he struggled to keep up with the rest of them—particularly when he fought his trombone through the two-and-a-half songs that passed when Sondra and Marcie disappeared into the ladies' room. It looked as if they were readying to leave.

"Man, you sounded choppy," Joe would say after the set's last song. "I haven't heard you play that bad since the tenth grade."

"Someone knocked the wind out of me," Franky huffed, still trying to regain his breath.

"Well, quit looking at those girls then."

Getting the wind knocked out of him turned out to be worthwhile. When the ladies' room door finally opened, Sondra and Marcie didn't march off to the exit but instead buzzed right back to the band's empty table. The moment he had thanked the audience for their applause, he dashed over to join them almost as fast as he would fly to the back table when he had to check on Ariel.

But surprisingly it was not Sondra—the object of his dizzying carnal preoccupation—that he first noticed upon sitting down. Instead he watched Marcie, for her attention curiously seemed to lie beyond the table. Contrary to her chirpy chatter with Sondra while Franky was up onstage, she hadn't spoken a word since he had rejoined them. Her eyes stayed mysteriously locked on the little makeshift stage as if the band were still playing, yet only one player remained.

"Who's that up there?"

Franky looked where she was pointing. Up onstage sat none other than his best friend and drummer for life. Joe, the guy whose career in romance had spanned but one or two miserable dates, sat hunched over on his stool with forearms resting on his spread knees as he studied the play list and tried to tap out both his nerves and the evening's coming songs.

"Who, him?" said Franky. "That man is not only the best drummer in the city. He's the best *man*."

Marcie grinned a little, as if she held a secret. Sondra, though, was more cautious on behalf of her friend. "He's that great, huh?" she said, blowing out a stream of smoke with puckered lips. "And how do you know that?"

"Simply because," said Franky, raising his chin, "he's been my best friend since the third grade. No one, other than his mother, knows him better."

Marcie bobbed her head nodding, but Sondra still scoffed. "You might be nothing but a slime bucket yourself, and that would make your buddy one too."

"That's true," Franky agreed. He gestured with his head toward the stage and Joe. "But just look at him."

Joe, totally ignorant of three people discussing him, was unknowingly enlisting himself in his own cause. He still tapped away, eyes lowered both in concentration and to avoid the eyes of others. The sight made Marcie giggle with affection, and even Sondra couldn't deny his authenticity.

"Now that I think of it," she said, "he does look nicer than you."

"That's because he *is* nicer," said Franky.

Marcie giggled and told him that Joe must be a real good friend. "I can tell these things," she said. "A friend and a real gentleman."

Franky was doing all he could to make his buddy look good, but if he was going to truly aid Joe's love cause, the time was now: He called the drummer's name across the room and waved him over. But Joe, who now could see two ladies at the table with Franky, answered with a return wave, feigning ignorance at the meaning of his friend's beckoning gesture. And then when he could feign no longer, he just shook his head in short, quick jerks while pointing downward toward his set list, conveying that he needed to study it.

"Excuse me, ladies," said Franky, getting up to saunter over to the stage.

The women watched the two friends go back and forth at each other like two hens jerking their necks back and forth in sync. As if escorting a blind man, he lifted Joe's arm and touched his shoulder to guide him off his stool. From there he walked his shaky friend to the table by holding onto his wrist with one hand and resting his other palm on the small of Joe's back. Before Joe knew it, he was sitting pop-eyed and facing two strange women. The drummer's speech faculties lost, Franky took the reins of the conversation.

Before long the boys had learned a little bit about their companions: Judging from Sondra and Marcie's disparate personalities, it wasn't surprising the two had found each other at work. During the war they had met at the great shipyard where the shore landing craft were birthed, the ones originally inspired by the swamps and bayous of Louisiana, the ones that crawled ashore like insects onto beaches in Franky's war.

"Sondra was the kind of girl my mama always said to stay away from," said Marcie with a mischievous giggle.

"When I first met Marcie, I thought she was so square I wouldn't be caught dead around her," admitted Sondra to the boys.

Joe still was saying nothing, and so Marcie turned the conversation to him. "Franky here says you're one of the best drummers in the city."

"Nah," he replied, head stiff. "There's plenty of 'em around here I'd kill to play like."

"Well, anyways," Marcie said, sighing so that her shoulders dropped, "too bad you're up there drumming. They should figure out a way so the boys in the band could ask a girl to dance."

Joey couldn't utter but one meaningless sound after that comment, let alone an intelligible word of any kind. Later, when the band had taken the stage again, as he kicked himself over his inability to speak, he told Franky, "I should've did what you did! I should've memorized how St. Francis talked." But as it turned out, Joe fared well that night, thanks to Franky's help and, more importantly, Marcie's disregard for coyness. The dynamics of the foursome worked out well for all: Franky's concentration on keeping his friend in the game helped steady his own quivering nerves.

"You guys could make a name for yourselves in the city," Marcie said at one point. "You're really good."

"The Franky Fritz Band won't make a name for itself in New Orleans," corrected Franky prophetically. "It will make its name in *America*."

Sondra turned to Marcie with a firm fold of her arms. "Ach! Talk about conceited. And to think you said he was nice!"

"She never said I was nice," said Franky. "She said I was a gentleman."

When the time came for the boys to head back to the stage for the final set, Franky thought to increase the chances of the girls staying at the table by ordering another round of drinks. Not until Nick showed up with the drinks did Franky scrape the bottom of his pocket to feel only a nickel and a couple of pennies. He kicked Joe under the table in a call for help, and the drummer—thanks to the fact that he boarded for free with his mother—pulled out his wallet from his back pocket. "Best investment I ever made," Joe liked to say in ensuing years.

When the set ended, the girls were still at the table sipping their drinks and waiting for the two musicians.

"I wonder what's on the jukebox," said Marcie, practically jumping up.

Joe shrugged. "Yeah, I wonder."

"Joe, be a gentleman and go look at the jukebox with her," said Sondra.

He tucked his chin down to his chest. "I can't do that. Franky's the gentleman."

"Yes, that's true," Franky said. "But I've been standing up all night and my feet hurt. You're sitting down when you play."

"Besides, I heard you're a gentleman too," said Marcie.

Joe had no choice but to accompany her. As soon as he eased himself up out of his chair, she glued her hand to the inside of his elbow to be escorted, and they started off, he stiffening his arm straight at his side and hobbling to the jukebox. Now the pair stood side by side over the shimmering machine that lit their faces, Joe standing straighter than his own drumsticks and Marcie leaning in, her shoulder reaching as close to his bicep as it could without making contact so that electricity danced back and forth between their arms. Meanwhile, the other band members, needing to pick up their instrument cases and belongings at the table, passed through like gulls swooping up fish so that they would keep out of the way of the boys' good fortune.

The next thing Sondra and Franky knew, Marcie and Joe weren't at the jukebox anymore but in front of the stage. The first notes of a song had sounded, and they were stepping into a dance, starting a sequence in which they would begin to discover each other through timid touch. She led him all the way, while he kept his shuffling feet close to the floor and struggled to tap them to the beat of "Romance

Me." Looking on, Sondra remarked how strange it was that someone so good on drums could be so clumsy on the dance floor. Yet the moment mesmerized not only the dancers but the two who watched them: They gazed upon the swaying couple and said nothing for several bars of the song, until Sondra slipped a comment into the silence, and it lingered like cigarette smoke.

"I would say those two might could fall in love," she said, never taking her eyes off of the dancers. "Except I don't believe in love."

The words resonated, as if Franky had been searching for them for years. Sondra had verbalized a notion that had already started to follow him, one that would gradually catch him and then burrow in like a feeding tick, and stay buried just below the skin for decades.

"Neither do I."

At that moment the two were entering into an unspoken pact. Franky had found a fellow philosopher, and one from his school of gloom at that. But the pact had nothing to do with the philosophical, but the physical. The sexual waters, which had been surging all along, swirled fiercely around them now and were about to hit flood stage.

"Love…" said Sondra, exhaling the smoke of her cigarette. "I'll let Marcie have that."

Their eyes left their friends to lock upon each other's.

"And I Joe," said Franky.

The mutual gaze spoke everything. They knew what was coming next.

After dancing through the two remaining songs they had bought from the jukebox, Joe and Marcie made their way back to the table. Marcie once again rested her palm on the inside of Joe's elbow in escort style, but this time he bent his elbow and held his forearm smoothly across his belly as she grasped onto the handle that he'd made for her. Franky couldn't stop watching in wonder. In the two minutes and forty-six seconds of the first song, Joe had passed through a rite of passage.

"I think my best friend just became a man," he said, his eyes following the approaching couple. "I wonder what I've become."

Sondra's foot, which grazed his big toe underneath the table, stirred him out of his momentary reflection. When Marcie and Joe sat down, Sondra and Franky traded a glance, and with one mere statement, their pact took concrete form.

"I'm not feeling well, so Franky's gonna take me home now," announced Sondra. As she stood up and gathered her purse, she sent a cursory glance Joe's way. "Now, you be a gentleman and take Marcie home."

Before Joe could answer, Franky had grabbed his horn cases and was starting to bolt with Sondra. Joe was caught looking at Marcie, who stood there clutching her purse in both hands.

"I better not walk alone," she said.

Joe, now transformed, as Franky had observed, spoke eloquently and simply: "Now, I wouldn't let you do that."

Marcie and Joe would tell their versions of the story a thousand times: Arm in arm the two walked together. He could have been escorting an elderly lady across the street, he took such great care in walking with her—plus, as he later would admit, he wanted to prolong the walk until forever. When they arrived at her doorstep, he called upon his only source of romantic knowledge—Hollywood—and kissed the back of her hand.

"You act like the fellas in the movies," said Marcie.

Joe could only shrug because he knew no better. Again, though, words dropped into his head, as if he was Franky speaking as St. Francis. "With you it's like I *am* in the movies," he answered.

Franky and Sondra, meanwhile, charged back to his apartment on Frenchman Street. First they kissed hard standing by the window and then they kissed hard with their glued torsos sliding off the couch and their legs entangled on the floor. Perhaps because he was older, or perhaps because he didn't care, Franky kissed Sondra with greater ease than he ever did Muriel.

Gradually the pace of the hard kissing slowed. After a few moments to catch their breath, they took the great walk into the bedroom while holding hands with a distance between them. At the foot of the bed that Franky was supposed to have shared with Muriel, they shed their clothes like a comfortable couple at home preparing for bed on a weeknight. But the passion quickened again as soon as bare skin rubbed.

Since Franky's sexual history was brief and sparse, comparisons may have been inevitable. Posted atop her body and right in the midst of the act, he stopped, arrested by a revelation.

"I don't feel anything," he said, panting. "This feels good."

Sondra noticed he was still, so she stopped too. Catching up to the words he had said, she looked at him with her head tilted, and then with shortened breath demanded to know just what he meant by saying he didn't feel anything! But before Franky could explain, she lay back and sighed.

"Never mind," she said, "I think I know what you mean." And they started up again.

FRANKY DIDN'T SEE much of Sondra after that, or speak of her, other than to deflect questions from Tim such as, "You made it with her, didn't you?" Without words, the bandleader and the woman had inked a contract specifying the terms of engagement: one night and one night only. The long-term implications of that evening, meanwhile, proved opposite for another couple. The very next day Joe told Franky he'd found the girl he was going to marry, and he would turn out to be right. The two became a pair almost immediately, notwithstanding Joe's occasional social misstep. He tried, for instance, to take Marcie on their first date on his bicycle, which he wanted to flaunt because he had just received a "motorize your bicycle" kit in the mail, bought after seeing an ad in the back of a boys' magazine, which he read even though he was no longer a boy. In spite of the blunder, they immediately began going out on weekly dates—to the movies, the soda shop, the bowling alley. With the band struggling, Joe was in the same financial situation as Franky, but Mrs. Randazzo, who had little money to spare, was so ecstatic her son had found a girl that she funded the dates herself. The couple's mutual understanding of the relationship's permanence was almost instantaneous.

Franky, meanwhile, had stepped into a contrary permanence. On the night that Joe found love, Franky officially turned his back on it. A brief sentence—*I don't believe in love*—uttered from the mouth of a one-night stand, had touched his self like his tux. Sondra's influence on him was slight, yet he found comfort in hearing his own framework for living verbalized, a framework that he had already more or less constructed but now could speak.

Now, if only the Franky Fritz Band could find its voice.

Chapter 10

THE KNOCK SOUNDED when Franky and Ariel were standing right inside the door. They were getting ready to go for their big outing that only one of them had been anticipating forever. Franky looked at his watch.

"Ten-oh-three," he said moments before the knock, holding his wrist a distance from his eyes. He was the first in the band to go nearsighted, but he still refused to buy glasses. "I guess Bobbi can't make it. We're supposed to go without her if she wasn't here by ten."

Even though Ariel had agreed on the outing to the junior college for registration, she stood sullen, hands in her pockets.

"Figures. We might as well not even go."

Franky played down her teetering sentiment by letting his chatter clip along. "Now, it's not a big deal, you'll still get to see her. She said to give her a call from a pay phone after we've finished registering so she can still meet us for lunch afterward." He glanced at his daughter, whose face hadn't changed. "Too bad, though. She sure was excited to witness her 'little girl go to college,' as she put it." Ariel rolled her eyes. "But you'll have other, more important milestones for Bobbi to witness—like graduation."

Franky hadn't been this buoyant in weeks because the band was doing so terribly. Thank God for Ariel going to college, he had told Bobbi the day before. "Otherwise, I wouldn't have a thing to be happy about."

True, Ariel had agreed to enroll, but she had done so with the enthusiasm of a sweltering swamp-day afternoon. Evan would be returning to New Orleans in a couple of weeks, so Ariel's life for the coming months was taking form: attending classes, working on her art, and being with Evan.

"Do you have your forms?"

"Yeah," said Ariel, tilting her head, impatient.

"ID?"

Tap tap tap.

They both jumped a little at the sound of the knock because they were standing so close to the door.

"Well, what do you know," said Franky, all the more buoyant. "I guess Bobbi's coming with us, after all."

At the prospect of Bobbi, Ariel's apathetic eyes flickered while her father opened the door. But the mere flickers were about to turn to flares of joy.

"We thought you weren't going to make—"

Franky wasn't able to finish the sentence. Or he just stopped speaking because it wasn't the *right* sentence. No, it wasn't Bobbi at all.

"Evan!" Ariel cried.

There he was slouching before them, trademark torn jeans and all, appearing on the stoop from out of nowhere like a ghost seen in a flash of lightning. Speaking not another word, Ariel gasped, and the two embraced, leaving Franky standing there to watch.

"I did it," he muttered.

The two didn't seem to hear. They were still embracing, Ariel's cheek against his slight chest. Both pairs of eyes stayed shut.

"I did it," he repeated.

They kept embracing while he stood there. Seconds passed—maybe even minutes, at least by the measure of Franky's miserable mind.

He cleared his throat. "Come now, Ariel, let's get going. Registration closes at noon."

Finally, Ariel opened her eyes and turned toward him, aware of his presence for the first time. "They're open tomorrow too, so let's just do it then," she said. "That'll be better anyways, so Bobbi can come."

Before he could open his mouth to answer, she had turned right back to Evan and started chattering. "You're home early!" she said. "What happened?" And he told her how he just couldn't stand being without her, so he had to get back. They talked on, and for a period of time they were all alone because to them Franky, who stood silent beside them, didn't exist. To be sure, he had been turned to a statue by Evan's unexpected arrival. Then they did something that as Franky later told it, shocked him. Like a band that has played together for years, they started out the door together in perfect sync, without communicating to each where they were going or even that they were going at all, chattering all the way through the sound of the door shutting. They were walking off into the sunset, or into another world, never to return.

They didn't go far, though. Looking out the peephole, Franky found them sitting on the stoop, holding hands and still talking. The cadence of their conversation had slowed, and their voices came through only in indecipherable muffled tones. A calmness surrounded the scene, which was a faraway curved globe because it was viewed through a peephole.

"She's gone," said Franky, even though she stayed on the stoop. Then, in defeat, he detached his eye from the peephole to find his easy chair.

They never left, literally at least. Within a few minutes the door opened again, and they shuffled in, still talking away, apparently never having stopped from the time they stepped out in the other direction. Franky, who was sitting with a *Times-Picayune* in his lap, looked up. They continued their conversation without acknowledging him, yet they made their way to the couch and plopped themselves down just a few feet away. They went on about their future together, using words that young lovers speak as naturally as words for food, words like *forever*.

But it was the word *commitment*—as in their *commitment* to each other was forever—that unglued Franky's lips.

"Commitment?" he echoed.

The two turned, noticing him for the first time, so he continued.

"You keep saying *commitment*," he said, rising out of his reverie. "Well, you made a commitment to *me*." He was suddenly fully sober. "And now you think you can waltz back in and save the day, do you? Sorry, son—that's not going to happen." He paused, as if considering whether or not to say something. "No, you can't just waltz in and take back a job you walked out on. The Franky Fritz Band will have to decide if you're in or not."

Franky was not stupid. In spite of himself, he was smart enough to leave the door open for Evan, the band's spark, to play with them again. He glanced at the two of them together, waiting for Evan to respond. This was the young man's moment to apologize, to say he'd like his spot back. But defying the intensity of the person speaking at him, Evan answered with his trademark shrug:

"I'm not into commitment, man."

He added something about "except for Ariel, that is," and the two gazed raptly at each other. Franky's mouth opened for a moment before words formed, and when they did, they came out slow and smoldering. With each sentence tempo and volume built. "You kids don't get it, do you?" he started. "You don't get commitment because you don't get music. This is a business, son—and when you're in the music business, you've got to show up for your gigs no matter what. Haven't you ever heard the expression *the show must go on*?" Before long he was almost yelling. "Music is a marriage—a *marriage,* for crying out loud. You've got to be committed to it! You've got to be committed to your bandmates!"

But Evan still stayed calm. "You keep saying 'the music business'—that's for you old-timers, man. My people, we don't need business anymore. We just play the music."

The bandleader shot up out of his chair. Ariel wrapped her arms around herself and scrunched her shoulders, waiting for her father to clock her boyfriend. But he didn't raise a fist; he only raised his finger and pointed it. "I'll tell you what, son, you can forget any gig with the Franky Fritz Band, that's for sure."

He turned and started off; there was nothing like a stage exit to ensure one got the last word. But Evan had some news to share.

"That's cool," he said to the bandleader's back. "I'm not looking for a gig anyway. We've got other plans."

Franky stopped and turned around. Glaring, he rested his hands on his hips. "*We* have other plans, huh. So you found some other fool players for you to eventually walk out on, have you? Well, good luck to them!"

"No, I'm not talking about any band. I'm talking about me and Ariel—*we've* got other plans." Franky bristled, but Evan continued, seemingly unaware. "We can't be apart." Turning to his girl, he grabbed hold of her hand with both of his. They exchanged brief smiles before her head bowed back down. "So around the time you go out on your next tour, we'll be doing some traveling ourselves—out west."

A friend had a band out in San Francisco, see, and they needed a sax player. A happening scene had coalesced in the Bay City, and "everyone" was headed out there. The best part, though, was that this friend of Evan's knew some cat named Bill Graham who ran a joint called the Fillmore. In August, the friend's band was tentatively scheduled to be on the bill. As if to convince Franky of the joint's legitimacy, Evan said that years ago the Fillmore used to be a dance hall—"the Ambassador, or something."

Franky lit up a little. "The Ambassador has music again?" But then he shook his head, warding off the reverie. "Rock music in the Ambassador," he grumbled. "That's worse than when they turned it into a roller rink."

Evan sighed, for the first time showing a hint of impatience, but then he gathered himself. No, it's not like that, he said. "Rock is a vital new musical force—just like your music was—"

Pow!

Franky stomped the heel of his shoe on the hardwood floor. Fists clenched, he was ready to do whatever it took to keep Evan from finishing the thought.

"My music," he said with his teeth as clenched as his fists, "is *still* vital."

They stood before each other, one ready for combat and the other slouching. Evan's slouch, though, had turned uncharacteristically defiant. Arms folded on his chest, he rested his weight on one hip while his dark eyes squinted as if he were taking a drag on a cigarette.

"Come on, Evan, let's go."

Still sitting, Ariel was tugging gently on his arm. But he brushed her off.

"Your music is okay, I'll give you that," he said, still glaring at Franky. "But rock is where it's at."

Franky's chest, bigger than his body from blowing horns, heaved with each breath he took. Neither the older nor younger man had yet to unlock eyes. The words came out in the quiet rumble of finality.

"*Your* music is nothing but a fad—it'll be dead and gone tomorrow." He took a half step forward and raised his finger. "So don't come running to me when that happens, son, because, so help me, you'll never play with us again. And if I can help it, you'll never play in this *town* again!"

That was it. Evan grabbed Ariel's hand and pulled her up off the couch. Having grown as red as Franky, he faced him one last time before turning toward the door.

"I thought you were cool, man, but you're just like the rest of the old-timers."

Standing full and tall like a soldier from Franky's era, the young musician faced the older bandleader dead-on. For the first time he was looking down at Franky because he'd lost his slouch. And then he said what everyone knew but what no one would say aloud in front of their charismatic leader:

"Face it, Franky Fritz. You need me more than I need you."

Franky just stood there. Ariel, her hand in Evan's, stepped toward her father, as if a burst of compassion threatened to well over and cause her to embrace him. But she stopped, and stayed planted where she was, between them, silent. When Franky finally opened his mouth, he spoke as softly as he spoke when he used to put Ariel to bed, only he still faced Evan.

"Get out." He grabbed Ariel's free hand so that two men now held each of hers. "Get out, and stay away from my daughter. You'll take her west over my dead body."

The two men glanced over at her. She didn't move an inch. Instead she just looked down toward the floor.

"Your daughter can decide for herself what she does," said Evan.

Ariel slowly shook her head in protest of the moment of forced choice. Then she made her decision. Head bowed in a way that could be construed as either meek or defiant, she slipped her hand out of Franky's and stepped toward her boyfriend.

"You were the one who always taught me to do my own thing," she said to her father. Then she lowered her head again and started off. "Come on, we'd better go."

It was Evan, not Franky's daughter, who glanced back over his shoulder after they'd stepped out onto the stoop. So at the moment Ariel closed the door shut, each of the two musicians caught the other's eye.

* * *

BOTH LUCKY STARDUST and a possible deathblow came all in one night for the band.

Franky's brainstorm to market the group in other parts of the country as an authentic New Orleans ensemble had yet to reap any new business. While he thought he was onto something, neither he nor any of the other guys had figured out how to land gigs beyond the local area, for distance alone prevented them from just showing up in person and making a pitch. The idea seemed just one of the zillion that shrivel up like a burned piece of paper, its ashen form floating away in the breeze until it disintegrates into nothing.

"We've never sounded better, and hardly anyone knows it," said Al after a gig at Nick's.

"Sure we've never sounded better," Joe said, "but we're still missing something. I can't put my finger on it. You know—a little spice, a little Tabasco or something."

Franky stopped putting away his cornet. "*You* of all people should know what we're missing," he said. "We're missing a girl. We're missing a chick singer."

Only problem was, how to get one. Most of the boys could barely get a date, let alone a capable female vocalist for the band.

Some weeks later they were playing Nick's, where only a bare core of the usual loyalists had shown up. Nick didn't overlook the fact that the crowd was sparser than usual, repeating his tired threat to put an end to the weekly arrangement. "You should be paying *me* to play here," was the inevitable comment.

"That's what I've always loved about Nick," said Tim, shaking his head. "He's so original."

All night Nick kept grumbling about firing the band. As the night wore on, the annoying drone of the bar owner's empty threats grated deeper and deeper on Franky's patience. Any moment he was going to open a valve to ease the building steam inside of him.

"Keep your mouth shut with Nick, Franky," warned Joe. "I wanna keep our one and only gig."

"Of course I'll keep my mouth shut," answered the bandleader, exaggerating his incredulity by spreading his arms open. "It would be absolutely stupid of me to get smart with our employer." Oh, but by the way, he added, "There will be a change in the play list for the next set. We're going to open with a different song."

"Oh yeah?" Tim said. "And what song is that?"

"Don't worry about it. You guys play a little better when you're tense."

"Ah jeez," said Joe. "We're in trouble."

When the band had assembled to start the next set, Franky began with introductory remarks as he often did, but this time his address to the audience sounded more like a farewell than an introduction.

"Ladies and gentlemen, I think it would be safe to say—" He paused for dramatic effect as the audience quieted. "I think it would be safe to say that if our Tuesday-night tour in this den of inequity ever came to an end, I trust you wouldn't come here anymore."

A murmur rippled through the little pack of patrons, while Nick glared at Franky. Al, meanwhile, appeased the fretting Joe by telling him not to worry because Nick didn't know what *den of inequity* meant.

"What?" called a middle-aged bachelor. "You gonna stop playing here?"

"Of course not, Ronnie," answered Franky. "But as I said: If we *did* stop playing here, I trust you folks probably wouldn't show up anymore."

"Ain't that right!" called out a woman. "I know I wouldn't come to this rat hole, anyway!"

Chuckles erupted, and others murmured in agreement. But growls came from behind the bar. Nick leaned toward the stage, watching every move of Franky's, palms resting on the bar and elbows projecting out into the air.

"And if we did stop playing here," said Franky cheerily to the audience, "I would make the following announcement…"

Franky started to give the count, but the rest of the boys, who had just been informed of the song choice, dropped their instruments to their sides and stood frozen and staring at their leader. Al stepped over to Franky.

"What the hell was that?" he whispered. "We can't play *that* after you gave it that intro!"

"Don't worry," Franky whispered back. "Nick will never get the insult. He won't know the song."

But Al was as rigid as concrete. "We ain't playin it. When Nick hears the lyrics and puts it together with that intro, he's gonna run us out!"

"Trust me, it's not like he's hearing the lyrics—we're doing an instrumental version."

Incredulous, Al looked at him for a moment and then shook his head and returned to his stage position. He gave a grudging nod to the other boys, who had been watching for his okay.

"As I was saying," said Franky, now addressing the audience again, "if we stopped playing here at Nick's, this is what I would say…"

The controversial song that they were fussing over? The 1923 standard (and Franky Fritz Band staple), "Who's Sorry Now?" which by then had already been recorded by a host of acts (including Benny Goodman, one of Franky's favorites) and even recently had enjoyed a modest revival, via a Harry James Orchestra rendition that charted.

In the here and now of Nick's, though, the title of the song said it all, its sarcastic question speaking to the bar owner. But the boys were supposedly safe from his wrath because Nick, who had spent his whole life ignoring music, would never even recognize the tune, or so Franky gambled. To Nick, music was at best background noise, in one ear and out the other, and Franky knew that about the bar owner from the start. Even back when he and Joe first met him and were caught in the intoxication of landing their first steady gig, Franky intuitively understood the bar owner's kind. At the time Joe couldn't stop talking about "what a nice man Mr. Nick was" to let them play in his bar. But in spite of the good cheer of the moment, Franky saw him in another light.

"I don't trust that man," he said. "Music doesn't move him."

Of course, the boys could never be certain that he didn't know the song. Almost everyone back then knew it, even those folks whose skin didn't tingle at the sound of a good melody. As they played the first notes, the boys all peered past their horns and drums and double bass to keep one eye on Nick. It was a wonder Joe could even keep his beat, but something had changed in him since he'd started dating Marcie: He'd lost most of his jitters and had become a relaxed fellow overall (moments like this notwithstanding).

The hotheaded owner was still glaring up toward the stage as the musicians moved through the first bars of the song. Having been party to Franky's introduction, a hint of puzzlement now tinged his usual scowl as he searched for any insult that might be passing above his head. Finally he shook that head like a wet dog and went back to wiping the bar top.

"Who's Sorry Now?" turned out to be such a crowd-pleaser that several audience members jumped up to dance. It may not have been the hottest of songs, but the way the Franky Fritz Band played it, the number's lilting beat, tempo, and tune all blended together just right to give off a happy feel that proved infectious to anyone within earshot. By the middle of the song any of the sparse audience members who weren't skipping around the dance floor were at least moving their heads from side to side and tapping their feet.

The irony of such a happy melody carrying the title and lyrics of "Who's Sorry Now?" was not lost on the band members. During a rehearsal when the band was first learning the song, Joe, who had already fallen deeply in love by that time, ruminated on the peculiarity of such a fun tune being coupled with a rather vengeful message. It just didn't seem right, he said, and yet somehow the song worked. But Franky thought he understood the appeal of the tune perfectly:

"What could be more fun than vindication?"

On this night at least, vindication sure seemed like fun. The gyrating audience soaked up the band's energy, fueled in part by the satisfaction Franky gleaned from insulting his employer, which is always fun. The boys, already admiring of Franky's verbal skills and wit, were now becoming flat-out awed by their leader. He could do just about anything and get away with it—except land them steady gigs.

But then something happened. The audience liked the song a bit too much for the band's own good, and that meant trouble. One particular woman on the improvised dance floor was so taken by the swaying fun of the tune that she jumped in to offer a little vocal help, partially humming and partially singing the simple yet direct words:

Who's sorry now?
Who's sorry now?
Whose heart is achin' for breakin' each vow
Who's sad and blue, who's cryin' too…

Her singing probably wasn't loud enough for Nick to hear, but it was plenty audible for Joe's hair to stand up on end, just as in the old days, pre-Marcie. As he drummed he made a *shhh* pucker out of his lips while his eyes bulged wide to help send his urgent message across the air to the woman. But she was having too much fun to notice.

Ted LeBlanc's eyes, meanwhile, were also fixed on the woman, but his look bespoke of a different interest. When a break in his part came and he was able to separate his lips from his saxophone's mouthpiece, he leaned into Franky's ear as the bandleader kept playing.

"She actually sings pretty good," said Ted. He leaned away for a moment, then he returned to Franky's lobe. "I don't get it, though. She's only kind of good-looking but I can't stop watching her."

Franky glanced at her and shrugged. "She's not much," he answered in between notes.

Yet he couldn't help but watch her and listen. She actually didn't sound bad—amateurish certainly, but not too bad. As he played, he noticed that Ted hadn't taken his eyes off her.

"Quit staring," he said, leaning over toward the sax player. "She's with a date. You don't want to get the dickens beaten out of you, do you?"

Catching himself, Ted followed the advice and looked away. "Why do you always say *dickens*? I never hear you curse."

"*Dickens* is worse than a curse word," said Franky.

He was right about the woman's date and the danger he posed to anyone ogling her. Slouching in his chair and using his fist as a pedestal for his jaw, the man fixed his eye on his dance-leader companion as if he owned her—or thought he did. He wasn't the biggest guy in the world, but he sure didn't seem friendly. Meanwhile, the woman, charismatic in an unintentional way, was attracting the attention of everyone in the room. With folks clapping to her lead, she sang louder and then louder.

"Come on everybody!" she said. "Everyone join in!"

So they did. They started singing along with her:

…You had your way
Now you must pay
I'm glad that you're sorry now
I'm glad that you're sorry now

The song spoke directly to Nick, that was for sure. Each time the band took the tune back to the top, more people started singing along with her, beginning with the treacherous lines, *Who's sorry now, Who's sorry now*. Worse, the woman kept coaxing them along: "This is fun! Now everybody, together!"

There was no way that Nick didn't hear the lyrics by now. Yet still he fought to put on the appearance of not taking notice by pacing back and forth and wiping the bar with his rag; if he didn't appear to notice the lyrics, he wouldn't have to make a scene. Then something worse happened. The gaggle of dancers, lined up in a couple of rows like a dancing Broadway cast, sought to bring the surly bar owner into the fun. When they came to a verse's last line, which went *I'm glad that you're sorry now*, they wagged their index fingers in unison straight at Nick. The mundane woman with magnetism had stirred up the crowd into a frenzy of fun.

The boys looked over at him. Rage reddened his face, and his head craned across the bar. Now there was no way he could publicly deny the taunting. So came the eruption, made stronger when embarrassment slammed into pride. He leaped out from behind the bar like King Kong offended.

"*Stop!*" he hollered. "*Stop!*"

Having anticipated the explosion, the band halted instantly. The sudden silence left the singing voices of the preoccupied audience to trail on for a few measures longer until, voice by voice, the tune petered out. Their bodies stopped moving to the music that was no longer. An old man sitting in a rickety wooden chair, who must have been hard of hearing and drunk, was the last to register the abrupt song interruption, for when the rest of the room had gone silent, he sang yet one more line:

Now you must pay.

Everyone stood frozen, staring at Nick. The barman was pointing straight at the boys onstage.

"Get the hell out of my bar!"

After needing a moment to catch up to what had just happened, the boys shuffled off the stage and began packing their instruments. The audience members, meanwhile, wandered back to their seats as if they had been hypnotized, not fully comprehending the double meaning that Franky had given the song and therefore not knowing the cause of Nick's eruption. The owner now focused his attention underneath the bar, where he searched for glasses to clean.

"We'll see who's sorry!" he barked, seemingly shouting to himself. "We'll see who must pay!"

The patrons began to murmur among themselves, but still the boys didn't say a thing to one another, instead keeping their heads hung low. Franky had blown it for them. His arrogant barb had gone way too far, and now they all would pay. A tenuous calm, the kind that befalls space when everyone knows the worst of a conflict has passed, drifted into the room, and people's shoulders began to loosen. Nick, who like the boys was still keeping his head down as he self-consciously tried to stay busy, hadn't said another word. A minute or two passed.

"Hey, stop it! You get lost, buddy!"

Now, yet another eruption had obliterated the growing calm. But the voice wasn't Nick's. It wasn't even the voice of a man. Right on the heels of *Get lost buddy* came a *slap*—the jarring sound of open hand on flesh. Every head of the handful of patrons left in the bar turned toward the source of the sound.

There before them stood none other than the cheery song leader of "Who's Sorry Now?" She glared down at her seated date, pocketbook in hand, with her knees bent in an action stance and her free hand clenched into a fist like a crumpled tissue. Then she looked up. With the sudden awareness of all the eyes fixed on her, a need to blurt out an explanation overtook her.

"He tried to feel me up in public!"

Everyone looked at the man sitting before her. Silence. Folks needed a moment to figure out what had just happened and how to respond.

"You heard her—get lost, buddy, and don't come back!"

It was Nick who had broken the silence. Coming out of their shock, patrons murmured agreement, which had the effect of coaxing the barman on. "The ladies in my establishment get treated like ladies!" He had found an opportunity to shed his bad-guy association, and so he added for good measure, "Did you hear what I said, fella?"

The man sullenly rose from his chair and stepped away, sticking his chin out and pulling up his trousers in an attempt at maintaining his tough self-image. The bar door shut closed behind him. Franky wasn't paying attention to the guy, though. Never having taken his eyes off the violated woman, he studied her curiously. The woman brushed dirt that wasn't there off her skirt and snug pink sweater. Then she stopped what she was doing to confirm that all eyes had gone back to her, a realization that again pushed her to find something to say.

"I swear," she grumbled, swiping up her belongings from the table, "I can't find me a good man for the life of me."

The woman seated herself again, smoothing her dress against her buttocks and down the back of her legs before making contact with the wooden chair. Next she tugged on her sweater, took a quick sip of her drink, and felt the back of her hair. Franky had been watching her every move, even now as she stood up to leave.

"It's her," he said to his bandmates.

The boys groaned. "He's looking at the women again," said Al to the other boys. "First he says shit to get us fired, and now he's looking at women again. Now I *know* he's lost his marbles."

"He's found the girl he's gonna marry—just like me!" Joe said.

But Franky wasn't listening to Al or Joe. The woman's every move spoke of a presence, a sensuality—all augmented by a lack of self-awareness. The boys, meanwhile, were busy grumbling along with the other patrons about what a jerk the woman's date was. Al said something about "how come the jerks get the pretty girls," and Tim said, "Go for it, Franky—you're a nice guy."

But Franky wasn't listening. He just kept nodding in thought, until the band members noticed his trance.

"Look at her," he said. "That, boys, is our singer."

He was stricken—business stricken, at least. But the woman had marched out of the bar, perhaps gone forever, before he could oil his joints like the rusted Tin Man and take action. Stirred from his trance by the *clap* of the barroom door, he jumped up from his seat to bolt out. He didn't reach her for a full block, at which point he leaped in front of her to block her path. Gasping for breath, he couldn't speak at first, and so he just pushed his business card into the befuddled woman's hand. She held it up with two hands:

Direct from New Orleans
The World-Famous
Franky Fritz Band
Featuring
Franky Fritz:
"The Man of Many Horns"

"Be there Thursday at five," said Franky, panting and pointing to the address, which appeared on the backside because the jumble on the front was too long.

The woman was still studying the odd card, confused. "Huh?" she said. "Where's that?"

"On Frenchman Street. It's my apartment. It's where we—"

"I beg your pardon, buster! What kind of a girl do you think I am? Just because you saw another man treat me like a—"

She raised her pocketbook over her head, but before she could release her cocked-back arm and smack him, Franky jumped out of the way and onto the street. "Ach!" she said, dropping her arm back down to her side. She hadn't smacked him, but she had won anyway, because with the sidewalk now clear again, she could huff and march on. But Franky wasn't ready to give up. As if floating across a bandstand, he danced back in front of her, blocking her way once again, this time with his forearm half-raised to deflect any oncoming pocketbooks.

"I'm not talking about you as a *girl*," he said. "I'm talking about you as an entertainer. As a *singer*."

The young woman's eyebrows rose. Turning away, she propped her hands on her hips. "Only me," she said, shaking her head. "A guy goes and feels me up, and it gets me a chance at show business."

Franky pulled out his handkerchief and patted his forehead. She too was wiping her brow, because in New Orleans even standing still in night air causes sweating, and so Franky offered her the handkerchief. "That's right, this is not about men," he said. "This is about business. This is about 'Who's Sorry Now?'"

The woman took the handkerchief, dabbed her forehead, and then studied Franky narrowly.

"I'm done with men," she said. "Kaput."

"Well, I'm done with women." He accepted the handkerchief back. "*Kaput*."

She paused to consider that. Then her cheek muscles eased and her purse dropped to the ground.

"My name's Bobbi," she said, grabbing his hand with both of hers. "Bobbi Roppolo. So you liked the way I sing, eh?"

Sliding his hand out of hers, he took a step back. "Easy, now. You could use a little work, frankly. I can see you've had no training, that's for sure." Bobbi grabbed her pocketbook and started to cock it back again, but it dropped back down to her side after he added, "I was more impressed with how the audience responded to you."

She put her purse to her bosom and her eyes dropped toward the crucifix resting below her collarbone. "My friends always said I could make the devil himself happy if I tried."

Franky gave a bored sigh. "The devil, maybe," he said. "Franky Fritz, never."

The two continued to size each other up. Franky studied her as if she were auditioning for the band right then and there. She, meanwhile, looked at him as if she were considering whether to stoop so low as to work with him.

"You're not like the Franky Fritz on stage," she said, breaking the silent impasse. "You seem kind of serious and boring."

She added that he acted "like an old man even though you look like a little boy," to which Franky responded she'd be well advised to focus on herself rather than him, for he had proven himself by launching a band and running it successfully "for months."

"Worry about yourself," he said. "Worry about your vocals."

But by then Bobbi had gone back to glancing back and forth between the business card and the quirky bandleader.

"*Man of many horns*, eh," she said, having missed Franky's lecture. "Jeez, that does sound like some kinda devil or something."

CHAPTER 11

ARIEL DID COME back that night after the standoff between Evan and her father—but only because the young couple wouldn't be leaving for a few days and she needed to pack. For Franky, her return represented one last chance to save her. For Ariel, it was one last chance to have her father understand.

She had plans, she explained as they sat at the kitchen table, where she'd set out two mugs and a pot of steaming coffee, the local brand with chicory for bitterness. He refused to sit, though, and so she began talking anyway while he paced about. She wasn't going to just follow some guy out to California, not her. A friend of a friend of Evan's had a gallery out in San Francisco, so she would be able to "get advice from a real artist" and kick-start her career by having some of her pieces shown at the gallery. Heck, she'd even take some of her artwork that had piled up around the house and sell it piece by piece on the trip out west.

"Who do you think is going to buy it?" her father asked. "The guy who pumps your gas?"

"*Maybe*," she answered.

They had a little money saved up to get out there, anyway. And make no mistake, she'd be self-sufficient—she wouldn't be dependent on any man, "so if that's what you thought, think again." Besides, Daddy, she added, switching tone, all would work out because these days you didn't need anything material, and even if you did, well, Evan knew people out there they could lean on. That's what it was about these days—shedding the material world and everyone helping each other out.

Franky scoffed at that one. "You're just kids, you don't know anything," he said, still pacing. "A roof over your head is material. *Food* is material. You think people don't need to eat anymore?"

But look at Evan, she answered. "Look at how talented he is—you're the first person to know that." She paused at the thought of her love, and her cheeks softened. "He's going to be so successful out there—I just know it." But then she looked around at her surroundings—the walls of a home that still stood after a century-and-a-half in the only American city that seemed ancient, a city where all was old and forgotten by all people except for brief days when they came and left as tourists. "He can't be here, he just can't!" she blurted out. "This place is stuck in the past—in music and everything else too!"

Franky threw up his arms and spun around. Everyone knew that he took any insult of New Orleans as if the city were his very self. Of course, the city *was* a part of him, which is why criticism of anyone's hometown can spawn a person's battle stance. "For crying out loud, Ariel, he left the band! All the things I taught you about love aside, how could you follow someone so irresponsible all the way out to California?"

Steadfast in the face of her father's storm, she sat back in the kitchen chair and folded her arms. "We count on each other," she said, pushing her chin up. "He's committed to his music, and he's committed to me."

Franky stopped again. An incredulous gaze appeared and stayed. "Committed? *Committed*? That irresponsible lout doesn't know what commitment is!"

Up until that moment, she had kept her cool. Even now she didn't yell. Instead the words themselves were as violent as Franky could ever know, and they thundered all the louder by the nearly whispered delivery.

"Evan was right about what he told me," she said. "You fucked me up."

He was used to her foul language, but he still stood there frozen in shock. He had bequeathed that mouth to her even though he himself never uttered a curse, for she had grown up with a busful of musicians. What she meant by that came out hours later, after the fight's intermission. Evan had told her she wasn't brought up in a healthy environment because as a child she lived in bars and hotels and tour buses. If that weren't bad enough, the worst act of all her father had committed against her was a mental one: He had brainwashed her to deny love. But Franky had an answer for that one, or at least a question: "I wronged you by teaching a truth that would protect you?"

And so began Act 2—and then 3 and 4, and so on, as the days went by. The argument raged like a biblical rain that poured for days without showing any sign of abating.

"I love him, and I'm leaving," said Ariel later that night, through the blurred vision of tears. "You can't stop me!"

And he couldn't. He could rant all he wanted about how she needed to go to college so she didn't have to depend on a man, how one of the few good changes happening these days was the opening up of new opportunities for women, how Evan wasn't to be trusted—he could say all these things, he lamented to Joe, but he still couldn't control what she did. So began the quiet, the hollow kind that grows out of a rift between loved ones. They lived in the house together for a few days, hardly speaking. Sometimes Ariel never came home at night, so Franky lay awake with his eyes open until the sun came up. Years working in a career that took place after dark tended to keep him up anyway.

* * *

NOW THEY FINALLY had a "chick singer," as Franky said. Bobbi could traipse through such numbers as "Loved You Yesterday" and "Skee-dattle" like an almost pro who, while not technically perfect, boasted "some decent raw material," to use Franky's description following her audition at the band's practice.

But what the band didn't have was a single date lined up. Even Tuesday nights at Nick's had been erased from their calendar, thanks to Franky's ego. No one bothered to tell Bobbi the band had no gigs lined up, though. The days passed and every day she would call Franky asking about "the next show."

"I'm deciding which to choose," Franky would answer. "There are so many, it's a little difficult for a business manager."

Being a sensible woman, Bobbi didn't immediately quit her job at the shipyard that once built the amphibious vehicles—the same place where Sondra and Marcie worked, incidentally. In fact, Bobbi knew of the two women and vice versa, although that was about the extent of it. While the two friends worked in the clerical offices and talked about such things as the newly available Dictaphone that was advertised as being able to record bosses even when they had cigars in their mouths, Bobbi, in contrast, was Rosie the Riveter come to life—even somewhat in looks. Her frame, though shapely, was perfect for her job of building boats.

What made matters worse for the band was that November was approaching, and in January Franky would have to report back to his father his gross earnings for the year, as required under their unwritten contract, which stipulated that he needed to increase his earnings by 5 percent each year. If he didn't start getting some dates these last two months of the calendar, he would find himself peddling ladies' shoes.

Bobbi soon suspected that there were no gigs at all from which to choose. One day she marched over to Franky's apartment and demanded to see the list of possibilities. Not able to produce any such list, he came clean and admitted that times were tough, that the calendar was blank.

"Great," said Bobbi, tossing up her arms, "I won an audition for a pretend band."

Wait, said Franky, he had a plan, and it was just a matter of figuring out a way to implement it. He told her about the idea of taking the band on the road and billing themselves as an authentic New Orleans band. "That's why I put *Direct from New Orleans* on my business card," he explained. He went on and on about how he just knew that good things were in store for the band, if only they could figure out a way to make some connections in places far away, where New Orleans musicians weren't a dime a dozen. Bobbi just stood there listening to the ranting; it was one of Franky's longest lectures, spoken almost all in the tone of a plea. Finally, she interrupted when Franky said he just knew they would become "famous in the middle of Ameri—"

"I got an aunt in South Bend—South Bend, Indiana."

Franky stopped his monologue to glare at her. If he was going to be interrupted, it might as well be for a good idea. "So what?" he said after a beat or two. "A lot of people have aunts in a lot of places. That doesn't mean they've got connections. It's all about connections." Obviously she didn't know that because she wasn't in the business.

"She *is* a connection," Bobbi interrupted again. "She works in a dance hall."

Now Franky's ears perked up. South Bend had an established dance hall, just as most towns did. "Your aunt works at the famous Palais Royale?" he blurted out. As a music fan who had been lustfully absorbing all the jazz information he could get his hands on ever since he was a kid, Franky knew every tour stop across the country the major bands hit, the Palais Royale in South Bend included; such luminaries as Glenn Miller and Tommy Dorsey had played there. He had read about the Palais Royale down at the public library when he was replacing his St. Anthony fixation with his jazz obsession. To play the Palais Royale! Perhaps the band's fortunes were turning.

He was off and running again, talking about the prestige of the Palais Royale, and how wasn't this a stroke of luck! She let him go on for a bit while she folded her arms, until she interrupted him again:

No, her aunt didn't work at the Palais, she said. "It's close, though. Just around the corner. And the name is almost the same, anyway."

The club where her aunt worked was but a dingy little hall, certainly nothing compared to the South Bend venue that Franky knew. The much humbler joint where Bobbi's aunt tended bar stole the little it could from its famous second cousin—namely, the inspiration for its name.

"It's called the Poor Man's Palace," Bobbi said. "The name is in American so the college students and young people can afford it better."

Franky's buoyant demeanor deflated, his giddiness turning to grumbling. "Poor Man's Palace—just terrific," he said. "It sounds like it'll be worth the thousand-mile trip." But Bobbi ignored him and continued. She had spent a few summers with her aunt and had even learned a few dance moves at the Poor Man. ("Where do you think I learned to move like how you saw me at Nick's?") It wasn't such a bad place, she insisted. A little rough around the edges, sure, but it was a start. And she loved Aunt Jess more than anything in the world. The woman was "a good-luck charm" for Bobbi, she explained. "*You* of all people should know how a person can be a good-luck charm—you've got Ariel." She explained further that "when the time is right, I'm gonna move up to South Bend and be with her forever, because she's the only one in this world I love."

Franky argued back like a man only half-listening to a conversation because it was all for naught anyway. Even a no-good joint like this place in Indiana couldn't give the band what it needed at that moment—a gig right *now*—for venues booked bands months in advance.

Bobbi just shrugged after Franky's rant trailed off. "Well, who knows, let me write Aunt Jess," she said. "Can't hurt anyways."

In the next days, which turned into a week and then more days, Franky forgot the ludicrous ideas told him by his new singer, who had only proven to him that she didn't have the acumen to contribute a lick to the business side of things. Meanwhile, one day Bobbi showed up on Franky's forlorn doorstep with an impatient knock. When he opened the door she didn't even say hello.

"You better start packing, we gotta be up there on the twenty-second."

She had landed them a weeklong gig, she said, which may have sounded like great news, but not to Franky.

"What sort of club would give a weeklong gig to a band it had never heard?" he asked. "And what decent club would still have a whole week open in less than a month?"

"Yeah, it's true their calendar is flexible," answered Bobbi, "and they do book bands late. After all, the Poor Man ain't the Palais Royale. But don't forget: My aunt promised the owner we were from New Orleans."

Franky's scheme of marketing the band's hometown had worked. Pleased with the success of his *Straight from New Orleans* branding, he bought into the idea of the trip to South Bend. After all, it was a college town and students had been some of his favorite patrons at Nick's. Still, he bristled at admitting any idea of Bobbi's was a good one. She grandly announced that if the tour was a success, she would quit her job because "I'm the best one there. I can get it back anytime." From then on, when any of the boys expressed any negativity about the trip's outcome, she pepped them up with the official Rosie the Riveter slogan: "We can do it!" But she generally didn't have the same patience with Franky, who was supposed to be the leader.

"All I can say is, if we're going to travel all that way up there, this dance hall had better not be a dump," he said one day.

Bobbi just glared at him, incredulous. "Where do you think you've been playing, anyway—the Ritz? I'll guarantee you one thing, all right: the Poor Man will be a step up from Nick's."

Franky had no answer to her pointed words. Regardless, they would be hitting the road—it was their last chance for survival. The trip, Bobbi explained, would actually be affordable. The crew would pile into Tim Callahan's Hudson and with some luck they'd make it to South Bend with pocket change to spare—assuming the clunker could make it. They could stay with Bobbi's Aunt Jess, who would even cook them meals. And if they stocked the car with stacks of sandwiches to eat and iced tea to drink, the only real expense would be gas. Heck, they could practically get up there for free, Bobbi said.

So the musicians packed up their brass tubes and drums and strings and a few changes of clothes, nestling the coveted instruments in the protection of the trunk and stacking the less important suitcases of clothes on the car roof, and off they went. Joe's mother, who was worried sick about her only child leaving the city limits almost for the first time, supplied the sandwiches out of the ham she had cooked the preceding Sunday, along with a thermos full of strong coffee and chicory. "Save this for the drivers, now," she said, handing the hot thermos through the passenger window.

But what about Ariel? For the first time Franky would be without her for more than a night. Having made arrangements for her to stay with Mr. and Mrs. Fritz, he began the trip actually looking forward to the break from parenthood. "It's like having a real job," he told Joe as they drove away, "only the five o'clock whistle never blows."

CHAPTER 12

HE LEFT WITH the band for the next tour because the show must go on. He did not even say good-bye to Ariel, but that wasn't his fault, for she hadn't been around the house at the time he left. Ariel and Evan would be heading west, at an unknown time that depended on when a friend, who was a mechanic but only on the side, could succeed in putting a new clutch in Evan's rusting '57 Fairlane.

From the first moments of the tour, Franky barely spoke to anyone, though his demeanor wasn't one of anger. As he helped load the bus at the band's meeting place—the parking lot of a Schwegmann grocery in Mid-City—his head stayed cocked diagonally down. His vacant eyes held fixed that way for the entire tour except while he was onstage, when he became Franky Fritz of the World-Famous Franky Fritz Band because of course the show must go on. So in the tour bus's wake as it pulled away, mixed in with the fumes and kicked-up dust, an uneasy stalemate hung in the air between father and daughter.

Even though Franky put on his stage face when he took to the bandstand, club-goers answered neither to his wit nor his riffs, perhaps because sometimes an astute audience can read a performer's heart, and this performer's daughter had just left him. The entire band, meanwhile, followed their leader's lead so that their musical juice leaked away, trickling somewhere off the bandstand and onto the tile floor backstage. Reflecting the band's sluggish energy, or maybe just because their music was passé, audiences grew sparser and sparser. When Ariel left to go out west, so did what remained of the band's fortune, it seemed.

Someone else had left the band too, of course. Franky found himself caught in a moment of melancholic reflection at one point of the tour, during a conversation with Joe at an all-night diner after a gig. As if momentarily forgetting Joe's presence, a thought escaped from his lips:

"If only Evan—"

Glancing up at his friend, he stopped himself before admitting to the rest of the statement. But Joe, of course, knew how the sentence ended, for everyone was thinking the same thing. He later repeated to Bobbi how Franky had almost said it himself: "If only Evan were playing with us, maybe things would be different."

Everyone knew their leader could never actually say that. Evan, the potential savior of the band, was also the thief of his daughter.

So never mind the band. The greatest worry was Ariel. Where was she? Was she safe?

"Don't worry, Franky," said Joe. "She's fine, I just know she is. And she'll make it to college yet—she's too smart not to. Heck, practically the whole band has been planning that out for her since she was born." He slapped the table. "She'll come back safe and then go off to college—that's how it's gonna be."

"If only I could make her go to college like I used to make her go to school," said Franky.

It wasn't the way everyone expected things to turn out for Ariel, that was for sure. A whole band of doting adults had been pushing her toward a higher education. Yet looking back, harbingers may have peeked out along the way, even the haunting kind that make time stop. The memory of those telltale moments—or, Franky wondered aloud, were they simply Polaroids of his failings as a father?—kept bubbling up as he tried to figure out what went wrong, using his friend Joe as a sounding board.

While the father-daughter pair were traveling on tour once years ago, Ariel had discovered the word *why*. She had driven her grandfather crazy with it, Franky later learned, and now she was ready to start in on her father. She was lying on her stomach on Franky's bed and drawing on scrap pieces of paper with crayons, which now came in more than the old standard eight colors, while her father stood nearby in the bathroom shaving. These days she had been asking for more and more paper, which Franky kept flowing because it occupied her during long, empty hours on the road and even at home. He always bought plenty of good paper, but he inevitably ran out on tour, at which time he fed her scraps so that she wouldn't either starve an artist's death or start in on his sheet music or tour ledger. Bobbi and Joe and the rest of the band had begun to marvel at her drawings, gushing with congratulations for them and asking to have some for their Frigidaires.

"Why do you do music, Daddy?" she asked.

"Because I have to," he replied.

"Why do you have to?"

He halted his shaving and peered out of the bathroom and saw her drawing with the focus of a jazzman.

"Because I'm an artist."

"Why are you an artist?"

Franky stopped again. The pause suspended the moment before he answered. "Because that's who I am," he said, and went back to his shaving.

Ariel was stumped, because the next logical question in this typical children's *why* game was a clumsy and confusing sentence for a young child to build: *Why are you who you are?* At a loss, she put down her crayon. What she said next, since it came out of nowhere, caused Franky to cut his neck so that blood streamed off his Adam's apple in a serpentine trail clear down to his collarbone: "Then why don't I have a mommy?"

Franky needed a quick answer. "Because she's not here."

"Why isn't she here?"

"Because I'm an artist."

"Why are you an artist?"

"Because that's who I am."

He had stumped her again by coming full circle, and so she returned to her drawing. Then with nothing left to say, she singsonged: "I'm an artist too."

Franky almost cut himself again. Her arbitrary pronouncement recalled a childhood moment of his own: When after learning of the great Bix Beiderbecke, he randomly told his father that he too would be a jazzman.

Before returning to his razor strokes, he sighed and shook his head. "Bite your tongue," he said and then resumed his shaving. "Bite your tongue."

But she didn't seem to hear him, or didn't understand the expression, and so she kept on with her crayons. Placing his razor back into his styrene travel case that he got free with the razor, Franky told her about how he had established a college fund for her. Practically from the time she could talk, he began telling her about going to college, almost with as much frequency as he told her of the fallacy of love.

Now she had cast aside both lifelong lectures—she had said no to college and yes to love.

* * *

SO THEY WERE off, on their "big national tour," as they started calling it. The trip itself might have been a great adventure, but because of budget constraints it turned out to be a grueling endurance test, one in which the crew rode day and night. The roads weren't built for speed, and the wartime national speed limit of 35 had been lifted only recently. Tim drove mostly, with Franky and Bobbi spelling him along the way. The thermos of coffee lasted not much farther than Jackson, and so by Memphis all the drivers agreed they needed to stop for more. They refilled their big thermos at a roadside diner somewhere on Highway 51, the road that seemed to have no end. The caffeine salve didn't help, though, and they wondered aloud why the coffee was no longer helping them stave away the fatigue. Bobbi, a seasoned traveler to the middle of the country, told them the reason.

"The farther from New Orleans, the weaker they make the coffee," she said. "So by the time you're in the Midwest, it's just dirty water."

By the time they arrived on Aunt Jess's doorstep they were all so bleary-eyed and sick of ham sandwiches that when she asked them if they wanted something to eat or whether they'd rather go straight to bed, each of them hung a vacant gaze upon her without opening their mouths. Standing there in front of her house, she couldn't get over the stack of suitcases, which included Joe's entire drum kit, piled like a rickety city skyline on top of the Hudson. "Jeez, what is this, *The Grapes of Wrath*?" she said, taking a drag on her cigarette. "Where's Henry Fonda?"

The weeklong run at the Poor Man hardly got off to an encouraging start. On the first night, the band played to an empty bar, save two or three college students trying to escape the murmuring calls of their books. Just before the first set, Joe launched into his fatalist drone, worrying out loud that the band wouldn't have enough money even to make it back home, and that as a result they all would probably be found dead somewhere in Tennessee along the side of a dark two-lane highway, or perhaps washed ashore along the banks of the northern Mississippi River, or maybe even lying dead in some Chicago back alley with fifty bullet holes pocking their bodies, the victims of a gangland shooting. Franky, who normally was patient with his lifelong friend, this time had one simple message for Joe: "Shut up."

The hall was so empty that the words reverberated through the dead space, repeating two or three times, as if the message was being spiritually delivered to the unspoken fears of the other band members as well. Keeping his game face, Franky carried through with his plan, on stage acting like the true professional he was fighting to become. It didn't matter that but a couple of skeptical patrons stood below them at the foot of the stage. The Franky Fritz Band was going to knock their socks off—all four of their socks. The band's leader would make sure of that.

When all the members had taken their places on stage, Franky approached Aunt Jess.

"Here," he said, giving her an index card. Handwritten blocky letters, all upper case, ran across every other line. "Read this into the mike—and make sure you say it *exactly* as it's written."

Aunt Jess studied the card, her lips moving silently to the words on it:

> *Ladies and gentlemen, may I have your attention please. I've gotta tell you, you're in for a special treat tonight. Straight from New Orleans, Louisiana, the birthplace of jazz, please give a warm welcome to:*
> THE WORLD-FAMOUS FRANKY FRITZ BAND!

Aunt Jess screwed up her face. "This isn't right," she said. "You're not world-famous."

Expecting the objection, Franky answered without missing a beat. "Of course we're world-famous," he said. "*A*, New Orleans is famous for jazz. *B*, we are from New Orleans, and *C*, we play jazz. Therefore, we are a world-famous jazz band."

It was actually Al Jolson and the power behind his *World's Greatest Entertainer* moniker that gave Franky the idea to call his band World-Famous, he'd admitted to Joe. Aunt Jess stuck the card in her pocket, shrugged, and said, "I like it. You got a real business sense."

A few minutes later, when Franky gave the signal, Aunt Jess stepped up to the microphone. A white bar apron wrapped around her waist, she stood before the vacant hall and announced the handwritten message laid out before her. Her reading skills were not the best, for the normally boisterous bartender read in the monotone of a zombie: "…you're-in-for-a-special-treat-tonight…the-world-famous-Franky Fritz Band."

"A little more enthusiasm tomorrow night, please," whispered Franky as he took over the spot in front of the microphone, horn in hand.

That first night went as well as it could have, considering the sparse attendance in the cavernous hall. Playing music was always a salve on the band members' spirits, and little by little they forgot they were playing to an empty room and instead rejoiced in their music, working themselves into a groove while laughing and exchanging smiles from unspoken jokes as they played, giddy with the revelation that they were making music a thousand miles from home. The powerful addition of Bobbi, who exuded spunk, helped feed the band. In addition to bringing her usual happy self to the stage, the surroundings gave her an extra punch of energy and joy, for she was back with her Aunt Jess in a hall that to her held an enchantment that only past moments in youth could have spawned. During summers at the Poor Man, she and Aunt Jess later recounted to the boys, Bobbi had danced her first steps as an adolescent (with Aunt Jess as her partner), passed through the rites of a summer crush (the object being the son of the building's maintenance man), and developed a bond with her aunt that a thousand miles and nine months apart could never break. Watching band after band pass through the Poor Man's Palace, Bobbi had learned a thing or two about the thrill of showbiz, at least the small-city variety. She thrilled in even the mundane side of the business: watching bands set up and put on their stage faces, play their gig, break down, and finally pack up and rumble off in their rickety little buses.

"You were around all that booze when you were so little?" asked a shocked Joe the next morning after hearing the stories of Bobbi's summers.

"It wasn't so bad," said the singer. "Besides, most nights back home there was more booze in my daddy's belly than there was in the Poor Man."

As it turned out, the two or three university students that made up the entire patronage that night must have been mavens, living in the very hub of the college social scene in South Bend, because on Tuesday the audience multiplied to around fifteen, and then Wednesday's total climbed to twenty, and still more showed up on Thursday. By Saturday, the biggest social night of the week, the band was pumping out a groove for a few hundred dance-happy students and young couples. Never mind a name for the band's style; regardless, the South Bend dancers' feet soaked up the music like old beer coming out of the parquet wood floor.

The irony of the band's first-time road success was that they had generated interest by promoting their New Orleans origins when in fact their sound was much closer to swing. Yet while no one seemed to care a lick, a know-it-all in any crowd can't fight opening his mouth, and so a skeptic called out during one night of the run, "I thought you were from New Orleans!"

Before the comment could so much as register in the minds of the audience members, Franky conjured an answer and spoke it into the mike: "Would you like to see our driver's licenses, officer?"

Scattered laughter echoed through the hall. But the challenger wasn't discouraged and wanted to flaunt his knowledge. "You don't sound like you're from New Orleans, and you sure don't *look* like New Orleans jazzmen," he said. "I know my jazz music, and that was Benny Goodman you just played. Benny Goodman isn't New Orleans jazz. Besides, New Orleans jazzmen are colored."

Franky laughed without smiling. "Stick around a little while," he said. "You might learn a little something about jazz."

"I know jazz, and I'm telling you that was Benny Goodman."

Others nodded in agreement and shrugged. As far as they knew, they'd just heard Benny.

"Son," he began, even though the kid was within a couple of years of his own age, "I don't care if we were playing 'Mary Had a Little Lamb' and our skin was colored green. If you really knew jazz, you'd hear New Orleans in our horns. You'd hear it in our beat."

The audience shrugged in understanding, and before the boy could answer, Franky launched the band into their next deafening New Orleans-tinged swing tune.

Playing to their biggest crowd of the week, the band ended their Saturday night gig on a high. "They were more fun than our crowd at Nick's!" said Joe after the show. But after a short night's sleep with the boys scattered about the floorboards and couches of Aunt Jess's house while Bobbi slept with her aunt in her double bed, they awoke to a disturbing truth. Their "big national tour" had consisted of a mere one venue, which left them stranded on an island—farther from home than any of them could imagine, without a moneymaking gig in sight. A thousand miles separated them from the Vieux Carré - "civilization," as Tim started calling New Orleans. Financially, a weeklong run at one venue called the Poor Man hardly made for a successful tour, given that their modest take would barely get them home. Worse, the Hudson was now making a clunking noise, and so they knew it would be foolish to aimlessly take to the

Midwestern roads in search of other gigs without any booked beforehand. Even Franky wasn't his normal upbeat self. After being away from Ariel five days, he was missing his daughter. Not being able to hold it in any longer, the mention of her name slipped out at the breakfast table.

"I wonder what Ariel is doing now," he pondered aloud.

"Ah Jeez, first Muriel and now Ariel," Tim said. "I thought this business about missing girls was all over."

Adding a sting to the moment: They had spent a windy and frigid November week in the open heartland, and the travelers who came from the world of bayous, swamps, and glaring wet heat were feeling a harsh cold they had never known, one that made them homesick for New Orleans.

Nevertheless, their spirits couldn't help but rise a little once Aunt Jess started feeding them eggs, bacon, toast, and coffee. The warmth of the morning sun coming through her lone kitchen window coupled with the heat floating out of the big iron radiator almost made them thankful for the cold outside, which for the first time in their lives gave them the delicious contrast of this toastiness inside. And after failing to get a potent cup of coffee on the road, they had been surprised to find the oily brew that Jess served up to be far more like the New Orleans version than the rusty water being percolated in every other South Bend home.

"My little girl over here always complained," said Jess, gesturing toward her niece with her cigarette. "So when she comes I have to triple the grounds."

Franky, who had been exchanging subtle barbs with Jess all week, raised his eyebrows. "Ah-ha," he said. "So now you admit that coffee, like most things, is best in New Orleans."

Aunt Jess gave an exaggerated eye roll while she worked the skillet. "No, I just boil water on the side and add it to mine," she said.

Franky scoffed. Obviously she still hadn't learned what good coffee is, then.

That did it. She was forced to interrupt her skillet work to deal with this young kid.

"You may act smart," she answered, one hand resting on her hip and metal spatula held in the other. "But it's easy to see, you don't have a clue." Before Franky could answer, she turned to Bobbi and said, "And Southerners say *Yankees* are uppity!"

The boys watched the interchange keenly. She had done something with ease that few could manage with Franky: She had gotten the final word.

"It must run in the family," Joe murmured to the others, gesturing toward Bobbi.

Strong coffee and eggs weren't the only blessings that Aunt Jess cooked up for the band. An idea popped into her head while she was feeding the group of ravenous and appreciative young men. As she dropped a second round of fried eggs onto Joe and Al's plates, she announced, "I've got a friend in Gary. A bar manager."

The joint where the man worked served as a little dance hall, and Aunt Jess thought she could convince her friend to let the boys play a night or two. Al chimed in that he knew Gary because that was where the nucleus of one of Tulane's great football teams had come from. On game days, Al had parked cars for 25 cents in the driveway of his uptown house near the stadium.

"And why would this friend of yours do that?" asked Tim, killing Al's moment of nostalgia. "He doesn't even know us."

"That's simple," Aunt Jess said. She used to date him when he lived in South Bend, and so he was willing to do just about anything for her—all she had to do was ask. Strolling back to the iron skillet of bacon and spitting grease, Aunt Jess explained with a shrug: "He really loved me, but he snored."

For a moment everyone stopped eating except for Bobbi, who was chewing her toast between her gums, causing a smacking sound. Even Tim, the emerging playboy, couldn't help but raise his eyebrows. Noticing the silence, Bobbi stopped chewing and tried to address the shock in the room, but she addressed the wrong issue.

"She can't have babies."

The only one among them who believed in Aunt Jess's ability to make the gig happen was Bobbi, who had grown up hearing story after story of her aunt's romantic exploits. "The funny thing is, she always ends up friends with them," the woman's niece reflected. "I don't know how she does that."

Standing over the stove with the spatula in one hand and a cigarette in the other, Aunt Jess explained that the bar in Gary would be perfect because instead of risking a motor trip in the ailing Hudson, they would be able to just hop on the South Shore train, which passed right through Gary. And if they were feeling really adventuresome and wanted to test the waters in other towns as well, they could continue even farther on the line, to Hammond or East Chicago, in search of a club to crash. Instantly, the boys' ears perked up.

"We're gonna play Chicago!" Ted blurted out.

The other guys, however, only snickered. Unlike their naive bandmate, who had been awestruck at the mere sight of the Franky Fritz Band at Nick's in New Orleans, they weren't about to swallow that preposterous claim. Chicago, of course, was the only city in the world that rivaled New Orleans for its jazz history. To play in that city would be a triumph, a major stop on the road to the big-time, a dream so big it had practically gone undreamt. Cognizant of the source of their snickers, Bobbi set the boys straight.

"She never said Chicago, you dopes," the vocalist corrected. "She said *East* Chicago. East Chicago, *Indiana!*"

So the band lugged a change of clothes and their instrument cases onto the South Shore train, full drum kit and all. On this trip, a train and not a car carried them, yet the travelers once again found themselves headed for a destination they had never heard of, a place where a tourist would never think to go.

CHAPTER 13

FRANKY WAS GOING crazy. Still no word from Ariel. He was preparing to hit the road in a matter of days for the band's next anemic tour, but he couldn't even give his daughter his itinerary because he had no means of contacting her. Nearly two months had passed since the day she hopped in "that *Evan's*" car, the '57 Ford Fairlane with a trustworthiness that was dubious, and started heading west without a destination address to share.

"She might need rescuing, and I won't even know where to rescue her!" he told Joe.

But then a letter came the very day before the band was to leave.

Dear Daddy,

It's a really happening scene out here. Evan's friend wasn't lying, he really knows Bill Graham at the Fillmore. You would like the Fillmore, on some nights anyway—it's not even rock acts all the time. Matter of fact, we just got to see Count Basie play there! I hope you're still not mad at Evan, or at least you can forgive him. I know you don't like to talk about certain kinds of love, but isn't that all that matters? That's what people out here are saying anyway. I know we're all young, but I hope you see our point, and it's not the kind of love you don't believe in anyway, the man-woman kind. Anyway, I hope you can please forgive Evan. It was my decision to go, so you shouldn't blame him.

I wish I could give you a phone number and address to contact me, but we're not really staying anywhere in particular. Don't worry, though, that's how people just do it here. Evan's friends usually let us crash with them, and even if not, the weather is nice and no mosquitos. I don't have much money to call but will be in touch.

Love,
Ariel

How thankful Franky was to hear from her, just to know she was okay. And at least she seemed relatively healthy, he commented to Joe. Yet she did not mention the art gallery, or a gig for Evan at the Fillmore. Other letters came, but they said the same batch of not much: talk of freedom and new ways, love, and a lot of the other garbage you were hearing on the news that the young people were supposed to be saying.

"She doesn't give any information!" he told Joe.

That is, she wasn't offering the concrete fodder that people all through history reported first and foremost: matters of food and shelter. She had said nothing of whether she'd found an affordable yet clean boarding house with other girls, whether any meals were served there, and how much money she had left for groceries after paying for her room. Worse, she never mentioned any of the horrific topics heard on the news that you would wonder about if you knew your kid was in San Francisco that summer: all the drugs and the images of people on the streets who, when you saw their eyes, no longer looked like people.

"Is Ariel still Ariel?" Franky wondered aloud, and Joe consoled him, assuring his friend that she was.

But who knew? His universe was so different now, he said. Men were flying around in space and even planning to touch the moon. Here on earth, the music he loved, which was so special that he thought it would last forever, was dying—while the young people were putting things in their bodies that rendered them not of this world, at least so it seemed when you saw them. It was as if for the first time in its history, the world was becoming another world.

As Aunt Jess told it, Michael Kawalski played half a season with the Chicago Bears before being cut. The reason: "Coach told me my body was right, but my head was too nice too match it." That's what he always said with a shrug that suggested he wasn't much for football anyway. Still, if his body didn't carry him to gridiron stardom, it at least got him in the door of the entertainment business. Any joint that wanted an imposing bouncer around to make a patron think twice about losing his cool would be happy to have Mike Kawalski on site. That's how he got started, Aunt Jess had said, and now he had moved his way up to bar manager at this little second-rate dance hall known as the Avalon in Gary. Because the place wasn't exactly a shimmering beacon of gentility on the middle-class dance-hall circuit, he did use his vocational gift to throw out an occasional ruffian every so often. However, the most commonly carried-out duty, a mandate handed down directly from the owner, was to tap the shoulders of couples getting fresh on the dance floor or in the shadowy corners of the hall while the deafening bands played. Another difference between the Avalon and some other joints: Black patrons—and black bands—were allowed into the hall, and that tended to make the jazz less fluffy and passé, even though the hall was buried away on a side street in Gary.

When the band members arrived, Mike was mopping the dance floor. "We got a pretty nice bandstand," he said, pointing toward the stage area. "I could get you a Coca-Cola if you want." That afternoon he shuffled out front of the hall with a tall wooden pole as Bobbi and the boys were going off to grab some dinner, and the musicians didn't pay attention to what sort of work he was going off to do. So when they arrived back at the hall with their bellies full and their bodies hungry only to play music, they jolted to a stop smack in front of the hall, in the exact spot where they had left Mike behind. Heads cocked upward into the sky as if they were watching fireworks, they gazed up at the marquee, on which hung a freshly arranged set of big, blocky letters:

FRANKY FRITZ BAND FROM NEW ORLEANS

For the very first time the group's name graced a marquee. The letters hung there, suspended above their heads, as if passersby were supposed to know who in the world the Franky Fritz Band was. The cluster of musicians all stood there, relishing the moment of pride. But not Franky; in him the marquee had spawned another idea. He disappeared through the doors to go looking for Mike. If passersby weren't familiar with the name of the band, "they at least should know the affiliation," he told the bar manager, and so he pulled the shrugging man back out front with the tall pole and a stack of more letters. Hoisting up the pole as Franky watched with the eager eyes of a guy convinced of his bright idea, Mike hung the letters that spelled Direct From New Orleans and The World-Famous, which he placed right above Franky Fritz Band. Franky couldn't contain his excitement, saying they were onto something. His bandmates, meanwhile, responded with shrugging approval, except for Slim Jim, who nodded his head up and down as if in a trance.

"It looks amazing," he said, gazing up at the completed marquee. "I think you're an even better businessman than a musician."

Not long after, an occasional pedestrian was seen pausing in front of the sign, and Jim, who stationed himself beside the box office window for the next 100 minutes, claimed to have witnessed as many as seven cars slowing down while passing the marquee.

Such sightings proved a harbinger for the coming night. Granted, every night people showed up at the Avalon to dance as long as *any* name graced the marquee, and most of the folks who flowed in that evening surely hadn't a clue whom the Franky Fritz Band was; they were just out for a good time. They got more than they expected. Everyone who showed had a rip-roaring night, and the crowd turned out to be the biggest the band had ever entertained with the exception of the Mid-City parade during Carnival. After the show, Mike Kawalski insisted that the taglines on the marquee, *Straight from New Orleans, The World-Famous...* must have brought in at least a few curious customers, for he had never seen such a crowd for a brand-new band.

"Sort of like a freak show at the circus," he said, "when you have to pay to see what's in the tent."

As the band members packed up their instruments, Mike, who was busy fiddling with the cash register behind the bar, paused in his work to tell them to come back any time. "You're good for business," he hollered across the empty room. Just before he started punching the keys again, he added, "And tell Jess I said hello."

With a successful night under their belt, the band decided to try their luck in another town along the South Shore line, just as Aunt Jess had suggested. Next stop on her suggestion list: Hammond. After getting off the train there, they gathered by a bench on the platform, having piled their suitcases (mere laundry sacks for Joe and Al) and instrument cases next to it. The gray skies matched the dreary industrial landscape. As they stood clustered on the cold, empty platform, the balloon of confidence that had inflated from the previous night's gig now sagged. The realization had reached them that they were no different from hobos: They had arrived at their destination, yet they had nowhere to go.

"Bobbi, let's go find a place to play," said Franky, breaking the spell. "You fellas stay here and watch the stuff."

Nobody argued with that proposition. They all couldn't be wandering about town with all those bags and instruments. And after the week at the Poor Man in South Bend, Bobbi had emerged as a leader of sorts herself. She had taken audiences to levels of enthusiasm that the band without her had never achieved, earning her automatic respect among the boys. She was not only a fine singer—she was an entertainer, and this pushed her to the front of the band right alongside Franky.

"Where to?" said the cabbie.

"Where there is music," said Franky.

The cabbie, who hadn't paid attention to who was getting in his car, turned around to frown at the nut who had spoken. He laughed with a snarl, as if his time was already being wasted. "What are you, some kind of tourists got off at the wrong stop? If you want to hear music, go to Chicago. Hop on the train, fella. You got a couple more stops yet."

No, Franky insisted, they hadn't gotten off at the wrong train stop. They just happened to be in Hammond, and they wanted to hear some music later that night.

"Just take us somewhere cheap," Bobbi interjected. "You know—where a cheap band would play."

Franky shot his usual glare reserved for her, but she must have spoken the magic words because the cabbie instantly came up with a possibility. He knew of a little joint that sat practically a stone's throw from the last downtown building, a joint he once hit four nights a week, "back before I got an old lady," he said. "They used to have some music there sometimes, but I dunno if they do that anymore."

After driving out to a part of town where buildings became spaced farther apart and where there was some confusion as to whether they were driving through a rough city neighborhood or a tough farming area, the cabbie dropped them off in front of a brick box of a joint where an unlit neon sign hung in its lone front window. As the hack rolled away, the muffled crunch of the tires on the gravel parking lot disturbed Franky. "It sounds like something suffocating," he said. "Or something empty." The drone of the cab's motor evaporated, and they still hadn't made a move.

"This place don't look so good," said Bobbi, surveying the bare structure.

"Relax, some of the best music in the world is played in places that look like this." But with scanning eyes Franky too was studying the building and failing to start toward it.

"Yeah right," said Bobbi. "Sort of like Nick's. That one band that used to play there, they were *world famous*."

She was right. The place looked neither more nor less seedy than Nick's—but Nick's resided on the comfortable streets of their hometown. Also, unlike Nick's, which was squeezed anonymously amid rows of Creole cottages and an occasional corner store, this building stood alone, surrounded by nothing but a gravel parking lot, like some rural jailhouse.

"A cat wouldn't perch where we're standing," said Franky out of the blue, hugging his arms to his body. "They're smarter than we are—they favor protected areas."

The wind kicked up and the air grew colder. At the same time, the sun slipped out from behind a cloud to reflect off the bar's window and throw a glare in their eyes so that they could barely make out the unlit neon sign. *Art's*, it read.

"See?" said Franky, pushing some zip into his words to try and change the air. "Art. *A-R-T*. I like the place already."

They started for the door, which opened right up. The lone room was square and empty, save a man behind the bar reaching into cardboard boxes and stocking the underneath of the bar. They'd witnessed the scene a hundred times before and they would see it a thousand more. With the bar hiding him, he came into view at intervals, and even then, only his shoulders and back surfaced.

Finally, his head peered over the bar top like a rat coming out from a hole.

"We're closed," he said. "It ain't lunchtime yet."

He went back to his stocking work. Still standing by the door, Franky looked at Bobbi and put his index finger to his mouth, a command to let him do the talking. They started for the bar; all they could see still was the hump of his back surfacing at intervals, like the whale in *The Book of Mammals* from the St. Francis school library.

"Sir, an opportunity has walked through your door."

The man looked up with a scowl on his face, but then saw Bobbi for the first time. The scowl turned to a hungry grin as he looked her full over. "A sweetheart, eh? Yeah, now there's an opportunity, all right. How much?"

Bobbi's arm jerked and started to cock back, but Franky grabbed ahold of it before she could hammer him with her pocketbook.

"Not *that* kind of opportunity," he said. "An even better one."

Disappointed, the man swatted his hand at them and went back to his stocking work. "Ain't no better opportunity then a broad, so if that ain't what you're talking about, get the hell outta here."

"Of course there's something better. *Money.*"

The man stopped what he was doing and half-raised his head. ("Mention money, and it gets them every time," Franky liked to say.) The bandleader slid one of his business cards across the bar. "That's right," he continued, "we're going to do you the favor of playing here tonight. Now *that's* an opportunity!"

"Ah Jeez, another band," the man grumbled. "We gave up on that last year. Like I said, get out."

"I don't suppose the chance doesn't come along often for you to get a real *touring band* in here. Why, we've come all the way from the jazz capital of the world: New Orleans, Louisiana!"

The man looked up with squinted eye and then finally bothered to take a glance at the business card. "World famous? I never heard of ya."

"They love us in Europe," said Franky.

"Everybody knows Chicago's where the best jazz is. New Orleans ain't got nothing on Chicago." He half-disappeared again, the lazy whale hump rising and then plummeting again into the sightless depths behind the bar. But at least the man didn't repeat his demand for them to leave, and so Franky and Bobbi kept standing there until he had to say something to break the silence—either by continuing the conversation or by throwing them out. "New Orleans, eh?" the man said. After a few more moments he stopped and stood up fully, his face now reddened from bending over for a long time. "And what kind of a band *on tour* has to go begging to find places to play?"

Franky shrugged. "We're coming from Chicago, and we've got a date the day after tomorrow a few towns over," he lied. "We have the night off, we're bored, and we've got some new material we'd like to try out." He leaned toward the man and lowered his tone. "You don't think we'd be stupid enough to pay those hotel prices in Chicago, do you? So here we are." He watched the barman, gauging whether his words had taken hold the least bit. "But never mind, then. If you don't want a real-live New Orleans band to play because you're afraid we'll be better than your Chicago bands, we'll just be on our way." He nodded at Bobbi, and they began to start for the door.

"I don't got the money to pay no band," the barman said.

Franky turned back around to face the man. He folded his arms, and his head tilted from side to side a couple of times. "Well," he sighed, "I suppose we've got nothing better to do tonight. If you let us pass around the hat, we'll call it even."

The man shrugged, which apparently meant that he accepted the terms, for he walked away without telling them to get out.

CHAPTER 14

Bye-bye ... Forever!

That wasn't what Ariel had said before leaving. It was a song.

Considering the title, you'd think Franky penned the lyrics, but not so. Even though Franky and Bobbi were oil and water in real life, the writing duo was in sync on the whimsically bitter songs. Looking back, that was even true from the moment they met, when "Who's Sorry Now?" brought them together. And it was true now, with Ariel gone, even as the band was failing, because no band can live forever.

But maybe sparks of life—those thrilling creative sparks—could still emerge, even now as the band fought for its final breath. On this morning, one among the dizzy million in which Franky awoke to the thudding thought of his daughter's absence, Bobbi showed up to go over the books with him and discuss a strategy for drumming up more support for the next tour—and, of course, to try and help him get his mind off Ariel for a moment or two. But he was in too foul a mood to do much of anything. Besides, Bobbi didn't help with her grumbling that she was about ready to "quit this tired band," sell her place in Mid-City, and make good on her lifelong plan and move up to Indiana to be with her beloved aunt.

"It's rock 'n' roll that's killing the big bands," said Franky. "That's what's doing it, you know." He started complaining about how the world was going to pot, how men were wearing their hair like women, and how, sacrilegiously, drugs were being mistaken for the authentic feeling one got from music.

Out of the boredom of not getting anything done, they meandered over to the piano, where they started punching out absentminded melodies and mumbling along meaningless lyrical fragments that would make them both forget about the ailing state of the band.

The exercise turned out to be as effective an escape as an old musical watched in a dark movie house: Before they knew it, they were doing some serious composing. "This sounds good," said Franky, keying a few notes. "Then this … (*tap-twinkle-tap*)… then this …" Bobbi nodded along, following his fingers. But she didn't always agree with where those fingers led.

"No, bonehead," she said, reaching in front of him to bang out a few notes, "it should go *up* here, not down—like this: da-da-duh-da!"

He was listening too hard to bother with her insults. "I like it," he said, and he jotted down the notes into his spiral book of blank music lines.

Once he became aware of the roll they were on, he flipped on the reel-to-reel tape sitting next to the piano to capture the runs and irresistible hooks that were flying around the living room like mosquitos. It was one of a thousand moments proving that the lifelong vocational companions were compatible only in music. Throughout the haphazard process she intoned mindless placeholder lyrics just to have something to sing along to the melody they were birthing, but some of those random words eventually floated around into sequence to form phrases that fit, at which point she scribbled them down onto the envelope of Franky's electric bill:

Stay away from me baby
And I don't mean maybe
This LADY is better than you!

So the tune was an entirely collaborative effort. Before long "Bye-bye … Forever!" which held the potency to fill millions of bitter people with the joys of validation, was primed to bring the band good fortune. The final verdict on the song came from Joe, for universal understanding among the band members stated that the otherwise quirky drummer was a soothsayer in anything music.

"This one could be bigger than 'My Baby's Gonna Cry'," he remarked when the band members heard their leaders tap out a stripped-down version on piano with Bobbi only half-singing intermittent notes. The others murmured in agreement, feeding off the underlying excitement. "We'll be the toast of the town everywhere we play," said Slim Jim. "Heck, Pops still makes hits, so can we."

The great Louis Armstrong had released his last big hit, "What a Wonderful World," not too long before.

"*Bye ... bye ... forever*, said Tim, drinking in the sound of the three words. "So much more timeless than love, peace, and harmony."

Franky, though, was still thinking about "What a Wonderful World," even though "Bye-bye ... Forever!" carried a contrary message.

"Well, we're not Pops," he said. "But Pops can at least give us hope. The old guys always have."

When creative flow comes, so does business flow—at least that's how it always worked with Franky and Bobbi. With "Bye-bye ... Forever!" in their pockets and, in the minds of the band members, poised to chart, the two leaders got down to the business of finding enough tour stops to hit the road one more time. Many of the places they used to play had long since shut down, but with a little ingenuity they found replacement venues: an outdoor party at the home of a college president in Champaign, Illinois; a "first annual" jazz festival in a new, suburban Washington, D.C. planned community that also was planning out future traditions; a veterans hall in a coastal Massachusetts industrial city with a one-room whaling museum.

Buoyed by the hope of "Bye-bye ... Forever!" all band members were more ready to hit the road than they had been in years. The irony, though, was that while *they* were ready, the song wasn't. Perfectionist Franky hadn't settled on an arrangement to his liking, and so the band was still toying with it in rehearsal when the time came to hit the road.

"We're leaving tomorrow," said Tim at the final rehearsal before the tour. "Just pick one of the ways we've tried it, and we'll go with it. This is our last hope!"

For some reason Tim seemed not only annoyed but even fretful about the whole situation, the others later recalled in hindsight, once they'd learned why. Joe, who had some experience with nerves himself, later said that he'd even spotted dappled perspiration on the sax player's forehead. The others generally agreed with Tim's point of view, but perhaps their hunger for more success wasn't as urgent. They just figured Tim needed the money more than they did, which would be typical, for he had been the worst among them at saving any of the fat pile of cash the core members had earned through the band's heyday and beyond. Nevertheless, Tim made his best point of all when he added: "Heck, Franky, you play the best when you improvise anyway!"

It was true. And speaking of improvising, Franky had inserted a solo on a muted trumpet that was beginning to catch fire. But while he normally might have been swayed by Tim's urging, he wouldn't budge.

"This might be our last chance," he told both Tim and the rest of them, "and we're going to make damn sure we get it right."

But as each tour date got checked off on the calendar, Franky never became satisfied with any one arrangement, even by the time the band's rickety bus pulled into the final tour stop of St. Louis. In that town the dance hall they used to play had closed down years before, while even the smaller nightclub they'd subsequently moved to hadn't asked them back, and so the venue to which time had relegated them was a downtown veterans' hall, where they would play for a small room of aging soldiers in awkward red blazers and their spouses. On this tour as well, some of the club owners, spooked by dwindling audiences for the Franky Fritz Band (or any such old-style ensemble), insisted Bobbi and the boys be paid through a percentage cut from the evening's profits rather than receive their usual set fee. That meant there was no telling how well or how poorly the tour would go.

"Let's play 'Bye-bye...Forever!' tonight," said Joe. "What do we have to lose?"

"No, said Franky. "I want to go home and play with it some more. I work better at home."

Everyone, even Joe, was exasperated with Franky by this point. And then came Tim's news. He hadn't said much until now, and it was strange because all tour long he had been moaning about why didn't they play the song and even why weren't they practicing it more. Now, though, his tone was uncharacteristically coy.

"Uh, Franky?" he said. The bandleader turned, perhaps sensing Tim was about to drop some bad news on them. "We don't have a choice. We *have to* play it tonight."

Franky glared at him. They had no choice but to perform the song, Tim explained, because he'd "arranged for someone important to show up."

"Oh, really," said Franky. "And who might that be?"

"Sid. He was planning to be in Chicago, so I got him to drive down."

Sid—as in, Sid Simeo, their old record producer. Tim had spoken with him before the tour began and asked if he'd be anywhere near St. Louis when the band arrived at the end of the tour; he *must* hear their sure-shot hit, Tim told the producer. Simeo lived in New York, but he always had spent a lot of time in the Windy City, particularly now that he was semiretired. Simeo, the boys all knew from years ago when they first started working with him, used his music-biz travel to womanize.

"I thought it was a sure bet we'd be playing it every gig by now," said Tim, palms open.

The statement came out in humble tones that no one had ever heard out of Tim or his sax. But Franky was livid. How dare Tim make business arrangements on the side without even letting him know! The bandleader lambasted him clear up until the start of the show—time that might have been used to practice the song. Sure enough, when they took to the bandstand in the veterans' hall, at a table to the left of the dance floor sat Sid Simeo, smoking a cigarette and giving Franky a nod when their eyes met. The first set came and went, and still Franky refused to lead the band into the song.

"The new tune isn't ready, so we're not playing it," Franky told Simeo at the end of the set. "I don't know what Tim was talking about."

Simeo wasn't the kind to raise his voice when he got hot under the collar. He just took a drag on his cigarette, eased out a breath of smoke, and said, "You mean to tell me I just drove three hundred miles to hear you guys play the same old dead songs?"

As with all comebacks, Franky didn't miss a beat. Yet this time he summoned no insult. "As I was saying, you're gonna love it. It'll be the last song of the next set."

So they would play the tune, after all. Still, Franky complained among the band members through the whole break that "Bye-bye … Forever!" wasn't ready. They could get through it, but the tune was not yet coated with that certain ineffable sound he knew the band could wring out of it, he said. Franky behaved almost as if the song, or the band, were snake bitten.

THE AUDIENCE OF former soldiers and their wives was sparser than expected. But still the ones who showed up cheered the old sounds as if they had just come back from the war. From the opening song of the next set, Franky donned his stage face, seemingly leaving his worries back at the break table. The rest of the band members knew full well, though, that "Bye-bye ... Forever!" stayed parked in the front of his head, for when the time came to play it, he turned around and shot them a glare. With his mouth beyond the microphone's reach, he muttered: "Anyone screws this up, you're dead."

He had never said such a thing before; he was different these days. It was hardly the way to instill confidence in the players—surely he knew that much.

When he turned again to the audience, the bright stage lights illuminated his face, and the old pro's usual aplomb switched back on, just like those very lights that had found him again. He stepped up to the microphone to introduce the world to "Bye-bye ... Forever!"—the tune that would launch the great Franky Fritz Band's comeback.

"Take note of these notes," he pronounced. "You'll be hearing them on the airwaves."

Yet in spite of his trademark cocky words, his voice echoed around the hall like that of a preacher speaking in an empty church and suffering a crisis of faith. Franky's lofty intro had set the standard at gold, and all eyes in the modest crowd gazed upward at the bandstand. They were eyes touched by the small hope of catching the energy they remembered once zinging about the Franky Fritz Band. Feeling their want like fingers reaching up and touching him, Franky dashed into the count with abandon, perhaps at too fast a tempo:

"Uh-one, a-two, a-one-two-three-four!"

The rhythm started pulsing and the horns started swaying. Peripheral vision met peripheral vision among Bobbi and the boys, the kind of glances that musicians make when they need to guess one another's next move. And then Bobbi's voice came in:

You said you loved me—

She stopped. The music that swirled around her vocals went in a couple of different directions, with Al's sax trying to find her and Franky's trumpet refusing to follow. Bobbi, who almost never made musical mistakes, had come in on the wrong measure.

It wasn't such a big deal, really—she and the rest of the band recovered from the gaffe, which passed largely unbeknownst to the audience. After all, these were pros playing, and the listeners didn't know the song anyway. The crowd jumped up to dance and even gave a short cheer at the end, but their quick return to their seats revealed their disappointment that the energy they felt years ago had once again eluded them. Nevertheless, Bobbi had done a right fine job delivering the rest of the number, bellowing lyrics that the band members all hoped soon would be, paradoxically, beloved:

> *I'll meet you sweetheart, at the white cliffs of Dover*
> *I can't wait to see you—when Hell freezes over!*
> *To think, us in England, I've never been there, ever*
> *So bye-bye my sweetheart*
> *(boom-boom-boom/tap tap)—*
> *—For-ev-er!*

"You ruined my song." Franky said at the break. "Thanks to you, we're finished!"

"*I* ruined *your* song," she said. "Don't talk to me about *your* song. It's our song—and I didn't ruin nothin'! You did the count too fast, and it screwed me up."

Never mind those two. Only one hope remained for the whole evening, really for the whole tour: Sid Simeo. The producer, who was notorious for his lack of expression, was rumored to have tapped his foot. After the set, the whole band wandered over to his table to say hello but really to hear what he had thought. They all waited with held breath for him to open his mouth. Yet in six words he expressed a combination of sentiments that left them confused:

"I hated it. I'm in love."

Franky protested with a *What do you mean, you hated it?* Simeo explained further. He didn't like "Bye-bye ... Forever!" because it just so happened that during that particular month he was in the middle of one of his extramarital affairs, except "this time I really love her." The affair was based in Chicago, from where he had just come, and so he could do nothing but relate all moments, both waking and sleeping, both musical and mundane, back to her.

"Yet again," Franky muttered later in the evening, "love ruins everything."

Franky had to blame somebody, so he kept blaming Bobbi. They argued clear on through the break about how she had messed up the song, and they argued onstage with their eyes, just as they always did, only this time the friction surpassed that of any previous occasion, for there was not a dash of fun in the exchange. When a biting lyric came, Bobbi sang it straight across the stage at Franky, almost hissing the words, even when they played the new tune again in a futile attempt to change Simeo's mind:

Stay away from me baby

And I don't mean maybe
This LADY is better than you!

As the last set drew to a close, they both appeared to forget about the spat—yet their scowls were not replaced with smiles. The waning moments of the music meant that the band's two de facto business managers next had to face the reality of hard numbers: Franky and Bobbi would do the books and see if the band had made any money on the tour.

After the gig this particular hall manager normally liked to approach Franky and talk about making arrangements for the next date. He did not say a word this time, instead choosing to help the bartender restock the booze while avoiding eye contact with Franky.

"We're losing St. Louis," Franky murmured to Bobbi. "Imagine that: relegated from a dance hall, to a room where they play checkers, to nowhere at all."

Bobbi shrugged, and the two leaders scooted in their chairs at a cocktail table near the stage to get down to business: entering in the books the tour's final line item, that night's gig, and doing the arithmetic. Joe, meanwhile, broke down his drum kit and the others smoked cigarettes and milled around.

"I think this one might have put us over the top," the drummer called from the bandstand, trying to shoot some encouragement everyone's way.

Eventually the band members gravitated in a circle around the table while Franky performed the final arithmetic equation with the no. 2 pencil he kept in his briefcase along with his ledger and tour-date contracts. Sure, the boys knew they would get paid regardless of the tour's success—Franky would always see to that—but the trip's bottom line foretold the ifs and whens of the next tour. Quiet, they all gazed at him. Franky tossed the pencil on the table and shook his head. He then looked up, noticing for the first time the group that had encircled him.

"After expenses," he said, "the band lost twenty-seven dollars and thirty-two cents."

No one knew what to say. Jim and Tim looked at each other, while Joe's eyes sank.

"My take could be a little less next time," said Jim. "I don't mind." Others murmured in agreement. The boys started chattering that they'd figure a way to make it work for the Franky Fritz Band—they always had and they always would. After all, they said, they had a pair of leaders who over the years had instantly solved every problem and turned them into one of the most durable big bands in the country. But Franky sobered them before they could whip themselves up into any more of a can-do state.

"I don't know when next time is."

It was true. There was no next time lined up. Sure, some clubs had asked them back for another date, but several others on their tour route hadn't, making would-be gigs so far away from one another that a tour wasn't really feasible.

Then Bobbi spouted out what everyone must have been thinking but didn't dare broach. "Oh shoot, Franky!" she said, flinging a drumstick of Joe's into the air. The stick bounced and clacked on the dance floor, rolling until it fell still. "Maybe it's time you faced the music. Maybe it's time you start thinking about calling off the band. I mean, a coupla decades is a pretty damn good run, ya know."

No one said a thing, either yea or nay. Slowly, Franky pivoted toward her, fuming.

"You—" He spoke through clenched teeth. "First you come in on the wrong measure and now you talk such nonsense? Why, I ought to fire you right here and now!"

"You can't fire me and you know it!"

Luckily, Tim stepped in. The accounting books were painted red, the bandleaders were bickering, and so there was only one thing left to do, according to the sax player.

"We're getting a drink," he said. "Franky, you're coming with us too."

Franky never did that, of course, but Tim kept after him, in part to keep him from fighting with Bobbi.

"C'mon, Franky, let's go. When does the whole band ever get together anymore?"

Everyone waited for the bandleader's reply. His answer was surprising, and perhaps even foreboding, for he actually cursed:

"Ah, jeez. What the hell."

Clearly, it was a poignant moment, perhaps an omen of change. The scene, in fact, reminded Joe of the last occasion Franky drank— when he was being dragged out by his buddies on his foiled wedding night.

* * *

LAST ON THE line came East Chicago. The boys had learned from Bobbi that the city wasn't part of "the *real* Chicago," as Tim had started calling it, but who could blame them for being just a little excited about playing in a town so close to the Windy City, and one that shared the same one-and-only name, at that? Someone unfamiliar with the area easily could figure that East Chicago might own at least a hint of the glamor that shimmered from its famous neighbor. *East Chicago* surely sounded nicer than Hammond or Gary did, that was for sure.

But any remnant hopes that the Indiana border city had snatched a crumb of its namesake's glitz were dashed away as soon as the train pulled into the station. It wasn't the industrial look of the town that deflated the air inside the band's hopeful bellies. Railroad tracks, and consequently the train stations along them, were often found in seedy parts of any given city. What darkened their eager eyes turned out to be a couple of messages announcing the entrance to the city, one painted across a distant municipal water-tank tower, the kind that squatted with a roof on top of it, and the other emblazoned on a small billboard right along the station platform. Both messages, which attempted to market the city, came from other eras and therefore failed miserably, or at least they didn't speak to the modern musicians gazing at them. First they saw the message on the water tank:

EAST CHICAGO, IND.

THE ARSENAL OF AMERICA

Tired from travel, their excitement over their little tour fell to the ground with the mere feathery nudge of those few simple words. Even the resilience of their leader Franky seemed spent.

"Have I reenlisted without knowing it?" he said to the train window.

The second sign, which also belonged to some other decade, wasn't much more tourist friendly than the first:

WELCOME TO EAST CHICAGO, IND.

WORKSHOP OF AMERICA

They all gazed through the train window at the cityscape of brick-and-mortar factories and warehouses, all looming as a backdrop illustration, visual proof, for the two signs.

"Jeez, and I thought South Bend was bad," said Tim, voicing the others' thoughts. "Yep, it's almost exactly like the real Chicago, all right."

"Hey, crybaby," Bobbi said, "how many times do I have to remind you: We used to play at Nick's."

After they had all plodded off the train toting their bags and instruments, she grabbed Franky's arm and marched him off to go hunt for a place to play. "Let's show a little more spunk in front of the band," she said, pulling him along by the arm. "They look to you for their moods. You know that."

"I'm tired too. I wonder what Ariel is doing."

She stopped, took a breath and nodded. "I know," she said. "I miss her too, so I can imagine…." Her voice trailed off, and they were about to duck into a cab, so she turned back toward the train platform and called out to the boys her Rosie-the-Riveter mantra with her fist in the air: "Hey fellas, over here! 'We can do it!' "

At the first hall they went to, the bartender told them they already had a band booked that night, and the man at the next stop said only, "No vacancy," without so much as giving them a glance. They were on the verge of their first failure of the mini-tour and they hadn't even been aiming high. The band had enjoyed a few high points, but they had turned such a small profit on their South Shore tour that any stops that yielded no gig could easily turn their bottom line from black to red, given the seven additional train tickets those stops burned. Even Bobbi, gasping her last breaths of spunk, started to sound more like Joey than herself.

"We're just like the Cubs," she said, shaking her head. "We're gonna strike out. That's how my aunt says it. We're just like the Cubs 'cause we're gonna strike out when it counts."

They were headed for strike three. That's when a cabdriver, after much thought and many shrugs of *I don't know*, offered a suggestion. "Well, there's the Just Like Home," he said.

The *Just Like Home?* That didn't sound like a dance hall, said Franky.

"It's not," said the man. "It's a family restaurant. But try there anyway."

A family restaurant? That made them skeptical, but they had little choice but to give it a try in spite of the cabdriver failing to elaborate further.

The place wasn't too shabby looking, it would turn out; at least it was nicer than the Hammond venue they had played the night before. Yet the size and shape of the room gave it a hopelessly awkward feel.

"What is it about this place?" Bobbi said with her arms folded as they stood looking in from the doorway. "Goldilocks wouldn't know to say too big or too small."

They would later learn that she had put her finger on it; like the Franky Fritz Band itself, the room hadn't found its audience. *Otto's Just Like Home*, as the sign out front read, had struggled for several years, because it was too small to be a real dance hall, yet too spacious to find its niche as a cozy restaurant or bar. The building's original intent (men's lodge?) was unknown, but it surely wasn't meant to be a restaurant. Whatever it had been, Otto had bought the place at a bargain rate a few years back with grand visions of repurposing it. Because of this ambiguous atmosphere and the resulting weak sales, the owner was always changing his business. At the moment, kielbasa and meat loaf were the orders of the day, but during intervening years Otto had made several attempts at turning the clumsy room into a mini-dance hall. ("Show business is where the money's at!" he would explain to anyone who would listen.) And then when dance crowds proved sparse, Otto would have the building resume its previously abandoned family-restaurant career: The fickle businessman simply filled the former dance floor with four rows of rectangular tables strung together, each partnered with long wooden benches that had previously lined the walls for flirting dancers.

"This is a family town," he would announce upon making the change, "and families need to eat!"

Only problem was, in that atmosphere the arrangement resembled a prison dining hall more than it did a family eatery. Reflective of the building's own fickleness, old Otto had changed the poor room's life purpose at least five times in as many years. At the time of that first attempt at a Franky Fritz Band tour, the place had been stumbling along through its present restaurant incarnation for several months, and now rumor had it that Otto was on the verge of changing up his business yet again.

"It might be just a restaurant now," the cabdriver told the bandleaders cryptically, "but it wouldn't take much to get him to change it to a dance hall."

Count on the business duo to get the job done. With each stop, they had been refining their sales routine, and they always used the band's New Orleans roots as their prime selling point. That was enough to convince the owner who, living up to his flip-flopping reputation, proved no match for the pair. Best of all, because the awkward venue was a restaurant at the moment, the owner had not a single band scheduled on the calendar. Franky and Bobbi seized the opportunity. By the time they bounced out the door of Otto's family restaurant, they had landed a five-night gig for the World-Famous Franky Fritz Band at the newly named Otto's Ballroom. And by the last of those nights the awkward room was brimming to capacity. Suddenly the room had found its purpose, it seemed, for the space was like the band itself: not too big, not too small, and always seeking an identity. The room was made for the Franky Fritz Band's stature and size alike.

The group arrived back in South Bend on a high, and Aunt Jess greeted them with yet more good news, telling them that the owner of the Poor Man's Palace—who did little more than come in once a week to do the books and tally the profits, leaving Jess to run the place—wanted the band to play there again on Saturday night. Naturally, another band was already booked, but the owner had been so impressed with the crowd for the Franky Fritz Band that when Aunt Jess had mentioned they would be back in town in a few days, he jumped at the opportunity to book them, even though he would have to pay the other band as well. That ensemble, a small-time Chicago outfit that had become a dance-hall staple outside the city limits, couldn't complain about getting paid in full for a half-night's worth of work, but they certainly weren't happy when they learned the Franky Fritz Band would be headlining.

Back at the comfort of Aunt Jess's and the Poor Man, band members, particularly the leaders, began to develop trademarks. For the stage Franky sported his tux and drenched his hair with a bucket of tonic; for her part, before gigs Bobbi rubbed her whole body with Cashmere Bouquet talc—"the fragrance that men love," according to the magazine advertisement, as well as a means of absorbing stage sweat. Last of all, she pulled on a pair of Glamour Girl nylons to give an irresistible shimmer to her legs, which men and boys had begun to ogle if they weren't gazing at her bust.

For the New Orleans gang, the second set of dates at the Poor Man's Palace was icing on the cake. The Midwest tour had been a smashing success by their standards, for they would be welcome back at every one of the venues they had played.

CHAPTER 15

AFTER THE BAND members dropped off their instruments in their rooms, they started trickling down to the bar. They had much to forget about and much drinking to do. The tour's level of success had been officially learned only a few minutes prior, but an air of foreboding had hung over the entire trip. Perhaps sensing the possibility that this was the last stop of the band's last tour, in spite of their tight finances they had decided to relive their heyday and stay at the Hotel Majestic as opposed to the usual roadside inn on the outskirts of St. Louis they had been patronizing during these recent, leaner days.

Tim pushed his favorite drink on Franky and, to the sax player's surprise, the bandleader downed the 7UP and gin in four or five gulps. "Look at you," said Tim, watching the thin man cock back his head. "The last time I saw you with a drink in your hand, Muriel had left you."

"It's worse this time," answered Franky, staring over the top of his glass. "Not only is music leaving me, so has my daughter."

No one had believed either Franky or Bobbi would end up coming down to the bar because of their spat, which had flared up again after the bookkeeping caused more sour moods. But there was Franky now, sipping his 7UP and gin, and so at this point only Bobbi needed to appear. And she did.

"Oh—you decided to come down, I see," said Franky.

"Oh—*you* decided to come down," said Bobbi. "Never mind, I'm going up to bed."

She turned to march right back upstairs. Joe, however, protested and convinced her to stay, reiterating Tim's comment about the band never being all together offstage anymore. "Just keep your back to him and you'll forget he's even there," he murmured with his back to Franky. "I do that sometimes myself." Then he faced both of them and ordered in full voice: "Now you two be good and stay away from each other."

But they weren't capable of doing that. They picked up where they left off. Had they just started the bickering, drink may have fueled it further; however, because they had exhausted both themselves and all arguments in the debate, the alcohol instead softened their tensed muscles and caused the two opponents not to care so much anymore. After one drink, they had for the most part stopped arguing. The conversation instead morphed into a philosophical discussion about what makes a decent song and why the band had enjoyed so much success over the years. By the second drink, Franky, an inevitable lightweight given his teetotaling ways and his feathery frame, actually stooped to pay Bobbi a compliment. But he said it as if he'd lost himself in thought, with his shoulders hunched over the bar and his eyes glazed on the melting ice in his empty glass.

"First Ariel, and now music. Gone. I don't know what I'd do without you."

To everyone's surprise, Bobbi blushed. No one—not Franky, not Joe, not anyone in her band world—had ever seen Bobbi blush before. Gathering herself, she slapped him and said, "C'mon, Ariel will be back soon, I just know it." The other band members, who had been caught up in their own conversations and were ignoring the two, given that they'd been party poopers what with their bickering, all looked her way for a still-life moment, one that froze like a frame on film. They had not heard Franky's compliment, but just about all of them sure had seen her blush. And those who hadn't seen it got an elbow nudge from a neighbor directing them to hurry up and look Bobbi's way.

Jim broke the tableau when he said randomly, "You two should get along in real life like you do onstage."

They all went back to their jokes, drinks, and conversations. Prior to the interruption, the two leaders had been launched alone on a different plane together, freed from their usual way of interacting, and they floated right back to it. The dynamic had shifted such that only one parallel could describe it: They were free to behave as if they were onstage together. Suddenly any insult was not an insult at all, but a flirtation. Words were still communications, but they were physical touches between them, not abstract exchanges. So the conversation became an American tango, with Franky pushing toward Bobbi as she bent back, and Bobbi leaning toward Franky as he turned half away: They were moving through words and, in the festive racket that had resumed around them, no one heard them but themselves.

The others kept drinking, as did Franky and Bobbi. The pair's leadership position within the group usually caused their conversation to drift a step removed from the others anyway, and this time was no different: Their followers, getting drunker and less observant by the minute, occupied themselves with their own talking, ignorant of the verbal touches between the two. After some time, one by one the players went upstairs, first Jim, then Ted and Al, and so on, each bidding a cursory good-bye that lacked focus thanks to the booze. Only three remained, and two were drinking; Joe was now on his seventh Coca-Cola, keeping the sparring pair company. A nondrinker like his best friend, Joe had come down for people and not booze, and so he was the only sober one to notice that Franky had entered a sphere somewhere beyond his usual self. Judging from Joe's tapping index fingers on the edge of the bar, one might assume he didn't like the pages of sheet music that were turning.

"One more Coke, please," he said to the bartender when the man passed by. Franky looked at his friend, dismayed, and the man put another glass of cola in front of the drummer with the rote reaction and blank face that bartenders trademarked long ago. Joe then took his third-wheel status a step further: He grabbed his Coke, slipped off his bar stool, and shoved it smack in between Franky and Bobbi.

"With all that sugar you're drinking, it's no wonder you're not tired yet," said Franky, forced to make room.

"You've got that right," Joe said. "I ain't tired, not one bit. I could stay up all night if I wanted to. In fact, I just might do that."

As if moving in perfect awareness of each other onstage, both Franky and Bobbi leaned back on their stools so they could see each other across the wide arc of Joe's back. In unison, they shrugged: For the first time, offstage at least, they were on the same side, for the dynamic was not Joe and Franky paired together as it always had been, but Franky and Bobbi, and then Joe alone.

The three chatted until Bobbi said she was going off to freshen up in the ladies' room. That gave Franky a chance to speak to his friend, and what ensued was the only time on record the two ever fought. It only lasted the length of a hot tune—three minutes—but that was only because three minutes was the length of time Bobbi stayed in the ladies' room.

"What's with you?" Franky said, the moment Bobbi stepped away. "Go upstairs, already. What do you think, I need a babysitter?"

Joe just shook his head with a slow rhythm that foreboded doom. "I don't like the looks of this," he said. "It ain't good for nobody. Not you, not the band." He took a gulp of his cola. "Heck, Franky, Bobbi ain't no Sondra. If you're going to live like you do, *please* stick to strangers!"

Franky's neck craned and his eyes bulged. "Just what are you saying, anyway? Go on and say it! How do you, of all people—Joe the prude, Joe the guy who's had one girl his whole life—how do *you* know what's going on?"

"I just know."

"I'm having a drink with my business partner, for crying out loud!"

The bandleader went on from there: He was an adult, he could take care of himself, and he didn't need his friend telling him what to do! But next, a moment of reflection passed over him, for his voice quieted, and he spoke as much to his empty glass as to Joe.

"You don't get it, you have Marcie. All I've got is the band and Ariel—and she's gone!"

Joe softened at the mention of Ariel, showing it by staying quiet. With a sigh, Franky's tone and cadence again shifted. Look, he said, all he was doing with Bobbi was talking, so why didn't Joe just ease off? Go on upstairs and get some rest; he and Bobbi needed to talk about whether she still wanted to be in the band. Yet the drummer still didn't budge; he refused to go up to his room and let them be alone. Bobbi would be back at any moment, and so the two friends needed to get this resolved fast. Finally, Franky lost his patience, speaking to his friend in a way that he never had before:

"Go back to your room and write Marcie a love letter or something."

He could say pretty much anything to Joe—except mention his wife or their relationship in a negative context. The big guy steamed until his face turned red. Having turned back to the bar and his drink, Franky waited for an explosion of a response, but it didn't come. Joe was too angry to speak.

"Jeez, what a ball of fun you two look like."

It was Bobbi, walking up. Still, neither Franky nor Joe said anything. Both sulked into their respective glasses. At last, Joe stood up to go. Before Bobbi could say an innocent "Heading up for the night?" he erupted with a short burst.

"All right, I'm leaving!" he said. "But don't go and ruin the band by this!"

After he marched out of the bar, Franky and Bobbi gave another shrug, a drunken claim of ignorance that said, *What was that all about?* And then, within moments:

"I'm tired," said Bobbi.

"I'm tired," said Franky.

She stood up and swayed, and so he held her waist to help her regain her balance. They walked side by side, he grasping her hand with the unspoken excuse that she might fall otherwise. They climbed up the old hotel's great staircase, which turned once 90 degrees, and the whole way up he kept one palm on her forearm and the other resting on the subtly intimate spot on the small of her back. Later, while defending his actions to Joe, he said that what made his final decision was the warmth coming through her dress; the moist heat was so strong that it felt as if there was no dress between them, that he actually was touching her sweaty skin. "And that feeling of weight," he said. Maybe it was because she was drunk, but, "As we walked up the stairs, I could feel her leaning back into my hand a little."

Their rooms were side by side, so the moment of decision could be put off until the very end of their journey. "Do you need help?" said Franky, standing before the two adjacent doors. "Sure, I could use a hand," she answered, and so he took the key from her fingers, his brushing hers, and unlocked the door.

The sex came fast and even with a hint of love, although Franky would never use that word. Once in the room they came together as if they belonged together, as if they had known all along what was coming next, which of course they did. Pent up in their encounter of pure touch was all the months and years of their bickering and competing offstage, and their showbiz flirtations onstage. In the process of all the undressing and kissing, they stopped only once, when Bobbi said something to ruin the moment. Terribly, her blunder came at the worst possible time—when they lay naked on the bed outside of the covers, just before he was to enter her.

"You're so tiny," she said.

Franky was taken aback. He was ready to either reignite the endless fight they'd had that evening or leap out of bed and run for his clothes, which she had flung randomly about the room. But then she added: "You're so tiny, I could break you like a twig."

Franky paused for thought: She had been referring not to one body part—she had been talking about his entire body. So she wrapped his arms around his narrow frame and he wrapped his around hers, and they joined, coming together as closely as two can come.

AFTER FRANKY HAD slept with Muriel, he had awoken to an empty bed. This time, he was the one to leave his bed partner behind. They had fallen asleep in each other's arms, with their faces almost touching, suggesting their closeness might stay beyond the night. Eventually they separated, as lovers do at some point when they sleep, since holding each other grows uncomfortable. For Franky, though, the space created and his wakefulness gave him moments to consider the world beyond the bed. Before long he was slipping from the covers and gathering his scattered clothes. Bobbi stirred, and so he crept all the quieter, then gingerly stepped into his slacks, keeping his eyes on her to make sure she slept. Adequately dressed, he threw his tux jacket over his shoulder, turned and headed straight for the door. But he couldn't go without one final look, and so he turned around with his hand grasping the knob, looking at her as if it would be the last time he would ever see her. He took pause, and then murmured the thought that passed at that moment:

"Bye-bye...forever."

THE ENTIRE TRIP home, Joe drummed a pencil on an unfolded road map stretched between his knees. The hollow sound of tapping on paper that lay suspended over air created a hollow thump. The others had long since learned to tune out his constant drumming, but the sound pulsed even louder on this trip: Not only did he pound harder and with more intensity, but two of the people in the bus hadn't spoken a word the whole ride, amplifying all noise.

"Would you cut it with the drumming, Joe?" said Tim, finally losing his patience.

"Sorry."

And he stopped. But it started up again within thirty seconds as they barreled down the length of Arkansas.

"Hey, why aren't you two talking?" said Slim Jim.

Everyone knew the intended audience to the question. Neither of the two bandleaders responded, and so Joe answered for them.

"Because we're through," he said. "We're all through."

Franky just drove and gazed straight at the road, his eyes hidden by his eyewear of choice whenever he got behind the wheel of the old bus: decade-old aviator sunglasses that great generals of his war once sported and that, as advertised, boasted antiglare lenses designed for the armed forces. And Bobbi, she sat in back with Joe, her arms resting on top of the pocketbook in her lap. She had locked herself in that position for six and a half hours, not even climbing out of the bus during stops to use the bathroom—the strength of her iron bladder by now legendary among the male band members and even more legendary after this trip. At last, by the eighth hour, she used the bathroom at a filling station and then marched right back to her seat and reassumed her position.

When they pulled into New Orleans, Franky dropped Bobbi off first. He rolled up alongside her home and stopped to let her out, his head locked straight ahead as if he were a chauffeur. Bobbi, meanwhile, for the first time in hours, unlocked herself from her waxen pose and climbed out of the bus. Stepping away on the grassy strip by the sidewalk, she stopped and made an about-face. She stood there, glaring into the driver-side open window, before saying something that jarred every single person in the bus—including Franky, but for a different reason:

"Bye-bye…forever!"

The slam of the bus door punctuated the remark. From Franky's perspective, her words said it all: They told him she had been awake when he left her the night before, hearing what he'd muttered aloud to himself. The boys, meanwhile, watched her walk into the night, up her steps and into her home—the one she had bought with money from the glory days of the Franky Fritz Band, the one she had begun threatening to sell so she could move up to South Bend, Indiana, home of her only family, home of the only person who loved her.

* * *

PULLING INTO THEIR hometown from that first tour, the only thing on Franky's mind was seeing Ariel. He couldn't contain his excitement, skipping down the short walkway leading up to his parents' front porch.

"Where the hell you been?" said Mr. Fritz, with the light that streamed out from inside the house surrounding him. "You should have been home over a week ago."

Franky skipped right past him, marching up the stairs to his old bedroom, where he knew Ariel would be sleeping. All in a matter of a few swift strokes he gathered her belongings, lifted up the slumbering child, and eased his way back down the stairs with the trusting weight of his daughter collapsed over his chest. When he returned to where Mr. Fritz was still standing near the door, he stopped and said, "Becoming a famous musician—that's where I've been."

"Famous musician, nothing. You need to be a man and live up to your responsibilities."

He'd had enough of his father, but Mrs. Fritz tried to play peacemaker by explaining her husband. "Your daddy loves having Ariel," she would insist. "He just doesn't like to show emotion, except for grumpiness."

But never mind his father. In spite of the physical exhaustion from the long motor trip, through Franky's eyes the world looked perfect at that moment. He had just completed a successful tour with his band and Ariel was back in his arms. And his father did prove to be of some service, particularly for the longer term. The next morning, he marched right back up his parents' walkway, strolled into the house, and smacked onto the kitchen table the modest stack of cash that he and the band had earned on the tour. While Mrs. Fritz jumped for joy and gave him a big hug, Mr. Fritz showed a more understated reaction.

"We're taking you down to see Mr. Bernie first thing in the morning," he said. That was, of course, Bernie Levin, Mr. Fritz's accountant for his shoe business.

Back home in New Orleans, the band members reveled in their newfound success. Granted, the "World-Famous" Franky Fritz Band remained unknown in their own city. Still, they were able to boast to their friends, family, and especially themselves that they had done it: They had embarked on a tour of the Midwest and actually turned a profit, if a modest one. The mundane realities of the road had extirpated most of their romantic notions of musicianhood, but they nevertheless reclaimed some of that romance after experiencing the comforts of home, with each member moving through life's daily errands with the hidden awareness that they were walking and talking professional musicians. No one noticed them on Canal Street or at the corner store save an old high-school acquaintance or family friend, but they nevertheless walked as if they not only knew the source of their next paycheck, but that it would come from their love. And because they earned their keep from their love, they were among the few who walked down the street as if they belonged in the world.

Business manager Franky started putting together their second tour the very day after they had returned. Compared to previous business challenges he'd already confronted, this one was a pleasure to deal with. The band could count on four solid, multi-night tour stops, giving them a minimum of ten or twelve evenings' worth of gigs, Franky estimated. Moreover, when they had made their first tour of these four cities—South Bend, Gary, Hammond, and East Chicago—Franky had gotten from each one of the bar owners a reference letter, which he himself had composed and then asked them to sign, so as not to trouble them with the writing part. The owners, who were anxious for the band to return, gladly obliged when Franky explained, "If we get more gigs in the Midwest, we'll be able to come up here more." The letters were a strange mix of Franky's diction and his dubious attempt at sounding like the bar owner who supposedly was doing the writing:

> *Dear Fellow Esteemed Booking Manager:*
>
> *I am writing to highly recommend the Franky Fritz Band. Now I know why they are "World Famous." They play not only with fine musicianship but a showmanship that brings in the crowds and keeps*

them happy and on their feet. Boy, do the people dance to the Franky Fritz Band. And that makes them thirsty, so thirsty my bar had its third best night ever. I'm sure the next time they come (I made them promise they'll come back), I'll have my best night, now that the whole city of Gary already knows about this World-Famous Band from New Orleans.

Sincerely,
Michael Kawalski
Manager
The Avalon, Gary, Ind.

While the Franky Fritz Band's motor stayed mostly idle once Bobbi and the boys returned home, Franky made sure he put his free time to good use, working on the logistics for the next tour and arranging for a band photo shoot to get a few glossy publicity prints. As usual, he proved resourceful in finding a photographer they could afford, calling on a former high-school classmate who charged the rate of someone who, like the band members themselves, was trying to launch a career—in his case, off the flood of marriages and births happening at the time. For the sake of the camera, in her best cursive Bobbi drew up the words *The Franky Fritz Band* on a sheet of poster board and cut it out to fit on Joe's kick drum; the drummer liked the sign so much that after the shoot he kept it pasted to the drum for upcoming gigs. Franky, meanwhile, had the boys go see Mr. Mintz at his shop on Canal Street for some tuxedo rentals. The young bandleader had already bought two more tuxedoes from Mr. Mintz since that ugly week of his foiled wedding, and so he was able to convince him to rent the boys tuxedoes at a 60-percent discount provided they brought them back within three hours.

"I'll probably be buying tuxedoes from you for decades to come," Franky told Mr. Mintz, and he would be right.

The four reference letters and glossy band photo, topped with a separate letter of introduction from Franky and one of his specially made business cards paper-clipped to the top of the stack, all came together to form a professional-looking publicity kit for the band, one that he and Bobbi could use when they cold-called new bars and dance halls the next time they hit the road. Franky even bought a palm-sized Filmo 8 movie camera to show prospects grainy and soundless clips of the band in action, which he spliced (in very crude, jerky fashion) with shots of giant, cheering crowds that presumably made up their audiences—but were actually a parade crowd filmed during Mardi Gras.

As the next tour neared, Mr. Fritz became the central character in Franky's life. First, there was Franky's impending income deadline, which was coming the following month, and Mr. Fritz didn't let him forget it. And each day the tour drew closer, he griped all the more about Ariel staying at the Fritzes during his son's upcoming trip. The elder Fritz constantly made smart-aleck comments about Ariel's crying ("With those lungs she'll be the best horn player ever!") and complained of how she tired him out if she stayed any longer than precisely three-and-a-quarter hours. "And it's not right for your mother to have to work so hard at her age," he said one day when Franky was at the house. "She already did that with you, and look at the thanks she gets!"

That was it. Franky couldn't hold it in any longer. Mrs. Fritz had started to tell her husband to bite his tongue—having Ariel wasn't any work for her at all! But Franky interrupted her. Speaking to his father, he said, "Don't worry, you won't have to see your granddaughter for three whole weeks, if that's the way you want it. She's coming with me."

"No!" said Mrs. Fritz.

"Hip-hip, hooray!" said Mr. Fritz, swooshing his newspaper.

Bobbi was thrilled about Ariel going on tour. She had taken to the child the first time she met her and doted on her ever since. Defending the news to the protesting boys, she reasoned that South Bend, the first stop, would be easy because Aunt Jess loved to have kids around. "During summers she practically raised me at the Poor Man," she said. "When I was a baby, she tucked me underneath the bar."

With the car already jam-packed for tour number two, Ariel ended up spending over half the trip on Bobbi's breast. Franky, perfectly willing to get a break during the endless ride, was happy to take her up on her steady stream of offers to hold the child. The trip was so long and tedious, in fact, that even the guys eventually grew so restless, tired and bored out of their minds that their insecure sense of masculinity dropped on the highway pavement and they too demanded, "Lemme hold her!" Being passed around the stuffed car for hours on end, Ariel fared fine with Joe and Slim Jim, finding comfort in the great cushion of Joe's chest and, conversely, the concave curve of Slim Jim's upper body, the boniness of which must have felt much like her father's. She fared fine in Ted's arms as well, but with Tim and Al, she cried almost from the moment of contact and so they each quickly returned her. Other than Franky, though, no one took more interest in Ariel than Bobbi, for she always took the child with her out of the car at rest stops, she fed her often, and she even changed her diaper. And once they arrived in South Bend, Aunt Jess was constantly doting on her too.

"It's just like when Bobbi was little," she said. "I always loved being a mother without being a mother."

When they started playing their gigs, Franky still had to find ways to make sure Ariel was okay while he was up on the bandstand, but the stress was nothing compared to what he had endured at Nick's. At the Poor Man, of course, Aunt Jess was the manager of the place, and she was thrilled to have Ariel in the dance hall, for she'd already been through that with Bobbi. Thus, Franky didn't need to build a Fort Ariel. Moreover, he didn't have to worry about her while he was up onstage, for Aunt Jess was there to watch her. The next tour stop wasn't much more difficult, for Jess simply wrote a letter to Mike Kawalski in Gary telling him to "expect a baby." (*Don't worry, she's an angel—a music angel, and a good-luck charm!* she wrote.) By the time they moved on to play the next town after that, Franky had gotten so used to having Ariel out in the open at gigs that he grew emboldened. When the band arrived for its engagement at Art's in Hammond, he simply strolled in with her as if nothing was out of the ordinary.

"What the hell is that?" said the manager, looking at Ariel.

"It's called a baby," said Franky. "Have you ever seen one?"

"Get her out of here."

"She's with the band. No baby, no Franky Fritz. Didn't you read the contract?"

A baby wasn't in any of the contracts, but managers never bothered to double-check the fine print. So for the remaining tour dates, and any gigs from then on, Ariel didn't have to be hidden away. The band had built a little clout already; other than the back table at Nick's, the automatic admission of Ariel was the first item in their unwritten rider that they had garnered.

That clout came for a reason. The Franky Fritz Band drew big crowds in all four cities and on every single night of the tour. With the band's name having been affixed to calendars and marquees of each venue (including the words *Direct from New Orleans/ The World-Famous* preceding it) dance-hall goers for the first time could anticipate seeing them as opposed to just happening upon the show that night. As a result, crowds turned out strong on weeknights and they packed the house on weekends. The band even picked up two extra, smaller gigs on the trip when patrons in South Bend and Hammond approached Franky about playing a couple of holiday events including a Christmas party at a college dean's mansion, and so they stuck around a few extra days for yet more easy money. For the band, three weeks of dates meant a paycheck they had never seen before.

Moreover, increased profits meant more cash for them to invest in expanding the band's tour base. Two mornings after the final show, the boys piled into the car once again and headed back home—only without Franky and Bobbi, who stayed behind with Aunt Jess and plotted out possibilities for the bigger, better third Midwestern tour. Once the old Hudson, loaded full of their bandmates, pulled out of Aunt Jess's driveway and they had waved the car good-bye in the cold, early-morning sunlight, the three stepped back inside and laid out a map on the kitchen table. Jess hovered over them with a cup of coffee in one hand and a slim cigarette in the other.

"I'd try Skinner," she said, putting her finger on a barely visible dot on the map. "It's not too far from here, and they'll be impressed when they hear you're from New Orleans."

Franky also saw an intriguing town on the map. "Champaign," he read aloud. "I bet they would like someone in a tuxedo there."

But Aunt Jess said his assumption was wrong. "It's a college town," she said.

"Even better," said Franky. "The college students, they love music."

They continued through the routine, pricking Jess's sewing pins onto potential destinations as if the three were generals strategizing battle plans on a military map. Some pinpoints were big towns, others small cities. The next day Franky and Bobbi were off, back on the South Shore train with a couple of overnight bags and a third one stuffed with their slick new publicity kits. Ariel stayed back with Aunt Jess, who had a couple of days off. Once in Chicago, they caught buses the rest of the way, traipsing their way to the towns they'd literally pinpointed on the map. Having grown comfortable in their pitch, they had become true salespeople, moving on to the next prospect as soon as they got rejected. But the trip wasn't exactly smooth. When Franky and Bobbi weren't sweet-talking a club owner, they were bickering with each other.

"I'll do the talking," Franky would say seconds before they stepped through the doors of an establishment.

"Why should you do the talking?" Bobbi would answer. "You failed on the last three stops."

The relationship drove Bobbi to try such drugstore products as Henderson's Nervine, which was said to offer a calming medicinal effect. Somehow, though, they would gather their business demeanor just as soon as they walked through the doors, and then one of the two would start in with a spiel while the other would shove a publicity kit into the owner's hand, interject with a reinforcing comment here and there, and even take over if the opportunity arose. The one-two punch flowed into a definite rhythm.

"We're world-famous," Franky might say, "and—"

"From New Orleans," Bobbi would interject.

"Got a beat that's guaranteed, I say, to bring 'em to their feet."

"For us they gonna holler and give ya all their dollars."

And so on, and so on; not once did the pitch come out the same. During these sales presentations a battle often raged between the two, unbeknown to the listener, but the rivalry hardly lost them any sales. On the contrary, just as the duo's friction did on stage, it shot an electric current through the three-way dynamic, a sales voltage that the club owner often couldn't resist. The impromptu routine was so bizarre that it had the unintentional effect of disarming the dumbstruck listener to the point that he became hypnotized into putting ink on the dotted line.

The sales trip paid off. By the time they got back to Aunt Jess's house, they had secured another three venues for the next tour. They would now have no less than seven clubs to play, all of which offered multiple-night gigs, so that later when they had returned to New Orleans and told the rest of the band the news, the boys, of course, were ecstatic.

"Seven clubs!" Al said. "We might as well move up there."

Joe stiffened, and his eyebrows shot upward into half moons. "Move away?"

"Never," said Franky, waving his hands. "You have to keep them hungry for more. And if we moved, we couldn't say we were from New Orleans."

With no car to get back home from South Bend, the three took the train. Franky, carrying Ariel, boarded first, and then Bobbi followed after saying good-bye to her aunt. But as Bobbi put her foot up onto the step to climb aboard, Aunt Jess grabbed her shoulder.

"You keep it all business with Franky," she warned. "There's something wrong with that boy."

Bobbi looked at Jess as if she wasn't sure she'd heard right. "What are you talking to me for? You know he drives me crazy."

Jess nodded. "I know. That's when they're dangerous."

The train trip home was pure luxury compared to the cramped car rides. As for Ariel, with both Franky and her newfound best friend doting over her, she was content and mostly quiet. The two adults, meanwhile, glowed in both the beauty of the child and the satisfaction of business deals forged. Perhaps they were too tired, but they seldom bickered the whole way, the only arguing coming when Franky tried to take too much credit for landing the new gigs.

Because their marathon trip lasted till the end of the line at the bottom of America, many passengers around them came and went, occupying and vacating nearby seats. They shot Franky and Bobbi dirty looks when they bickered, but when things were quiet, some drank up with loving eyes the tranquil scene of man, woman, and child.

"What a beautiful baby," said one lady in a hat that sat high atop her head. Both head and hat tilted to the side as she spoke. "Such a nice family."

That misidentification happened at least three times on the trip, and it would continue to happen for years to come. Usually it generated a dirty look between Franky and Bobbi, causing the speaker to wonder what they had said wrong. Sometimes if he sensed the observer was especially prim, Franky would enjoy a bit of shock value.

"Thank you," he would say, "but the child is from another brief relationship of mine."

The comment silenced the woman in the hat, who put her gloved hand to her mouth and, as soon as etiquette permitted her the chance, snuck off to find another seat and distance herself from the sinful couple. On later occurrences, Bobbi might blurt out something before Franky could speak first: "I ain't married to that nitwit."

They had become the greatest of rivals. Rivalry, of course, breeds either respect or resentment.

CHAPTER 16

THESE DAYS WHEN Franky was home in New Orleans, a good walk was always the best medicine to clear his head, so off he went. When he took walks around his French Quarter neighborhood, no one gave him a second look even though he wore a tuxedo. The city's celebration of food, in combination with an economy that had slugged through the decades like a chronic weed-smoker, spawned a perpetual smattering of career waiters walking to and from work. On first glance, Franky merely appeared to be one of them.

But not on second glance. Without any particular destination, he walked upright and distinguished, much like the front man that he still was, as if he were conducting the jazz orchestra of everyday life about him. Whenever asked about his outfit, he had a simple explanation: "Why, I've worn it since the day of my wedding—you know, like Miss Havisham."

He strutted farther than usual today: up Dauphine Street from his home on St. Phillip, and then onto St. Ann toward Rampart Street, the French Quarter boundary where Creole cottages and echoing voices ended and car fumes and the din of steady traffic began. Across Rampart he could see the big sign of unlit bulbs spelling Armstrong Park, the words arching over the entrance in that happy and welcoming sort of way, just like the entrance to an amusement park. At dark the municipal-parks department still turned on the lights of that sign, making the arcade entrance all the more inviting—while, paradoxically, tour guides and any Joe on the street would warn you never to go in the park at night.

Franky was seen on this walk by a sporadic member of the band from years ago who, curious to see what the enigmatic bandleader was up to, followed him for a block or two. Franky wasn't marching as he normally did. He plodded along until he stopped and looked beyond the passing cars to the smiling park entrance on the other side of the street, the entrance shunned by everyone except those comfortable in the world of guns, drugs, and brown-bag booze. *Armstrong Park*, the sign said, as in Louis Armstrong. He clutched a lamppost in front of Rampart Corner Mart, where the cashier sat on a stool cooped up inside a booth of thick glass and iron bars. Franky stood gazing at the unlit park sign arching over the entrance, and then with the hot sun pressing on his taut skin, his eyes shifted down the block to the other end of the park and Congo Square. In another century, slaves had gathered in the square on free Sundays, birthing jazz on that very spot, according to legend. Next to the park lay Tremé, the storied jazz neighborhood, and right over there was the street that gave "Basin Street Blues" its name. Having intended to do so or not, he now stood on jazz holy ground, at the heart of music history.

He gazed back and forth between the Armstrong Park arch and Congo Square for such a long time that the watching ex-band member himself was hypnotized by the still scene of melancholy meditation. Then suddenly Franky shattered his own scene. He screamed so loud that even the whirring cars on Rampart failed to drown him out. More surprising still was that he cursed:

"I didn't fuck her up! I didn't fuck her up!"

His arms flailed out so that his tux jacket spread like the broken wings of a penguin. To anyone who saw, he was merely a man on the street lost in a haze of dementia, of which there were many in those days, especially younger ones. Thus, the cars and pedestrians all but ignored the lost soul who shouted and cursed at no one.

"They oughtta do something for them 'Nam vets coming home," said one passerby, shaking his head. "Giv'm a place to go during the day or something. Get'm some help."

The observing band member gave a short nod in answer to the comment, but he was too busy watching his leader, whom he had always known as the sharpest of men, great in both music and business.

* * *

GOING OUT ON tour, they conquered the new venues too. Around this time Franky invested in a travel clock, the kind that stood up by folding it into a triangle and that as long as you kept it wound, told you many things—not just the date, but even the day of the week, a useless feature to most people but a crucial one for someone living on the road. Also around this time Franky decided the band was pulling in enough money to add a few players. One-car tour transportation turned into three-car caravans. Unbeknown to the rest of New Orleans, a first happened: The band became integrated, beginning when the clarinet player Alvin Stokes joined the pack on tour and played with them on and off for the rest of the band's life.

Those auditioning had three requisites to fill: They needed to be damn good players, they needed to enjoy tingeing tunes with old styles, and they needed to have access to a car at least some of the time. From then on it would be at least an eight- or nine-piece band, with the peripheral players coming and going with each tour. During one tour in its heyday, the band traveled with as many as eleven players. Most musicians who came on board from then on ("the second generation," Franky called them) would rotate in and out of the band over the years. It wasn't that they weren't welcome additions; some of them just preferred staying off the road and gigging with local bands whenever possible. In addition, before long a new, more exploratory jazz was unfolding and some of them got heavy into these modern sounds—for like most any musician, if they got a chance to play what they wanted, they took it.

And another kind of music was soon to bubble up, one whose infant root strands were reaching into the rich, effluvial soil of Louisiana. One evening Alvin Stokes brought along a friend of his to a band rehearsal, some fellow from the Lower Ninth Ward, and told Franky, "You'd be wise to audition this cat." As it turned out, the guy played a piano like Franky had never heard, for the keyboard rolled along and somehow twinkled sweet and sensitive at the same time. Everyone loved the shy fellow (he reminded them of quiet Ted) whose name came out barely audible when Franky asked for it on that first audition. "Antoine," he whispered. "Antoine Dominique."

He sure gelled with the band that night. Bobbi even handed him the mike and he sang a couple of numbers with the same sweet tones that rumbled out of his piano. But in spite of what the young man had to offer, Franky showed ambivalence.

"There's something about him I don't like," he told Joe after rehearsal.

The drummer said that was only because Antoine Dominique was from the Lower Ninth Ward—which reminded Franky of the Ninth Ward, notorious home to Muriel.

"I know it's not 'cause he's colored—you're not like that," said Joe. And then he turned square at his friend and put his hands on his hips. "But you can't take it out on a fella just because he makes you think of your old sweetheart!"

Franky glared at him for mentioning Muriel. "Well, maybe," he said, "but there's something else too."

Maybe young Antoine Dominique caught on to Franky's chill and made himself scarce; or maybe he just didn't pursue a spot with the Franky Fritz Band because the group's music seemed passé. Regardless, Antoine didn't come around much after that and Franky didn't pursue him. Franky would move on to other things and so would Dominique, as time would tell.

Still, Franky pushed to grow the act. "The band's got to be big," he said again and again, even at a time when the music and the dance halls were dying.

"But, Franky," Joe said, "big is out."

"It sure isn't out with those people we play for." He stopped and held his palm to his heart like a stricken lover and added: "Think of our fans—we were lucky enough to find one another, and I won't be the one to desert the relationship."

Given all the touring he scheduled, some said Franky was a workaholic, that he drove his band too hard, but in truth he was only following his success much like anyone who has either ever fallen into, or fallen in love with, a vocational calling. New Orleans never quite embraced him and he knew he was lucky enough to find places where people did. The end result was that their popularity grew in all these far-off places, and the money flowed.

The core band members were getting used to life on the road. Each fell into a routine that carried them through the daylight as well as through the wind-down time late at night after shows. If Joe could find an all-night diner, he would usually grab Al or Slim Jim or one of the newer members to go for coffee and eggs. Tim went along with them sometimes, but only when he couldn't find "somewhere with Seven-Up and gin and nooky," as the young war vet said. The rest of the players followed either Joe's lead to a diner or Tim to a bar depending on their moods—or sometimes they headed straight to their motel room, particularly toward the end of a tour when they had grown weary. If Ariel was along, Franky would go straight back to the motel. Bobbi, uninterested in hanging out with a bunch of men, usually headed for her room as well. Many times, though, Franky, Ted, Joe, Alvin, and anyone else who was game would mimick when Fletcher Henderson went to the integrated dance world of Harlem's Savoy: The boys and sometimes Bobbi would hit whatever music venue was hottest. If it was a colored club and Tim had committed to going, he might hesitate, but all it took was one taunt from Alvin: "You scared of us coloreds or something?" That would shut Tim up and he would fall in line.

On one of those early trips to the Midwest, Franky and Bobbi walked back to the motel together, which had become their routine. Ariel was sleeping in Franky's arms, her cheek resting on his shoulder. "Mind if she stays with me tonight?" she asked when they got to the lobby. The gray-whiskered motel deskman, who was dozing with his head tilted back and his mouth puckered open, came to and peered over his reading spectacles.

"Be my guest," said Franky, and he handed little Ariel over to Bobbi.

"What is this, musical babies?" said the deskman. "Two parents, two rooms. Next thing you know, the kid will get one of her own too."

So through the years Bobbi and Ariel kept bonding, while the girl was introduced to the singer's nighttime feminine rituals that were alien to the motherless child: putting on her robe, brushing her teeth with toothpaste for "tobacco mouth," applying DreamFlower cream and powder to sustain her beauty.

After that third tour had wrapped up, Franky and Bobbi stayed behind again to go fishing for more venues and gigs, seeking to stretch their territory, as Franky was now calling it, even farther. Making their way in the direction of the more populated East, they secured dates in the biggest cities they'd ever played, snagging a gig in Cleveland and then another in Pittsburgh. The trip between those two cities was a new experience, for they passed over mountains, which they had never before seen. The rest of the band would repeat the experience a couple of months later, eyes shining with awe when the band drove into Pittsburgh after playing their South Bend-Chicago circuit. Joe was particularly insightful upon first seeing the Iron City, for the imposing mountains and rock inspired him to understand how the Midwest and New Orleans, which everyone had sworn were exactly opposite in every possible way, proved identical twins in one or two respects. "Louisiana and Indiana, they sorta rhyme, and they're both flat," said Joe, gazing up at the looming masses of rock surrounding them as they rode into the smoky town. "I never thought they could have anything in common till I was in a third place."

After Pittsburgh, Franky and Bobbi kept trekking farther east in search of more gigs, securing future dates in Harrisburg, York and Lancaster "P-A," as Jim liked to say. The band was rolling and gathering speed. Bobbi, who up until then still hadn't been sold on life with the Franky Fritz Band or its future, stopped talking about moving in with her Aunt Jess in South Bend and opening up "my own washateria" by answering an ad from the Aero-Matic Laundromat company, which promised amazing earnings of up to 8,000 dollars a year.

The itinerary they'd created for the next trip didn't exactly make for a national tour, but it was a step in that direction, for it spanned Illinois to Pennsylvania. Each time they pulled up at a new club, the first thing Franky did was hunt down the manager, shove an index card into his hand, and repeat the same words: "Say it *exactly* as it's written." The words, always printed by Franky's crisp hand, remained the same no matter the city they were playing, and they were the same lines he had given Aunt Jess to recite on that very first road gig:

> Ladies and gentlemen, may I have your attention please. I've gotta tell you, you're in for a special treat tonight. Straight from New Orleans, Louisiana, the birthplace of jazz, please give a warm welcome to: THE WORLD-FAMOUS FRANKY FRITZ BAND!

As the band played on, little Ariel tagged along all the way—happily hopping between the motels rooms of her father and doting Bobbi—to the point of her becoming the band's unofficial mascot. She was with them at gigs, and when she grew old enough to crawl, during sets she stayed in a crib or playpen or carriage—not hidden under some back table as before, but right behind—or even *on*—the bandstand. As she grew older and cried less, if the tune was appropriate she even served as a stage prop. For example, when the band played "My Baby's Gonna Cry," Franky and Bobbi, sharing the vocals, would strut over to the carriage and roll it back and forth as if trying to appease the delighted child as they alternated with each other singing the refrain: *My baby's gonna cry, what's the matter, why, my lady's gonna cry*. And how many songs of that era and since include lyrics with *baby*? So she was the perfect stage prop. While she stood in a playpen, they might go over and sing directly to her, belting lines like, *I love my baby* or *Baby baby I'm gonna miss you* or *Baby you're the prettiest thing these eyes have seen*. The audience ate it up. Whenever Bobbi or Franky edged closer to her on stage with a nifty little dance step or two, they would cheer and clap, and in response Ariel, sensing all the eyes on her and the good times bubbling over in the room, would bounce up and down, smiling as she held onto the side of the playpen. By then Ariel was practically a member of the band.

"She should be getting a paycheck too," said Bobbi.

"She is," Franky said. "I just opened a college account for her."

Franky's endurance for the road seemed endless, largely because of his teetotaling ways. And Ariel again played a part in his success in this respect, for her presence demanded that he be mature and stable, even on the road. She grounded him, much as spouses can ground each other—and so in that sense she replaced the woman that he never had.

But was she a handful. Ariel started saying words well before her first birthday, and like any child, in no time she was attempting to give a name to anything that walked into her world. One particular word, however, came later for the precocious child than it did for other children because she had no use for it: *mama*. When she did learn it—probably while playing with another little girl who lived next door to her grandparents—she latched onto it, as if she had suddenly become aware of what she lacked. In no time Ariel started calling every woman in sight *mama*, just as toddlers might say *dog* for every kind of animal they see. Worse, once she discovered the word, she didn't seem to want to unclasp her tiny fingers from the term no matter how hard Franky tried to pry them away. And as intelligent as she was proving to be, she refused to learn the nuance of the loaded word—specifically that it did not refer to every female who passed on the street. When he toted her around on errands to the grocery or the Hibernia bank, her calls of *mama!* elicited looks of pity from women. Seeing a father and toddler out shopping alone together, they may have read into the situation correctly—that she lacked a mother.

Of course, eventually Ariel did accept the nuance of the word *mama*—that it was not meant for all women. The term referred to only one person, and that person was different for everyone. For her, therefore, the sole individual could only be one woman.

"Mama!" she said to Bobbi one day.

The band was on tour, and Bobbi had taken her for the night. At first she laughed it off and ignored it, but Ariel was persistent.

"Mama!" she said, and looked for the reaction that she had gotten out of Bobbi the first time.

"I'm not your mama!" said Bobbi.

"Mama!" Ariel said the next morning.

"Would you stop it with the *mama*?" Bobbi said, looking in the mirror while holding her Pan-Cake makeup container in one hand and patting her face with the other. Ariel, who long ago had revealed her stubborn nature with her infamous crying bouts that wouldn't end, was now showing it in a new way. Meanwhile, Bobbi's adamant reaction only made it worse, for when the toddler realized she had the power to affect a separate being in such a way, she did it all the more—and made herself laugh every time. In addition to her stubborn side, she was showing her artistic and verbal proclivities early, through her discovery of the amazing powers that come with words.

"Mama!" she would say, and then watch Bobbi's face contort.

Not long after that, she learned that if she said certain other words, she had the power to make the faces of other big people change as well. She was growing up around a bunch of men—*musicians*, at that!—and so the language she learned did not become a young child.

"Shit!" she started saying. "Goddamn shit!"

The words came randomly, just like that. But as she got older, she learned to use phrases that approached the right context. At the pre-gig meal in a diner, for instance, the waitress might ask what the little girl wanted to drink. Joe, who always sat next to her in restaurant booths, would ask if she wanted her usual ginger ale when the waitress stood with pad in hand, waiting to take the order.

"Yeah, what the hell?" she would say. "One ginger ale, please."

The waitress might say something like, "That kid oughtta have her mouth washed out with soap," or maybe she would just shake her head, grab her pencil from behind her ear, and jot down the vulgar order. Regardless, language had revealed its power to Ariel, and so she kept swearing until eventually it became a part of who she was. On one occasion, when a fresh-faced bank clerk offered her a lollipop with the enthusiasm of someone assuming the little girl had never received such an offer when in fact she had received a thousand, her response came with not a trace of annoyance but only a simple shrug:

"Oh, I don't know, I don't give a rat's ass."

Ironically, around this time Ariel fixated on the popular and pure program *Father Knows Best*, which transitioned from radio to television. Little Ariel would sit there, transfixed and grasping in her little hand the new and wondrous remote control that wasn't all that remote because it performed its miracle by way of a cord that ran all the way back to the television. Even when the show was on the radio and Ariel was only an infant, Franky loathed it because he had already started his lifelong crusade against love and marriage.

"The only thing true about that show," he lectured to Ariel as she sat transfixed before the television, "is the title."

Meanwhile, some neighbor friends of the Fritzes reinforced Ariel's mother-father vision: Mr. and Mrs. Goldstein, Ariel observed when over at their house, slept together in the same room. Why did his father have no lady to sleep with?

She saw an obvious solution to this problem. At the start of a tour, the band pulled into the first town and proceeded through their routine, which is the only comfort on the road. They stopped in at the motel to check in and get settled before they would grab their preshow meal and then drift over to the dance hall and get ready for work. Ariel was used to the ritual by now, and so she stood there at the front desk listening to the familiar chatter that passed between the desk clerk and Franky and Bobbi. The clerk knew the band from previous visits, and so without asking how the arrangements would work, he turned his back to them to fetch two sets of keys on the wall. That was when Ariel, whose head hovered far below the counter so that she couldn't be seen, hollered.

"Just one room, please!" she said. "We're a family and so we sleep together."

Even Franky was at a loss for words. The desk clerk tossed bored glances back and forth between the two adults, waiting for an answer as to how to divvy up the rooms—or room. Beneath his graying mustache, his lips barely moved when he said, "Whatever you decide, I won't tell nobody. You know—kinda like attorney-client privilege." Down below and invisible, Ariel was chattering something about happy families when the man added, "Just make up your mind already."

That at last unfroze Bobbi, and so she whisked up Ariel into her arms. "She's something else, isn't she?" she said. "I love her like my own, but I couldn't last five minutes bunking with *him*."

Franky piggybacked onto that comment with a modest insult of his own, and the two entered into their usual back-and-forth bickering, against the backdrop of Ariel's whiny protests about why couldn't they ever all stay together in the same room. All was back to normal. In the quibbling, the equilibrium of the old ways had returned like the bubble in a carpenter's level. During the back-and-forth, Franky, seeing the situation as a teachable moment for his daughter, bent down closer to Ariel's level. "As long as you live," he said, "always stay in a separate room. Men give you nightmares."

At the mention of nightmares, she stopped her whining and looked at him with the big, oversized eyes of the child that she was.

Yet in the long run the motherless girl didn't stop about the two bandleaders getting married, and that pressure didn't abate as she grew older. She would blurt out to anyone who would listen (for instance, Bernie Levin, the band accountant), "Daddy and Bobbi are getting married," or ask while scribbling with crayons on the streetcar, "When are you two going to get hitched, anyway? A man and a woman get hitched when they love."

The moments caused discomfort, but for Franky they also represented learning opportunities. On these occasions he began to bequeath his beliefs on love's fallacy to Ariel at the earliest possible age.

"I'll teach her the truth," he told Bobbi, "so she never has to be lied to by some man."

Bobbi, who according to rumor had her share of bad men, nevertheless showed a lot less cynicism than Franky.

"You shut up about that," she said. "I see your point about the whole Prince Charming thing and all that, but you're gonna poison her."

Poison or no poison, he had a lot of work to do. Ariel, either because she intuitively saw her father's strange prejudice on this single topic for what it was or because fairy tales and other girls at school taught her the mores of the day, ignored Franky's lectures and kept talking about marriage. On one particular occasion, it was obvious where she got her romantic notion of weddings. A daughter from a famous New Orleans restaurant family got married one Saturday in St. Louis Cathedral, a place that Ariel had visited often, and the event was the talk of the town, with photos plastered across the newspaper gossip pages and front section alike. Everyone beyond Ariel's age knew St. Louis Cathedral was where the important and the famous married, and now she had acquired this knowledge for herself.

"*I'm* going to get married in St. Louis Cathedral too," she said after seeing the photos and asking her father about them.

So often, it seemed, she had that prophetic way of sounding—as children do, some more than others. In those days she even talked of weddings when she and her father would go to Mass at a small Catholic church in the Tremé neighborhood. They went because, like Ariel, the church itself proved prophetic: It miraculously (and surreptitiously) had initiated practices encouraged by the Second Vatican Council some years before the council even existed—that is, the Catholic priest and congregation celebrated Mass with vibrant gospel music. Experiencing the music as if they were at a concert in which they could participate, she and Franky celebrated right along with the congregation. The setting, meanwhile, moved Ariel to sporadically speak of weddings in churches.

As she grew up, whenever Bobbi and her father were together, she adopted *When are you two gonna get married?* as her personal mantra, even into preadolescence, the time of first crushes, when love is first understood and misunderstood. To be sure, she was third-generation Fritz, every bit as stubborn as her father and her grandfather before him.

CHAPTER 17

THE END OF the wait, the one that lasted almost forever, came on a Tuesday afternoon. Bobbi had just left, after bickering with him about what was wrong with the band and how maybe it was time for her to just up and go to South Bend to live with her Aunt Jess. Calling on the thousands of mundane hours they'd spent together, the leaders used bickering to get past their one-night union, which neither had mentioned. There was no need to.

So when the screen door opened and slapped shut with a cadence it had forgotten— *squeak,* one, two, *slap*—he wasn't in the greatest of moods, even though he now was trying to busy himself by making futile attempts at throwing out old things. He had just discovered a junkyard cornet underneath the kitchen sink, where its dulled brass, all splotched with black, lay nestled amid the plumbing pipes in a seeming tangle. He knelt there by the sink, holding it in his hands. Music, as usual, made his mind drift.

"Daddy, I'm home."

The voice broke the fleeting trance. Or maybe it entered the trance. Her inflection rendered the words neither an announcement nor an exclamation—just a simple statement, almost a question. The house hung quiet for a few beats. Franky dared not answer, for fear he had been hearing things.

"Daddy? Are *you* home?"

The junkyard cornet dropped out of his hand and onto the kitchen floor.

"Ariel? Is that you?"

But of course he knew it was she. There was no answer, not even the patter of footsteps on the hardwood floor coming toward him. Since she didn't come to him, he stepped forward, edging his way as one does when not wanting to be disappointed by a sight. His head slipped out of the kitchen ahead of the rest of his body, and there she was: still standing by the front door. Staying there, she seemed to question her welcome, whether the home was still hers.

"Daddy," she repeated, "I'm here."

Ariel hardly resembled herself. She looked thin underneath the clothes she wore: blue jeans with stringy tears in both knees and an oversized men's sleeveless T-shirt caked with some sort of engine oil or gunk, the shirt's loose fit making her already petite, braless breasts even smaller. Her brown hair, which couldn't have been washed in ten days' time, hung unkempt save for the ponytail that gathered a weak majority of her locks. The urge to embrace her was only Franky's second thought. His first came out of his mouth:

"You look terrible."

She looked down as if noticing herself for the first time and then started to mumble something about the car breaking down somewhere in New Mexico, and there being no money left, and—and—

And she burst into tears. With arms open, she stumbled over and embraced him, or let him embrace her. She was sorry, she said between sobs, sorry she didn't write or call except for a few times. At first she was angry with him for talking to Evan the way he had, and then after she stopped being angry...well, a lot of time had passed and so by then the habit of not writing or calling had formed, until finally—when she really wanted to talk—she was embarrassed about not being in touch and not having anything, and so on and so on. In the early part of the trip, Evan had caught on with a band, and then he caught on with another. But then the gigs dried up and he got dropped because music is a business and money was tight and the sax part of the group's sound was an afterthought anyway.

"I think Evan was just dreaming about the Fillmore," she said. Franky raised his eyebrows at the hint of bitterness in her voice. And then, at the thought of him, she added: "Oh—damn that *Evan!*"

Franky didn't say a thing, but a faint smile surfaced, betraying the appropriate reaction to his daughter's sobbing story of hardship.

"I couldn't have said it better myself," he murmured.

Not hearing, she continued. As for her own art, she had sold exactly one piece in two years, and that was accomplished only when a desperation for cash hardened her enough to use flirtation. Feigning keen interest in the profile of a youthful businessman at an adjacent café table, she sketched him with colored chalks and then handed him the portrait as "a gift, for five dollars." She and Evan survived without shelter for some time, living on the street right along with the hippies, as Franky had heard the suited anchorman call them on the television news. Near the end of her odyssey she reached a point where she had nothing to eat and even resorted once to panhandling when she achieved the human nadir of growing weak from hunger.

Her tears having emptied by the time the story ended, Ariel released a long breath, signaling she had let it all out.

"You were right," she said. "The old ways are better."

Franky, who had been listening with his eyes closed, nodded and smiled. "It's okay, dear," he said. "You're home."

Now they sat together on the couch, close and silent.

Calm, she started up again, saying how home was where she needed to be and how she still wanted to pursue art in some way. But she would do it by going to college—at home in New Orleans—and then maybe even going for her master's of fine arts "like this girl I met in San Francisco," after which she would enjoy teaching while still doing her own projects on the side.

Franky drank it all up, beaming with every vision she painted—and every new word about the future spoken without Evan's name. "You sound like me," he said in a moment of reverie. "I once dreamed of an artistic life that included schoolteaching."

She stared across the room to a wall, another canvas for the vision of her own future she painted. What a worthwhile life, she said—creating art and working with kids at the same time. Then she turned back to him, putting her hands on his knees. Would he support her in her pursuit?

"Of course, my dear!" Barely able to contain his glee, he gushed about how the college savings he had built up for her through the years remained untouched because he knew she would use it some day. "You always have a home, dear," he said. "You always have my support."

"Oh, Daddy!"

They embraced again, her head falling on his chest while she tapped a different reservoir of tears, the one tapped by happiness. "Oh my dear," he said, in near tears himself, "I'm so glad you're home. You know I would help you in any way I can, I'd do anything for my little girl." They stayed like that for a little while, just enjoying each other, snatching a speck of the time lost over the last two years. Franky smiled in contentment. The moment was so sentimental it recalled the days when Ariel used to be glued either to him or the new television.

"Yes, father knows best," he said almost in reverie. "Good name, terrible program."

But the funny thing was, as the great band historian Joe pointed out, as much as Franky hated that show, its radio and television run coincided almost perfectly with the band's best days. Joe, therefore, insightfully reasoned: If nostalgia inspired the program's success, nostalgia had something to do with the band's heyday too. Franky didn't talk to Joe for hours after that.

Franky slapped his knees and got up from the couch. "I'm so sorry you had to learn the hard way from Evan," he said, headed off to the kitchen for a glass of water and beaming at the notion of being right on the most important matter in the world: his daughter. "The opposite sex will always let you down. But not your father. Your father will never let you down!"

Ariel, who was now resting her cheek on the back of the couch with knees to chin, lifted her head and gave him a quizzical look. "Evan?"

A guffaw bubbled out of Franky. "I see you've completely put him out of your mind," he said, "which is for the best, of course."

She didn't answer until he came back, glass of cold water in hand.

"What are you saying about Evan?"

"Well," he said, shrugging. "I didn't want to be so direct, but it's good that he's gone."

She looked at him, squinting as if she didn't know the language he spoke.

"What is it, dear?"

"I don't think you understand," she said. "Evan and I came out of this stronger than ever. Now we know for sure what we always knew deep down: Our love is forever."

Franky later said he remembered the grandfather clock, the one his parents gave as a wedding gift long ago, *tocking* three times before he could reply; it was if he could feel a stroke coming on.

"But—" He stopped before pushing on. "But you haven't mentioned him. You cursed his name."

Her head lowered. "I've missed you, Daddy," she said quietly.

She spoke in hushed tones, muted either by a need to reset the moment or by the sadness of standing between two sides. Taking a deep breath, she reminded him of how she had walked through the door after two years, and they had so much to say, there were things they needed to work through. Sitting up to look him straight in the eye, she said, "Right now this moment has been about us. Just us."

Franky glanced away. Her hands slapped her knees and her voice lightened, yet stayed firm.

"But now that the subject of Evan has come up, we might as well talk about him," she said. "In fact, you might as well get used to hearing about him, and you'd better get used to him being around."

Never mind that Evan was still around; something else had just happened now. In a single moment, the room had spun around exactly 180 degrees from the position it had occupied forever. Stealing his spot at the podium, she had become the lecturer, the one with the wise tone. Franky was now standing before her, still clutching his glass.

"I raised her for twenty years only to take this role?" he said to the air.

Since he hadn't sat down, she pulled his arm until the dazed man dropped onto the couch. Some of the water sloshed over the side of the glass, wetting the cuff of his tux. Once sitting, he took a sip that forced his Adam's apple out when he swallowed, and she put her hand on his knee. But in spite of the gesture, she kept on with the unsavory words she was forcing him to ingest.

Evan and she had been through so much together, she began. They'd had some wonderful times out west, moments that glistened, when they both knew they were living in the middle of a stillframe in history in which no one who took part would ever forget: the air, the music, the community, the peace and love, which were two words that when put together didn't seem a cliché back then. But they also had weathered some terrible times too. There was no food, no money, no place to sleep except in the park, "and that was supposed to be cool, but I found out I like beds." In the end, "after the good times and bad," they came out of all the struggles stronger than ever—and wiser and more mature than before. Now it was time to act on that wisdom—"a wisdom of ages," she called it.

Dizzy from the room having turned around 180 degrees, he had been listening with his mouth locked half open. But *wisdom of ages* did it—he rolled his eyes and came to.

"Oh, come on," he said, swinging his piano man's index finger to interrupt. "Don't give me that baloney."

But she beat him to the starting line of speech, opening her mouth before he could continue. And what came out—the blasphemy she spoke—all the forces of the universe should have joined together to hold down, keep stuffed inside her, as far as Franky was concerned. The universe, however, was not on Franky's side these days, neither in music nor family.

"Like I told you, we're embracing tradition," she said, forcing a mood shift by scooting to the edge of the couch. "We're getting married!"

* * *

THEY TOURED AND toured. Always on the road, they drove their way into the years considered the band's apex, which came long after other big bands had died but mostly before a president was killed. A three-car caravan was replaced with an old bus that Franky bought up in South Bend through a connection of Aunt Jess's. The lone bus on the car dealer's lot, the salesman told him, had been owned by a Chicago swing band that sold it to the dealer after falling into financial trouble and eventually going to the grave where all the rest of the swing bands lay. "Perfect," said Franky, handing over the cash after a fair amount of haggling. "It's in the music family, so I know it will be good to us."

With referrals came connections and with connections came more gigs. They kept pushing their way farther east and then north, in the summertime making it as far as New England and Maine, where they played under outdoor band shells near Atlantic beaches that sported swirling rides and dirty boardwalks, or at Massachusetts amusement parks with whitewashed roller coasters and cinder-block dancehalls that shook when the coaster trains roared above. The band bus—with its old-time body that sported a curvy, bowed hood below the windshield—chugged up and down the East Coast, through New Rutherford and New Haven in the North, and Birmingham and Rockingham in the South. They hit their old haunts in the Midwest, swinging their way through South Bend and Gary and clear on to Omaha, and in between adding Minneapolis and Albany on their relentless club-date circuit. They got stuck in a traffic jam going through Des Moines and picked up a hobo when they bought their six bucks' worth of gas at a station in Dayton. Franky and his players even reached the West Coast, making it to clubs within just a few miles—but never within the city limits—of hip San Francisco. They played so much and worked so hard that gigs blurred together even though they had a howling old time at each and every one. On one of those blurry tour stops, somewhere between the Midwest and the West, they crossed paths with a nondescript fellow who entertained Franky with his verbal cool to such a degree that Franky thought he was a musician. But the guy said he wasn't, that he "just understood music like a musician, that's all." The fellow also complimented Franky on the band's performance.

"I dig you guys," he said, sounding surprised at his own reaction. "Your sound is dead—it's obsolete, man—but somehow you cats are still hot."

Struck by the young man's musical insight and unoffended by the part about their dead sound, Franky introduced himself and asked the stranger his name, which caused the guy to take a long drag on his cigarette.

"Just call me Sal," he said. "Sal Paradise."

Not until years later, when he was thinking about San Francisco because of his long-lost daughter, did the young stranger's identity pop into Franky's mind.

"So that's who that was," he mumbled one day over coffee with Joe. "Kerouac."

The memory conjured a parallel that struck him forcefully. He commented how he'd lived a life similar to the San Francisco legend's, traveling the country and married to the road; moreover, he had done so right around the same time as Kerouac, as if he and the quintessential beatnik himself were moving along two parallel lines but never touching—except for their predestined convergence at that very moment.

"I lived the life of the legend," he said, "yet the music didn't match." Perennially a little out of sync, Franky played the music that had come before the bop and post-bop that the Beats embraced. "Typical me," he said. "Alienated even among the alienated."

As for the moniker *World-Famous*, it eventually became at least a partial truth: The band did travel to the Canadian side of Niagara Falls for an occasional gig, playing for honeymooners who embraced dated music because they were in love, in a lodge made of logs that featured a giant picture window overlooking the falling water. And boy, was that a sight for the band members, because water didn't fall in Louisiana except for when it rained. Like clock time, the bayous flowed so slowly that the human eye could watch them all day and see not a drop of water move.

The fact that the group had grown so popular in many towns across the country caused occasional confusion and even disappointment among tourists who would journey to New Orleans on holiday and inquire about the World-Famous Franky Fritz Band. "Franky Fritz Band?" some local bartender or waiter might respond.

"Who dat?" The truth was, the band filled a market void in midsized cities still hungry for a place to dance at a moment in time when real dance music was quieting. There was no outfit out there exactly like the Franky Fritz Band, which played non-New Orleans music with a New Orleans spark and sported a front man and front woman who spiced up the show with fisticuffs spirited through melody. Fans latched onto the *Direct from New Orleans* moniker, claiming they could hear the exotic Louisiana bayou in the band's pulsing blasts of rhythm and sound—and maybe they could. But most patrons came just to dance and have a good time, because that's what the Franky Fritz Band was all about.

Thus, as jazz, innovative by definition, steamed ahead, Franky succumbed to arrested development, which ended up being good for his career. Some acquaintances said his paralyzed preferences had something to do with Muriel, that his music was locked into the era when they were together in high school, but others brushed aside this notion on the grounds that it was common for musical taste to freeze in time like a glacier at the exact moment that marks a person's coming of age. Whatever the reason, Franky just plain loved that era of jazz as well as earlier sounds, starting with his beloved Bix Beiderbecke.

To some extent he did appreciate where jazz was going, though. At one point, word got to Franky that he needed to go see a certain player. "You're a horn man," one musician told Franky. "You've got to go see Miles." The musician making the recommendation, in fact, played sax in Miles Davis's band and had become a friend in passing to Franky, for they ran into each other occasionally on the road. And so once on a free night during a long tour, Franky did catch a Miles show in New York City.

He loved every note. Franky subsequently touted Miles's genius to anyone who would listen—but then he would always add a side comment, wistful in its rhetoric: "Why can't folks love the new and the old styles too?"

Franky's friend the sax player, meanwhile, played on with Miles. But Lee Konitz nevertheless must have empathized with Franky's point of view. Some years later, he expressed regret about turning down a chance to play with Goodman, and from that regret he spoke a great truth. In an interview, Konitz said that "a first love always occupies a special place."

(That succinct and eloquent statement would live on—but the funny thing was, through the years its meaning erroneously evolved, leaving the music context behind: Purveyors of love stole the quote for use on romantic greeting cards and other sentimental pieces that could be sold in the marketplace.)

In spite of the changing times, the Franky Fritz Band flourished, not least because of the enigmatic allure of Franky himself. Onstage he would always say something counter to the mood, which somehow made the audience love him more. When the fans cheered after a particularly hot number, he might utter through the microphone with not a trace of emotion: "Would the journalists please stop throwing things." (Of course, there normally were no journalists in the audience.) Or over wild applause he might say something enigmatic yet strangely perfect in its timing: "Thank you, thank you. For the music that comes through me I owe everything to my second cousin Evangeline, who taught me how to make gumbo." Instead of simmering down the crowd with such a monotone delivery, somehow the confusing remarks (and sensual reference to food and exotic Louisiana) only augmented the energy that the band had built. Even at the beginning of the evening, before he'd captured the audience between his two spindly magician's hands, he might say something like: "I have a special announcement from the fire marshal and the dogcatcher: Absolutely no pets are allowed in the facility." After pausing a moment to see the crowd of perplexed patrons, he added: "The problem, you see, is that my playing draws animals to me like St. Francis." His arrogance was of the kind that did not repulse but instead confused and magnetized. But it was not only words that captivated them. His allure also had all the more to do with how he moved across the stage, floating coolly, almost ethereally, about his bandmates, somehow defying the hot tempo of the tune they were playing, as if the air—electric with jazz—were too much for his feathery weight to overcome. More than a man, he looked to be an apparition. Franky was coming to the point when he was at the height of his musical powers, when his very being was almost pure music. Inside every note he blew were the million he'd played and heard before, and so all the notes he ever knew welled up from inside him at every performance. In fact, the million notes of his history welled up not only in every present note he played, but in the silent space between those notes as well. He learned literally thousands of songs and taught hundreds of them to the band, for his musical memory was second to none. Some said too that even though he was over her, Muriel's memory gave his playing a certain edge that was unique to him alone. Yet in spite of all the success both musical and professional, those closest to him said a secret sense of earthly estrangement nevertheless weighed upon him. Here was a man recognized in dozens of towns across America but almost unknown in his own, a New Orleans musician who didn't play New Orleans music, a near-jazz virtuoso who didn't play the jazz of his time, and a young man who preferred being old.

DURING MORNINGS OFF the road, father and daughter enjoyed the various paces of a home ritual: a hot breakfast, followed by Franky shaving and washing up as Ariel drew on scratch paper, bounced around on his bed, looked at a book, sang to a record, or lay on her back chattering to herself about random thoughts passing through. As part of the permanent backdrop at home, the picture of Muriel still sat nearby on his nightstand. Franky once confided that at first the photo hurt because it was of his first girl, then it haunted because it had become a ghost, and then finally it generated nothing at all because it had become a piece of paper. When Ariel got old enough to start asking questions about it—if only absentmindedly since it had been there all along—Franky tossed it in the trash can. Eventually he would tell her the truth, which he had learned via word of mouth years before: Ariel's mother had died as a result of a fascination with ice. That is, having deserted steamy New Orleans for a new life after her pregnancy, she had moved up to a second cousin's home in Cleveland, and one cold day she was drawn by the allure of the cold, hard surface of a great lake, one that recalled Lake Pontchartrain back home for its sightless horizon. As it turned out, the surface was not as solid as it appeared because the harshest part of winter, the period that hardened cold water, had yet to arrive. She fell through.

So for opposing reasons, home was just as blissful as the road for Franky, where he saw America changing and growing fast. New Orleans, by contrast, was his haven of stability that stayed pretty much the same, even though the expanding city was crawling out to the alluring water of Lake Pontchartrain and the low-lying lakefront, which soon would be 100 percent safe from storms, thanks to the hard work of the levee board and the dollars from the national government that supported their big project.

"It's true New Orleans is growing too," he said to Joe one morning over coffee at their favorite pastry shop. "But everything still stays the same. This is the only place in all of America where everything stays the same."

CHAPTER 18

ARIEL WASN'T GIVING up. How mature she'd become, Bobbi and everyone agreed, how patient she was with him, how she tried to reason with her father even when he behaved like a child.

"It's official," proclaimed Bobbi. "The roles have been reversed!"

Weeks had passed since her return, and every time Ariel had tried to broach the topic again, Franky either changed the subject or gave a reason for needing to go out. Then one day when he came back from one of his increasingly frequent walks, she was there waiting for him. He headed straight for the balcony and she followed a minute later, holding two glasses of iced tea—a gesture of peace and an invitation to chat that took physical form. Franky sat in his wooden rocker, gazing through the Spanish-balcony railing of black cast-iron branch designs and down on the lazy activity of the more residential lower Quarter. The *klock* of a horse on pavement grew louder in the distance until it appeared with a carriage trailing it, rounding the corner where sat the pharmacy that hadn't changed in more than fifty years, although the soda-fountain counter and spinning stools, bolted to the floor with such strength that no one bothered to take them out, had been retired the year before. The carriage driver was telling the thirtysomething tourist couple seated behind him some historical lie about the pharmacy's previous incarnation, long before even the days of the soda jerk: Marie Laveaux's secret hideaway where she concocted potions of love and death. The little building over on Bourbon Street that most tourists and residents knew as Laveaux's, the driver said, indeed was hers as well, but this place was where she did her really powerful work. "Dat's where she got downda bidness!" the driver barked, turning around to bulge his eyes at the couple. They both leaned forward, listening intently to the histrionic driver, with not a speck of skepticism. Franky had once said he got the idea of peddling fantastic New Orleans legends around the rest of the country by hearing the carriage drivers spin their own tales of the Crescent City.

"God, it's hot out," said Ariel after watching the carriage man wipe his brow with a handkerchief folded into a square. Settling in the rocker next to him, she muttered something about San Francisco being cool. "Why don't you come in and we can talk?"

"I've always known your spirit wasn't from here." He took a swig from his glass. "I'm not even sweating. If you were from New Orleans, you wouldn't complain about the heat that way."

"It's your fault, you know. It's all that time I spent on the road away from here."

"Right." He gave a firm nod, staring across the way. "I never should have let you spend so much time on the road. Maybe then you wouldn't have traveled for two years with a rock musician."

Ariel gave a sigh and then turned to him. "Look, I need you for something," she said, sitting on the edge of her rocker.

Franky turned his head, his face softening on hearing words he hadn't heard from her in so long. Then he turned back away. "You're all grown up now. I didn't think you needed me for anything."

"Come on, Daddy. I need you for the wedding, for a—a *practical* reason. Practical's good, right?"

"How can there be anything *practical* about love? In fact, marriage is even less practical than love—because it tries to make love practical! How practical is that?"

She didn't answer at first, and Franky went back to staring across the street at the opposite balconies, where plants grew for miles out of pots and cascaded down the cast-iron railings like a jungle only partly tamed.

Then she knocked the wind out of him with a request that some call the greatest honor of fatherhood. Still sitting on the edge of her rocker, Ariel grabbed his hand with both of hers. "Daddy, I want you to walk me down the aisle," she said.

At first he acted as if he hadn't heard her. The black cast-iron balcony railings across the street were still there to look at, and they always would be. But when he did speak, he answered with the coldness of rhetoric:

"How can I walk you down the aisle when I don't believe in love?"

Her head dropped. Tears had already formed in the corners of her eyes when she said, "But I have no one else."

Those tears, only two or three, didn't soften him. Instead, like an allergic response to good medicine, they forced the opposite effect, triggering a rant. "My God, you *have* become a traditionalist, haven't you?" he said. "How could you ask me to do such a thing?" He went on from there: It was as if she hadn't heard a word he'd spoken all her life. He had raised her the best he could. Worked tirelessly to impart the wisdom that would serve her through the harshness of life. Toiled and toiled to teach her what he had learned. He had done it all for her!

"I thought I'd given you the most precious thing," he said, throwing up his arms. "I thought I'd given you what would protect you."

He had taught her love's falsity with devout fervor—and doing it through the kind of repetition one would employ when teaching the times tables:

> *... There is no such thing as love ...*
> *... There is no such thing as love ...*
> *...There is no such thing as love ...*

And he had done this—irony or no—out of *love*!

But instead of being touched by his conjuring her childhood, Ariel winced at the recollection. She shook her head and waved her hands as if shaking off a bad memory.

"Even during all the years I believed you about that," she said, "I still never liked when you actually said it."

EACH OF THE ensuing days, Franky gave a different reason why she couldn't marry "that Evan." One moment Evan couldn't be trusted because he had left jazz to play rock. The next moment, the reason might be more general: He was a musician and musicians weren't to be trusted.

"So I guess that means I can't trust you," she answered. "I should never have trusted your wacky advice."

As he tied his shoes and prepared to leave for a morning walk while Ariel finished her coffee and hurried about the place to go somewhere herself, Franky was muttering his latest set of protests—now he said something about how she and Evan weren't "the proper age."

Judging by her looks, that almost seemed true. Practically overnight, with a shower and shampoo, a good night's sleep in the clean sheets of her girlhood bed, and a fresh pair of clothes taken from her old dresser, she had transformed from that of a sad homeless woman to a fresh-faced, almost childlike Ariel. It was strange, though. Bobbi, for one, observed how one moment she looked at her and saw a sparkling young girl but then the next, a mature woman stood before her. In either light, "my little girl" looked more beautiful than ever, she said.

"Tell me I'm too young to get married," said Ariel. At this particular moment she was looking every bit a woman. "I dare you, Franky."

Standing near the doorway, he looked up at his daughter. Ariel had planted herself between him and the door, and she was demanding an answer.

He dismissed the notion with a wave of his hand. "No, you're not too young," he finally said. "You're too old. Love, my dear, is for the young."

The full extent of love was a childhood crush, he said, nothing but a childhood crush. And now she was going to marry *Evan the rock musician.* Since she blocked his path, he went on like this in a mindless musical solo—a bad one, the indulgent kind—until Ariel had had enough.

"Daddy, it's up to you whether you want to witness your own daughter's wedding."

Jolted out of his gritty solo, he could now see that the palms of her hands were facing him in a sign of surrender. Yet as he would later tell Joe, in spite of surrender, she paradoxically seemed in total control—of herself, maybe even the room. Hands up in surrender, yes, but she faced him square, fixing her eyes on him like a teacher making a point with a student one-on-one.

"It may be up to you," she continued, "but I can promise you one thing. The wedding is going to happen, whether you're there or not. And trust me—if you don't come, you'll be the only one not there."

Then her firm calm gave way. She now was visibly holding back emotion and its symptom of tears so that she could release the final thought following her, as thoughts do, one after the other in a chain.

"And I'm not sure when I'll be able to face you after that."

Now, though, she still faced him square. But Franky refused to meet her moistening eyes. Hands dropping down, she sighed and stepped aside, allowing him to move past her and out the door.

* * *

THROUGH ALL THOSE raucous touring years, Franky never drank a drop after the night of his wedding, when his friends had taken him out to do what they considered to be the only thing to do when you get left at the altar: Drink yourself sick. That night had made him so ill that he couldn't touch booze for a long time after that, until eventually he came to see himself as a nondrinker. That in turn made the emotional link stronger: The only time he had gotten drunk, it happened to be the most wretched day of his life. Joe's mother always had said that a person who goes to bed drunk doesn't get a healthy rest. "It's because you don't dream when you sleep drunk," she said. "Did you ever hear of a drunk that had a dream?" Later in the century Mrs. Randazzo's long-held belief was verified by science, which found that alcohol impedes the stage of sleep characterized by rapid eye movements—that is, REM sleep. Franky understood Mrs. R's theory, albeit in a more practical sense than the scientific explanation given some years later. "Of course a drunk doesn't dream," he said. "He gets it all done when he's drinking, so he's got nothing left when he shuts his eyes." Whatever the reasons, whether he thought it might impede his musical creativity or whether the association with his wedding night was just too strong, Franky left the boozing to others.

If a drunk dreams only in waking hours, Franky lived like a drunk even though he never drank a drop. He poured his imagination into his music and the band, which was cruising along with happy success. Now in a near-frenetic stretch of creative flow, he busied himself writing music and reconceiving arrangements to old tunes if he wasn't on the road. Joe would come over to his apartment so that they could pound out rhythms and scribble lyrics on scraps of paper strewn about his frail coffee table while Ariel crawled and shuffled about them, sometimes tearing to shreds the scraps of paper containing song words and notes that surely would have become famous. Or when the seed of a musical idea landed in the topsoil below his scalp begging to be watered, he would charge across town on the streetcar, electric with excitement like the power lines above his head, straight to Bobbi's house to bang it out with her on the piano. Why do you bother writing? he was asked occasionally. It's not as if you'll ever get a chance to make records. Nobody is recording your kind of music anymore; you came after your own time. But Franky insisted he wrote music just because he loved it, not to sign any record deals. "What else am I going to do when I'm not on the road?" he answered. "I'm not going to waste my time on love and girls, that's for sure." And then he would add: "Besides, a lot of people like to live in the past."

He said such things even at a time when the foremost feature of the residential skyline began to consist of wash hanger-like television antennas, while below those roofs, most radios had turned from wood to plastic and their dials came in circles instead of long rectangles. Like anyone in his position would, though, Franky did harbor the dream of becoming a hit-maker. Joe dreamt the same dream a thousand times too: As boys the two friends had spent hours up in each other's bedrooms playing records while dreaming and scheming about the wildly successful music careers they would build together.

One night an opportunity for the recording fame that they always coveted opened up in Passacken, New Jersey, a scruffy but active town that lived just across the river from New York. It boasted a giant coffee-roasting plant as well as a shoe factory—the latter facility causing Franky to learn the funny town name as a child by reading the words *Passacken, N.J.* on shipment boxes countless times back in the cramped stockroom of his father's store. The area was noteworthy for another reason, one Bobbi and the boys realized only when they saw a road sign that read *Hoboken to the right*. Passacken was almost right next door to the hometown of a giant entertainer of the time whom Franky always called "the other Frank" as if the superstar Sinatra and he were equals.

Only a few years prior, the band had made their first tour stop in Passacken, in the literal shadow of the Big Apple. So just as they had made it to East Chicago, Indiana, but not Chicago, Illinois, just as they had played Newark but not New York (Newark was actually a big jazz town), just as they had come within mere miles of playing all these famous cities, the town of Passacken promised to become a standard and antiromantic tour stop for the band. From that first visit it would remain a poignant place for Franky because there he picked up a copy of *the New York Times* one morning after their gig and stumbled upon a headline in the arts section that sent a shiver through him for its reference to home. *A Streetcar Named Desire* had taken the theater community by storm not long before, and there was now talk of a movie starring Marlon Brando, who had played the lead in the Broadway production. Haunting to Franky was that he had so often taken the *real* Desire streetcar to get to Muriel's house. Meanwhile, *Streetcar* the play was a story of warped love—and so, like *Great Expectations*, the Tennessee Williams work proved yet another blow to literature for Franky.

That association with Passacken never completely left him in spite of the good fortunes the town later brought. Those fortunes came when a certain fellow happened to be in the audience at one of the band's gigs, and yet he was nobody special: just some guy bored on a Thursday night, looking for something to do with his girl in a place no one would know him. This man, who favored talking out of the corner of his mouth to appear important, had driven over from Manhattan, beyond the world he inhabited so that he could be with the girl, who stood silently beside him. He explained as much to Franky; surely a touring musician could relate to a man's natural needs. "I got an old lady in the city," he said in muted tones. "Nobody'll see us here."

Franky rolled his eyes and started to move on, but the man tapped him on the shoulder. Hold on, he said, he had something to tell the bandleader that he wouldn't want to miss. Bored, Franky turned back around to face the hanger-on.

"I got a friend in the business," he said out of the corner of his mouth as if only Franky should be privy. "You should talk to him."

What the man was saying was, he knew a record producer. Truly he was someone who believed you could be important by association: First, he had sought out the bandleader—the room's center of attention along with Bobbi—and now he was dropping names.

Franky merely gave an "Oh, really?" before heading back up to the bandstand a few moments later, and that was that. But the next time the band passed through town the story picked up where it had left off. "Some cat wants to talk to you," Al told Franky when they were in between sets. Grumbling that he was tired, Franky shuffled out in front of the stage, where the same man was waiting alone. He told Franky he'd brought along "that guy in the business I was telling you about" and pointed to a figure standing in back with arms folded and his coat and fedora still on. Something about the way he stood told Franky this was no joke. When the time came to start the final set, he ordered his bandmates to "add some Tabasco like never before" to their playing, giving them a stern "trust me, fellas" look. Mostly they just shrugged; Franky was always telling them to do something or other for no apparent reason much like a coach telling his team to perform nonsensical exercises in practice. But of course Joe the worrier had to ask why. To keep the drummer's nerves from manifesting, Franky said only, "Because I have a friend in the audience."

At the end of the show, the man who talked through the side of his mouth introduced Franky to Sid Simeo, "the guy in the business." "I hope you enjoyed the show," said Franky, waiting for a verbal reaction to the band's performance.

"You were okay," Simeo answered with a shrug.

Joe, who had overheard some of this conversation and figured out who it was, stood in the background nearly in tears.

"We're better than okay," said Franky, putting one of his business cards in Simeo's palm. "We're from New Orleans."

Sid Simeo scoffed with a listless look on his face. "You were okay," he repeated. And then, just like the acquaintance who had introduced him, he said he had to "go and meet my girl I got on the side." The two men's respective affairs had made them friends.

So much for catching the ear of a big-city record producer. Disappointed himself, Franky tried to console Joe, telling him that the guy probably wasn't even a producer anyway. "*New* York and *New* Orleans, they're both very old in spite of their names," he explained. "And so they both have a lot of crooks."

So by the time the band got back home two weeks later, the shunning record producer had slipped far out of their minds. The morning after their return, Franky sat at his kitchen table going through the tall stack of mail that inevitably collected during tours. As a tool for this tedious process he had taken to using a letter opener made of "simulated whale ivory," as the engraved lettering said, a memento he'd bought at a regular tour stop in the coastal Massachusetts city where the only remnant of its glorious whaling past was a one-room museum and a statue of Captain Ahab standing in a grassy spot between two forking streets. The letter opener aided Franky in working through the tall piles that collected, but the task nevertheless always left him crotchety toward the end. This was his state when he came across, tucked toward the bottom of the pile, a typed envelope with a New York City return address. Opening it, he found a business letter, also typed, signed at the bottom by none other than Sid Simeo. The record producer would like to record some sessions with the band, the letter said.

Simeo wasn't anyone important, the band would learn once they looked into the man's background. Sure, he was legitimate, but not unlike the Franky Fritz Band, he was anything but big-time. For years he'd been cruising at an altitude of pressurized survival, suspended just above music-biz failure by limp breaths of a regional hit here and there, yet held down from further ascension by the rushing jet stream of unqualified success. But that didn't keep Franky from taking advantage of the opportunity. "We can sell records out of the back of our bus if we have to," he said. "We can sell them at our shows." So the band did go into the studio with Simeo, and they did get in some productive sessions; Simeo met them out in Los Angeles, where he also had some "personal business"—that is, he mentioned to Franky once they were out there, "another girl on the side." The band, by now flush with cash, made a little vacation of the trip, taking the Sun West Railroad out there because an advertisement in one of Franky's geographic magazines boasted how the trains sported a Vista Dome.

The best in the bag of singles they recorded: "My Baby's Gonna Cry," their old standby, their crowd favorite. More than a few copies of the single ended up selling and not just out of the back of the band's bus. The tune became a minor hit, charting for a brief three weeks, driven by their base of fans in second-, third-, and fifth-tier cities across the country. More significantly, it generated greater attention and loyalty among the band's followers in each of its staple tour towns. Franky had always dreamed of buying a home in the

French Quarter, and as the composer of the song receiving royalties, he soon thereafter realized his dream, even purchasing one with an automatic dishwasher. That was about the time that Joe and Marcie bought their place too, a lovely two-story home buried under the shade trees of a side street in Mid-City, a block from Bayou St. John. Continuing his preoccupation with two-wheeled transportation, Joe even bought himself a RoadKing scooter, which he would ride to each end of the city limits back and forth five times, from the Mississippi River to Lake Pontchartrain, whenever he wasn't on tour. Even though the band's good luck had started in New Jersey, Joe—who some said could occasionally be almost clairvoyant in his random insights—linked their success to New York. "We had good luck here because New York is like New Orleans," he said on one trip. He went on to explain: Their names both began with *New* even though they were both old, New Yorkers' way of talking reminded him of all the folks he knew back home even though New Orleans resided in the deep South, and both cities were "surrounded by swamp."

"Heck," he concluded during one tour, "I'm surprised they don't got gators up here."

There were gators lurking in the waters surrounding the band, though—namely, another musical phenomenon. A hint of this came when Franky and Joe stopped by a music shop off Canal Street to see how their record was selling. As they passed through the doors, they saw a familiar face in the window—on a poster. The big, friendly mug in the portrait photo gazed back at them in black-and-white.

"That's him!" said Franky, gazing at the serious countenance. "That's the one I never liked."

At the bottom of the poster, it read

New Orleans' Own: Fats Domino

They didn't know the young man staring right back at them as Fats Domino, though. It was Antoine Dominique, Alvin Stokes's shy friend who had awed them at rehearsal that one evening. Franky and Joe raced into the record store and asked the man behind the counter to play the new Fats record for them.

"Everyone wants to hear it," said the bored shopkeeper. "They say radio stations are playing it as far as Detroit." Then the man, who looked tired and ready to retire, added, "Everyone's going for that race music nowadays."

As they listened, Joe nodded his head and tapped his foot, but Franky shook his head.

"It's good," he said. "It's different, and it's good. Now I know why I never liked him."

But Franky was cooking up his own music during those days. Life and music at this point were one in the same, for music was all he lived. His playing was so potent that on occasion respected musicians from regions the band played might stop in and catch a gig. Often they would award the man in the tux the compliment of all compliments for a jazz player:

"He's one bad motherfucker."

CHAPTER 19

MOST FOLKS DESIRE the life gift of finding a rock—someone who stays the same through all the years and in spite of all swirling, surrounding circumstance. That person may serve as confidante or counsel but not necessarily so; a rock is simply consistent, both in action and interaction, as a friend or when observed. Of course a rock is born by perception; moreover, any gift can be misunderstood or conjured for misuse.

Ariel had turned her back on Franky, and now Bobbi (who seemed to take the opposite side on everything these days) was siding with her. So it was no surprise that at this point he called on his best friend the harmonious drummer. He summoned Joe to the haven of the French pastry shop where they met for coffee some mornings in between tours—although he didn't really summon him since they probably would have gone anyway. More and more they seemed like retirees, drinking coffee in a shop at home instead of a diner on the road.

The moment the bandleader stepped up to the table, he started venting to his seated friend, who had already ordered two coffees for the both of them. How could the two people closest to him expect him to participate in something he had renounced? How could he bless a life-altering mistake that his own daughter was about to make? Could Joe believe it?

But when he paused to allow his friend to insert a consoling remark, Joe refused. "I think you should do this one small thing for your daughter and go to her wedding," he said. "Make her happy and walk her down the aisle." When he got only a glare back, he added, "You can be pretty stubborn ya'know, Franky."

The Mad Soloist reacted as though the drummer had just sworn allegiance to rock music. In that moment, something had changed about Joe, or at least about their relationship. First Ariel, then Bobbi, and now Joe?

"She's going crazy and rebelling," he answered, overlooking the comment. "That's what she's doing—just like all the kids are doing these days. She's going to go and ruin her life by rebelling." Franky lamented that everything around him had changed these last few weeks. His daughter was getting married. Folks were throwing hints at Franky that it was time to break up the band. Bobbi was acting funny; maybe she'd be the first one to quit.

"Even you've changed, Joe," he added. "You're speaking up."

The drummer ignored the comment because his mind still mulled over Franky's take on Ariel. Joe could be philosophical at times, everyone knew, zinging profound statements during random moments and with no self-awareness. "But, Franky," he said, "if she's rebelling, she's doing it by acting old-fashioned—she's getting married to her sweetheart, just like they always did."

Franky didn't respond, instead raising his brows in a half-listening way to consider the notion. Meanwhile, Joe, never good in math or logic, added up in his head what he had just said, number by number.

"If you go by the old ways," the drummer wondered aloud, "can that still be rebelling?"

Franky paused to consider that one. Maybe his friend had a point, he said: Ariel's behavior was all his fault because "the values I taught her were ahead of my time." If he only had taught her how *wonderful* love and marriage were, he reasoned aloud, she would have dismissed the notions and instead devoted her energies to fighting institutions with the rest of her generation, rather than embracing them. He was in the middle of one of his introspective soliloquies now, speaking as if Joe wasn't even there. The drone went on, like a whirring top, and Joe, unable to get in a word, didn't interrupt for a while. Then finally:

Clink!

Franky stopped. Joe had slammed his empty cup on the table with such force that it made a jarring crash, like a judge calling order.

"Forget all that stuff for a change, willya?"

After he spoke, the sudden awareness of the crashing noise of the cup seemed to surprise even Joe, for he looked around to see a few heads turned their way.

"Listen, Franky," he said, quieting his voice and leaning in a little. "Growin' up, you were always smarter than me, that ain't no secret." He stopped to smack his lips and shake his head as if he were too perturbed to finish his thought. "But I gotta tell ya. Letting your crazy wedding mess you up for the rest of your life has got to be the stupidest thing I ever seen."

Franky's mouth grimaced shut and his neck cocked back like a coiling snake. No one had spoken so directly to him about what everyone knew, the reality that didn't require an expensive psychologist to figure out. But Joe wasn't finished. His pithy phrasing shrunk still further in length, only to gain in power.

"Just because your wedding got ruined, it don't mean you gotta ruin it for your daughter!"

The bandleader's body had turned to stone. When it showed signs of movement, it came only in the form of a couple of jerks. He spoke into his empty cup.

"I once thought my own wedding would be the death of me," he said. "But instead it's my daughter's that will do me that favor."

Joe let out a frustrated sigh. "There you go with your sayings again."

When Franky looked up, he saw that his friend was shaking his head with his arms folded across his chest. "Jeez, even my best friend is deserting me," he said, disgusted. "Next thing you know, you'll say you want to break up the band too, just like Bobbi keeps hinting at."

It was meant only as an aside, a half-serious statement. Yet Joe's eyes widened. The off-the-cuff remark turned into one of those pregnant moments when a loaded topic is grazed. Avoiding Franky's eyes, Joe gave a shrug. That was his only response.

"Why don't you just tell me right now?" said Franky, leaning over the table. "Do you want to be a part of the next generation of the Franky Fritz Band or not?"

Head bowed, Joe said in almost a whisper, "Sometimes you gotta know when to end a good thing."

Franky set down his empty cup with a *chink*, crumpled up his paper napkin, and tossed it on the table. "Well, what do you know," he said, nodding. "You *are* deserting me."

Joe could only shrug again. The drummer put his hands to his knees to rise up out of his chair and muttered something about Marcie expecting him. Then, to Franky's horror, he sighed and mentioned the last good song the bandleader had written—horrifying to Franky because the title served as terrible parting words:

"'Bye-bye… Forever.' That's a good tune, I'll give you that."

The drummer had paid a compliment, but the title left Franky speechless. It kept coming from the mouths of all. Before he could answer, Joe waded off, his person dwarfing the little café tables and chairs that he squeezed by, while Franky sat alone, an empty cup with a coffee stain on its side sitting before him.

The Mad Soloist now stared out the window, where Joe reentered his picture-frame of sight, taking pause before starting his trek home. The drummer, Franky's lifelong backbeat, shook his head in slow rhythm and shuffled off.

* * *

HE NEVER HAD a woman, although he had plenty of women. When the band started enjoying some road success, the ladies started coming to him like lured dragonflies, and he was there waiting, happy to feel nothing, which is what he had learned from his encounters with Sondra. The skinny stick of a man, with his terse ways that somehow sprinkled mystery, drew women to him almost at every stop. To this group of fans nothing could be more alluring than a man with a microphone levitating above the throngs, thanks to the mundane prop of a three-foot plank stage. Each night they gazed up at the man who worked by playing, while patrons danced and drank, all under a hypnosis conjured by the playmaker who churned out fun from his instrument as if it were the wooden bucket of an ice-cream maker.

Around this time he started to hate returning to his bed at night—alone at least. After he learned from Sondra that it felt good to feel nothing, the first of the women to come his way was Betsy Thomas. They met when she and her friend Rita, both local college students and music fans in Champaign, approached him to tell him the band "was nothing special." Franky had noticed Betsy while he was playing, even though she stood far from the stage, leaning against the back wall and sharing cigarettes with her girlfriend. She hadn't so much as tapped her foot to Joey's beat; that's what first made Franky notice her. But she stayed, not because she and her friend were enjoying the music but rather they were having fun mocking it. After the final song had ended and the band started breaking down, she finally detached her shoulder blades from the back wall and sauntered over to tell him that she had been victimized by false advertising. The marquee outside had said *Direct from New Orleans*, and obviously this band didn't know what New Orleans music was all about. "It's like those signs at the carnivals," she said. The marquee, she continued, mimicked the tall claims boasting of the *World's Only Human Lizard* that allegedly slithered in a cage just inside the entrance to a dark carnival tent. "And then after you pay your thirty cents, it turns out it's nothing but a man painted green. That's you and your band: the man in the tent painted green." Besides, she said, the way Franky walked about that bandstand with his nose up in the air, he acted as if he were a musician in the purest sense. "If you think you're so cool, why do you play all that old stuff?" she said. "Bop is where it's at."

Franky told her he loved the new music but that he was doomed to playing the songs of his adolescence. And besides, he said, consider the band's unique arrangements: "Sure, we may play the old songs, but just listen to how we play them." Picking up his instrument cases to head toward the bus, he told her to come back and listen more carefully next time. She shrugged, giving a nonchalant *maybe*, but before she left she turned back around.

"I will say this," she said. "You do blow a sweet tone."

She did come back when the band came to town, although she still leaned against the back wall like the femme beatnik that she wanted to be. This time, though, when Franky glanced toward the back as he played his horn, he caught her nodding to the beat on a couple of occasions.

"I've got her," he said through the side of his mouth to Al, who was standing on stage next to him.

Just as she had before, she approached him after the show, a professor come to give him a grade. As Franky stood on the stage putting his horns into their coffins in anticipation of daylight, he glanced up with indifference. She walked as if the grade that she was about to dole out would be a failing one, and this assumed criticism somehow aroused Franky. But when she met up with him, she didn't hand over a piece of paper with a *B* or an *F*. Instead she said, "The songs you play are old, but I dig you. I can tell you're still one of us."

Her friend wasn't there that night, so what she meant by *us* was in question, although Franky assumed he knew. "Of course I'm one of you," he said, kneeling by his cases. "The question is, are *you*?"

She responded with a *What the hell are you talking about*? "I *am* us, or I wouldn't be saying *us*."

Not necessarily, said Franky. Anyone who wanted to prove who they were had to live who they were. "Betsty the Beatnik!" he said. "That's your name—Betsy the Beatnik!" She recoiled in ire when he raised the possibility that she might only be a pretender, a poseur. "I'm not sure," he said, looking her over. "I haven't quite figured you out yet." And so as Bobbi and the boys gathered their things on the stage, the pair proceeded to debate the philosophical and the abstract. Who was he to accuse her of being a pretender? she said. He claimed to be a true musician, but he merely recycled old music. To that, the twentysomething Franky said, "I may be an old man, but at least I know who I am." The conversation followed them out the door because Franky could never let go of an argument and apparently neither could she. So without breaking stride Franky handed Ariel to Bobbi for the evening and marched off with Betsy, both of them prisoners to the back-and-forth, which dragged them in cuffs block after block from the club to a twenty-four-hour diner, where they could argue more.

Eventually, the argument started to peter, as it inevitably had to at some point, and the slowing beats in the dialogue made the two cognizant of the fact that they were a strange man and a strange woman sitting together at two o'clock in the morning. Now the conversation, all this time revving with competition and coffee, started to sway more like gin. The great debate had become a dance, one tinged with the smell of impending sex.

"If you are who you say you are," said Franky, "you need to prove it to me."

She took a bored drag of her cigarette as if she didn't need to prove anything. But then she stood up from the booth and he stood up from the booth, and they slid down the street, hand in hand to his dark motel room. This night he would not have to confront his empty bed alone. He never even switched on the light and she didn't ask why.

Betsy the Beatnik came around when the Franky Fritz Band pulled back into town, and they repeated their rendezvous many times, until on one tour she didn't show up. She was merely the first, anyway—the first of many to keep Franky from having to face the emptiness of a motel bed. There was, for instance, the school of women who behaved more like Mary. For nights on end she stood at the foot of the stage gazing upward, eyes following the leader of the band as he floated about the stage, with horn and voice issuing and answering challenges with Bobbi, his nightly sparring partner of the stage. Mary looked at the pair as if she were watching a romance picture and imagining herself in the leading lady's role instead of Bobbi.

"You're a great jazz player," she said after so many nights of gazing. She had edged her way to the table where he was taking a break between sets. What aroused Franky, though—starting with his curiosity—was that the coy girl had been hiding something behind her back. Now she unveiled it, putting it before him: a Bix Beiderbecke album. "Will you sign this?" she asked. "You sort of sound like Bix."

If he had been capable of love, she would have won it right then. Instead, Bix Beiderbecke made mild attraction turn to lust. From her perspective, meanwhile, the stage man's music and movement had left her awestruck, giving him trancelike powers over her for the entire night and making her do things she might not have done otherwise.

They came, one by one, like a string of train cars: rebellious and trendy types like Betsy, naive student music lovers like Mary, older cynics like Sondra, and a hundred other variations on a thousand themes. Regardless of personality and background, they all said of him things like "really arrogant but I could go up to him because he's so skinny," and "he's conceited, but gentle—in that musician way," and, "I wondered how those long fingers on his horn would feel on my body."

Franky struggled with insomnia most nights, which is why he said he preferred never to go to bed alone if he could help it. He did have an explanation for his own sleeplessness, whether he believed it or not himself. After being onstage and playing music (or writing it) all night, he'd already spent all his dreams long before climbing into bed. To be sure, the way Franky floated about the stage and generated song, it really was as if he were occupying a dream world, or maybe creating one. And if he had any reverie left in him after a night of playing, he most likely spent those remnants between the legs of a woman.

A child discovers everything, though. Along with all the talking coming out of Ariel was her walking. Now that she was strong on her feet, her independent soul spoke all the more. Whether in a grocery store or at the zoo not far from her grandparents' uptown home, if she desired something, if something drew her interest, she charged after it before an adult could hold her back—sending Franky, Bobbi, or even Joe scampering for her while she darted for the elephant or the tiger or the bear exhibit. She would even scamper up the zoo's famous manmade mound of dirt, Monkey Hill, the highest point in the city that was constructed to teach New Orleans children what a hill looked like.

One night on the road, before Franky had quit sex as a companion, Ariel awoke in the midst of a bad dream while staying in Bobbi's room. Her guardian for the night awoke only when she heard the clinking of metal and chain against wood. Opening her eyes, she saw Ariel, the resolute walker who always had to be watched, stretching high toward the door latch. She stood just tall enough to reach the latch on her tiptoes, Bobbi could see, and so it would have been only a matter of time before she had gotten out and left into the middle of the night.

"Honey, where in the world are you going?" said the singer, sitting up so that the covers fell to her hips.

"I want to see my daddy. I had a bad dream."

The guardian held out her arms in the darkness. "Come here, darling, come see your Bobbi."

With head bowed, little Ariel pattered toward the shadowy silhouette of comfort and climbed up at the foot of the bed. Once atop the mattress, she shifted into a speedy crawl so that in no time she lay nestled on the bosom of the singer. "Tell me about your nightmare, honey," said Bobbi. "It will help to talk about it." Ariel had dreamed of a big band, she explained, like the one her daddy and Bobbi led. Only this band of men was nothing like theirs. This was a band of goblins, and their instruments were axes and reapers. Instead of playing trumpets and trombones, they waved their tools in a chopping motion, until in unison they all stood up and left their seats to march out into the audience, where Ariel sat. At that point she experienced a common nightmare failing: Her feet had turned leaden. As hard as she tried, she couldn't flee half as swiftly as she knew she could. The grim musicians were going to get her.

"It was sort of like 'The Sorcerer's Apprentice,'" she said.

Bobbi rolled her eyes. "Your father shouldn't have been playing that for you on the hi-fi," she said. "And that *Fantasia* movie they made—that's supposed to be for kids?" Bobbi had nightmares too, she explained with empathy—they come to most everyone, but they weren't real. This very night, in fact, she herself had been having one, although she didn't want to go into details. "It was about a man," she said. "You'll learn that those are the worst kind, even when the dreams are fun." Ariel perked up on hearing the comforting fact that everyone had bad dreams, which seemed to add credibility to the assertion that they weren't real. Eventually, after having calmed her down, Bobbi said, "Would you like to sleep with me tonight?" Ariel nodded a silent yes, and so Bobbi tucked her in beside her and then turned on her side to go back to sleep.

But then Ariel's goblins came back: Once again, she climbed out of bed. She picked up a key on the nightstand—Franky always gave Bobbi a key to his room when she had Ariel—and shuffled through the darkness for the door. This time, having practiced once before, she swiftly unlatched the door and passed through it without awakening her guardian. Alone, wearing her flannel nightgown in the frigid northern darkness, she shuffled to the next door, her bare feet tapping the cold concrete of the walkway. The key turned in the lock, and Ariel peered in. Both moonlight and a beam from a parking-lot lamp streamed through the doorway as soon as she cracked it open.

Strangely, the room hardly stood still. Sheets rustled as if they lived. Perhaps one of those night goblins was attacking her father. She pushed the door open a little wider.

"Who's there?" said Franky, craning upward. "Bobbi? Is there something wrong with Ariel?" With the door wide open, light from a nearby streetlamp spilled all the way to the edge of the bed, and so Ariel could see that not one but two bodies lay there—and coming into focus now was the rising hip of a woman who lazily turned on her side. "Ariel, dear, what's the matter?"

But she didn't say what was the matter. She didn't mention her nightmare yet because a stranger was in their company.

"Daddy, why are you giving that lady nightmares?"

Slipping past the line that separated the stream of light from the darkness, Franky climbed out of bed in his boxer shorts and walked his daughter back outside with his hands on her shoulder and arm.

"Why are you giving that lady nightmares?" she repeated, her hand in Franky's while he walked her back to Bobbi's room. "You said if men stay in bed with ladies, they give them nightmares." Now they stood outside the door of Bobbi's room. Franky was gazing down at his daughter, his back bent almost to 90 degrees as in a Norman Rockwell painting of adult and child, but he still hadn't found anything to say. Ariel added: "And I know it's true, because Bobbi just told me something like that too."

That made Franky find his voice. He hadn't been giving anyone nightmares, he insisted. The lady with him was a friend, and so he was being nice to her.

"No, I don't think so," she said, refusing to accept his answer. "That's not nice."

Franky cocked back his head in reaction to her firmness.

"I wasn't giving her nightmares," he repeated. "I'm trying to *help* her with hers, just like I do for you, right?"

Finally giving Franky at least some hope, Ariel paused to take this in. But then she shook her head and folded her arms in the cold. "I don't think so," she concluded with finality. "The way she was wiggling, it looked like she was still having her nightmare."

Now Franky was forced to lie further. He was known among adults as the wizard of words, getting himself and his band out of almost any pickle, but he wasn't succeeding with his own child. Yes, he insisted, she was only moving around because she had previously been "excited by the dream." By now Franky had opened the door to Bobbi's room and guided his daughter into the doorway. Again,

Ariel contemplated his father's words, and again her response took Franky aback:

"Well, if that's really true, why don't you help Bobbi with *her* nightmares?"

This time she didn't wait for Franky to answer with another lie. Without unlocking her gaze, she pushed the door closed.

CHAPTER 20

BOBBI PICKED A good day to end it all. The rain had been coming down all morning, stopping only recently. And when the rain fell on the French Quarter, the residue of memory—which always hovered low, just above the rooftops of New Orleans in the thick air—descended down clear to ground level, carried there within the vessels of the fat Louisiana raindrops. The band saw plenty of precipitation while on the road in other places, and the sight of it would always take Franky back home. "It rains bigger in New Orleans," he often was heard saying. "The drops are bigger there, but more calm and sad."

"S'down, Franky," said Bobbi. "Right here. I got somethin' I wanna tell ya."

It was a command, not a request, even though Franky stood inside the door of his own house. Still, after she marched past him and he closed the door behind her, he obeyed: He took a seat on the couch where she pointed.

"I know what you want to talk to me about," he said, trying to seize some control. "Ariel's my daughter, and so it's none of—"

"Never mind Ariel," she interrupted, dropping down in the easy chair across from him. She perched on the chair's edge so that her fellow bandleader hovered below. "Although, how you're acting toward your little girl is disgusting."

She was so fed up with Franky and "this business about the wedding" that she couldn't even talk about it right now. Besides, "It's no use anyway," she said, "because I'm convinced you don't have a heart." Franky started to utter protests of *what do you mean*, but she told him to shut up.

"Like I was sayin,' forget Ariel. This is about us."

That quieted him. Two beats passed while they faced off, and then she jumped up and started pacing, going back and forth twice. Then, widening her shoulders and setting her hands on her hips, she stopped to face him square. With chin raised and chest out came her great announcement:

"Bye-bye forever, Franky! I'm going to the one I love."

His head tilted, eyes narrowing in puzzlement. Then, seeping over that first face came a vacant gaze. Franky slouched back into the couch like a man forty years older.

Almost to himself he uttered, "I didn't know there was someone else."

She didn't answer, letting the moment pass after having given difficult news. Or perhaps she was enjoying the effect a little. He, meanwhile, regathered his Franky front; his voice came through strong again, with that edge he had picked up only in recent years.

"So you too have given in to love, have you?"

Bobbi's jaw tightened and a crag formed between her eyes. A subtle taste of bitterness, which must have been lingering in her mouth all along, came spitting out in verbal form.

"What do you know about love?" she said.

The metronome-like grandfather clock, never having stopped talking for twenty-two years, beat on for a couple of measures.

"I don't know a thing about love," he admitted. "But I know about friendship, and you know it."

"I'm not so sure about that, Franky. After being with you for so long, I'm not so sure you know about *any* of that stuff."

She continued from there, and her talking didn't seem to go anywhere at first. Of all things, she started rambling about the state of music, her audible thoughts sounding like Franky himself as she riffed on the subject of how a rock band gives only a few musicians jobs and can still make all that noise. "Damn those amps," she said. "They make four or five people sound big. And damn all those multiple tracks they can layer in recording studios nowadays—they've got machines that make 'em sound big too." Any other time Franky would have been interjecting verbal nods of agreement, taking the ball she served him and adding a new spin to it. But he stayed in his shell and let her go on. She was going to the one she loved.

Inevitably, her ramble slowed like a car that had lost the foot on its gas pedal. She'd made her money, and so it was time to face the music and move on. Since Aunt Jess wasn't getting any younger, now was the time for her to move up to South Bend "while we both can still have some fun."

Yes, her dear Jess. It turned out that her aunt, Bobbi finally got around to clarifying, was "the one I love."

Still submerged in thought, Franky gazed vacantly in the direction of Ariel's room. "A family's love," he said, nodding in agreement yet still defeated, "the only love."

Bobbi just shrugged and neither said anything. Like the spaces between notes that form music, it was becoming a conversation of air-conditioner drones and grandfather-clock *tocks* as much as it was of words. Then Bobbi shifted gears, offering up some concrete detail to her plans. She and Aunt Jess had saved up enough money to buy the Poor Man's Palace, which was available for dirt cheap because the place had been vacant for years, after no one came to dance anymore. Franky interjected, saying it was "the stupidest idea I've ever heard" because the Poor Man could never draw a crowd for big bands these days, and so she would be throwing her money out the window.

"It would be best for you to stay here in New Orleans," he said. "Stay here at home and help me figure out how to fix the band."

"Shut up and let me explain. You might think I'm stupid, but I'm sure not going to open up a dance hall in these times."

But, she continued after being interrupted, the Poor Man "still has music in its boards." At that, Franky bucked up a bit, looking her way and listening more actively, which spurred her on to build on what she had said. That's right, the Poor Man could still be a music venue with the right owners who would be able to awaken it.

"Maybe the Franky Fritz Band could help wake it up," he said with a pensive nod.

Bobbi threw her palm his way. "No, Franky, I'm not talking about any old Franky Fritz Band playing there."

Then she offered the single detail of her and Aunt Jess's business plan that she had held back—its shock made all the more potent by how it contradicted all that she had just lamented about music.

"Aunt Jess just signed the papers for the place. We're gonna open up a rock club."

Even the air conditioner and the grandfather clock stopped. That's how Franky recalled it, anyway. His mouth roared open in a blur of words: He railed at her, calling her a turncoat and a disloyal business partner and everything else that would hurt an old friend, until finally he threw up his arms in futility because there was nothing else to do.

"Who cares what you do?" he said. "You're not the Bobbi I thought I knew!"

She must have been prepared for the reaction and she certainly knew her news would hurt him. That's probably why for the first time ever she let him speak to her that way. She didn't say a thing, and so he kept on. He might have droned on for years, a strategy that could have kept her from ever leaving for South Bend, but she knew him too well for him to succeed at that ploy, and so she finally interrupted.

"Damn it, Franky!" She threw her purse down on the floor—a last-ditch weapon that always made him stop. "Don't you get it? *You won't break up the band, so I gotta break it up for you!*"

She took a breath, which calmed both herself and the room a little. Once again she tried to elaborate on her reasons for heading off to South Bend. She was leaving because it was time to leave, and there really was nothing here for her anyway. She was tired, tired of working with the world's most stubborn bandleader, and even tired of New Orleans—tired of being drenched in sweat three seconds after leaving the house, tired of the giant cockroaches that flew in the air when they got excited, tired of the parades that closed the streets to traffic for two weeks around Mardi Gras. She was sick of this cesspool of a swamp, where the poor stayed poor, where an interstate highway now cut through the middle of the city on concrete stilts, where they now played football indoors inside a spaceship downtown, where a levee system was being built "that won't work anyway because the levee board is corrupt so their project will be too," and where racism was still as popular as music, even though the rest of the country was supposedly changing at least a little. This laundry list she recited revved her up again, until she was speaking rapid-fire bullets. So came her summary.

"I'm tired of New Orleans, I'm tired of the band, and frankly *Franky*, the thing I'm most tired of is *you!*"

Franky's neck jutted backward. He glanced her way, then toward Ariel's empty room, then back toward her, yet never reaching her eyes. She had said it all, laid it all out on the table. It was as if he'd been left with a choice of giving his blessing, as with Ariel's wedding. Finally his gaze settled on the coffee table and stayed there, his forearms resting on his knees.

"Go then," he said, waving her away with head dropped from fatigue. "Just go. Leave me to the dogs like Ariel, I don't care."

Bobbi stared, incredulous. Then, coming to, she shook her head and obeyed his command.

* * *

EVERYONE SAID ARIAL'S talent might match her father's in whatever she chose to do. She showed promise in school—when she went to school, that is. From the time she was a toddler Franky regularly said the word *college* right along with his anti-love teachings, even linking the two by telling her that education would free her from depending on men for anything. As for a field to pursue, he told her she needed to study something practical such as bookkeeping—or if she worked hard, and because the world might be changing soon for women, law or medicine.

"As your grandfather always used to tell me," he said, "they can take assets from you, but they can't take a skill."

She would pursue a skill, all right, but it wasn't exactly the practical kind that Franky had in mind.

Once in school, she still toured with the band all summer and on any holidays and vacations; in fact, even if she had but one day off, Franky would take advantage of it and get her out on tour with the band so that he could spend more time with her. She'd end up being with the band for what amounted to a long weekend, and then (when she was old enough) catching a train home to New Orleans, where her grandmother would be waiting anxiously at the station. Sometimes she'd join Bobbi and the boys in the middle of a tour, and Mrs. Fritz would accompany her all the way to wherever they were. Ariel's truancy rate was high, and Franky made sure he knew exactly how many days she could miss per grading period without automatically failing. That she performed relatively well in school in spite of her truancy rate was testament to her intelligence.

It was a wonder that she ever passed her English classes, given her father's attitude toward the subject. As she grew older and was assigned stories and short novels to read for homework, she brought them with her on the road. Franky allowed her to complete her assignments, but he didn't let the sight of his daughter reading fiction pass without a grumbling comment about "the nonsense they teach kids in school." On the contrary, *Sputnik* was wonderful from Franky's point of view. When the Russians launched the fear-spawning rocket a few years later, he was elated that the school board at last was coming in line with his way of thinking, emphasizing math and science over letters. "You see?" he said of the Russians. "I bet *they* don't spend so much time on stories in school, and look where it's gotten them!"

Through the years the persistent questions about mothers and marriage kept coming and coming like stinging rain—until one day they just stopped, which was when Franky knew Ariel had reached adolescence. During this time Franky advanced his unorthodox teachings with his daughter, for he wanted to make sure she stayed away from the illusion of love. Franky, who denied the existence of many things, had a perfect lab test to verify whether or not virtually anything was real, a test he would explain often to her. The test was practically as pure as science, he liked to say, and it was beautiful in its simplicity: "If you can pay for it, it's real."

Even something as intangible as music passed the test, he explained: One could pay for music. You can buy a record. You can pay to hear a band play. Music, therefore, was true. You could even pay for physical love. "But can you pay for the other kind of love? Certainly not. Case closed." And young Ariel nodded her head.

While Franky taught her from early childhood about sex, Bobbi was her teacher in other matters. She showed the growing girl her Peter Pan-brand bra, which was said to offer a rounded silhouette rather than a pointy one. She explained to Ariel that she would need to choose between a napkin and a more modern solution, the tampon.

Another indicator signaled the dawn of her adolescence, this one a concrete and harsh one. Franky shuddered when she pulled it from her book bag one afternoon after getting home from school. It was surely an innocuous assignment to most parents, but to Franky, it couldn't have been a more controversial book. He saw it lying there on the kitchen table, alongside Ariel's bag: Charles Dickens's *Great Expectations*.

"I see they're still teaching garbage," he said.

Franky told Ariel not to do the assignment. But she was a fourteen-year-old girl at the height of self-consciousness, and so she read it in secret because she didn't want to be different from the rest of her class. And she liked it too, which made her more interested in literature, which made her more interested in English teachers. Other than Ariel's friend Sue Nolan, Bobbi was the only one who held that secret, and only after it was all over.

Perhaps it was no coincidence that Sam Delacroix taught English because that subject was the obvious way to rebel against her only parent. He taught tenth grade, which was the year of *Romeo and Juliet*. Thanks to his vague references to big-city theater, he was known as someone who had dabbled in acting—off-Broadway (where the important plays were being produced, he told people) in New York. But according to stories that circulated in parents' circles, his only time spent in the entertainment business during his two-month stay in New York came as a twenty-five-year-old waiter in a small eatery. Still, to the students he was an unmarried teacher who had traveled and worked in New York City, not to mention acted onstage. The students at the all-girls school hadn't known many single teachers, especially ones younger than forty. "He doesn't have a family," said her friend Sue Nolan. "Wouldn't you just love to know what he does at night?" They chatted like that for hours over the telephone. Ariel was the first child anyone knew to have a bedroom extension phone, which Franky called a big mistake; he had spoiled the only child, particularly given that he refused to have the extravagance even for himself.

While the girls didn't know what an unmarried man did at night, they knew of one evening activity of Sam Delacroix's: attending rehearsals for *Romeo and Juliet*, a local production at Le Grand Theatre on the edge of the French Quarter. Delacroix was playing Mercutio, he told his class, and they were all invited to attend the performance for extra credit. For either education or egotism, Delacroix had scheduled his classes' reading of *Romeo and Juliet* just in time for the production.

The first time Ariel mustered the courage to speak to him, her attraction manifested itself in the form of combativeness. The day they started reading *Romeo and Juliet*, she approached him after the bell.

"My father doesn't believe in love—the kind between a guy and a girl, at least."

Mr. Delacroix put down a red pen and looked at her, bemused. Then a knowing smile surfaced onto his face, and he nodded at her. "I can see where you got your intellect."

Ariel couldn't help but blush. From there they waxed philosophical about the nature of love versus its falsity. After a few minutes Ariel thought she was chatting so intelligently—largely by regurgitating things she'd heard her father say—that she thought she had outwitted her teacher. Bouncing on her toes beside Delacroix's desk, she suggested that she be excused from the assignment based on "my superior understanding of the topic." But Mr. Delacroix had other ideas. Ariel's precociousness was all the more reason that she *must* read Shakespeare, he said. "Besides, it's good to have our presumptions challenged—particularly the ones that our parents imprint on us."

"I like *that* idea," she said, nodding.

She started coming by his classroom every day after school. As he marked up papers at his desk while expounding on drama and literature to her, she would linger nearby, sometimes in the student desk nearest his, sometimes bouncing around his chair and peering over his shoulder. Sometimes he stopped grading papers altogether and just chatted with her, and they segued from the topic of love in literature to love in life, and to which guy from the brother high school was going steady with what girl.

"You follow me like a puppy dog," Mr. Delacroix once told her.

Surprisingly, she didn't take offense to this. "You're lucky I like you," she said. "I ignore everyone else."

Which was true. This teen had gone the sullen route, one of those girls who pride themselves on their frown. In fact, her father had not seen her smile since the end of ninth grade, even when he tried to be witty with her, and so he began to enjoy the road more, while she stayed with her grandparents. She showed little interest in anything other than art, with the exception of—once during a random week as expressed to Bobbi—a beauty-developer product that "may increase your chest line measurement" through muscle building.

Meanwhile, she kept coming by Sam Delacroix's room after school, five days a week by this point. In the afternoons before they went their separate ways down the corridor, they lingered outside the classroom door and caught each other's eye at the last moment before Mr. Delacroix turned and rushed off to rehearsal. In that moment, sullen Ariel would fill the tiny space of silence with a smile that flicked on and dimmed almost before it registered. She spoke to no one about Delacroix, except her confidante Sue Nolan. Every night on the telephone, Sue listened with the interest of a teen to Ariel's tales of what she and "Sam," as she now called him, had discussed that afternoon. Thus, Sue readily accepted when Ariel needed a partner in crime to see *Romeo and Juliet* at Le Grand Theatre with her. Ariel had been shy about going to see her teacher perform, and so she waited until the very last night of the show to attend. The entirety of that Saturday was spent anticipating and preparing for the evening. In the morning she and Sue went down to Canal Street to shop for a new outfit that she would buy with babysitting money. She eventually decided on a simple skirt-and-blouse combination after walking up and down the shopping strip thirteen times and going into all of the department stores at least twice and smaller dress shops once. ("It's got to be classy and adult-looking—we're going to Shakespeare," she told Sue, who agreed.)

From the entranceway of Mr. and Mrs. Fritz's, where she was staying because Franky was on tour, off they went, more dressed up than her grandparents had ever seen them on a Saturday evening. The older couple, blinded by grandparent love, were perfect subjects to be fooled. "My smart granddaughter," said Mrs. Fritz as they stood just inside the door before they left. "I'm so proud you're going to Shakespeare on your own, even if it's for extra credit." Sue snickered without letting Mrs. Fritz see. "That's it—we're going for the extra credit," she said just before the door had shut.

But once the girls had settled into their seats at Le Grand Theatre and the curtains had opened, they were surprised to find that they enjoyed the production, especially after having become familiar with the play in class. "Hey," whispered Sue during the first few minutes of the performance, "they can say those old-fashioned words like they're really talking." The girls also were impressed by the significant amount of yelling by the actors, which kept them alert in the stuffy theater darkness that otherwise might have induced sleep. The spectacle of live theater entertained them much more any time

Mercutio Delacroix made a stage entrance, even though his sleeveless biceps were flimsy for a young man's. During those times, Ariel confessed, she didn't hear a word of dialogue and lost track of the plot.

The show finally ended ("Now I won't have to read the rest of it," said Sue), and the two girls, stiff from hours of sitting, pushed themselves out of their seats like two old women.

"Follow me," said Ariel, grabbing Sue's hand. Injected with a new burst of energy, they pushed their way toward the stage, against the stream of patrons shuffling to the main doors in back. To the right of the stage was an EXIT sign, and they passed under it, which led to a darkened passage, followed by a dimly-lit set of steps. They climbed them, only to be confronted by a shut door. With no hesitation Ariel pushed it open and they forged on as if they were doing something wrong. Now they were in a small area surrounded by three doors, and a drone of festive voices could be heard coming from somewhere. To the right was a door with an EXIT sign. In front of them was another door with the words PROP CLOSET on it. And to the left was a third door with a sign that said ACTORS AND STAGE PERSONNEL ONLY. They leaned in closer to the latter door—yes, the crowd noise came from there.

"This is going to be easier than I thought," said Ariel.

Still they hesitated, conscious of the hidden racket muffling through: all the shouts and cheerful voices, like sounds made by fans coming out of a stadium. The actors had finished their run, and they were congratulating each other and letting their friends praise them. With Sue peering over her shoulder, Ariel edged the door open, careful not to hit anyone on the other side given that the room sounded packed. As soon as the door cracked open, the rollicking racket jumped three notches louder as if someone had cranked the volume knob on a hi-fi. Men and women, all much older than the girls, were standing and milling around shoulder to shoulder, some holding champagne bottles above the level of the revelers. They squeezed through bodies trying to find the one cast member they knew, stopping with each passage to try and crane their heads over the taller adults surrounding them.

"Ariel!"

Delacroix, flushed with the triumph of a final performance, had seen them first. Ariel rushed up to him. "You were wonderful, Sam!" she exclaimed, and the three chatted it up as Delacroix, his fragile chest only partially covered in draped cloth because he'd stayed in full costume, took swigs from the champagne bottle he hoisted. When he stepped aside for a few minutes to talk to another actor, Sue said, "You talk to each other like he's one of us." Not only did they talk as peers, they talked on and on (mostly about Sam's performance), until eventually Sue got tired and bored. Ariel, feeling comfortable in the adult world she knew so well from being an only child and a touring-band mascot at that, put on her mature demeanor like a blouse and told her friend to go ahead and go home, that she would fine.

"We're discussing some serious things," she said. "We're discussing art. We can't stop now."

"But you're supposed to come home with me! Where you gonna spend the night?"

"Don't worry, I'll be fine. I'll just sneak back into my grandparents' house. They'll be asleep since they aren't expecting me."

Sue hesitated for just a moment. Then she raised her eyebrows and gave a sly smile. "Okay—as long as you tell me what happens!"

With Sue gone, Ariel and Sam Delacroix were alone among crowds of actors and friends, for no one seemed to pay much attention to them, save the occasional cast member coming by to slap old Mercutio on the back and laugh about a line that almost got tripped over or a prop that failed unbeknown to the audience. Eventually the herd of cast members, stage crew, and friends of the production started dissipating, and Sam and Ariel moved along inside the anonymous flow of people. According to the shouts, everyone was heading to Capulet's house for the cast party. Come along, said Delacroix to Ariel. "You can be my guest—that is, unless you have a curfew, which you probably do."

Curfew—the words of an adult to a teen. But a hint of a dare sounded somewhere in his voice.

"I don't have to be anywhere," said Ariel. "My dad's on tour."

Delacroix hoisted his bottle of champagne, took a swig, and then passed it over to Ariel. "Your dad understands how mature you are."

They drove toward the party from the French Quarter. Lord Capulet lived in a shotgun house not far from the big city park, where neither the poor nor the rich lived. For the first time now the two were quiet and alone, connected by the confines of a car riding down Canal Street as it darkened into its more residential section. She had stood by him at his desk as they reviewed her work, but they had never sat together like this, forced so close by the size of a fascinating little Japanese import car that Mercutio called a Datsun.

"Juliet was about your age, you know," said Delacroix. "You're actually even a year or so older."

Ariel folded her arms and tried to hold back a smile, staring straight ahead out the windshield into the darkness. "I know," she said. "I remember that from class. I understand why Shakespeare made her that age."

Now it was mostly darkness and quiet that filled the little space inside the car. The live oaks on both sides of the divided street filtered the moon rays into dappled light. Delacroix's car hummed comfortably because his pressure on the gas pedal was easy and steady, and he drove slowly but with purpose.

"We don't have to go to the cast party if we don't want to," he said.

Would she like to see his collection of playbills instead? He kept talking so that she didn't need answer just then. He had as many as twenty-two playbills from his short stay in New York, he said, and even a few from Chicago, where he visited periodically. He even could show her his prize possession, hidden in a cypress chest beneath his bed: a playbill from the original Broadway production of *A Streetcar Named Desire* with Marlon Brando. "I was there," he said, leaning toward her with the celestial eyes that he normally saved exclusively for the stage. "And you—you who loves theater too—you should have been there with me."

"My dad hates that movie *Streetcar*," Ariel said. She looked out the window, where the trees and the darkened homes passed by. "So yeah, I want to see it."

A few minutes later, he was reaching under his bed for the cypress chest. They sat side by side on the edge of the bed, looking at the theater souvenirs. After they flipped through the *Streetcar* playbill, he closed it shut and set it on her lap as if offering it to her, his fingers reaching over the paper to linger at the neutral position of her knee. She forced the leg still, and she gazed down at it so that hair fell alongside either side of her face to hide her eyes. He brushed her knee with the back of his hand so lightly that she could barely feel it. The hand passed over again, and then again, sensitizing the skin. She still did not move, and so he kissed her neck and then her mouth. She turned to face him directly, although her head stayed bowed as if she were still looking at the playbill in her lap. The next day, concluding an hours-long talk with Sue, she would describe the event in paraphrase: Her first kiss and her first man came all on the same night.

CHAPTER 21

"OH, DARLING, IT'S going to be so beautiful," Bobbi said. "I can't wait for the day."

"Yeah, and my bride is going to be the most beautiful thing about it," said Evan.

Ariel blushed a little. Franky, meanwhile, was not sitting at the kitchen table with the three conspirators planning a wedding. Instead he was fixing himself a sandwich, lurking in the background like a new pet that had disappointed its purchasers because it turned out to lack affection.

"Oh, I would *love* to get married in the cathedral—I've always dreamed of it," Ariel said. "Wouldn't it be just grand?"

"Not *would* be just grand," Bobbi corrected, "*will* be just grand. We're gonna get you married there, darling, you just watch. We've got a plan."

Everyone knew that when Bobbi set her mind to something, she would get it done—against whatever odds.

"Don't be ridiculous," called Franky, unbending himself from peering into the refrigerator. "Whoever heard of a Jew getting married in St. Louis Cathedral?"

"It's your fault, you know," said his daughter. "A Catholic setting feels right because of all the gospel Masses in Tremé you took me to."

"For the music. We went for the music. And maybe for God. But definitely not for the ritual."

Evan chimed in that he grew up Catholic, so it made sense in that way as well. Besides her comfort with a Catholic setting, Ariel admitted there were other reasons: The cathedral was a fairy-tale locale to many a New Orleans girl, for the historic church was the perennial heart of the city, the place for prominent members of the community and luminaries to marry. She had associated the church with romance since the day when she was a young girl that she'd learned of the wedding held by the famous restaurant family, the wedding that splashed across more than one section of the *Times-Picayune*.

"Once again, falling prey to society's lies," Franky interrupted. "Once again, falling prey to fairy-tale fiction."

"Ach!" she spit back, throwing down her pencil. And then she said it. She said the unspeakable. "Just because *your* wedding didn't work out the way you wanted doesn't mean mine can't!"

Franky stood there, dizzy and red—from bending low into the fridge and now from the attack. He had to lean sideways against the counter to support himself. Still, he hardly stumbled from the blind punch.

"That's right, I had a wedding in a Catholic church once," he said, jumping right up from the boxing-ring canvas, "and look what happened!"

But Ariel only shrugged and the wedding talk resumed with the working out of details. To conduct the ceremony, Bobbi had secured a justice of the peace: "Mr. Charlie," an old childhood adult neighbor and perennial bureaucrat who still refused to give up his city job even though he had already reached his maximum pension. As for location, they would never be authorized to hold a civil ceremony in the cathedral, and on top of that, they hadn't even booked the famous venue, anyway. Yet they had a plan, as concocted by Bobbi and Evan, to overcome such insignificant obstacles so that Ariel's dream of a cathedral wedding could be fulfilled. The ceremony would be so small that they would be able to privately pace through it in a spot somewhere along the side aisle of the church, hidden among the holy edifice's everyday activity—as the tourists wandered up and down the nave in sweaty shorts and weighted camera straps, as an occasional homeless man limped inside to rest his aching dirty feet in a back pew, and as alternating bodies of the rock-solid faithful and nearly hopeless knelt to light prayer candles before the Lady of Prompt Succor in the back corner. Amid this quiet movement of the weekday afternoon, a small cluster of friends gathered for the wedding would barely be noticed "if we do it right," said Bobbi.

The conversation was stressful for Franky, to say the least, but the main cause was what still hadn't been spoken. The trio at the table had talked for nearly forty minutes, and not once had anyone mentioned the part in the ceremony about Ariel walking down the aisle—and specifically who would walk with her. Clearly, the topic must come up.

Or maybe not. Perhaps Ariel, as she had claimed, truly had accepted she would have to forgo that one small part of her dream. So as he kept listening in on all the wedding planning, he began to think the jarring subject of father refusing to walk daughter down the aisle would not be broached again. He regained his usual aplomb. His pace around the kitchen quickened, for he had decided on his snack—a lettuce-and-cheese sandwich on rye with some speckled brown mustard—and so with a touch of verve he gathered the ingredients and then assembled the sandwich. Noticing him as he made an uncharacteristic gesture with his hands, Bobbi asked suspiciously: "Whatchya rubbing your hands together for? That sandwich don't look *that* good."

He carried his plate over to his easy chair in the living area and was just about to bite down on his rye-bread sandwich when Ariel turned to him. In her right hand she held a sharpened pencil, which pointed down onto a legal pad in writing position.

"So Franky," she said, getting ready to fill in a blank, "you come to your senses yet and decided to walk me down the aisle?"

The others stopped talking. They were just a few days away from the wedding, she explained matter-of-factly, and so "I need a commitment. You remember *commitment*, right?" Franky didn't say anything, so Bobbi jumped in.

"Don't worry about your daddy, sweetie," she said, glaring at Franky. "He's just a knucklehead sometimes. Look, if he don't want to walk you down the aisle, I'll do it myself!"

Franky raised his eyebrows before taking a considerable bite out of his sandwich, which crunched because the lettuce was iceberg. The *crunch* seemed to set Bobbi off.

"Didn't you hear your daughter? She axed you a question. Now, what's it gonna be—you gonna walk her down the aisle or not?"

Evan and Bobbi fixed on him, while Ariel looked down into her lap. Bobbi had forced his hand. He glanced at each of the three of them. Then he straightened up in his chair and put his nose in the air.

"I already told you. I refuse to participate in something I don't believe in."

Ariel was the one who had to absorb the blow, which knocked her into wounded silence. So it was Bobbi who reacted. All that had built up over two decades, all the disagreements, all the bickering, all the dimensions of their relationship never uttered, were ready to burst forth now.

"Franky, I swear by the Virgin Mother of God—" She stopped to attempt a shallow breath. "I swear by the Virgin Mother of God, if you don't walk your daughter down the aisle, you don't exist to me anymore!"

She punctuated her threat by bolting for the door and slamming it. Ariel started to cry, though no sound came from her.

* * *

EACH AFTERNOON, STARTING on the Monday after attending the great love story *Romeo and Juliet*, Ariel wandered like a Dickensian ghost to Delacroix's classroom after the last period. Every time, though, Delacroix was not there, apparently having disappeared within a minute of the final bell; maybe *he* was the ghost. Before the next weekend had arrived, in conversations with Sue she was calling him a jerk and every other name in her book—a book that had been written over the years with the help of a busful of male road musicians. Sue took up her cause too. When she went to her first-period English class with Delacroix, she scowled whenever the guilty teacher looked anywhere near her direction so that he would know that she knew all about him. The glares would surely compound his stress.

Ariel would not be deterred from seeing Delacroix alone one last time. Forging on with her routine, on the next Monday afternoon she made her way to the classroom as soon as the final bell rang, this time moving more like a menacing zombie than a harmless ghost. And this time she found her target.

He was sitting at his desk behind a stack of papers that he graded with a red pen. He looked up from his work, registering the situation. At the sight of him, she wavered, her strength seeping away onto the floor and out the classroom door like paint; his power over her was extraordinary, she'd found. The two made small talk. Reclaiming a smidgen of lost strength, Ariel finally brought up the night of the play in a conversational way. He only shrugged.

"I'm an artist," he said. "I'm not meant for any one person."

She gripped her hands into fists. She might have cried or she might have screamed. From one flash to the next, she seemed ready to do one, then the other. Delacroix raised his hands, either calling for calm or preparing to shield himself from impending attack. At that point, the sound that came out of Ariel's mouth in the end was neither a weep nor a scream. It was closer to a growl—but it wasn't directed at Delacroix.

"My father was right," she said, shaking her head. "My father is always right."

Then began the journey out of there. He failed to call after her—as a big part of her must have hoped. She moved, feeling his eyes on her delicate back while she silently gasped for air and floated out to the hallway. As if he hadn't selfishly taken everything from her already, on this occasion he must have stolen—right from under her literal nose—still one more thing: all the oxygen in the classroom, which he selfishly sucked up in the breath of relief that he took. Now leaning for support against the tile hallway wall with hand on chest, she seized back her breath after a few moments of panting. The meeting had taken everything out of her, for she could barely make it home.

Yet Ariel surprised Sue in the recounting. That evening over the phone, she told her friend the experience had been "fantastic and kind of exciting." She had brought this grown man to his knees. Delacroix practically had been shaking.

A couple of evenings later, Franky picked her up at her grandparents after returning from his tour. Even though she hadn't seen her father in weeks, she had been quiet in the car, the inside of which was veiled in darkness, as Delacroix's had been just a few nights prior. Her silence wouldn't have surprised Franky so much; the teenager was always sullen these days. Finally, staring straight ahead through the windshield, she spoke out of the blue.

"You were right, Daddy. There's no such thing as love."

Driving down St. Charles Avenue in the night, Franky turned toward her. He might have asked what in the world happened while he was gone for her to say that. His daughter's comment surely suggested something traumatic had come at her. Instead, though, a contented smile formed and he responded with no probe of paternal compassion.

"That's my girl," he said. "That's my girl." And they rode in silence the rest of the way home.

CHAPTER 22

THE SURROUNDS AT the wedding proved to be just as the planners had anticipated when they sat around the kitchen table to lay out the ceremony. The cathedral was a still pool that rippled only with occasional echoes: A few tourists wandered up and down the nave in sweaty shorts and weighted camera straps, an occasional homeless man limped inside to cool off and rest his aching, filthy feet in a back pew, and the patrons of the church—the rock-solid faithful kneeling alongside the nearly hopeless—lit candles before the Lady of Prompt Succor. They were in an old church—a silent place where everything echoes. On the stage-right side of the altar, a gathering of former bandmates and old friends clustered along the side aisle. Joe and Marcie, Al Butkus, Slim Jim Hebert, Ted LeBlanc, Alvin Stokes, and

Tim Callahan showed up for the makeshift ceremony at which their mascot, the adopted daughter of the band, would wed a musician of her own generation.

The group of old friends deferred to the discussion led by Bobbi and Ariel, who were telling Bobbi's old acquaintance the justice of the peace how the ceremony would go. Seeking confirmation from the city government official that she was keeping with tradition, Ariel would often stop to ask, "Is that the way they usually do it," and the tired-looking man would shrug and say, "Sure."

No one mentioned Franky's name. But every time an echo sounded—usually from a kneeler being set down or put back up or from a worshipper coughing in the middle of prayer—they all turned toward the back of the church. That is, everyone turned except for Ariel, who either was too occupied with the logistics of the ceremony or had given up caring whether her father showed up or not. She was right never to turn and look: Whenever the rest of the lot turned their heads, Franky never appeared. Eventually they all grew conditioned to the sounds that never signaled the father of the bride's arrival.

Meanwhile, Ariel continued to try and work through how things would proceed. Whenever she asked a question about the ceremony—such as, Should the justice of the peace say a few words before she walked down the aisle or wait to speak till she arrived?—old Mr. Charlie the justice would say, "Doesn't make any difference, ma'am. Whatever you prefer."

"But which is traditional?" said Ariel. "What did people do back in your day?"

That's when a different sound started. Footsteps echoed and they were hardly the squeaking of a tourist's tennis shoes. No, a certain staccato tapping suggested otherwise. The footwear must have been leather-soled, such as what a man might wear with a suit—or even a tux, and even the cadence of the steps echoed familiar. The grand entrance, though not of the bride, had begun.

One by one heads turned toward the back: There was Franky, marching up the nave, chin raised in the air in either defiance or dignity.

But if everyone else was surprised, Ariel acted unimpressed.

"Glad you could make it, Franky," she said upon his arrival.

Her father shrugged. "I figured it wouldn't hurt to watch." After an emphatic beat, he added, "Even though my daughter's marrying an unemployed rock musician."

She had already turned back to the justice of the peace, but that made her glance back at him for a moment before she could catch herself. So, in spite of his showing up, he wasn't going to walk her down the aisle after all. As Franky started off to head back into the sea of pews, Marcie called after him.

"Evan doesn't play rock anymore," she said. "He's going back to jazz."

Franky stopped in his tracks. He turned toward Evan, causing everyone to do so as well—which in turn compelled the young sax man, the living presence of the topic at hand, to elaborate. He did so with his usual shrug, explaining, "Rock's not where it's at for me. There's more freedom in jazz."

The older musicians nodded and murmured in agreement, and Ariel chimed in above the din. "That's right, Franky," she said, "and furthermore, Evan has a job. He already joined a band that makes a lot of money."

After just a few phone calls to let people know he was back in town, Evan had landed himself a permanent gig with a band that was selling out clubs by blending some old sounds with new. The unspoken truth hung in the air: Evan, whose chops apparently were coveted around town, was more employed than Franky was.

Franky offered a blasé raise of the eyebrows, turned around, and started off again—presumably to a seat in the second or third row. But no. Surprising everyone, he passed those first pews and kept going right back down the nave, marching like the soldier he once was, straight for the doors in the rear. The click of his tuxedo shoes echoed throughout the cathedral, and the spectators sucked in a collective gasp, all on behalf of the bride.

But then he stopped. With a near soldier's click of the heel, he spun 90 degrees and then slipped into one of the pews umpteen rows back. And there he planted himself, facing them. Apparently, the pew he had chosen was a safe enough distance from the lie that was love.

After he settled into the pew, the rest of them followed Ariel's cue and mostly ignored him while the two principals began to take their places. "We'll get started in a couple of minutes," said Mr. Charlie. "I gotta be back at city hall." Ariel seemed unfazed by the turn of events and her father's presence in the background. Speaking as if she were dictating a grocery list, she went on discussing with Bobbi how the retiring vocalist would walk her down the aisle—arm in arm, as Ariel said, "just like it's always been done," and Bobbi gushed about how proud she was to have that honor.

"Bobbi. Please come."

The voice was not Ariel's. It echoed from a distance and everyone knew its sound. The others gave but a glance Franky's way before going on with their conversations, making Franky seem like a difficult child being corrected by the technique of ignoring.

But Bobbi didn't ignore him. Instead she turned to look over at her lifelong business partner, sitting there alone amid the sea of pews.

"You bet I'll come," she said. She started marching down the nave, looking like she would smack him the moment she reached him.

But by the time she got there, or maybe because she thought she caught a shocking trace of humility on his face, she cooled off a bit. Taking a breath to recover from her purposeful walk, she turned back around in the direction from where she had come. Together, she standing and he sitting, they paused to look upon the gaggle of friends at the front corner of the church. Ariel's print dress of soft flowers swished off her leg as she bounced around in excitement; apparently, she wasn't too concerned with her father anymore.

"Boy, she makes a beautiful bride, don't she? It don't make one bit of difference that she ain't got a wedding dress on. Not one bit."

Sure enough, Ariel had found a dress residing at a three-way meeting point of perfection, where crossed the modern style of the day, the classic of yesterday, and the singularity of one's self, which is timeless. Evan, by contrast to the beautiful bride, stood off to the side in his usual torn blue jeans.

Franky didn't answer, although he too was looking in the bride's direction. His silence must have reminded Bobbi of her initial anger, because in a newfound huff she broached the topic that loomed on everybody's mind.

"I don't suppose you got me to come all the way down here to tell me you're gonna walk your daughter."

Franky sat in the pew, stiff and straight. It was as if he hadn't heard her. In fact, a beat or two passed before he registered that someone was speaking to him, for he gave a "Hmm?" But then, after all the buildup over all the weeks, he responded by almost dismissing the question.

"Oh," he said with a wave. "Of course. That isn't much of anything."

And that was it. The great dilemma over and done with, just like that. Bobbi studied him a moment before waving toward the altar to get the bride's attention.

"Hey, honey," she singsonged with zero enthusiasm, "he's gonna do it."

"Great," said Ariel in a matching tone. "So let's get going."

After the endless wait for Franky's answer, no one by now, it seemed, cared.

"Okay then," Bobbi said to Franky, grabbing his arm and starting off, "let's get going. Your daughter's waiting."

"Hold on a minute." He hesitated. "Please—sit down."

He sat there like a man bowed in prayer, and so, with an *ah jeez*, she acquiesced. "This better be quick, this is Ariel's moment," she said, sliding into the pew beside him.

"All the things you said the other day," he started. "You know, about being tired." He was sitting with his hands folded together in his lap and his shoulders rounded so that once again he looked forty years older. "I'm like you," he said. "I'm tired."

Sitting side by side, they both stared straight ahead as if they weren't supposed to look the other's way, like two rival mobsters meeting in a public place to make a deal.

"The Franky Fritz Band is done."

It was as if the world stopped spinning—and in fact theirs had. Everyone knew the World-Famous Franky Fritz Band was finished back when Bobbi said she was going to South Bend, but if anyone owns anything, it's the rights to one's name. Once Franky pronounced the band finished, everyone understood he wasn't going to try and press on, dubbing any old bunch of musicians the Franky Fritz Band. They all knew the Franky Fritz Band was ineffably more than just skinny Franky Fritz, child admirer of Bix Beiderbecke; Franky Fritz, failed groom of a foiled wedding; Franky Fritz, father of the bride.

The two coleaders looked each other over for a moment, two souls now officially retired from the only love each had ever known.

"Well, I'm glad you finally came to your senses—on two counts," Bobbi said. She patted him on the knee as she started to edge out of the pew. "C'mon, let's go. We've got a wedding to be in. Then I've gotta make Birmingham by nightfall."

That's right, she said, she was leaving for South Bend that very day, and she would be stopping overnight to visit a girlfriend in Birmingham along the way up.

"Wait!"

If his urgency didn't stop her, his hand certainly did. He grabbed her arm so she could go no further. For a moment they were locked in a stalemate, he sitting and she standing and pulling. "C'mon, Franky, stop it, let's go! We can talk after, at the restaurant."

"No," he said. "It can't wait. It has to do with the ceremony. So sit down. Please."

Bobbi's eyes shot upward toward the faraway ceiling of the cathedral, and she huffed. "Heavens to Betsy. He's gonna kill me yet, before I leave town!"

"You complain too much," he said gently.

"*I* compl—?"

"Come on, sit down, will you?"

She laughed at the irony of that one. Nevertheless, she gestured the sign of the cross and dropped down beside him.

Franky started: Everything around him was changing, he began. There was no band anymore, Ariel was getting married, Joe was acting like he wasn't Joe anymore. Even she was leaving. Everything, it seemed, was collapsing like jazz itself.

"Look," he said, "let's be reasonable. We've known each other for decades. It's not right you should go away just like that."

"It ain't right? *It ain't right?* What, do you control me or something? Well, I nev—"

"Just hold on," he said, raising both hands in surrender. "Okay, so it's right. It's right for you to go away, because it's your choice."

"You're damn right it is. I'm glad we got that straight, at least."

The voice of a woman broke the quiet of the cathedral.

"Hey, you two!" A couple of tourists and a handful of people praying looked up. It was Marcie, calling down the nave. "You comin'? You got a beautiful bride waiting here, ya know."

"Hold on," said Franky, "it's important."

He turned back to Bobbi. "As I was saying. Sometimes there are two rights."

"Oh yeah? Well, what is that supposed to mean?"

"Well..." He intoned the word as if asking a question to which he was unsure of the answer. "It could be right for you to stay too."

"Ah, come on, Franky, we've been through all this." She started reiterating what she said the other day about how it was just time to leave New Orleans and how she wanted to be near the only family that ever was family to her.

"But you have family here too," Franky said.

"I don't have none here I wanna know, that's for sure."

"Sure, you do."

"Yeah, and who might that be?"

Franky hesitated for a moment. Then he just shrugged.

"Me," he said with his palms open. "I'm family." When she didn't answer immediately, he added, "Or at least I could be—even in an *official* sort of way."

She gave him a quizzical look—her business partner had surely lost it. And so Franky continued on with what he was getting at. All his words rose and fell in a *let's be reasonable* tone. "Look," he said. "We've known each other for practically all of our adult lives. We've always been together more or less—not *together* together, mind you, but, well, you know what I mean…." He shrugged. "Together."

She let him keep talking uninterrupted—maybe because she couldn't believe what might be coming, maybe because she saw a stubborn friend talking with sincerity, or maybe just because she was curious to find out what the heck he was talking about.

"So I've been thinking, it would be strange to not have you around, and—"

"If you're trying in your own stupid way to say you'll miss me—okay, sure, Franky, I'll miss you too, hon. Now let's go."

He was losing her; he needed to cut to the chase. And so he went and said what he needed to say. The irony came in how he said it. All his life he had exploited his own talents for conjuring an ethereal world by mingling music and showmanship. But now, here within the mystery of a church, at the point of one of his life's greatest decisions, he tapped tones of the everyday.

"Look," he said, "we've got a justice of the peace right here. Why don't we get married too?"

Bobbi didn't move. Her eyes had been fixed on the bridal party in the front, and they stayed there. Then, slowly, she turned, reddening with rage. The universal question that usually softens a person had ignited the opposite in her. Bobbi's back stiffened straight so that she now hovered over him. Fists clenched and shoulders raised, she had taken her trademark stance known best by those who have been smacked by her pocketbook. Franky knew the stance from the very day he'd met her; since then, he'd always managed to jump out of the way. This time, though, he stayed, waiting for the blow. But she didn't smack him. She opened her mouth.

"What? Excuse me?"

He pushed through the moment with a shrug of reason. "Well, it's not so crazy, really. We've known each other a long time, and—"

"You don't propose to a girl like that!"

Dumbfounded, he gazed up at her with mouth agape. She continued: "Marriage, is serious business. And so is proposing. But you make it sound like you're asking why don't we go drink a beer!" Franky raised his finger in explanation, but she ignored him. "No indeed, weddings are sacred. They're witnessed by God. It's how I was brought up. I ain't like this new generation that thinks they can get divorced just like that, no sir!"

But Franky had an answer to that as well. "It's okay," he interrupted with a shrug. "It won't be a Catholic wedding."

She looked at him as if he had lost his mind, but he kept on. He had thought it all through, he said. He respected her Catholic upbringing, and so the civil ceremony made perfect sense because they wouldn't be married by the Church. With such arguments, he might have been convincing a club owner to give the band a gig. To his old friend of two decades he summed up the rationale behind his "I respect your faith" sales pitch in the following way, as if they had just met:

"If it turns out you don't like me, you can just divorce me."

She didn't answer him, but she didn't protest the logic either. She even nodded a tiny bit while processing it, and so, encouraged, he reiterated his various points with more zeal, even while she interrupted every so often with a "but." Eventually those *buts* turned into *ifs*, with the unspoken subtext, "*If* we were to actually do it," and without realizing it they moved on to the crucial terms of the hypothetical marriage, such as whether she would move into his home or vice versa, who would be responsible for dusting the piano, and whether the forbidden word *love* could be spoken inside the home when referring to both them and other couples.

The whole time, the group of friends and Ariel had been patiently waiting around while the two talked. They must have known the pair were discussing something serious. But Ariel had to interrupt at some point.

"Hey, you two, what's the holdup?" she called. Again the tourists and worshipers looked up. "Franky, if you still have cold feet about being a part of this ceremony, I'm not waiting for you to decide."

This time Bobbi answered. "Hold on, honey," she said. "We're doing some negotiating."

After a few more words between the two of them, Bobbi told him they couldn't make Ariel wait any longer. "So ask me again," she said. "And this time ask me nice."

Franky didn't kneel down on one knee, but he did turn to her in the pew and grasp her right hand with both of his.

"Bobbi," he said, dead serious, "will you marry me?"

She shrugged and raised her brow so that her pupils went to the corners in half-bored thought. ("I wanted him to suffer a little," she later explained to Marcie.) Then she shrugged again, as if she had been offered a cigarette.

"Okay," she said. "What the hell."

They were not finished, though. The negotiations continued while they walked back toward the gathering.

"You might be a decent songwriter, but you're illiterate in love," she said. "So *I'm* writing the vows."

Walking along beside her, Franky expressed skepticism at turning over the creative reins. "Just what, exactly, will I have to say?" he asked.

"Whatever I tell you to," she answered. "If you don't, I won't even need a divorce."

And here's a hint about the vows, she continued: "I'm not marrying anybody that doesn't love me." Franky didn't answer, instead bowing his head in thought as they walked. This marriage proposal wouldn't be as easy as simply reasoning out that they'd been together for so long, so why not get married?

The two arrived at the group, and the justice told everyone to take their places. No one gave Franky and Bobbi a second glance because their attention had turned to the ceremony that was about to begin. The majority of them shuffled over to the front two pews to take their seats for the show. That was when Bobbi made the official announcement.

"Oh, by the way," she said as the cluster broke apart to take their places, "the band is now folded. The band is folded, and me and Franky are gonna get married later today."

Each of them stopped in their tracks. Since all eyes were on her, she elaborated, but only on logistics. They would wait until after Ariel and Evan got married "'cause this is my lil' girl's day." Then she turned to her old acquaintance the justice of the peace, and called, "Hey, Mr. Charlie, you can stay another coupla minutes, can'tchya?"

And that was that. After a momentary initial jolt, there was a collective shrug. As far as the band went, the members in attendance were all at least okay financially from twenty years of straight touring and ready to move on to other projects anyway—ones with a more local focus. As for the unlikely marriage, the gathering of bandmates, who had spent tens of thousands of hours together and were already more or less married to one another in the first place, said little more than, "All right" and continued on their way to the pews. Three audible words did, however, float up above the shuffle and din.

"It's about time," said Ted, as much to himself as anyone. It was unclear whether he was referring to the marriage, the breakup of the band, or both.

Only Ariel reacted. She rushed over to Bobbi and embraced her. And then still holding her, in an "Oh my God" sort of revelation that such a thing couldn't possibly be true, she jerked her head back to study her friend's face, and said: "Are you sure you can put up with him?"

Only Joe was effusive in his congratulations to them both. "I'm so happy for you," he said. "I tell ya, you two were meant for each other."

The justice of the peace told everyone to take their places, while he stationed himself where the side aisle ended, alongside Evan and Bobbi. Ariel and her father made their way about halfway toward the back of the church for the big walk down the aisle. But then she stopped.

"Hey, wait a sec," she called from their starting position. Everyone looked the bride's way—except for Franky, who shuddered. Later he told Joe how the voice echoing down the nave conjured the voice of Muriel, standing in the very same starting position of a church, calling off his own wedding. But then Ariel jolted him out of his nightmare. "Why don't we all get married together?" she said. The day would be made more special because it was her childhood dream for her father and Bobbi to marry. "A little late, maybe," she admitted, "but my dream nevertheless."

The two couples quickly rearranged the ceremony to accommodate the additional marriage. On Ariel's insistence, Bobbi took her place beside Evan and the justice of the peace in the front of the church. Given that Franky was walking Ariel down the aisle, Bobbi assumed the position where the groom would normally await his bride; with Franky serving two roles in two different weddings, circumstances demanded that the traditional roles be reversed.

"Okay, let's try this one more time," said the justice of the peace. "Places, everybody."

Not so fast. Ariel halted the ceremony yet again—and this time it about made everyone's collective heart stop, for it threatened to kill the wedding before it began.

"Hold on," she said, turning to Evan. "This doesn't feel right."

Everyone gasped. By genetic inheritance, Ariel was mimicking a mother she never knew. Even Franky gasped—and he wasn't exactly crazy about her daughter's marriage.

Then Ariel continued: "Evan's in those damn torn jeans still." In a gesture at her surroundings, her open palm swept around in a half-circle. "If I get to have my wedding in this beautiful cathedral, my groom sure had better be dressed up!"

"It just doesn't feel right with him dressed like that," she repeated, and Bobbi and Marcie and Joe, after breathing sighs of relief, nodded and uttered a "yeah, that's true." But no one could do anything about it: They couldn't exactly run out and find Evan a new outfit. The justice of the peace had to be back at the courthouse on Tulane Avenue at three o'clock for a staff birthday cake.

"I got it," said Bobbi with her index finger up in the air. Everyone turned; this was the woman who had always given them good ideas. "Franky, go on and give your tux to Evan. It would look good on him."

Franky stiffened, incredulous. "Evan wear my tux?" he said. "Not if my life depended on it!" He hugged himself, apparently not being able to stand the thought of the tux leaving his frame.

"Come on, Franky," Tim called from the pew, "just lose the stupid tux for a change." Others murmured in agreement: "Come on, Franky, be a sport. You need to get a new wardrobe, anyway."

"But without it I'd feel naked," said Franky. "And it's my wedding day!"

"Not if you don't give up that tux, it won't be," Bobbi said.

As a matter of fact, she said, she had just thought of a condition that Franky needed to meet in order for her to marry him. "I want you to wear blue jeans for our wedding," she said. "*Torn* ones."

She was sick and tired of looking at him in that old tux. "If we're gonna be married, you need to change up your wardrobe a little."

The gathering in the pews murmured among themselves in hushed tones, as if they were attending a more formal ceremony and the bride was late making her entrance. Everyone looked Franky's way again; he was cornered.

"Oh, all right then," he grumbled, and proceeded to take off his jacket and unbutton his shirt.

They all formed a circle around him. Right there in St. Louis Cathedral he dropped his pants and then slid on Evan's blue jeans, while Evan stepped into Franky's tuxedo. For the first time since he was a teenager, the stage man was seen in public without a tux and, ironically, it was on the occasion of his wedding. Marcie, who was sitting with Joe in the front pew, studied Franky in his new outfit and said, "Not bad—you should dress casual more often."

But Evan was already struggling with the funny pieces of the tuxedo—the clumsy cuff links, the strange shirt, and especially the bow tie. Franky marched over to him.

"Give me that," he said, swiping the bow tie from him. "I'll show you how it's done."

Afterward, they all talked about the still frame that followed: Franky and Evan went face-to-face, nose to nose, like a mirror's reflection, as one tied the other's bow tie. They came almost as close as a kiss, but neither seemed to notice, for they were too busy working on the tie. Once again, the justice of the peace, annoyed from all the starts and stops, told them to take their places, and this time the ceremony did get started. Arm in arm, Franky and Ariel walked down the aisle, albeit just a short 100-foot stretch along the side of the nave, so as not to draw too much attention to the surreptitious ceremony taking place among a handful of tourists and worshippers.

"You're walking me down the aisle," said Ariel. "You're really doing it."

"No, you're walking *me* down the aisle," said Franky.

"I don't think so."

"I think so."

When they arrived at the corner off the altar, Evan and Ariel turned to each other and held each other's hands. The justice of the peace gave the couple the traditional blessing they wanted, and he did it in hushed undertones so that the gathering wouldn't draw attention. But when the bride and groom kissed, everyone forgot themselves and erupted in a cheer, which sent waves through the cathedral before the pool flattened again to its prayerful state.

Then it came time for the older generation to marry.

"We've written our own vows," said Bobbi to the justice, stepping forward with her arm interlocked in Franky's.

"Yeah, they do that these days," said the justice. "You wouldn't believe the things I've heard."

He said a few words of introduction, and then instructed the new couple to proceed with the vows. They turned to face each other, and Franky, having taken note of how Evan and Ariel had stood, clasped each of Bobbi's hands. A smile came over her face, and some intoned *ahs* rippled through the group.

"That's sweet, Franky," Bobbi said. "Now repeat what the man tells you."

Standing straight, Franky nodded an okay. Bobbi shoved a scratch sheet of paper into the hand of the justice and told him to please read the vows for Franky to recite. Even though she had only a couple of minutes to write them, the talented lyricist produced material both elaborate and specific:

"I, Franky Fritz," said the justice, "of the Franky Fritz Band…"

"I, Franky Fritz of the Franky Fritz Band …" the groom answered.

"…promise to break up the band."

"…promise to break up the band."

"I, Franky Fritz…"

"I, Franky Fritz…"

"…did not think there could be love…"

Franky nodded grimly at that one. "…did not think there could be love…"

"…until I met you."

Franky stopped. He looked at Bobbi, then at the justice. Everyone leaned forward in their pews, glued to this moment in the ceremony.

Bobbi repeated for the justice, "...*until I met you*, Franky. Say it: *until I met you.*"

Franky hesitated more, and so Bobbi folded her arms and huffed that they might as well all go home now. Franky tried to be conciliatory, but only in his own way.

"It's not you," he said. "It's just that I'd be admitting I was wrong for all these years."

Protests bubbled up from the audience:

"Ah, c'mon Franky, just say it."

"Admit you love her, Franky!"

"Don't be a jerk for a change."

"Okay, okay," Franky said, glancing toward the pews. "Go easy on an old friend, will you?"

Again he got in his starting stance, standing up straight and grasping hold of Bobbi's hands before asking the justice to please continue. Softened by his touch, her face relaxed.

"I, Franky Fritz, did not think there could be love," said the justice.

"I, Franky Fritz, did not think there could be love," Franky repeated.

"Until I met you."

"Until I met you."

Another small cheer bubbled over from the pews. Later some said it was in response to the professed love, while others said it was because Franky at last admitted he was wrong.

"My darling, I am so devoted to you . . ."

"My darling, I am so devoted to you . . ."

". . . that I promise never to stand in the way if you dump me and want to divorce me."

". . . that I promise never to stand in the way if you dump me and want to divorce me." Then mumbling under his breath to her, he added, "*Dump* and *divorce*. Nice alliteration."

The lyrics to the vows went on for a few more verses that by Bobbi's design were both romantic and contractual. Finally, after Franky had successfully recited all she had written, she concluded the song with an accepting nod and an improvised line of her own.

"Okay," she intoned, "Against my better judgment, I love you too, Franky Fritz."

From there she turned the reins back over to the justice of the peace, who did whatever he had to do to make everything official. At the end he asked if they wanted him to say, "You may kiss the bride," and, after giving each other a glance, they said *sure*.

A few coughs could be heard among the congregation; a kiss between their two coleaders would seem downright strange to everyone attending. So the bride and groom made the traditional embrace little more than a peck. A little more.

CHAPTER 23

IN THOSE FIRST weeks after the marriage, they had business matters to take care of—namely, tying up the loose ends of shutting down the band. But the ensemble's death turned out to spawn a modest musical rebirth.

It all started when Franky, having plenty of time to think nowadays, still couldn't get that flyer out of his head that had ignited the demise of the band—the one he had seen stapled on the wall in a diner entrance while traveling west on a tour that was no longer spirited:

The Davenport Jazz Festival
Presented by The Bix Beiderbecke Preservation Society
-featuring the music of Bix-
Come Experience the Legend of Davenport!

But now the flyer wasn't depressing him—it was spawning visions of fun.

"All the miles we've logged on the road, and not one time have we traveled for pleasure," he pointed out to Joe. "What do you say we take our first retirement motor trip?"

Franky and Joe and Bobbi and Marcie piled into Bobbi's Dodge La Femme, which by now was motoring through the interminable years of an automobile between new and classic, and headed north. But this time they weren't traveling to South Bend to launch a tour. Instead, they avoided any of those new interstate highways, which Franky said "carved New Orleans in half like a butcher's knife," and followed the familiar Mississippi because not only was it their hometown river, it passed through their final destination of Davenport, Iowa too.

Going to Davenport was like going home, for Franky behaved like his childhood self once he got there, hearing all that Bix-inspired music packed into one weekend. Like a boy toting his mitt to a ball game, he even hauled his old Conn Wonder cornet to Davenport. And boy, the players weren't half bad for some random small-town festival. After watching a band called the Beiderbecke Bombers whirl through a set that included "Riverboat Shuffle," "Davenport Blues," and "Squeeze Me," he made his way up to the stage to congratulate them on the set. They got to talking, and Franky introduced himself.

"Franky Fritz? The Man of Many Horns?" said the man who played trumpet. He was younger than Franky but not by much. "I used to see you play when I was in college." Hoisting his horn out in front of his barrel chest, he added: "You're the reason I left college to follow this piece of metal."

The man had left school because of him. Franky beamed. He had been a successful Bix evangelist and had never known it.

Thrilled by the presence of his personal legend, the trumpet player begged Franky to join the band onstage for an improvised number during the next set. After some coaxing Franky agreed, and he scampered back to the car to fetch his horn. Up onstage the Mad Soloist jammed along on a lengthy version of "Ace in the Hole" to the cheers of the crowd, and even sang a few bars on the next tune when the trumpet player thrust the mike in front of his face in the middle of the song.

The audience ate it up. They roared when Franky played a short solo, and a cheer crescendoed when the barrel-chested trumpet man barked into his microphone above the swaying music: "Ladies and gentlemen, in person before your eyes, the Mad Soloist, the Man of Many Horns—the legendary *Franky Fritz of the World-Famous Franky Fritz Band!*"

Once again, after years of stale performances, his walk became an act of floatation across the stage. The happening was so special and electric that Joe allowed himself to be coaxed by the band onstage to sit in on drums for a couple of numbers, and when the Beiderbecke Bombers found out Bobbi Roppolo was in the audience, they dragged her up to sing a number too. Before the festival had ended, Franky had been inducted as a full member of the Bix Beiderbecke Memorial Society, and he was invited back the following year for a paid gig.

Around this time a new movement was arising in New Orleans, one that would become one of the ancient town's greatest traditions, even though it was the only place in America already bursting at the seams with so much tradition that it presumably couldn't fit any more inside its city limits. A jazz festival was being formed, and the brand-new event was in need of talent. As usual, Bobbi, who it was said knew everyone in the entire city below a certain class, was the catalyst: An old friend of hers was involved in the organizing of the new festival. His acquaintance with Bobbi, in fact, made him one of the few residents of New Orleans aware of the Franky Fritz Band and its almost national following once upon a time.

So Franky, teeming with newfound confidence after conquering Davenport, assembled the core members of the band once again. Playing with the energy of retirees who garnered the universal spirit that it was "just like the old days," they took the festival by storm, at least among the modest cluster of aging revelers dancing in the sun-soaked grass before the fairgrounds stage. Various iterations of the band played at both festivals every year. They became famous in faraway Davenport and they grew to be fan favorites at the New Orleans event as well, but only among a small cluster of festivalgoers. Continuing to follow Franky was a penchant for success limited to faraway places and among individual clusters of fans connected only by highways.

But only somewhat. The band's steady following at the New Orleans Jazzfest spawned opportunities for occasional gigs at bars and events around town throughout the year—just enough for the feel of Franky's horns to stay familiar and his playing to stay sharp.

Meanwhile, having tasted the jazz-festival circuit, he fine-tuned his perception that the music he loved was dying, a perception cemented when he first saw the Bix festival flyer in the diner while on the road. He verbalized the changed worldview some years later, when an exciting jazz radio station with no commercials was launched on the far left of the burgeoning FM dial. The station came via a new concept called public radio.

"It's not a relic," he said of his jazz. "It's just nonprofit."

Still, the topic always weighed on him, and he never quite came to terms with certain things about the world. He couldn't get away from the notion that his favorite styles had been replaced, pushed aside to make room for the next thing, and the next thing after that. According to his friends, years later he was cranky for six days straight after he read a passage in the autobiography of Miles Davis, whose every musical turn Franky had followed through the decades, ever since he was urged to go hear the innovative trumpeter. The passage went

> *I never thought that the music called "jazz" was ever meant to reach just a small group of people, or become a museum thing locked under glass like all other dead things that were once considered artistic.*

At first Franky refused to say a word about the quote, but after those six days of grumpiness, he confided to Joe that he agreed "at least in spirit" with the words and that he knew what Miles was "trying to say, anyway."

FOLLOWING ALL THOSE years together, the sexual energy that made for such great stage chemistry between Franky and Bobbi didn't translate in the bedroom. On their first night together they each removed all of their clothes in the methodical way of washing up, then slipped naked under the covers, where they hugged while lying on their sides and touching each other's skin. In the daytime, they didn't touch much, for the couple was far too used to communicating any affection through the airwaves and from short distances such as across a bandstand, or through barbs and bickering, which was the primary means of spousal communication that Franky had absorbed from his parents. But they came together quietly at night, loving each other's middle-aged bodies, which they both agreed somehow seemed strange and new, yet familiar all at the same time. While they rediscovered each other from their one-night stand on the road, which was hardly remembered because of drunkenness anyway, they came together in the routine way of couples who have been with each other for years, maybe because they had been. Their familiarity left little room for romance, except for a few random moments that would always take each of them by surprise.

"Doing it with you," Franky reflected with a shrug one night as they lay together on their backs, "it's nothing new, really."

Bobbi glared at him, but before she could react to the seeming insult, he added, "Over the years we already did it a hundred thousand times—in the film reels inside my head, that is."

A smile broke over her face. "Oh, Franky," she said, "that's the most romantic thing I've ever heard!"

When they slept, she always put at least one toe to his boney ankle, and he at least one musician's fingertip to her scalp. They were touches that, if not signifying passion, signified their fate.

The band members had long since grown addicted to debating and discussing their leaders the Mad Soloist and the femme vocalist; thus, wherever those players' lives took them, they kept at it. They marveled at how Franky—who had always lived and died in his music career by being one, then two, then three or four steps behind the latest musical fashion—after all the years that he and Bobbi had been together, had proposed marriage. He did it years after he might have done it, but maybe back then it wouldn't have worked out anyway. He did it in a place where everything stayed the same, and yet nothing did except for the heat and the poverty, not even the very earth under his feet, which he later learned from a newspaper story was washing away, disappearing into the Gulf. He married her right around the time that the levee board was squandering money while it only partially built a flawed system, a corrupt wall around a bowl of a city where the scientists said it was just a matter of time for a perfect storm to come through and drown the stubborn old metropolis—a storm even greater than the one that caused the coffins to float down the streets like pirogues, greater than the one that separated the dog from his indifferent master, maybe even greater than the bitter contents of anyone's memory. It was too late for Ariel to have a true mother growing up, but not too late for Bobbi to be a life force. Too late for "Bye-bye . . . Forever!" to ever chart, but not too late to rewrite the refrain.

ACKNOWLEDGEMENTS

AT THE TIME I began *The World-Famous Franky Fritz Band*, jazz intrigued me, but I had spent little time with it. Music is music—so goes one of the novel's undercurrents; therefore, on that level, time period and genre become only secondary in the story. Nevertheless, before long, I'd become a fan of jazz. In working on *The World-Famous Franky Fritz Band*, I'm grateful to have had the opportunity to gain a new friend in this amazing art form.

I am far more grateful for the people who have provided help along the way. John Paine was instrumental in helping to shape an early draft. John is a pro of pros, and I'm so glad I found him. His suggestions were crucial, as was his personal touch. A writer's goal is to choose the right word for the right place, and the same might be said of a coach in sports. I'm not sure John would consider himself a coach, but he nevertheless is an outstanding one. Aside from tinkering with the Xs and Os of the novel, he always seemed to provide just the right word—usually one of encouragement—at just the right time, practically all the way up to publication.

Richard Klin gave the book one of the final reads, and it turned out to be a crucial one. In addition to providing some great feedback, he identified a historical error that otherwise might have haunted me. I'm grateful to have had such a top-notch writer read the book and provide valuable input on several issues.

I'm blessed to know a hugely talented artist, Joshua Budich, creator of the cover illustration. When I first saw it, I thought he'd stepped into my head. (Good thing he's a friend, not a foe.) On a side note, I love the fact that in both Rich and Josh, I unintentionally found two guys who themselves have put the lens on art and artists—subjects that run through *The Franky Fritz Band*—in their own work. (For Josh's art, check out joshuabudich.com; for a look at some of Rich's projects, go to richardklin.com.)

While the story was envisioned in a fictional, perhaps parallel, America, historical and musical sources came in many forms. Ken Burns' *Jazz*, particularly the book companion to the documentary film, proved most helpful for music history. Alvin G. Gottschall's *Growing Up in New Orleans* was crucial in the merging of the yesterday in my imagination with the memories of an actual person. Jean Pierre Lion's *Bix: The Definitive Biography of a Jazz Legend* provided key information, and thanks go to the Bix Beiderbecke

Memorial Society for the group's informative website, and promotion of the man and jazz itself. A look at commercial advertising is a terrific means of understanding another time; in that regard, adsource.com, a database of historical advertisements, was of huge help. "The Conn Loyalist" website (cderksen.home.xs4all.nl), run by Christene Derksen, provides a wealth of information for anyone interested in Conn instruments.

A big tip of the hat also goes out to the countless jazz CDs and books on World War II and music whose pages I flipped, and websites that I surfed, all of which flavored the pages of *The Franky Fritz Band* in some way or another. Special thanks go to Dave Molenda, friend in soccer and kindred spirit in some intangible way, for indulging me in email conversation concerning impressions of certain Midwestern towns and landscapes.

Tim Canan, being the usual great friend and person he always is, once gave me a random gift for no particular reason after making a trip to San Francisco and visiting the famous City Lights independent bookstore. The item he brought back for me: Kerouac's *On the Road*. Gifts for no reason can be the most special kind. I had yet to read the classic, so if it hadn't been for Tim's thoughtfulness, Sal Paradise would never have made his cameo, brief but meaningful. Thanks, Tim.

Guy Kawasaki's *APE* was instrumental in teaching me about publishing—*artisanal* publishing, as he calls it. Now that I've been through the multifaceted process, I can see why.

John H. Matthews was a godsend during the time that the *Franky Fritz* train was reaching the publication station, providing support in the publishing process and developing the website cjlevesque.com. John is a creative renaissance guy, wearing hats (fittingly, he's a creative hat wearer, in fact) including photographer, Web designer, video producer, and, most recently, novelist. His debut novel, The South Coast, was released in 2013.

Notwithstanding the fictional-America viewpoint taken, any mistakes are my own and not those of sources, inanimate, virtual, or human.

The fiction-writing passion bubbled up—that is, beyond the latent and fearful state characterized by the notion that *other people are novelists, not I*—while I lived in New Orleans. I first shared that joy with Harold Ellis Clark, partner in crime and now, years later, an accomplished playwright and writer in multiple genres. After meeting in Martha Corson's wonderful class (thank you for your teaching, Martha), Hal and I comprised a two-person (sometimes three) writers' group back then, and those Saturday mornings at Rue de la Course coffee shop were often the highlight of my week. That was years ago, yet his feedback on my writing from those days and general encouragement surely informed these pages. Once *The Franky Fritz Band* got rolling, another writers' group came to my aid. Many thanks to Regina Johnson, Sharon Ritchey, Tara Taffera, and Suzanne Steward for their helpful feedback during the book's early stages and for sharing with me in the joy and tribulations of writing.

The act by an unpublished author of writing a novel is, particularly in this modern world that's driven by data and odds, a foolish waste of time, on paper (pardon the pun). Yet still, we beat on, boats against the current ... to quote Fitzgerald out of context. On that level, the greatest thanks go to anyone who's ever spoken a word of support or shown a face without judgment for this writing endeavor. The long list of people starts with my mother and father, Paul and Beverly Levesque, who have given a respect, of a kind that will always move me, for whatever crazy new life plan I might have schemed up through the years, including the quiet announcement that I was at least going to *try* to write novels. Through either their blood or their values, they passed along this support, respect, and absence of judgment straight to my brother, Marc Levesque, and sister, Paula Betzold, whom I thank dearly for the same. Jeff Betzold, my brother-in-law on paper but really just my brother, has given me that same gift.

To continue on with this theme, no one has given me more than my wife Nancy. The dedication speaks for itself. Ricker and Caroline, uncle and aunt to Nancy and now me, you already know that part of *Franky Fritz* was written at your beautiful Maine camp. Talk about inspiration. Thank you. And thank you for the years of lobster and wonderful memories.

ABOUT THE AUTHOR

C.J. Levesque has been a professional writer for more than 15 years. Prior to that, he worked in social services and as a teacher in New Orleans. He now lives with his wife and two rescue cocker spaniels in Baltimore, where the football team takes its name from an Edgar Allan Poe poem.

Made in the USA
Lexington, KY
15 July 2014